D0065924

Also by Jean Thompson

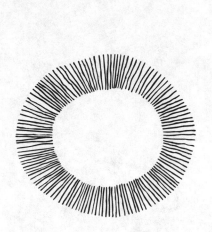

Wide Blue Yonder

A Novel

Jean Thompson

Simon & Schuster

new york london toronto sydney singapore

Simon & Schuster
Rockefeller Center
1230 Avenue of the Americas
New York, NY 10020

For information about special discounts for bulk purchases, please contact
Simon & Schuster Special Sales: 1-800-456-6798 or business@simonandschuster.com

Designed by Jeanette Olender
Manufactured in the United States of America

10 9 8 7 6 5 4 3 2 1

Library of Congress Cataloging-in-Publication Data
Thompson, Jean, date.
  Wide blue yonder : a novel / Jean Thompson.
    p. cm.
  I. Title.
PS3570.H625 W5 2002
813'.54—dc21   2001034157
ISBN 0-7432-0512-X

Acknowledgments

My sincere gratitude to Henry Dunow and Denise Roy for their expertise, enthusiasm, and unfailing support. Many thanks to others who helped: Stephen O'Byrne, Adrienne Kitchen, Carolyn Alession, and my friends at El Centro por los Trabajadores.

Part One **June 1999**

There Is Always Weather

Beige Woman was saying Strong Storms. She brushed her hand over the map and drew bands of color in her wake. All of Illinois was angry red. A cold front currently draped across Oklahoma, a raggedy spiderweb thing, was going to scuttle eastward and slam up against your basic Warm Moist Air From the Gulf. The whole witch's brew had been bubbling up for the last few days and now it was right on the doorstep. Beige Woman dropped her voice half an octave to indicate the serious nature of the situation, and Local Forecast nodded to show he understood.

Then he got up to see if the coffee was ready. It wasn't quite; he stood watching it drip drip drip. When he poured milk in his cup it swirled like clouds. The sky outside was milk as well, milk over thin blue. Local Forecast stood on the back porch steps and turned his nose to the southwest, where all the trouble would come from later. He sniffed and squinted and tried to tease the front out of the unhelpful sky, but it stayed as shut as any door.

Back inside it was Man In A Suit's turn. He stood, palm up, balancing Texas by its tip. Texas was green today. Florida was full of orange suns. Man In A Suit tickled the Atlantic coastline and whorls of ridged white sprang up, high pressure. Then jet stream arrows came leaping out of the northwest, blue and swift, full of icy glittering.

There was always Weather. And every minute there was a new miracle.

Coffee and cereal, then fifteen toe touches. Fat Cat rubbed at his ankles and got in the way. He couldn't reach his toes anymore. He got all purply and out of breath. He was old. Plus it was humid this morning, 93 percent, as you might expect on a Strong Storms day. He let his head hang and peered at the screen from between his legs. He had a glimpse of upside-down palm trees, which puzzled him for a moment before he straightened and collided with the couch, anxious to get turned around and watch properly.

Tropical Update. He'd almost forgotten, with all the storm news. It was June the First, official start of Hurricane Season. Now he'd missed it and would have to wait through twenty minutes of insurance commercials and such before the next Update. He settled back in the couch. Fat Cat poured into his lap and solidified there, thrumming away. The big map was on and he fixed his eyes on the exact center of Illinois, You Are Here, the place the Weather lived.

Of course, you didn't get hurricanes in Illinois. You couldn't have everything. For hurricanes there were special people to show you how bad it was. The ocean going lumpy and gray as the storm moved in. Then came the galloping wires and sideways rain and the riven treetops. The announcer all tied up in a parka hood and staggering to keep upright. Water droplets blurring the camera lens. Local Forecast felt his heart grow large, thinking of their bravery. Sometimes if it was really bad, they were only voices on the phone, a lonely scratched-up sound that left you to imagine the shriek and slam of those water-soaked winds, the darkness closing in.

The blue screen came on. The Local Forecast. Blue blue blue, deep glowing indigo, like an astronaut would see from outer space. As long as there was the blue, there would be Weather.

He had to pee. He always had to pee nowadays, nothing down there worked the way it should. He got up, spilling his lapful of insulted cat. And wouldn't you know, when he got back from flushing, the Update had started and any second now they'd show the names. Names for the new hurricane season, storms that hadn't been born yet. Ocean currents not yet warmed, wind: not yet beginning to eddy. Come on come on come on.

Arlene, Bert, Cindy, Dennis, Emily, Floyd, Gert, Harvey . . .

His eyes stopped right there. Harvey was his other name.

And since there were, as Man In A Suit said, an average of nine named storms every season and six hurricanes, the odds were on his side. He pitied people with names like Rita or Stan, who were pretty much out of the running. Hurricane Harvey! The mere possibility sent him bounding around the room, making hurricane noises. Hurricane Harvey, a spinning white spiral tilting now toward Florida, now toward the Bahamas, considering a jaunt up the East Coast. People boarding up windows and laying in batteries and bottled water. Waves eating beach houses bite by bite. Of course you wouldn't want anyone to die. He'd feel terrible. He hoped at least he'd be an American hurricane, where they could handle these things a little better.

Meanwhile there were Strong Storms to worry about, no more than twelve hours away. His skin prickled with energy. Godamighty. He stood in the shower and yodeled. The steam from the shower mixed with the clammy air so the shower was more or less wasted, but who cared. He hopped around the room one-legged to get his pants on, then fell back, oof, on the bed. He paddled himself upright and launched himself out the front door, but first he turned the sound down on the Weather so they'd get a break from talking while he was gone.

There was one street you walked to get to the grocery and another street you took on the way back. Local Forecast kept his feet moving smartly along in spite of the heat. Humidity was down to 84 percent, still darn high. The miserability index. The grocery doors whooshed open and the cold canned air blessed the back of his neck. Lettuce bread lightbulbs cat food hamburger hamburger hamburger. He grabbed a cart and skated down the aisle.

"Whoa there, Harvey."

Bump bump. Local Forecast looked up. The carts were all tangled together in a chrome thicket. The stranger made a tsk sound and reached down to unhook them.

"What's the big hurry? Not fixing to rain, is it?"

"Sunny, high in the mid-eighties. Becoming cloudy by midday. Showers and thunderstorms possible by late afternoon. Some of these storms could be severe, with heavy rains and damaging winds. Chance of rain seventy percent."

"That so," the stranger said agreeably. He had a big pink face and shiny eyeglasses. Local Forecast waited for him to go away but he turned his cart around and walked it alongside Local Forecast, like the two of them were mothers pushing baby carriages together. "Well, then I'm going to need some rainy-day groceries."

He steered them down the produce aisle. Grapefruit mooned at them. The pears had sly little puckering faces. There were apples polished like headlights. Heaps of green things, cucumbers and celery and mops of spinach. They were nothing you could imagine inside of you.

"Are you eating enough vegetables, Harve? Roughage? Antioxidants? Important stuff at our age."

Local Forecast ran his cart into a pyramid of cantaloupes and stood there, trying to remember. Lettuce bread.

"How about some oranges? Vitamin C."

Local Forecast shook his head politely and righted the cart. He fumbled with a lettuce, then decided against it. The store had too many lights and big slick puddles of shine lay all over the floor. He ended up at the meat counter, clutching the edge of the case as if it was the rail of a ship. There were trays of pink, skinned-looking things down there in the frosty air.

The voice was at his elbow again. "Lean meat and nothing fried. That's the ticket."

Local Forecast waved a hand, the way you'd brush at a fly.

"Harvey, don't you remember who I am?"

He stared up at the pink face until eyes came out from behind the glasses. Two wriggled eyebrows and an upper lip scraped as clean as the veal cutlets in front of him. Ed.

He must have said it out loud because the stranger (*Ed?*) pumped his face up and down. "That's right. Ed Pauley. Sure. You remember. I've known you ever since high school. Time marches on."

Time marched on. Local Forecast could hear it making gravelly sounds while he thought about School. He had it in a book somewhere at home. Mostly he remembered yawning. Luxurious, ear-splitting yawns that squeezed tears out of the corners of his eyes. There was a lot of yellow afternoon light and chalk dust hanging suspended in the slanting rays. His slumping behind polishing the softened wood of the desk. Rows of necks ahead of him. More yawning.

"The glory days," Ed said. "We were football conference champs three years running. Football wasn't your sport, was it, Harve? You were more of a track-and-field guy."

Breathing through his mouth and his lungs filling up with pain. Legs on fire. But was he running to something or away?

"Harve? Wait for me."

Ed pushed his cart double-time to catch up. "What's this, a race?"

Local Forecast was looking straight at the green cans, so he put some in his cart.

"I sure as heck hope you have a cat."

He kept talking alking alking alking, but Local Forecast wasn't listening. School came before the Weather, he was sure of it. And other things had happened in between. Were they in a book too?

He put some more things in his cart, gave the checkergirl money and she gave him money back. Brown pennies; he turned them so the Lincoln heads all faced the same direction, then he put them in his pocket. He walked down the going-home street, trying to get his mind around a thought that was like a stone in his shoe. It was about Football Ed turning into Old Ed and time marching on.

Back home. He dumped his groceries in the kitchen and turned up the sound on the Weather. Red Woman was standing in front of a map of India, a place that didn't interest him much because it was always hot and always the same flat green-blue. The only really good weather was Local. He got the book for School down from its shelf. It was sticky maroon leather with white letters on it: THE BULLDOG, 1949. There was a cartoon bulldog shouting through a megaphone. The book flopped open to one page, like it always did, and he lifted it up to his nose to see.

It was a boy in trackandfield clothes. His arm was hauled back and there was a whaddyacallit. Javelin. He was throwing a javelin on a black-and-white day in 1949. Local Forecast studied it, then rearranged the book on the coffee table so that the javelin was going west to east, the way the Weather traveled.

The boy in the picture had shiny hair and a smile that lifted up one side of his mouth. His bare arms and legs were ropey with muscle, pointing in all directions, like he was trying to scramble out of his clothes. Local Forecast rapped the top of his bald head with his knuckles. Knock knock. He unzipped his pants and regarded his legs, all fattypale and sad. Look at that. But there was the name under the picture: HARVEY SLOAN.

So the boy in the picture was the old Harvey, who was really young. And he, Local Forecast, was the new Harvey, who was really old. No wonder he got so confused. The boy in the picture was aiming the javelin at the farthest point he could see, which was 1949. Somehow it must have kept going and going, because it found him everytime he opened the book. This old-young Harvey must have wondered how everything would turn out. "It's OK, really," Local Forecast told him. "We've got a house now, and Fat Cat, and the Forecast comes on every ten minutes."

But there was more to it than that, he knew. He was leaving things out. He knew he was and it made him feel guilty. It was a terrible thing to fall into the hands of the Living God no no no no southeast winds five to ten miles an hour barometric pressure twenty-nine point eight six and falling.

There were other people in the book too, Football Ed and pretty girls. If you made a book of them now, they would all be old. He knew what came after old.

After old, they closed the book on you. That's the story of my life, people said. Everybody had their own book. Beginning, middle, end of story. Then Uh-Oh. That's what people said. Not that anybody ever came back to tell about it, except maybe Jesus and he didn't stay very long. You probably weren't allowed to come back. It was a terrible thing.

All the storybook of his life he was afraid. He forgot why. He was just a scairdy. They'd tried to beat it out of him. It was a terrible thing to no a terrible no no.

He stood up, forgetting that he had his pants undone, had to stop and hitch them up. What if it was all just another kind of forecast, a prediction nobody checked up on?

He kept very still. The television chattered away. What if it was just them trying to boss everything? The way they had it set up, Heaven sounded like more School, and that was if you even got in. In Heaven you still had to be you. Oh, he was tired of he. Of trying to remember and trying to forget. It all weighed you down so. He hadn't led a good life. Box of snakes no no no no patches of heavy dense fog, visibility less than a quarter of a mile.

Say you could forget even about forgetting, once your poor old leaky body quit on you. He was something clear and cold, like the jet stream, his mouth full of blue roaring. Whambang! Or just a little ruffle of wind over warm Pacific water, wind that pulled the water right up into it. Then something gave it a push and it meandered toward California. Stopped to spit snow on the near side of the Sierras. Sailed right over the Rockies, really something now, a genuine System, leaving green tracks all across the map. It tore up a chunk of eastern Colorado and sent a whole plateful of lightning rattling down on Nebraska. Why, it might even end up in You Are Here, setting off sirens, then raining itself out somewhere over the Ohio valley.

He didn't see why it couldn't be that way. Everything explained in terms of wind and water and temperature. Pure and simple. He wanted to tell the young man in the picture that a great many sad things would happen but that it would turn out all right. He wanted to tell his old man self the same thing. He wanted to catch that javelin at the end of its perfect rainbow arc. All you had to do was concentrate.

But later that day, watching the southwestern sky turn the color of steel and the dogwood leaves show their pale undersides in the shrilling wind, he wasn't so sure. He was still afraid. And would there still be Weather, if he wasn't here to watch it?

Land of Lincoln

There were places like Springfield that used to be important but were now only good for being state capitals. Josie Sloan enjoyed saying this about her hometown, in the way you can enjoy a grievance. It was a dump of a place that thought it was hot because it had the governor and a batch of blowhard legislators that the truly braindead voters of Illinois had elected. Nothing ever happened here and you could die of boredom a dozen different ways. You could spend your days roaming the aisles of the Dollar General, stuffing your cart full of depressing ticky-tacky, or you could marry one of the local oafs and have baby races with all the other oafettes, or you could wipe down the sticky counter of the Taco Bell for the twentieth time so the same fly could keep landing on it, like Josie was doing right now.

It was two o'clock in the afternoon and nobody was ordering tacos or nachos or watery sodas. Moron, which was actually the nickname he preferred, was scraping down the grill and kicking up grease smells. Bonnie was on the phone with her loser boyfriend for one more of their extended love chats. The fly circled fatly around the room, as if it was bored too, and landed on one of the *Star Wars Phantom Menace* posters. She hated *Phantom Menace*. She was never even going to see it. Outside the glass and concrete-made-to-look-like-stucco box, a steady stream of traffic went nowhere. She was seventeen, with nowhere to go.

Bonnie hung up the pay phone in the vestibule and came back inside, looking dreamy and smug, the way she always did at such times. "How's Curt?" Josie asked for politeness' sake.

"He's great. We're gonna rent a garage for him to work on the Camaro—he decided on the color. Candy-Apple Red."

"That sounds awesome." Bonnie never seemed to realize when Josie was making fun of her, and in truth Josie lost track of things herself. Because even though Bonnie had buck-teeth and an ass like an upholstered chair and Curt was prime oaf material, the two of them were happy, pathetic but happy. Josie thought there was something stingy and separate about herself that would keep her from being happy in any of the obvious ways.

Bonnie ambled over to the heat lamps and checked her lipstick in the metal reflection. Moron was belting out some hip hop song about death threats and the Internet, wa boom, wa boom, wa boom. Josie would get off work in two hours, unless while she wasn't paying attention she'd already died and gone to hell. Taco Hell.

Bonnie poured herself an iced tea and wedged one hip against the counter. "Stick a fork in it."

"Yup."

"At least the Prince of Darkness left early." This was the manager. Even the jokes were nothing new. Bonnie said, "So . . ." as a kind of invitation.

"We're still broken up and it's going to stay that way." Josie shoved a stack of napkins in the dispenser so that it was impossible to draw out less than ten or fifteen at a time.

"Who're you going out with now?"

"Nobody."

Bonnie tilted her head but didn't get to say anything, because right then the door opened and two little kids with their hands full of grubby change came in. So Josie didn't have to hear one more time how hot Jeff was and other of Bonnie's opinions. She didn't hang out with kids like Bonnie and Moron at school, they weren't really her friends. They were Taco pals, that was all. Bonnie and Moron and their crowd were the lumpen, low-expectations kids, while Josie and her friends were crammed full of expectations: SAT scores and college, the school newspaper, plays, sports, things that looked good next to your picture in the yearbook or on those college applications, what a bunch of nasty little tail-chasing careerists they all were.

Josie went back through the kitchen, pretending they needed more sauce packets, and sneaked into the walk-in refrigerator. She sat down on a cardboard box of lettuce and started counting, *one two three,* up to the hundred or so that she figured she could get away with before she had to get back. A hundred wasn't enough time to even start thinking about all the fucked-up things she had to deal with: Jeff, how many weeks months years she'd feel bad about him, *ten, eleven, twelve,* her scummy job, which took her all the way up to *forty, fifty,* her mother, *sixty,* her father, *seventy,* her father's nincompoop wife, *eighty, ninety,* the rest of her life, a big fat zero. She was only a dumb kid in a dumb town and there was nothing special about her even though she pretended there was. She was stuck here with everybody else in the everyday everything. *One hundred.* Josie stood up and headed back to the front counter for another round of fast food fun.

Half an hour before quitting time, the sky framed in the glass windows was piling up clouds like a stack of dirty mattresses. Moron and Josie pushed the door open and tried to smell rain in the air. Moron was bummed because he had his motorcycle. "Shit. Figures. The one day this week I bring it." Moron's real name was Jason. He had slick, dyed black hair and subscribed to body-building magazines and he was supposed to graduate this year but hadn't wanted people getting the wrong idea about him.

"Maybe it'll hold off," said Josie. "I'll find out." She put a quarter in the pay phone and dialed. He picked up on the first ring.

"Local Forecast."

She pictured him sitting on the sloping corner of his old couch, which was exactly the color of canned tomato soup, his knees pointed at the television. "Hey, Uncle Harvey, it's Josie. Can you tell me when it's gonna start raining?"

"At three forty-five P.M. Doppler radar indicated a line of strong storms extending from Beardstown to Carlinville, moving northeast at thirty miles an hour. Tornado watch is in effect for Tazewell, Mason, Sangamon, Menard, and Logan Counties until seven P.M."

"That sounds pretty heavy." Josie did some quick wind speed and distance calculations. They could just make it, she figured. "How are you, are you excited? Make sure you go down in the basement if it gets really bad."

"Persons in the watch area can expect wind gusts up to fifty miles an hour, torrential rains, damaging lightning, and possible hail. Conditions are favorable for tornado formation. Be prepared to seek shelter."

"Yeah, that's right. Thanks, Uncle Harve. I gotta run. Be careful, OK?"

She hung up and Moron asked, "Does your uncle work for a TV station or something?"

"He's really my great-uncle," said Josie, not wanting to get into a discussion of Harvey just then. "Come on, we've got to be ready to punch out the second that clock turns."

She drove home through streets that were alive with wind: stray bits of trash skittering across the pavement, flags snapping, trees trying to turn themselves inside out. The western sky was dark and swollen but the rain hadn't come by the time she pulled into her garage. Her mother wasn't back yet and the house was dark. She left it that way, liking the feeling of gloom as she walked through the downstairs. In the kitchen the answering-machine light was blinking, probably her mother, so she ignored it. Five o'clock in the afternoon and there was that eerie nonlight you imagined a total eclipse would be like. Thunder rolled out of the sky's open throat.

Josie rummaged in the refrigerator. The beam of light made the room even darker. More thunder. She closed the refrigerator, fished a joint out of her backpack, and stepped out the kitchen door to watch the show.

The first brittle lightning showed above the treeline. It was going to be a great, ripping storm. She felt almost happy standing there, she felt careless and dramatic, like someone in a movie. The first rain spattered down, a few unserious drops.

"Hey, Jose."

She yelped. His face was a pale circle, floating toward her from the back of the yard like a balloon. "Jesus *Christ*," she spat, furious at being so scared. "What the hell are you doing here?"

"Nothing."

"That's such a stupid thing to say." She crossed her arms. The lightning was really starting to rock. He stopped a few yards away from her and just stood there, looking pathetic. "Well, you better go now."

"I walked."

"One more bright idea."

He didn't say anything. "You are such a pussy," she told him. He'd set her up. Totally. She stared at the joint she wouldn't get to smoke now. The rain started in so hard and fast that she had to raise her voice. "Hurry up, get inside."

He was happy about this, he was getting his way, but he had to act like it was no big deal, like he was so cool that he just naturally slouched his way out of a thunderstorm. While he was still in the yard there was a giant BOOM and the sky split open with white electricity and he jumped for the door.

Josie stepped aside to let him enter, then she turned on the light, not wanting to sit in the dark with him. He shook himself like a dog. "Woo-ee!" he said, instantly cheerful.

"My mom's on her way home."

"Uh-huh." He tried to smooth his hair with his hands, then gave up and went into the bathroom off the pantry for a towel. She hated how he knew where everything in her house was. She hated his stupid blond good looks that let him get away with things. He was exactly like some big dumb collie that once you petted it, forgot all about everything it had done wrong.

When he came back in she was sitting at the breakfast table watching the rain bounce off the concrete patio. It was doing that, bouncing. You could see the drops land, then go straight back up. Amazing. Jeff moved behind her chair and pretended to be watching also. She could see him reflected in the lighted window. He was looking down at her, his mouth held shallowly open. Josie bumped her chair away from him. "What?" he said.

"Go sit down, OK?"

"Jeez. Attitude." But he flopped into a chair across from her. The wind was banging thunder around like the sky was a kitchen full of pots. It was a wicked storm. She wouldn't be surprised if there was a tornado out there with her name on it.

He said, "Come on. Talk to me."

"We already did that."

"I mean ordinary, what's-new talk, not your usual tragic bullshit."

"Go to hell, Jeff."

"You know what your problem is? You don't know what you really want. You get PMS or something and all of a sudden you're too good for me or anybody else. What'd I do that was so terrible anyway?"

"You're a collie."

"Huh?"

"It's not PMS. It doesn't have to make sense to you."

"Good, because it doesn't."

"Sorry." And she was. She used to be so crazy about him. He was her boyfriend, that was how you were supposed to feel. You were supposed to keep feeling that way but she didn't, it had worn off. The lightning seemed to be coming from all directions. She didn't believe this. It was like *Wuthering Heights* or something. Except that he wasn't Heathcliff and she wasn't Catherine. They weren't souls bound together throughout eternity. Maybe nobody was these days. There was only the everyday everything, people grubbing for money or tedious fun, and maybe he was right and she wasn't too good for anything.

"I just miss you, OK? So shoot me." He reached across the table and stroked the inside of her arm. "You ever wonder what it's like to do it in a big storm? Huh?"

"No," she said, both to his hand and his question. But her skin was doing a treacherous, creepy sort of dance, and beneath her skin she was going crazy.

"Just for fun. It wouldn't have to mean anything."

"Oh, good."

"We can do it the way you like it."

"You always say that."

"Come on." He was behind her again, his hands exploring, pinching slyly.

"What about my mom?"

"No offense, but I don't want to do it with your mom."

She laughed and the laughing turned everything loose inside of her. Josie grabbed his hand and they scrambled into the front room, where they figured they could see if the car was coming. For some reason it was lighter in here. When she skinned off her shorts and underpants her bare self looked exceptionally naked, moon-colored. He kept his clothes mostly on, in case they had to stop. The head of his penis kept getting tangled up in cloth and butting loose. A tornado was probably going to rip through the house and carry the two of them, still stuck together, up into the air and deposit them somewhere very public. He smelled like the towel he'd used to dry his hair, a laundry smell. The thunder passed overhead, taking its quarrel eastward. She kept slipping off the edge of the couch. It kept not fitting in right. That was OK, it was just for fun. It wasn't really the way she liked it. Oh well.

He was so pleased with himself afterward. Good boy. She couldn't really blame him. It was his nature to want what he wanted. To know what he wanted. "Hurry up," she told him. "You really have to go. I'll give you a ride home."

He would have rather hung around and stayed for dinner and acted like everything was back to normal, but she was going to win this one. If they stayed together for the next fifty years, she knew exactly how everything between them would play out. She thought about writing a note for her mother but decided she felt too mean. When they were getting in the car he went to touch her hair, missed, and swiped her across the shoulders instead. When she turned to look at him he gave her a loose smile that was like an apology for itself.

"You're so pretty."

He wasn't all bad. Not even mostly. He was just himself. She made him crouch down as they pulled out of the garage. Good thing, because wouldn't you know it, just as she was shifting out of reverse, her mother's car appeared, headlights bearing down on her like a charging hippopotamus.

"Shit. Stay down." At least it was still raining hard and her windows were fogged. She opened hers just enough to wave. Her mother's face, already angry, leaned out of the car, her mouth moving. She was saying why didn't you answer the phone, fold the laundry, start dinner, where do you think you're going? Josie waved and sped off.

Jeff sat back up. "Why've I got to hide?"

"Because she doesn't need to know my business." She slid in the Paula Cole CD and turned the music up all the way. By the time they reached his house she couldn't stand it one more minute, wanting him gone.

"So, I guess I'll see you later." He waited, half-out of the car.

"I don't know, Jeff." The rain had turned down one more notch, a gray screen with the evening light filtering in behind it. It was tired, just like she was.

"What does that mean?"

"It means I don't know." Everything she did was a mistake.

His face closed down. "Fine. Be weird." He slammed the door behind him. God she was the most fucked-up mess.

She didn't want to go home just yet to do the Mom thing, so she kept driving through the rain-softened streets. There was a big tree limb lying on somebody's lawn. Josie wondered what kind of tree it was. Trees were one of the million things she knew absolutely nothing about. The lawns themselves were that luminous, nearly radioactive green that you sometimes got with storm light. The gutters were loud with running water. But the storm itself was over. Everything was over except for her, Zero the Great, who would keep staggering on until she collapsed from total idiocy.

You could still drive through the cemetery even when all the historical stuff was closed. Josie figured the weather would have chased all the tourists off and she'd stand a good chance of having Abe all to herself.

It was a little embarrassing; she didn't tell people about her Abe fixation. After all, growing up in Springfield meant you pretty much had Abe for breakfast, lunch, and dinner. It was like this was Rome and he was the pope. Among Josie's friends, who had been taken on tours of the Lincoln Home and the Old State Capitol every year from first grade on, who had been made to memorize "O Captain! My Captain" and had watched unlikely looking tall men growing chin whiskers for pageants, it was obligatory to affect a certain casual boredom regarding Abe. She understood all that. She wasn't sure why it worked differently on her. It was just one more thing about her that was weird.

Everybody knew about Young Abe, poling his flatboat up and down the wide rivers, way before he even thought about being famous. Then there was Lawyer Abe, riding a horse miles and miles of muddy country road on the Illinois circuit, winning cases with his folksy wit. Candidate Abe, speechifying from a flag-draped platform. Then President Abe, carrying the terrible weight of the war and the entire wounded country. You saw it in every line of his face. It broke her heart. You couldn't believe you could feel that way about history, something in a book, but it zinged her every time.

Then there was Dead Abe, who she was on her way to visit. Josie turned off of Walnut into Oak Ridge Cemetery. The fine screen of rain was still falling and the road was edged with shallow puddles. The big oak, she knew it was an oak, thank you very much, had shed patches of leaves like handfuls of torn-out hair. She drove past the monuments for Vietnam and Korea. There was one other car in the parking lot, a family with two little kids who looked like they'd waited out the storm here. They were just now getting out of the car and wandering around, trying to salvage some of their Historic Springfield day. Josie ignored them and parked at the farther end. She waited until they gave up and drove off. Then she got out and hiked over to the statue.

This was an enormous, oversize bronze bust of Abe, emerging from a rough-edged granite boulder. For years people had climbed up to rub his nose for luck, polishing it shiny. The rest of him was all dark and gaunt. Poor man. He'd never been good-looking. They'd done the best they could with the portrait but it was still a pretty gnarly face, all jawbone and sunken cheeks. The shiny nose was a further indignity that he bore with patience and good humor. If Abe was still around, you could bet he'd have something wry to say about it. Like the time visitors came to the house to see Mary and he told them she'd be downstairs as soon as she got her trotting harness on. Mary said Oh Mr. Lincoln, and got that look on her face.

Josie retrieved the joint she'd held on to all this time and fired it up. "I know," she said. "One more stupid idea."

Abe just stared ahead with his usual bronze forebearance. He understood everything. He'd seen a cruel cruel war and men in numbers no one had imagined until then, dying either very fast or very slow. Brother against brother. Josie didn't have a brother but she thought she knew something about a house divided against itself.

Josie's mother owned a store downtown called Trade Winds. It specialized in high-end printed fabrics from places like India and Bali. You could buy lengths of cloth or you could buy it made up into tablecloths and bedspreads and napkins and pillow covers and diaper bags and kimono jackets and checkbook covers and every manner of cutesy gewgaw. It was a fun look, her mother said. A casual, country-yet-sophisticated, fun look. It made Josie want to barf. The whole house was full of printed cotton that always smelled of some faint, stale spice no matter how many times you washed it. When she was fourteen Josie had declared war by tearing down her peach-and-white-vine-printed draperies and replacing them with miniblinds. She'd done away with the peach-splatter bedspread and slept beneath a truly hideous synthetic black fur throw. She still had that thing somewhere at the bottom of her closet. Her mother had pronounced it unsanitary, which at the time had seemed like a validation of everything she hoped to accomplish with it.

They fought over everything, and the smaller and stupider it was, the better. The ghost of her mother's lipstick print on the rim of a mug in the cupboard. Josie's trashy music. Her mother's fake, plummy telephone voice when she was talking to somebody she wanted something from. Josie's refusal to pluck her eyebrows. And so on. In Josie's opinion, her mother was crabby from the strain of trying to pretend everything was perfectly fine, in the face of adversity they were soldiering on, they had risen to the challenge, blah blah blah. She should just give it up, admit that as a family they were basically dirt soup.

Josie's father hadn't lived with them since she was twelve. He'd married somebody named Teeny. Imagine. A grown woman.

The most depressing thing was how people, her parents and everyone else, wasted their lives and didn't seem to realize it. How they settled for such pitiful scraps, attached themselves so passionately to everything that was small and dull. Her father existed only to accumulate more money. Her mother's mission was to cover as much of Springfield as possible in smelly third-world cotton. The president of Taco Bell dreamed of the perfect taco. Abe had freed the slaves and preserved the Union. There was absolutely no comparison.

As for Josie, she would no doubt trudge through another year of high school, then go to the state university's local campus and emerge sometime later with a degree equipping her for some as yet unknown but irritating career. A statistically normal Springfield citizen. Yet everything in her cried out against this, kept insisting in the face of all common sense that she was meant to be something extraordinary, splendid, remarkable, live the kind of life that hadn't been invented until now.

The sky was beginning its long decline toward evening. A little sun leaked out from beneath the rolling edge of cloud and lit Abe's nose with somber glory. "Tell me I won't grow up to be exactly like everybody else."

Abe didn't answer back, which was another of his truly excellent qualities. Josie finished her smoke and scuffed over to the car.

Only June, and the summer was already settling into a bad pattern. Life with Mom and Taco Torture. She had to work every day that week. When it wasn't busy it was very slow. Time was a five-hundred-thousand-pound monster, lifting one giant foot an inch at a time. After the lunch rush the Prince of Darkness had them doing things like scraping gum off the bottom of tables and polishing all the unpolishable aluminum in the place. "Time to lean, time to clean," he kept saying, just for meanness. He was a fattish young man who wore sleeveless undershirts beneath his corporate button-downs. Little tributaries of sweat snaked down the bulging geography of his neck. His hair was receding in a weird pattern that left a point in the exact center of his forehead, just like the old pictures of Satan. "Sloan! You call that clean?"

"What's wrong with it?" asked Josie blandly. She considered quitting. It was the kind of job that you imagined yourself quitting from day one.

"I pity the guy you marry, princess. Pay attention here. First you take your little hand and wrap it firmly around the sponge. Then you apply your basic elbow grease, like so. No, your highness. Allow me. You don't want to wreck your manicure. What's that color, huh, Slacker Sapphire?"

Later, after the Prince had gotten bored with abusing her and retreated back to his nasty little office, Josie thought more about quitting. There had to be easier ways to earn gas money. Someone in the Taco Hell corporate headquarters had lost it and replaced the chain's spuriously festive colors, red, green, and gold, with an even worse combo of pink, green, purple, and red. You could see both color schemes in evidence, like an evolutionary struggle between two repulsive species.

Bonnie said, "Hey. Feel like playing?" Josie shook her head. "Come on. Your turn first."

It was a game they played when they were feeling particularly raunchy. They had to imagine doing it with the first man who walked through the door. It was truly sick, considering the clientele, enough to put you off sex entirely. "Come on," Bonnie insisted.

"Yeah, OK." She'd sunk this low. It was a gross-out game. Usually you got stuck with some bald type.

"He has to be somebody at least our age, though. Not a kid."

"Whatever." Maybe she could get a job at the Cinema. She could watch the movies in ten-minute chunks. Pour butter goo on the popcorn. Give in, live the Springfield life, die quietly. She wasn't even looking at the door when it opened but Bonnie's face made her turn around.

Josie saw the uniform first. A cop. Then she saw him. Dear Lord. He paused at the head of the little post-and-chain maze that herded people toward Order Here, scanning the menu. Outside of a magazine, she'd never seen another human being look this good. He had the most beautiful throat. An architecturally perfect column of marble skin. A statue in uniform. Dark dark eyes. Everything inside her stopped. Like going right up to the edge of a cliff and balancing there.

She was aware of Bonnie shuffling and nudging and silently carrying on, but she paid her no mind. His lower lip was caught between his teeth, making the color bloom in it. Then he was moving toward her through the maze.

"Welcome to Taco Bell, can I take your order?" The idiotic

mantra. Her voice a squeak. She couldn't even look at him directly so she stared at his blue blue shirt and silver badge.

"Yeah, how about . . ." He paused and she dared to lift her eyes up to the beam of his face. He was doing that lip-biting thing again. His teeth. His dark, level eyebrows. His voice, God, sometimes she thought the thing she loved the best about men was their voices. "Two of the Baja Steak Gorditas and a large drink."

"For here or to go?"

"To go, please." Damn.

Josie repeated the order, forcing Bonnie to turn and reluctantly begin fumbling with the bags and cups. Josie announced his total and waited while he reached for his billfold with the same lazy movement you might use to scratch a not-very-pressing itch. There was an actual gun and all that other police stuff on his belt. Every molecule of her body felt scrambled, as if she'd been microwaved. She actually felt dizzy. She didn't trust herself not to fall in a heap. His hand warmed the air above hers as he passed the money to her. Say something. If she didn't say something, she might as well commit suicide.

"Arrest any bad guys today?" Just shoot me.

"Not yet. My shift hasn't started." He smiled, but the smile settled somewhere above her head as he waited for his order to come up. Frantic, she attempted to get some part of her being to function properly. Mouth, hopeless. Feet, gone. Her eyes were open but they were connected to something other than her brain. Name tag. Name. Tag. Focus. It said M. CROOK. A cop named crook? No way. Rings? Nothing. Glory be. But already he was picking up his food, telling Bonnie he wanted hot sauce, rattling ice cubes into his drink, fifteen seconds away from disappearing forever.

The door opened and closed behind him. Bonnie already had her mouth working, saying, "I don't believe it, he was like . . ."

But when she turned around, Josie was no longer there. She was out the backdoor of the Taco Bell, tearing off the stupid hat and sending it skating across the parking lot. She was diving for her car keys. Everything within her had started up again. She had stepped off the cliff edge into brilliant air and she knew now what splendid shape her life was meant to take.

She would fall in love.

Service Engine Soon

There was nothing wrong with the car, they said. Everything checked out, oil pressure, battery, emission control. They swore up and down. Elaine, a woman who was no longer impressed with promises and who didn't mind being difficult, made them go through it all over again everytime the light came on. Difficult was now called "assertive" and was a good thing. She figured that sooner or later they'd get tired of dealing with her and fix the damn car. It was driving her crazy. Literally. She'd forget all about it, she'd be behind the wheel, hands, feet, eyes doing the car thing, her mind lightly tethered, free-floating, enjoying the ride. Then the light would go on. A pinprick of worry puncturing all that good feeling. Elaine tried ignoring it. It was, after all, only a stupid lightbulb. But it was taking on a life of its own. She tried to predict it, outsmart it, by doing things like not using (or using) the air conditioner. No dice. It was becoming a superstitious tic she used to measure the success of her days: light off, good; light on, not so good. She kept waiting for the car to do whatever it was threatening to do so she could drag it back to the dealer in triumph.

Meanwhile, she had other problems. Ed Pauley was doing his fussy best to make his interminable point. Elaine kept nodding to show she was paying attention, and also, she hoped, to hurry him along. Finally she found a place to wedge in an interruption. "Ed,

I agree with you, it's a matter for concern. But why not tell Frank? After all, Harvey's *his* uncle."

Ed puffed his cheeks and pretended to think about this. Frank was the last person to be useful in any human crisis. They both knew this and she was mildly curious as to how he would avoid saying it. Finally Ed put on a thoughtful face and said, "Of course. Absolutely. But I kept thinking how much Harve's always taken to you and the little girl and I thought, well, maybe he'd enjoy seeing you."

Meaning, you could divorce a guy, but because you were a woman, you were still on the hook for the family obligations he couldn't or wouldn't take care of. Elaine tried to imagine what Frank would say if she was the one with the crazy uncle and somebody asked him to deal with it. She watched Ed gaze around the shop at the fabric displays. Every surface was heaped with color and pattern, like yards and yards of butterflies. Clearly none of it interested him. More womanish business, Ed's face seemed to say.

Elaine said, "I've always been fond of Harvey too. He's never hurt anybody but himself."

"That's what I'm worried about, Mrs. Sloan—"

"Lindstrom."

"Beg pardon?"

"Lindstrom, not Sloan."

Ed nodded to indicate that he would forget this immediately. "When I saw him last week I had to wonder if he was taking care of himself."

"He always has. Cashes his Social Security checks. Pays his bills. Functions. It might not seem like much of a life to you or me, but you can't decide those things for people."

"He was buying cat food."

Elaine said patiently, "He's got a cat."

"Oh. I was afraid . . ."

"I can buy him vitamins, but I can't promise he'll take them. I can make a doctor's appointment, but there's no guarantee I can get him out of the house."

"If you could just check up on him, that would ease my mind," said Ed, still concerned but beginning the process of handing off, retreating. She supposed she was only annoyed at him because he was trying to get her to do the decent thing, what she should have done anyway, regardless of how richly Frank had deserved divorcing. Poor Harvey. What had he done to deserve his lonely life?

Ed Pauley was the same age as Harvey. There had to be a little anxious itch behind his good-neighbor concern, it had to be anxious, watching yourself age in the mirror of your friends' faces. Ed's own pink face was deflating, losing air. A big, bulky old man, going soft around the edges. Elaine didn't know him all that well personally. He was only the kind of man you knew publicly. Chamber of Commerce Ed, Kiwanis Ed, glad-hander Ed. The hometown lawyer made very good. The thriving opposite of Harvey. Productive citizen. Wife and kids, grandkids. People to take care of him in his golden years. As Harvey had her, sort of.

Because now that the obligation had been laid on her, she'd see it through. She believed in responsibilities. Acts of charity. They were positive things that you could balance against all the wreckage and mistakes of your life. So far she had a business that worked, a marriage that hadn't, and a daughter that the jury was still out on.

After five years of grinding effort, the business was about to become an overnight success. A Chicago store was planning on carrying her line of home accessories. Elaine imported most of the fabric goods directly from an artisan's cooperative she'd organized in rural India, in Bihar. Twice a year she went there to tend to its affairs and determine her new season's order. She had invested in the rebuilt dye works and the water system that processed the industrial waste and provided the village with sewage treatment. There were times she marveled. It almost seemed as if all she had to do was aim herself at a goal, and after a time it was so. She understood those fables where someone smote the ground with a magic staff and a city, or a castle, or a fruited plain sprang forth. They were shorthand for enormous amounts of unimaginable labor. The cooperative kept fifty women employed in sewing circles where they produced gold-thread embroidery and tissue-fine blouses and other handwork, for the only money they had ever earned. When she visited, the women presented her with wreaths of hibiscus and offerings of food and tea and tiny bottles of Coca-Cola. Children in school uniforms lined up to sing songs. The plant's managing committee strung a banner across the main entrance, WELCOME TO MOST FAMOUS AND BEAUTIFUL LADY. She had accomplished many solid, productive, useful things. She had done what she could. You did what you could, but there was still the rest of India. And there was still Uncle Harvey.

Elaine said, "I know what Frank says about Harvey. But what do you think happened to him?"

Ed did the cheek-puffing thing again and his eyes searched the ceiling, as if he needed a space clear of color in order to gather his thoughts. "Did you know that he was in the school glee club? Harve? Sang at all the assemblies. Tenor, I think he was." Elaine must have looked impatient, because he raised a hand. "What I'm saying is he was as normal as pie. Just like anybody else. Or normal enough. Quiet. His brother, that was Frank Senior, he was the one everybody remembers. The war hero. Harvey was always sort of, 'Oh, him too.'"

The door to the shop opened, a customer. Elaine said, "Be right with you," and Ed was left dangling in mid-story. Elaine tried to prod him along. "By the time I knew Frank's dad he was pretty sick. I don't remember him saying anything about Harvey."

"Oh, he wouldn't. None of his folks liked to talk about Harvey. They had that old-time religion. It didn't allow for making mistakes."

The customer came up and stood behind Ed, making a point of waiting for her, so Elaine was forced to shoo Ed away just as he was on the verge of becoming interesting. He said good-bye and took himself briskly out the door. But glancing out to the sidewalk, Elaine saw him becalmed there, hands dangling at his side, squinting first in one direction, then the other.

When she drove home that evening she was cautiously pleased to note that the dashboard light was off, as it had been for the last couple of days. She fixed herself a sandwich, then contemplated the telephone for a melancholy time. Calling her ex-husband was a necessary first step. She had to get Frank's nominal permission before she embarked on any enterprise involving Harvey. She had learned over the course of her marriage, and especially after it, that the simplest matters could grow tentacles of suspicion and intrigue if she failed to take into account Frank's sense of his own sovereignty and territorial rights. If, for example, she wanted to arrange a birthday party for their daughter (back in the days when Josie would have tolerated such a thing), it was best to proceed by complaining, vague about birthday parties and how much trouble they were. At the time of the divorce settlement he had made a video of the house and its contents, complete with his narration: "Here you see the front vestibule, which, due to floor tile I installed in 1989, has appreciated at least twenty-five per cent in value." He wanted to know why Josie had insisted on getting a driver's license at age sixteen rather than the more insurable eighteen; had Elaine put her up to it? Every transaction was like negotiating with the North Koreans. No one had forced her to marry the man. She picked up the phone and dialed.

Teeny answered with her melodic, three-syllable hel-lo-o that sounded like a door chime. "Hi, Teeny, it's Elaine. I have a question for Frank, is he there?"

"Elaine. How are you? I can't remember the last time we talked. Ages. You just keep so *busy*."

Teeny's way of annoying Elaine was to adapt a particularly gracious tone, tinged with sympathy for the fact that Elaine had to work for a living. "I'm fine, Teeny. Yeah, I have been busy. I'm sure Frank's busy too. This'll only take a minute."

"Oh, he's out by the pool. He just loves that silly float chair with the can holder built in. Paddles around like a big old water bug. Hang on while I walk the phone out to him. Honey? Honey, get that thing off your head."

The phone was muffled then. Elaine heard some bumpy, cottony sounds that she took to be conversation. It's Elaine. What does she want? I don't know, she didn't say. Well, tell her I'm not here. I already said you were. Christ.

"Hello." His aggravated voice. She knew it well. She imagined him paddling around like a big old water bug in plaid bathing trunks. His white knees pointing east and west. Zones of pink sunburn crawling up his arms and shins and down his neck.

"How's the water?"

"What?"

"Nothing. Your uncle Harvey's scaring people again."

Swallowing sounds as Frank hoisted his drink. "What did he do, a rain dance in the park?"

"No, he's just being himself." She related Ed's account.

"Ed should maybe keep his nose on his own face."

"Yes, but I don't want people to think we weren't watching out for Harvey." It sounded rather bald, put that way, as if they cared only for public opinion.

"Huh." Frank mulling the data. His mind was like one of those games where you put a marble in the top and it threaded its way through a maze and popped out the hole in the bottom. You could follow the process all the way through from beginning to end. "Does he belong back in a home or something?"

"I don't think so. Not yet." She hated talking about it so glibly. Institutional life for Harvey would mean the dementia ward and the kind of pills that made you fall asleep in a chair. "Somebody should go check up on him," she said, and waited.

"Check up. Like, go talk to him and see if he knows what day of the week it is? Don't they have somebody from the county who does that?"

Elaine kept silent. Part of the marble-in-the-maze routine was Frank's compulsion to say something cheap like that. In the background there was the sound of a television commercial played at top volume for the space of a remote's click. The receiver was muffled again. When Frank came back he had the edge of his private conversation, a leftover laugh, in his voice. Probably Teeny had taken off her swimsuit top. "Maybe you could run over there next week. You're closer."

"Sure. You're welcome."

"Just don't get him all worked up so he starts expecting things." Meaning money, she supposed. Snake. "You know, Frank, I don't think of Harvey as crazy. More like he's on this different plane where there aren't any good or bad people, just good or bad weather."

Frank considered this for a moment, then surprised her by asking about Josie. "She's fine. At least, she's healthy enough. Good vital signs. Of course, she glowers and slouches around the house and acts like she loathes every minute of existence."

"What's wrong with her?"

"She's a teenager." Elaine regretted it the instant she said it. A stupid remark she didn't even mean. If Josie had heard it, she'd take it as one more piece of evidence that would weigh against Elaine on the unforgiving scale of her daughter's heart. She amended herself. "She's just very private. Very closemouthed. I figure it's the boyfriend."

"She has a boyfriend now?"

"Hello, Frank. She's had the same boyfriend for more than a year. Jeff, the Hormone King."

"What's that supposed to mean? What are the two of them up to?" Sloshing sounds. Frank agitated, perhaps even capsizing. "Don't you keep track of them, for God's sake?"

"Frank, relax. Joke." Smart mouth, stupid brain. Why could she never resist her own cleverness? "I'm sure they aren't doing anything. Besides, I think they broke up." In fact, she was sure they were doing everything. Nothing evidentary, like condom wrappers or suspect bedsheets. On those occasions when she had come home late from work, she'd found them sitting blankly in front of the downstairs TV in poses of lustless disinterest. But she *knew.* "I'll go see Harvey and call you back if anything needs to be done, OK?"

When she hung up the phone she let her breath out, looked around for someone to complain to, and as usual found no one. Perhaps she should get a dog, or a lover. Josie was at work. She'd started a new job hostessing at night in a franchise steak house. While it was a step up from fast food, it meant she kept later hours and left the house looking alarmingly dressed-up and older, in an unwholesome sort of way. There were dangling earrings now, and a lot of smudgy eye makeup, and clothes that approached some borderline of too short or shiny or tight or sheer. Elaine was tempted to speak with her about the Business Wardrobe. Which would no doubt go over just as well as the famous Sexual Responsibility and Contraception talk.

She tried to remember that time when everything between

them had been simple, or at least straightforward. She had to go back a long way. Josie had been a sweet baby, an exceptionally golden, beatific child. All right, so she was her only child, and it wasn't as if she could make impartial comparisons. But there were the pictures, the videos, the memories. She and Frank had never been anything other than an awkward mismatch, even back when they were too young and hopeful to realize it. Yet somehow they had come together to form this perfectly symmetrical and prepossessing creature. They'd even been happy, from time to time. You couldn't take a picture of that. It didn't hold still long enough.

Maybe they should have been guided by that fitful happiness, tried harder later when the marriage took its sour turn. Would it have been better if she and Frank had toughed it out, made the usual compromises, resigned themselves to a life of low-grade hostility and disappointment? Elaine had asked herself this many times, and the answer always came back the same. No, for her. Frank, who knew? Yes, for Josie. Even a remote and clueless father on the premises seemed better than the wound inflicted by his absence. In spite of all the paperback books and counselors that told you how to help your child articulate, process, manage, and come to triumphant terms with the family crisis, nothing went according to the script. Instead, a blank and resentful screen had descended on her daughter's face at age twelve.

At this same time Elaine had taken the first of many deep breaths and struck out on her own. Nothing had come easily, but she could look back now and give herself credit for whatever success she'd pried out of life. She'd had her share. No complaints.

And yet. And yet. Something kept nagging at her in the same way the dashboard light did. Off and on. Undiagnosable. A twitch or an itch that said something was out of balance, overlooked. Something she had done or left undone. An anxious edge to even the best of times. She was forty-five. The wilting prime of life. She had friends who had taken up the serious practice of yoga, or started on antidepressants, or embarked on the sort of wilderness expeditions that required you to collect dew on plastic sheets for your drinking water. All of them trying to commune, or connect, or revitalize. She understood their not-enoughness. The fear that they were not happy enough, or valued enough, or beautiful (still beautiful!) enough, or fill-in-the-blank enough. The modern disease. Life as ten thousand screaming television channels projected on an empty screen.

She was startled to hear the garage door opening. Eight-thirty. Josie home unexpectedly early from work. Elaine, who was sitting vacantly at the kitchen table, composed her face to look interested and welcoming. "Hi honey." A neutral, cheery, daughter-greeting tone designed to deflect antagonism.

"Hi." Josie swept past her to the refrigerator. One syllable for three. What would happen if she didn't say anything? Would Josie speak, or would they circle each other in silence like fish in an aquarium?

"You're off early."

"Yeah, it was slow, they told a bunch of us to go home." She emerged from behind the refrigerator door with a bottle of iced tea, which she opened and drank half of, then returned to the shelf. "This one's mine, OK?"

"Would you like some dinner?"

"No, I'm going out again."

"Oh. Who with?"

"Jenn and Tammy. Tammy's folks just got a new pool table."

Her eyelids fluttered. Elaine took this to indicate that the evening's plans had nothing to do with pool, and possibly nothing to do with Jenn or Tammy. Was it good or bad that the girl at least bothered to lie? Was there any way you could ask your child to at least please keep herself alive? Tonight she was wearing a black knit dress with a white stripe around the edges of the neck and straps. Her thin arms were bare and suntanned. Her legs were propped up on high heels that made her mince a little, and her dark blond hair was pulled off her neck so that there was one long line of her from head to toe. Elaine could have started in on the makeup, but decided not to. It wouldn't be long before the girl wouldn't have to pretend at being an adult.

Josie noticed her staring. "What?"

"I was just thinking how nice you look tonight."

"Oh."

There was How was work, and Drive carefully, and Make sure you're home by midnight. Instead Elaine said, "I'm going to go see your uncle Harvey tomorrow. Would you like to come?"

"Did Dad put you up to it?"

"No, I put myself up to it." Josie raised her eyebrows but didn't ask. "I thought I'd stop at the deli and get some sandwiches. Make a picnic out of it. I know he'd enjoy seeing you."

"Do you think so, Mom? I mean, does he really pay attention to anything but the stupid Weather Channel?"

"Of course he does." More certain than she felt. "Anyway, the important thing is that somebody has to take care of people who don't have anybody else."

Josie's face lit with a sudden delighted grin. "You mean like I'm gonna have to take care of you someday, huh?" She wiggled her fingers in a cheery wave as she headed upstairs. "I'll go if I'm up, OK?"

The next morning Elaine made sure she was up, even though it meant Josie sulked against the car door, her hair unwashed and her opaque sunglasses flying like a black flag. What did you do last night? None of your fucking business. One more conversation not worth having. It was a perfectly beautiful summer day, a sky full of whipped-cream clouds and clear light. They drove through downtown, past Trade Winds, its window elegantly turned out in blue chrysanthemum print bedding. She wished she was there, at her place behind the counter, where the only problems were those of money. Past City Hall and the big hotels and the Lincoln Home with its constant line of summertime tourists, descending block by socioeconomic block to Harvey's neighborhood.

At the deli Elaine bought turkey sandwiches and soda and potato salad and chocolate chip cookies. "Here," she said, handing the bags to Josie, who had remained in the car listening to obnoxious music. "Make yourself useful."

"Give me a break."

"No, you give me a break. Were you drinking last night? I want you to tell me the truth."

Josie tilted her head to catch the stream from the air conditioner. "Why? You wouldn't believe me anyway."

"Try me."

"I wasn't."

"I'm very glad to hear it."

"Why are drinking and drugging the only things you worry about? That is such a joke."

"Well, tell me what else I should worry about. Please."

"Just . . . everything. Life." Josie raised one hand to sketch out some vast and cloudy shape. By then they were turning into Harvey's driveway, a gravel track with a stripe of weeds growing up the middle. Elaine shut off the engine and they sat for a moment, taking in the place. Josie asked, "Does he know we're coming?"

"I called and told him." In response, Harvey had recited the month's rainfall totals. Maybe this hadn't been such a good idea.

When she was a small child, Josie had called Harvey's place the Crooked House. Its white clapboards shed a few more nails every year. The porch sloped downhill. Moss was growing around the shingles and the little stovepipe chimney. Elaine promised herself that she would at least pry enough money out of Frank to fix the roof. There was an old-fashioned glider on the porch, the kind that moved with a rusty noise, and a plastic whirlygig in the shape of a duck with paddling wings. Sunflowers and hollyhocks grew in one corner of the yard. Lined up on the front edge of the porch, along the windowsills, and on the surface of a sawed-off tree stump were countless small clay flowerpots and plastic tubs. Each of them held some sprouting or leafing or blooming plant. There were marigolds and spider plants and something that might have been lettuce, fantastically gone to seed. A tough-looking nasturtium. A sweet potato set to root in a glass jar. A row of stubby carrot tops in cottage cheese cartons. Morning glories propped up on sticks and beginning to strangle the neighboring begonias. The house resembled a child's zigzag drawing or something from a down-at-the-heels fairy tale. All the window shades were drawn down at lopsided angles. The Crooked Man and his Crooked House.

The front door was open and through the screen they heard the steady, uninflected voice of the lady weathercaster. "Harvey?"

Elaine couldn't see him in the TV-lit dimness. Josie edged up behind her with the groceries. "Should we just go in?"

Elaine reached out and plucked the sunglasses from her daughter's nose. "Just hold on a minute. Harvey? Yoo hoo."

Josie muttered, "Yoo hoo. Incredible."

"Hush." Harvey's dome-shaped forehead appeared around the corner of the kitchen doorway, then he ducked back out of sight. "Harvey, are you hungry? We brought you lunch." Again the head-ducking, then the head was followed by the rest of his elongated timid self. "Oh look, Harvey, Storm Center's on."

He moved in front of the television to watch the weather map. Elaine opened the screen door and motioned for Josie to follow her inside. She set the paper sacks on a table, then slipped into the kitchen to look for plates. The kitchen was enough to break your heart. She found three mismatched plastic plates in a cupboard, pink, green, and turquoise, fork-scarred and shiny. She decided against pressing her luck with glassware; they could drink from the cans.

When she went back in, Harvey had hunkered down on the floor in front of the television. Josie loitered by the door, still uncommitted to entering. Did she have to be beaten with a stick to get her to do anything? Elaine unwrapped the sandwiches and scooped out potato salad. Thank God for plastic forks and paper napkins. "Would you like Coke or Sprite, Harvey?"

She held the two cans up before him and his hand closed around the Coke. Elaine settled discreetly on the couch and offered him the green plate. He raised it to his nose, then his hand closed around the sandwich and he took a bite. Crumbs dribbled from his old soft lips. It required a little more effort to manage the potato salad, but soon he was working away at it. Behind them, Josie rummaged in the paper bag, making three times the necessary noise.

Harvey's gaze stayed fixed on the television. The map showed a bulging line of dark green, busy over Minnesota. What was it about his face that made it seem just slightly out of focus, like a television getting bad reception?

"Goodness, I hope that old storm won't come our way," said Elaine, just to keep up the pretense of normal social interaction. "What do you think, Harvey? Is it going to storm?"

"Ne. Ne." His mouth full of bread and potato salad. He shook his head. Swallowed. "Frontal system over the upper Great Lakes will remain nearly stationary through tomorrow, with thunderstorm activity expected along a line from Minneapolis east as far as Detroit."

He still hadn't looked directly at her, nor even at his food as he lifted the plate to get it closer to his mouth. Were they making him nervous, or were they just voices unaccountably escaped from behind the screen?

Elaine heard something scrabbling beneath the couch and lifted her feet in alarm. She'd forgotten Harvey's awful cat. As if you could forget it for a minute, the smell and all. A claw shot out to snag her shoelace. From the corner of the couch frame a hairy tail swished back and forth with an angry beat. Perhaps the creature sensed she was a threat to the household and its grimy routine. Elaine flicked a crumpled bit of sandwich wrapper to the floor and the cat emerged to pounce on it. Then, discovering it was useless, it turned to stare at her with its flat yellow eyes. It scratched its chin with a back foot, fleas, probably, and stalked out of the room.

Harvey had eaten everything; he still held the plate, as if unsure what to do with it. "How about some more potato salad, Harvey? No? Look, I brought Josie to see you."

Elaine motioned her forward. Josie squatted on the floor next to him. "Hey, Uncle Harvey, how's it going?"

He raised the green plate up to the level of his chin, then let it fall. His free hand reached out to Josie and touched a stray piece of her hair. A nervous giggle slid down Josie's throat. "Jeez, my hair looks like ass today."

"Watch your mouth, young lady."

"Oh you don't care, do you Uncle Harvey? Look, he likes my earrings too." They were dangling Austrian crystals and they caught the light in a pretty way. One slice of rainbow prism landed on his face and he smiled his crooked smile.

"Mom?"

Josie was pantomiming something, a fluttering gesture with one hand at the bridge of her nose. Did she want her sunglasses back? Elaine reached for them on the table next to her, but Josie shook her head, mouthed something. I. I. I what?

Then Elaine understood. She got up from the couch and went to stand behind Josie. Another commercial was on and she watched Harvey jerk his head toward the noise of the jingle. His eyes were cloudy, like chips of old ice. Cataracts?

He must still see things. The weather maps, colors, lights, and if he sat close enough, words on the screen. Josie was giving her an agonized look, as if there was something she should be doing. "Let's go out on the porch a minute. We'll be right back, OK, Harvey?"

He nodded, or at least Elaine imagined he did. She opened the screen door and stepped out into the strong sunlight, so much brighter than inside She understood that he probably kept it that way so he could better see the television. She understood why nothing in the house was either entirely dirty or entirely clean.

Josie followed her outside. "Oh man. His eyes look so *creepy*."

"Keep your voice down." Elaine paced the narrow length of the porch. There was a red plastic milk crate upended midway. She lowered herself onto it, smoothing her flowered skirt around her. She was getting too old and too fat to wear such things. She looked like a wallpapered cow. "We have to figure out some way to help him."

"Like get him to go to an eye doctor? Good luck."

"Just let me think a minute." What if Harvey needed surgery? What about informed consent? Could you explain to him about hospitals, or injections, or anesthesia? How could you even test his vision in the first place?

The alternative was to leave him alone until his eyes got so bad he'd be groping around on his hands and knees to find things. They'd left him alone for too long already, they being herself, Frank, the community of souls. Elaine looked out at the beautiful day and the crazy little potted garden and the ragged summer-green grass that Harvey still cut with a hand mower. Why did any of it ever have to change?

Josie said, "You can tell him he's going to some sort of weather convention."

"And then what, tie him down? I don't think so. He needs to be able to cooperate."

"Well, doctors treat babies and vets treat animals all the time without their cooperation."

"Your uncle is neither a baby nor a stray dog."

"I didn't say that."

"Let's try for constructive suggestions, all right?"

"Like nothing I say would ever be any good. Thanks a lot." Josie turned to go inside and let the screen door whack shut behind her. Elaine stayed where she was for a time. Always one of them was tinder while the other struck the match.

When she did go back in the house, Harvey was seated on the couch. His usual spot; you could tell from the broken-down springs and the pattern of food stains, like another kind of map. Josie was standing between Harvey and the television, a chocolate chip cookie in each hand. "Ready?"

She'd draped an old wool muffler, something she must have found in a closet, over the top of his head so it covered one eye. He looked ridiculous but docile, like those pictures of dogs dressed up in hats and sunglasses. Now she was the one comparing him to a dog. Josie brought one hand and its cookie very gradually forward until he reached for it. "Great! Now where's the other one?"

She fussed with the scarf, rearranging it, then repeated her drill with the other eye. When Harvey had a cookie in each hand and was trying to get both into his mouth at the same time, Josie smiled at her mother, sweetly smart-ass. "I'd call that cooperation."

Elaine went to see what she could do about the kitchen. She filled the sink with dish soap and scrubbed everything in the cupboards, then started in on the cupboards themselves with the last of some Spic and Span she found under the sink. The stove would be another day's work, but the inside of the refrigerator could have been worse. At least he had actual food in there. As she was tackling the floor, washwater soaking through her front in big damp patches, she heard Josie's breezy laughter. Of course, it wouldn't occur to her to be in here doing something useful. Her knees were wet. She really shouldn't have worn anything nice.

Finally the kitchen was subdued. The rest of the house would have to wait until next time, or maybe she could get a cleaning service to come, if she paid them extra. Josie and Harvey were sitting next to each other on the couch, watching the screen intently. "Hey Mom, did you know they might name a hurricane after Harvey? Cool, huh?"

"That was on the television?"

"No, he told me." Josie flipped her hair off her shoulders in a way that Elaine found irritating, although she usually managed not to say so.

"Really, Harvey? Would you like that?"

He only blinked his cloudy eyes, not looking at her, and pushed the last of the cookies into his mouth. She persisted. "I think I'd probably like it. All the excitement. Special coverage, I bet."

Josie giggled. "Hurricane Mom."

Very funny. "So Harvey," Elaine angled herself to stand in his line of vision, such as it was, "could we come back and see you sometime soon? We could go to the park, have ourselves a real picnic."

He leaned forward, hands on his knees, to take in the details of the Local Forecast for the four-thousandth time. How could anybody stay fixed on this stuff day in and day out? The temperature puttering up or down, wind shifting by inches. Wouldn't it be better to look out the window and be surprised once in a while? Harvey belched mildly. She had not really expected an answer from him. She packed up the sandwich wrappings and empty soda cans. "Josie?"

"Bye, Uncle Harvey. It was great seeing you." Josie kissed him on top of his shiny head. Elaine noticed, and wished she had not, that the old man had an erection.

Elaine led the way to the car, Josie dawdling. "Hurry up, I have to get back to the store." She felt irritated in complicated ways. She had imagined herself bestowing her generosity and good intentions on Harvey, imagined his simple gratitude. She had imagined that she would fix him somehow. She was irritated at Josie for frisking around and playing the favorite (if she only knew the effect she had!), and at Harvey for not being fixable. She couldn't decide exactly how to worry about him, what might happen to him, or perhaps what he might take it into his head to do.

Once they were driving away Josie said, "What did he do before the Weather Channel?"

"I have no idea. He didn't really talk to you, did he?"

"Sure he did. You were in the kitchen. They had this thing on about famous hurricanes, and he said, 'Harvey's on the list.' I said did he mean the list of hurricane names, and he said yes."

Elaine wasn't sure what to think. Everything would be so much easier if there was some way to get through to him. "I don't suppose he said anything else."

"He said, 'It's a terrible thing to fall into the hands of the little dog.'"

"What in the world?"

Josie shrugged. "Don't ask me." She reached for the radio, then thought better of it and slumped back in her seat. "What happened to him anyway, or was he always nuts?"

"He had a nervous breakdown."

"What exactly does that mean? Is it like a computer crashing?"

Elaine glanced over at her, but Josie was peering through the windshield, her forehead puckered and serious. Perhaps they could manage an actual conversation. She said, "I wasn't there. It was a long time ago. Your father was just a kid too, so this is what they told him and he told me. Harvey had a job driving a taxi. I know. Imagine. He must have been in his late twenties then. He drove the cab to St. Louis and ended up at the police station there, saying he was lost. Crying and blubbering. No clue that he'd driven a hundred miles. Couldn't remember where he lived. So your grandpa had to go to St. Louis and bring him back, and when he didn't calm down or get better they sent him to the hospital at Manteno and that's where he stayed for twenty years."

"No way."

"I don't know what they'd do for somebody like Harvey now. Back then it was electric-shock therapy and big doses of thorazine. I don't imagine the family went to see him much. It wasn't encouraged. Then . . ." Elaine sighed. She felt as if she were recounting the history of an old sad war. "Times changed. The big push was to deinstitutionalize, that was the word, mental patients. Put them back in the community and make counties and towns responsible for their care. Except they didn't get any care. Harvey's one of the lucky ones. Your father's family bought him a house. A lot of them just ended up walking the streets."

"Yeah, but what *happened* to him?" Josie demanded.

Not having listened to a word she'd said. Let it go, Elaine told herself. Trust your daughter to let you know when you were being a total bore. "Your father's folks just said he was always weak in the head. That's the way they talked."

The car was quiet then. Elaine thought of other things they might talk about, conversations that, in some ideal world, you might imagine having with your nearly grown daughter. What things made them happy and what things made them afraid. Advice about college, boys, the future. And how you seldom realize you are making a choice, an important turning down some forked path, even as you are trying to be watchful of that very thing. Like trying to see a clock's hands move or trying to catch yourself growing older. Maybe you could see it from outer space, but not close up. Maybe only after you lived a life could you stand back and see its shape and pattern, everything you'd been staring at all along, like those magic eye prints that were so popular a couple years back. Here was knowledge or happiness or desire, whatever it was that knit everything together, here was your name written smaller and smaller, good-bye, good-bye . . .

There was traffic making itself known. She had to come back to the moment, get busy with the mechanics of driving. Josie sighed and her hand spider-walked toward the radio knob. As if there were any subtle way to start that particular music. Elaine opened her mouth to say something exasperated. The dashboard light blinked on and stayed lit.

The Criminal Mind

Friday afternoon and LAX full of people in a hurry to get everywhere in the world. At peak times the airport achieved the population of a small, restless city: business drones with cell phones, packs of slow-moving, cool-walking teenagers, parents herding kids, skycaps pushing wheelchairs loaded with the apprehensive elderly. There were Taiwanese whose hand luggage consisted of plastic shopping bags, Israelis, Filipinos, sunburned Germans who always seemed to be hefting sports equipment, Indian ladies in saris. Snatches of unknown languages, Russian maybe, or Portuguese. Rolando Gottschalk, heir to all the Americas, liked the big airport. It was one place that even his improbably named and ancestored self might be inconspicuous.

He was leaning against a wall, contemplating one of the security checkpoints. The lines were long and travelers were shifting luggage straps from shoulder to shoulder, crowding into one another with no place to go. Although the weather in Los Angeles was summer-perfect, there was fog in Seattle, there were high winds in Phoenix and thunderstorms over the Great Lakes. There were delays and cancellations, everything backing up, people getting fretful. The five no six security types at the checkpoint were hollering at everyone to step here and stop there and raise your arms, and wasn't it great what a cheap coat and tie and an ID badge could do for your ordinary dirtbag's sense of personal power and self-worth.

Rolando picked up the flight bag at his feet and joined the stream of passengers rounding the turn from the ticket counter and slowing as they hit the pileup at the checkpoint. He managed to walk without making any actual forward progress. Echoes bounced and splintered on the tile and glass surfaces. There is a quality of light that is only found in airports, glass reflecting glass reflecting sky. The shrill sunlight bored into his skin layer by layer, warming him, making him sleepy and easeful. He felt like a snake, a magnificent coiling snake, filled with danger and hot blood.

Directly ahead of him was a vacation-bound family, Mom and Pop and three mid- to pint-size kids, distracted and squabbling about who had the tickets and who had to go to the bathroom. Rolando increased his stride so that without rudeness he entered the checkpoint line before them. He was, at this moment, the least memorable traveler in the airport, a thin young man in a wind-breaker and dark work pants, thin mustache, green eyes a little too close together in his brown face. When he reached the X-ray belt he placed his flight bag neatly on its side and stepped through the archway. Nothing metal or suspect in his clean, anonymous pockets. On the other side he paused to remove his windbreaker. Behind him Pop was emptying a noisy river of keys and coins into a tray. One of the kids was acting up, whining, and Mom was saying, "Of *course* you want to go see Grandma," and Pop was emitting a little cloud of peevish exclamation points like a car-toon, and it was the easiest thing in the world (the irritated secu-rity guard repositioning the family's mountain of carry-ons), for Rolando to drop his windbreaker over their camera as he bent to retrieve his flight bag.

Moving neither quickly nor slowly he sought the thickest part of the moving crowd. At the first restroom he entered a stall to ex-amine the camera, a Canon with many desirable features, and placed it in the flight bag. He flushed and washed his hands and made his usual looking-in-the-mirror face, a stone-cold dead-eyed gaze that did not acknowledge the thing he most hated about his reflection: his peanut-shaped skull and kinked red hair. At a snack bar he purchased and ate a slice of pizza and then, when he felt his heart slow to normal resting rate, he retraced his steps and sauntered past the checkpoint. Heartbeat was the clock that never misled you. So that when he walked out through the baggage claim doors and something in the brassy exhaust-tinged air made his pulse quicken he decided that contrary to his plan, this would not be the best place to acquire a vehicle and instead took his usual bus home.

He was superstitious in these private, idiosyncratic ways, unlike his candle-lighting German-Irish-Mexican mother, who sometimes confused the characters in her telenovelas with the saints, unlike his long-vanished Jamaican father who, it was said, had believed in mojo and those voodoo deities in charge of sexual function. Rolando collected smooth pebbles, which he got to know by touch. (Even now he was fingering one caught in the seam of his left front pocket.) He had never owned a calendar and there were times he could not have said what day of the week or even what month it was. He preferred it that way, so as not to lose his own rhythm, that heartbeat clock. He believed that as long as he never flew in an airplane his life was safe. He regarded five-dollar bills as unlucky and avoided receiving them in change. He loved the sun, and on a day like today, when it rode the sky for many hours, he knew that things were working toward some unknown but beneficial end.

After stopping at the home of an acquaintance to dispose of the camera, Rolando approached his own residence on foot. Except for a time in Silver Lake he was too young to remember, he had lived all his twenty-two years in El Este. With his oddly constructed and pigmented face, he could be made into anyone's enemy, an outsider anywhere. Even among Mexicans he ran the risk of being mistaken (and beaten) for a Guatemalan or Samoan. But he was most at home here, in the little pastel houses and tiendas and baleful asphalt. He was more Latino than Black and more Black than Anglo, although the moment you looked at him any of those ways, you began to have doubts.

As soon as he walked in his front door the phone rang. He answered in a flattened voice. "Hello?"

"Rolando?" Ascending plaintive female screech. "Where you been?"

"Busy."

"All week? Don't give me that. Why you don't come around like you said?"

He looked over the room for something to distract or fortify himself but found nothing. The place was a shithole. That was why he was leaving. "I'm busy with I'm gonna be out of town for a little while."

"Out of town where?"

He picked a name. "Texas. San Antone."

"You not going no place without me. Your worthless self promised. Or was that just your dick talking? Lando! You listening to me?"

He held the receiver away from his ear and searched for a cigarette. The phone sounded like a bee in a glass jar. When there was a pause in the noise he said, "It's just some business I got to take care of. It's nothing personal to do with you."

"Business. Your only business is making nasty-ass trouble for me and everybody else. Hear me good. Don't you come sniffing around once you get back. Not if you was to come crawling. Shithead. This is it, finito. Bum voyage."

She hung up. Rolando sighed. He was going to have to leave before she changed her mind and started in pestering him again.

He would have to tell his mother something too, once she got home from work, and she would not be so easy to handle.

If you say to anyone, Tell me your story, there is always a starting place. Rolando was not in the habit of talking about himself, but if something could have crowbarred the words loose, he would have begun with, I had three older brothers. The fathers of the brothers were men named Sergio and Jesus and so they had turned out more or less normal-looking. From an early age they took to pounding on him. It was amusing to them to see how easily he could be made to land on his diapered bottom and squawl, like a superior sort of toy. When he was a little older they invented elaborate routines and strategies to trip him up and send him tumbling down stairs or into unyielding objects. When it came to something basic, like hitting, their efforts were thorough and varied. They employed flat-handed slaps to the back of the head, knuckles to the ribs, a thumb that hooked you just under the chin, the sudden wrench and pop of a twisted arm. It didn't help that his mother defended him and doted on him and punished the others for his every bruise and blood letting. The brothers had long ago moved on to their own forms of trouble, but from them he learned lasting lessons of guile, silence, speed, and vengeance.

From his growing-up years he learned other things. That the evil-smelling ditch behind the garage was an excellent place to practice feats of balance and acrobatics. He knew the wealth of tastes available at the corner store, dulces and gumballs and red-hot potato chips and Nehi flavors, and the melting in the mouth when you had a craving for one certain thing. How to make a gun that shot bottle caps, with considerable impact, out of a sanded piece of wood, a nail, and rubber bands. How to ride double on a bike, how to latch on to the bumper of an accelerating car in order to prove skill and bravery. Pussy. You din't even half-try. Screw you fuck face, screw you puta mamma. They loved the way those words filled up their mouths. Other boys learned that while the standard insults were acceptable, they must not call him Nigger Lips or Brillo Head, not unless they wanted to risk an all-out attack in which the standard rules of combat did not apply.

He was secretive, solitary, on the edge of every group. He kept his eyes open for opportunities, he prided himself on his perfect, better-than-twenty-twenty vision. It was amazing, the number of people who never really noticed anything or took proper precautions. It was also a matter of pride that he had never actually been arrested, although he had been asked many times by the police to justify his presence on the streets, his identity and his intentions, as part of a public safety policy that protected certain neighborhoods from the people who lived in them. From time to time he worked at one or another small job, but for the most part he was engaged in the acquisition of certain items of personal property from careless individuals. It was a way of getting by; he couldn't remember ever feeling guilty about it. A kind of harvesting, wherein people with too much of things, money that might go sour or bad, were relieved of its burden.

But he had begun to chafe at his old routines. There was a narrowness in his life. He felt he had never really decided on a course of action, only drifted into things. He had cloudy dreams of all the places he had never seen, all the lives it might be possible for him to live, once he broke free from his origins. He had been saving up money bit by bit, fifteen hundred dollars. Counting it out felt like flexing a muscle. He had a sense of possibilities, of unknown currents in himself. Anger had been his only fuel and power, the thing he could most easily lay hands on and call forth. But what if he possessed other qualities and strengths, previously unsuspected? If he could not change his face or his history, he might yet breathe a different air.

He might surprise them all some day, him, Rolando Got Jack, target of a thousand jokes and fists. He might return with his pockets full of wealth, as wise and smooth as one of his mother's brown saints. Anything could happen.

But first he had preparations to make. That evening, after his mother had finished disbelieving his story about San Antonio, he stepped out into the street. Paused to get a cigarette working. Children called out to each other in the rose-tinged dusk. Traffic noise, never very far away, crested and receded like the ocean. Although the air had cooled, the pavement still smelled hot. There were other smells too, something balmy or fruity, with a faint underlay of stink. The things they put in the air nowadays, the sweet was probably just as bad for you as the stink. He walked to the end of the block, nodding to people sitting out on lawn chairs, people walking dogs, and although none of them individually was anyone he expected to miss, he would miss the whole of them.

On the avenue the night would just now be getting underway, the cars cruising slow and soft through the wash of lights and music, the sidewalk busy with sellers of CDs and silver and T-shirts, doorways propped open for a glimpse of the ruby-lit darkness inside, and everywhere the beautiful, beautiful girls . . . But he steered clear of all this and hiked on as far as the small, nearly grassless park. Two younger boys were playing basketball in a circle of streetlight that lit them like a stage. He had never been much of a player, but he loved the tart sound of the ball on cement and the boys' excited, swaggering voices. And the view from the park's little rise, the pink smear of freeway lights and beyond them the distant mountains, black except for the small trails and constellations of brightness, like an upside-down universe. He would miss all this too. It disconcerted him to discover such feelings in himself, soft places that sent out eddies of confusion just when he needed to be straightforward and clear.

He caught a bus on Whittier, transferred downtown, and disembarked in a neighborhood that had often suited his purposes.

Quiet, but not so much that a pedestrian would attract undue attention. In Los Angeles it was often a very suspicious thing to be a pedestrian. Nice houses, these. Little bungalows with red-tile roofs, brass gadgets on the front doors, fishponds, somebody's idea of a statue. A place he wouldn't mind living himself, if not for his prejudice against any wealth that could not be carried by hand. He strolled past the car he had already picked out, a sky blue Ford product with enough of the new worn off it so that people might have grown relaxed about things like alarms. His heartbeat was so sweet and steady, you could have used it to keep time to a waltz.

These things were not difficult, given the proper equipment, experience, and opportunity. A final look around. Pop the lock, strip the wires, fire it up, and go. They never knew what hit them. Out on the boulevard and merging with the traffic, a model citizen obeying all vehicular laws. Oh, he was slick. He sang himself a little slick song as he fooled with the radio. Half a tank of gas in it. These folks were absolute princes. He could tell they were the kind to have excellent insurance. He wished them well. Thirty-eight thousand miles on it, practically new. He took further inventory. Box of Kleenex. Change caddy with a handy roll of quarters. If he'd called Avis and told them what he needed, he couldn't have done better.

There was a nice tape player, with auto-reverse and a lot of settings that would be fun to fool with. Already he had begun to think of it as his car. Groping around, he found a single cassette in the console, homemade by the look of it.

He popped it in and weird shit started coming out of the speakers. Chimes and flutes and bird noise. And here he thought these people had taste. He was disappointed in them, he was personally saddened. He reached to eject the tape. That was when the angel choir started up.

Layers of sound so beautiful it made him see colors, white and candy-cane pink and sunburst gold. The angels climbed stairways of luminous chords. His heart climbed with them. Crazy! They were just singing Ohhh, but like nobody's business.

Then the voice started. A man's voice, welcoming and easy, the voice of your best friend. "Life," it said, "can seem complicated. We all know the feeling. Worries about work, health, relationships, money. Worry on top of worry. Times we feel we hardly have room to breathe freely, let alone relax, clear our minds, and focus on what's important to us. For the next hour I'd like you to join me in a journey toward harmony and greater self-knowledge. Remember, you are not alone." The angels sang a little riff. "When the world swirls with formless chaos, when fears and troubles mount, remember that forces for peace and understanding are all around you. You are a cell in the body of God. You are a cell in the body of God." The words echoed and reechoed. The angels were going nuts. "You are a cell in the body of God. You are a cell in the—"

Rolando punched the eject. New Age crap. Great production values, feel-good bullshit for people whose biggest problem was how to pay for their tennis club membership. Man, he was glad he lifted their car. He should go back and burn their house down so they'd get a feel for what real trouble was. Real was his nose twice broken, so much for breathing freely. Real was the tattoo on his right shoulder, a snake coiling around a rose whose petals dripped blood. Real was a lifetime of jobs like the one at Planet Chicken, clearing away half-chewed lettuce and cigarettes put out in coffee cups and worse. Real was the deck stacked against him since before he was born. If there was such a thing as the body of God, then he was an abscess, a tumor, a stinking boil.

This was how the anger came over him, all at once in a black wave. Once he reached his own neighborhood he parked the car two blocks away and slipped inside the darkened house where his mother slept. His duffle was already packed. He took the roll of money from its hiding place, also the gun he dared some fool to make him use. Then he was gone for good. He pulled away with as much speed and noise as he could muscle out of the engine and hit the freeway, heading east.

Part Two **July**

Global Warming

Something was wrong with the hot. It kept getting more. There were places like Texas that you expected to crisp up every summer. But this was different. Cities far up north zoomed into the nineties. Out east it quit raining. There were serious charts that showed the rainfall deficits, nine, ten, fifteen inches. Yellow patches crawled across the map; they meant drought. It was the worst one this century. Or maybe second worst. Scientists had measured the polar ice caps and the glaciers in Alaska. There was no doubt about it. Everything was melting.

For all have sinned and fall short of the glory of God.

Local Forecast watched the bubble of hot air floating over You Are Here. Every day the bubble grew a little larger. He could feel the weight of it. All the folded places of his body stuck together. The thermometer outside the kitchen window rode a rocket. Fat Cat stretched out on the floor by the fan. You could have tied it in a knot. All afternoon the big yellow sun beat beat beat against the window shades. The air slowed down to nothing.

Man In A Suit said, drink plenty of fluids, limit exertion, wear comfortable, light-colored clothing, avoid alcoholic beverages. He did all that. It wasn't enough. It just got hotter. He filled dishes of water for the exhausted birds. He ran bathwater and paddled around in the tub until his hands got pruney. In Chicago the power kept failing. He didn't like to think about things like that.

He imagined giant wheels and pistons grinding to a stop, electricity leaking out of the long black wires. Everything was breaking. What if the water was next?

It was the Year Of Our Lord Nineteen Ninety-Nine. Something big and bad was coming.

The grass was turning yellow. He dribbled the hose on it but he wasn't rain, he didn't do it any good. Here and there they got a thunderstorm, then the sky shriveled up. He worried about the farmers. If the farmers didn't get rain, they couldn't grow food. That meant hard times. People going hungry, starving, as the oceans rose and covered up Washington, New Orleans, Los Angeles. Tall buildings going down like sand castles. Now cut that out. It was scairdy talk. You could get in trouble. Crying I'll give you something to cry about.

His head hurt. When you stayed in the tub too long, your brain wrinkled up. Daddy was dead. Mamma was dead. Frank was dead. Sometimes he missed them but not really. They were in Heaven. Heaven was like a football game they had the best tickets to. Daddy slept the sleep of the just. Sometimes he snored. You could creep right up to him and look into his mouth, the black place the snores came out of. His tongue was sticky. The corners of his mouth were sticky. The snores blew little sticky pieces back and forth like curtains in a window. There was a smell too. It was amazing that such a smell came out of Daddy, a purely evil smell. It started down where the snores were. Like there was something bad black inside that only came out when Daddy slept. It spoke in the language of snores. Very carefully he leaned close in so he could feel the rumble all through his head. He listened hard. It was saying all the words you weren't supposed to say. It was pleased with itself for getting away with such a trick. Daddy's eyes opened no no no 30 percent chance of showers late, then clearing and continued warm.

He was still in the tub when Yoo Hoo came. He didn't hear her until she walked right up to the bathroom door. "Harvey? You in there?"

He gave a little yelp and knocked the water this way and that. He was embarrassed not to have his clothes on. "It's all right, Harvey, it's only me. I'll go wait on the front porch. I have a surprise for you, OK?"

Local Forecast let the stopper out of the tub until there was only him left in it. He didn't feel clean, just naked. He ran to his closet and got dressed as fast as he could. Then he could relax. There was only one Yoo Hoo today. She sat on the glider next to a big gray box. "Whew. I just don't think it can get any hotter. I brought you an air conditioner, Harvey. What do you think about that?"

Local Forecast had forgotten shoes and socks. He felt bad about his feet. They were so long and white and fish-shaped. He tried to walk them back under his pants legs. "An air conditioner. Do you know what that is?"

He reached out a finger to touch it. It felt cool. Yoo Hoo said you plugged it in. "We could put it right next to the television. I honestly don't know how you've gotten by without one all this time. Can you help me lift it?"

He wasn't much help on account of still being mortified about his feet. He bent down close to try and see them better. They looked like something that had grown moldy in the ground, big pale moldy roots. She said never mind, she could do it herself. She kept talking to show him how easy it was and how much fun. He liked her. She smelled good. "We just need to—prop it up right here—get it more . . . unnhh. When's the last time you had this window open? All right. Ready?"

It started up loud. The window rattled and shook. Then it kicked out a little cold air. Yoo Hoo got all excited. She said for him to get his shoes on. "We'll go for a drive, and when we get back it'll be all cool. How about that?"

It was a wonderful thing. It was cold-in-a-box. Instant October. "Harvey, I promise you nobody's going to take it away. It'll be right here when you get back. Now where are your shoes?"

She talked so much she got him out the door. His eyes hurt. The hot was too yellow. He stopped his feet and tried to get his mouth moving. "Daddy said."

"What's that, Harvey?" She leaned in close to him. She had a face that asked questions even when she didn't talk. "You know what would be a good idea for you? Sunglasses. Here. That better?"

"Daddy said the world shall be destroyed by fire."

"Slow down, I can't understand you. Are you worried about the car? The car has air-conditioning too. I promise I'll drive extra careful."

The world flew by in bits and streaks. Its colors were melting. The glass was rolled up. On the other side of it things zoomed toward him, then away. "I bet it's been a while since you rode in a car, huh, Harvey? Can you even remember the last time?"

His stomach flipped up and down. The last time you. He had glasses on his nose. How did that happen? He missed the Weather. Had he remembered to turn the talking down? Daddy said it was the last time he was going to put up with that sort of nonsense. He was a bigboy now, old enough to know the difference between right and wrong. Local Forecast squeezed his eyes shut. He heard the calming voice of Beige Woman, talking about all the Weather that was happening in places a long ways away. The Weather was one thing that was nobody's fault.

Except for Global Warming. He gave a little hot-and-cold shiver. All this while he had tried not to think about it. He forgot what he did wrong but it was bad. He told Mamma he was sorry.

Mamma said Turn not to the right hand nor to the left: remove thy foot from evil. Mamma's hands were afflicted. She rubbed them with salve but the skin stayed cracked and raw. When she washed his face her hands scratched him. The salve smelled like glue and mothballs. Global Warming was what happened when your feet did evil. He had sinned and fallen short. Whatever he had done, was it bad enough to burn up the whole world? The smell was horrible. He could feel his stomach rising up his throat.

"Harvey? Do you need to stop?"

She came around and opened up his door and he put his head out and spat up a little on the pavement. "Oh dear," said Yoo Hoo. "Maybe this was just too much too soon. Here, take this and rinse out your mouth."

With the car stopped he felt better. He leaned back so his head was in the cold and his feet in the hot. "I was going to take you to McDonald's but I don't know what that would do for your stomach."

"Supersize it!"

She laughed and said she guessed he watched enough television to know about McDonald's. Was he sure he felt up for it?

"Quarterpounderwithcheese!"

Local Forecast and Yoo Hoo sat in the car, eating out of paper bags. They had big wet paper cups full of ice and pop. Everything was so good. His mouth couldn't get enough. He licked the salt from his fingers. Yoo Hoo said Slow down, don't make yourself sick again. But she was laughing, she was in a good mood. He scrabbled around in the bottom of the bag. All gone. He belched.

"I usually don't eat junk food. You won't tell on me, will you, Harvey?" He was supposed to say something, either yes or no. But the only thing that came out of him was another belch. Pretty soon he was going to have to pee. Where were they anyway? It was full of trees he didn't know.

"Most days I just eat at the register. A salad or something. It gets so busy. Then I go home and I'm too tired to fix anything decent. Josie's hardly ever there anymore. I pour a glass of wine and fall asleep in front of the TV. Not much of a life, is it?"

Trees and cold air whooshing up from the innards of the car. He liked the car. It was big and smooth and the seats were the color of vanilla. If you had the right kind of car, you didn't have to worry so much about Global Warming. You just drove somewhere cooler.

"All I do is try and keep one step ahead so the business doesn't go down the tubes. I've seen it happen. You don't stay sharp, you're history. So everything's haggle and push and pinch. I have to remind myself the whole rat race was my big idea. Nobody said I had to run an import business. I feel like Alec Guinness at the end of The *Bridge on the River Kwai,* do you know that movie? After he's tried to stop his own army from blowing up the bridge, and he slaps his hand to his forehead and says, 'What have I done?'"

Local Forecast really really really had to pee. He opened the car door and ran into the trees. The trees were all too skinny. He ran a little farther but the heat made him wobble and he still had the glasses banging on his nose and finally he just couldn't wait any more and unzipped right where he was and did it on the ground.

It felt so much better. He couldn't see much of anything because of the glasses but there was a lot of loud talking. Somebody was saying Police. Then Yoo Hoo was at his side, turning him around and telling him he had to come with her. She told him to do up his pants. He was so embarrassed. The Police were like Daddy.

When they were back in the car Yoo Hoo said it was all her fault. She should have been watching out, taking better care of him. "Next time you tell me if you have to go, OK?"

So he was in trouble again. Oh, bad word. Frank said he was going to get it now. Frank was a pistol. He whupped the Germans. He had a uniform and medals. He had answered the call of duty. Frank said the Army didn't take sissies. One look at him and the Army would laugh itself blue in the face. That's why he didn't go to war. He was just as glad. He never liked loud things and the Army was full of them.

He liked running, back when his legs worked. He could just stick his head in the air and go and go. Nobody could catch him. It was one more thing he liked about the Weather, it was fast. Mamma Daddy Frank were slow, because they were dead. He ran past them and waved. He climbed the clouds like steps.

The car stopped. They were back home. "Yoo Hoo," said Yoo Hoo. Are you listening? Are you understanding?

He was so fast, her words couldn't catch up to him. Her words rose to his ears like fish bubbles coming to the surface of a pond. If he closed his eyes, he could pretend he was running. The car door opened and she tugged on his arm. He liked not looking. He cheated and opened his eyes a little going up the stairs. "I don't suppose you've ever locked this door. That's something you should really get in the habit of doing. Do you even know where the key is? Never mind. I'll look for it."

He kept his eyes shut and felt around for the couch. The Weather was talking so he knew exactly where he was. The air whistled with cool. He grinned out loud. When he sat down on the couch, Fat Cat thumped into his lap. Man In A Suit said, Record heat continues in the central plains, midwest, northeast, and southeast. But inside it was perfect. He petted Fat Cat. Even his fingers were happy.

Local Forecast must have fallen asleep. He woke up but he kept his eyes closed. He had such a funny dream. It was about the Army, where he'd never even been. In his dream the Army gave him a medal. It was for fast running. He forgot Yoo Hoo was still there. She said, "What are you doing with those glasses still on? How can you see anything at all?"

She lifted them off his nose. His eyes were still screwed shut. "Look at me, Harvey. I have to show you how to turn the air conditioner on and off. In case you get too cold. Right here. Harvey! It's important."

Local Forecast opened one eye. She showed him On and Off. Sometimes she acted like he didn't know anything.

"I cleaned the bathroom and brought you some supplies, toilet paper and Comet and stuff. And kitty litter. You definitely need kitty litter. Now I want to talk to you about something else. Are you listening? Are you hearing?"

He pointed to his ears. He had closed his eyes again but he could feel her looking at him, deciding things. "Fine. I'd like to take you in for a checkup. Just your basic physical. How long has it been since you've had one? Never mind. I'd almost rather not know. I promise no one will hurt you."

He wondered if she lived anywhere she would be going back to soon.

"And an eye exam. I'm very concerned about your eyesight. You might not even notice because it's a gradual thing. I'm hoping there's something they can do about it. We'll see what the doctor—"

no no no no doctor no no no doctor run bad word feet bad smell hot hot run no no no no

Desperate Diseases

Josie couldn't decide if it would be better to be the victim of a crime or to have him arrest her. There were advantages to both. It was sexier to be the arrestee. A girl gangster, tough and sneering, being manhandled into the back of a squad car. Oh yeah? Make me, copper. A cigarette dangling from her pouting crimson lips. He would have to handcuff her. There would be this incredible dynamic between them, an initial antagonism that masked their smoldering . . . nah, no good. Cheese-o-rama. This is your brain on love. Every lame MTV video and bad movie she'd ever seen was infecting her. Anyway there were consequences involved in acquiring an arrest record, plus she didn't really want to take up smoking.

So what was she supposed to do, pay somebody to mug her? Join the force? Tammy said, "What if he's gay?"

"Oh thank you. Thank you very much."

"Seriously. He's too perfect. If he's not gay, then he's every gay guy's fantasy."

She never should have said anything to Tammy. Too late. She'd wanted to show him off. So she'd driven Tammy to the Super Pantry where, if you parked and pretended to use the pay phone sometimes around three-thirty in the afternoon, you might be rewarded with a brief but unobstructed view of Officer Crook, sauntering into police headquarters across the street.

Sometimes he was already in uniform, sometimes not. He didn't wear anything gay, just ordinary shirts and jeans. Tammy was full of shit. There were probably gay cops somewhere, but not in Springfield. The M was for Mitchell. Mitch. She knew that from the phone book. He drove a black Acura with a sunroof, license plate KCX 767. None of the things she could find out about him were any help. He was still sealed up inside his beautiful self.

"So how are you supposed to hook up with him, assuming he even likes girls?" Tammy was acting like it was so hysterical but Josie could tell she was impressed with him and trying not to be.

"I followed him home one night," Josie admitted.

"Stalker!"

Try every night last week. She was beginning to think he wasn't much of a cop, not to notice her. A couple of times he stopped at a sports bar she was afraid even to enter lest her arrest fantasy come true. But most often he just went home. He lived in an ordinary apartment building, a place for people who didn't care where they lived. That was sort of disappointing but maybe he had it fixed up nice inside. She tried to figure out which windows were his but everything was curtained over and blind. So she'd sit for a while longer in the parking lot, watching bugs that were as stupid as she was battering the false moon of the sodium-vapor streetlamp. The air at midnight was just as thick and humid as it was at noon, worse, almost, because the black choked you. She would drive home feeling she had begun something terrible, reckless, and greedy that would come to no good end.

There wasn't room in her now for anything but love. It weighed her down, it fought to burst out of her. She was truly miserable, and at the same time she was exalted. She couldn't believe that no one noticed. At night in her bed she made love to her fingers, calling forth every scrap of him, every image that was no longer a memory but a picture of memory, and the more the actual fact of him receded, the harder she urged her body, until it seemed that when she made herself come, she had somehow embraced him. At other times she knew very well that a love that fed only on itself was unreal, unwholesome. Something had to happen.

She was sick from the heat and sick from desire that went nowhere. You couldn't forget about the heat for a minute. One of the hottest Julys on record, they said. The air conditioning at home wasn't working right; it couldn't keep up with the temperature and poured out a thin tepid soup. So that both awake and asleep she felt gritty and dragged out. She slept as late as she could and most days she woke up to an empty house. In the kitchen there would be a coffeepot burned down to sludge and a note from her mother: Hi Sunshine, don't forget whatever tedious thing she was supposed to do around the house. Have a great day! Sunshine. Her mother was not being sarcastic. She was incapable of such a thing. But how could anybody look at her crazed and hangdog self and think Sunshine? And what was Mitchell Crook doing at this exact same instant?

Tammy said she should just forget about it.

"How old do you think he is anyway?"

"I don't know. Twenty-one or -two."

"Try twenty-six." Tammy had a jolly look on her face.

"Like you know shit about him."

"Fine. Have it your way." Tammy went back to picking at her eyebrows in the mirror. She was thinking of getting one pierced and was trying to decide if she had the right bone structure to carry it off.

Josie thought that Tammy was somebody she could see herself not being friends with someday. Sooner or later they would have some really gorgeous fight and all the little things that irritated them about each other would burst into flame. "All right," Josie said. "Give."

"I asked my brother if he knew any fag policemen."

"No more gay stuff, OK?"

"I asked him if he knew anybody named Crook and he said there was a Crook a year ahead of him. So I found him in Kent's old yearbook and he was Class of '91. Do the math. At least twenty-five and probably twenty-six."

That was Springfield for you. There was no such thing as a handsome stranger. Everyone had already been discovered and colonized. Twenty-six. Some of the air went out of her. That meant when she herself was thirty, he would be almost forty.

"So anyway, Miss Jailbait, unless he's some kind of child molester—"

"Just shut up, all right?" It was a matter of pride now. If this was really love, it didn't matter. Besides, it wasn't that he was too old. It was that she was such a little underaged twerp and no one would ever take her seriously.

Her new job was a big improvement simply because the place was about two months away from going out of business. So she got off work early almost every night and could prowl the streets, looking for love. The restaurant was called Beefeater's. The conceit was that diners were in Merry Olde England. When she was in the mood to think that such things were funny, Josie imagined opening a restaurant with the daring concept of eating right where you actually were. A purely Springfield ambiance. It would be called Abe's, and decorated in a corn and soybeans motif. The menu would feature food that could be eaten with the hands.

The cook at Beefeater's had a cough that sounded like it came up from the bottom of a coal mine, and his feet were giving out or maybe it was his knees so he spent most of his time drinking coffee at the break table. The steaks had names like the King's Ransom and the Queen's Fancy and he screwed them all up so bad the joke was the little flags saying RARE or MEDIUM were going to be replaced by ones labeled E. COLI and BURNT COW'S ASS. The manager was a pimp. The dishwasher would probably turn up on *America's Most Wanted* someday. Josie handed out menus to the few customers dim enough not to have gotten the word yet. "Was everything all right?" she asked them as they paid their bill under the fake heraldic banner that marked the cash register. "Come back and see us again soon." Smiling her most delighted, innocent smile and would life ever offer her an opportunity for anything but screaming irony?

Her mother said, "I can't believe you're at work until all hours. So why don't you tell me what you do instead?"

"Mom, it's summer."

"What's that supposed to mean? Just because it's summer I'm not going to worry about you? Let me remind you

That You Are Still A Minor And As Long As I Am Responsible For You oh, did her mother ever say anything that wasn't a completely canned speech? Every time she opened her mouth Josie imagined an audience of chairs springing up before her, like her Women In Business meetings.

It was Sunday morning, one of the few times neither of them had to be someplace else and so they were stuck in the house together. Her mother had fixed some runny scrambled eggs that neither of them really wanted, in an attempt to make it a festive occasion. Her mother was wearing another of her print caftans. She had about twenty of them. Josie thought they were like carrying a sign that announced: I Have Let Myself Go. You could still see where her mother had been pretty, in the arch of her eyebrow and the way her hair swept back from her forehead in a smooth dark curl. But the skin underneath her eyes and chin looked muddy and stretched, and if she, Josie, ever put on weight like that, so her arms jiggled and her boobs stuck out as square as a drawer in a file cabinet—

"—asked you a question, Miss."

"Come on, Mom." She acted bored, which could always disguise her not paying attention. "I just hang out with kids. We do stupid stuff like go to the Super Pantry. Drive around. It's not like there's anything to do."

"There's enough for you to get into trouble. Whatever you're doing it better not be something you don't want me to catch you at. Now listen up. Your father and Teeny want you to go with them to Aspen the end of August and I think it's a good idea."

"Well, I think it's a completely rancid idea, Mom!"

"You just finished telling me there's nothing to do here."

"I'd rather be bored than tortured. Besides, I have to work."

"It would be the week before school starts. You'll have to quit anyway." Her mother was logical at all the wrong times.

"They don't really want me to go. They just want to be able to say they spent money on me so I owe them something. Besides, Aspen's full of women who wear fur coats with cowboy boots and guys—"

"Have you ever been there?"

"—guys with fake hair and big turquoise rings. I've seen their pictures. All their friends are like that, rich and awful. They sit around and drink and think they're so hilarious. Besides, Teeny's gross."

"Yes." Her mother sighed. "She is that."

"She'll make me fetch and carry all her stupid hats and sunglasses and I'll have to go shopping with her at horrible boutiques that sell shiny jumpsuits and leopard-print sweaters and she'll try on these horrible expensive tacky clothes and ask me how they look—"

Her mother was laughing and trying not to. Laughter was spurting out of her closed lips in little snorts. "All right. So much for Teeny. But your father would still like to spend some time with you."

"Sure."

"Come on, baby. I'm trying to be a good custodial parent here. Don't sabotage me. It won't kill you to spend a week in a fancy condo with mountain views."

"You're forgetting the views of Dad and Teeny acting like total cow flop."

"Now that's just mean."

"Last time I went over there for dinner, Teeny played her exercise video the whole while and Dad stayed in the bathroom for forty minutes."

"Your father isn't that good at expressing his feelings."

"Because he doesn't have any. How about what I want to do, doesn't that mean anything to him?"

Her mother began to look very patient. "Maybe if you invested some effort with him. Changed your attitude."

"Why is it always me that has to do stuff? Huh? Why don't you ever tell him to invest some effort or change his attitude? Does he get some kind of special lifetime credit just for being around when I was born?" They were going to make her do this, go on the vacation from hell and waste her last free week, a thousand miles away from Mitchell Crook who didn't know she was alive.

"As a matter of fact he does. And so do I. That doesn't mean parents are perfect. It doesn't mean we don't have to do our part. But we are your—what? What is that face supposed to mean?"

"Why do you always talk like that? Why do you always think you know everything? God. You don't know fucking anything."

"That's enough of that kind of talk."

"Fuck fuck fuck fuck fuck fuck fuck." But the splendid anger that had propelled her was already trailing off, and her mother was giving her a saddened, superior look.

"All right," she said. "Thank you for your elevated and mature contribution to the discussion. I think I'll let you talk to your father yourself about Aspen. I can't imagine he'll really want to take you anywhere."

The caftan billowed and frumped its way out of the room. Stupid stupid stupid stupid.

Abe was a great father. Even when he was president he'd make time to kiss the boys good night. Mary said he spoiled them. Two of them died. Little Eddie and Willie. They died of things like scarlet fever and typhus or something else that nobody died of anymore. It was terribly sad. She sent her sadness across the years. She always felt it reached him somehow, just as his wisdom and suffering reached her.

Maybe she should go ahead and die. Or almost die, so they'd feel sorry for her. She knew it was a childish way of thinking, but her whole idiot self was turning into a mess of impulses and shrieking nerves, and if someone had proved to her that in her next life she would come back as Mitchell Crook's dog or Mitchell Crook's parakeet, anything that was allowed to look on him awake and asleep and remember, dimly, that she had always loved him, she would have said yes, gladly, let me die.

Since she was not dead she did things like call his apartment on nights she was certain he was at work. So she was a stalker. It wasn't anything she couldn't deal with, now that she had absolutely no pride. It was a sickness, the following and the calling. A secret sickness that she only pretended to want to cure. How weak, degrading, shameful it all was. Once she had said these things to herself she was free to go ahead and do what she wanted. She always blocked her phone number in case he had Caller ID or some other kind of police superscanner. The phone rang four times before his machine picked up. "Hi, Mitch here, I'll get back to you." Plain and simple. Eight syllables. You could have set them to music. The sound of his voice was a drug that she only allowed herself every so often. And once when she'd miscalculated and he answered with a breezy hello, she dropped the phone as if it burned her. The actual fact of him was just too overwhelming.

Some nights she drove out to Lake Springfield, just to depress herself further. It was a tame sort of a lake, with a soft mud bottom and water the color of tea. There were fish in it, sure, people caught them and ate them, even though there was supposed to be some disease you could catch from swimming in it. There were places kids went to drink beer and mess around. She and Jeff had done that, plenty of times. She heard he had a new girlfriend. She guessed she was glad he wouldn't be hanging around pestering her, but there was something irritating about it also.

She drove through all the places she imagined police might patrol. The public housing complexes, the crumbling, deserted edge of downtown with its welding shops and gaping warehouses. The mall where scuzzy kids her age hung out in packs, and the truly awful liquor store that looked like it got robbed about once a week. From time to time it occurred to her that it was genuinely dangerous to be in such places. She took pride in this. It made her feel she was finally accomplishing something. And when a black guy in an old rattletrap car pulled up next to her at a stoplight and said, in a bored voice, "Hey, you want your pussy licked?" Josie only said, "No thank you," and drove on.

She almost never saw a cop car. You'd think there was no crime here, along with all the other things they didn't have. She certainly never saw Mitchell Crook. She had no idea what beat or territory he covered, which was what kept her from doing something like burglarizing her own house and calling 911.

Then one night, in the gasping middle of the heat wave, when the lead story on the local news had been the death of six hundred chickens after a poultry farm's cooling system failed, her luck changed. She'd gone into Blockbuster to kill some time when sirens started up, a whole howling chorus of them. Everybody else in the store looked around for a startled moment, then went back to flipping through the videos. But Josie was out the door and across the parking lot in a dead run. She could still see the taillights and revolving flashers at the end of the street, about to be swallowed up by darkness.

On a hunch she gunned the car after the now-vanished lights, then swung left onto Sangamon Avenue. She rolled down the window to hear an echo of sirens. They were headed out to the west edge of town, where the Auto Zone and discount grocery and Farmer's Service Co-op gave over to a new subdivision of little square houses, like a child's blocks, before the monotonous fields began.

Was it a fire? Josie couldn't tell. A fire was of no use to her. No, she saw the string of winking lights clearly. They were turning into the vast concrete apron of empty parking lot around the FS Co-op. She cut behind the shopping center to the service road that ran along the edge of a stray cornfield. This was far enough away that she felt inconspicuous, although she could still see. They were police squads all right, three of them. She felt an unmistakable sexual tickle, God, what kind of freak was she becoming?

She left the engine running for the air-conditioning but turned the headlights off and stepped out of the car for a better look. To one side of the Co-op were big above-ground ammonia tanks, a smaller tank for kerosene, and a row of tractor tires, man-high, bags of mulch and peat moss on pallets, straw bales under a tarp, and piles of gravel and landscaping stone. Now that the squad cars were here nothing seemed to be happening. She could see a group of men standing around in the headlights, although her view was obscured and she was too far away to hope to make anyone out. It had to be almost ninety degrees still, and wet-blanket humid. Sweat felt a half-inch thick on her skin.

Then two figures emerged from the far corner of the building where they must have been crouching behind the ammonia tanks. They ran toward the cornfield, almost straight at her. She was too paralyzed to move, and they didn't seem to notice her until they were almost upon her, and then the one in front skidded to a stop and the one behind cursed and nearly piled into him. When the first boy lifted his face she said, "Moron? Is that you?"

It was so dark out there she couldn't guess how she'd recognized him. Maybe it was the bulk of him, and the way he ran, heavily, with his shoulder tight and muscle-bound. "Josie!" he yelped, and the boy behind him said, "Shaddup, will ya?" in a loud whisper.

"What are you—"

But Moron had her by both arms and was half-lifting, half-pushing her ahead of them, across the road and into the cornfield. She was still sorting out her first surprise, and to be bundled along like this, to be enveloped in so much large and hot-smelling flesh, was an extraordinary thing. The corn was nearly head-high, a good crop year everybody said, not that she could ever remember a bad one. Corn just couldn't help but grow here. The wide green leaves slapped her face. The boy she didn't know was muttering curses.

When they were a few rows in, Moron loosened his grip and she said, more curious than anything else, "What is this, huh?"

Moron bent over with his hands on his knees to catch his breath. "Man, I suck. No endurance."

The other boy said, "I am going to kick Podolsky's ass big time. What a limp dick." Josie recognized him now, a kid with bad skin and long, weedy hair who hung out at the losers' table in the school cafeteria.

Moron said to her, "We were messing around in there and this guy Podolsky was in the car outside and we set off the alarm and he freaked."

"Oh. What were you looking for?"

"Just stuff. I thought maybe they'd have some tires that'd work on my truck."

"Don't tell her anything. Jesus Christ." The longhaired kid was crouched down in the cornstalks, peering back at the Co-op. "They're still out there. I don't think they saw us."

"How's Taco Swill?" Josie asked Moron, for something to say.

"Oh I quit not real long after you did. I got on at Plastic-Pak. It pays a ton better and I don't have to wear a stupid hat."

"Yeah. I got another job too." She was wondering what she ought to do about her car. Over the sound of the engine she could hear the tiny voice of the radio behind the sealed glass.

"So what are you doing here? This is too weird."

She couldn't invent anything that made sense, so she mostly told the truth. "I heard the sirens and followed them to see what was happening."

"Yah?" She couldn't tell if he disbelieved her or if he'd just run out of things to say. He was quiet, peering through the thick-planted rows. Even hunkered down he looked absurdly large and visible, like an elephant trying to hide behind a picket fence.

"Well," said Josie, "I should probably shove off now. You boys take it easy." She stood up and started back toward the road.

"Whoa whoa whoa." Between the two of them they hauled her back down. "That's not a good idea right now," Moron explained.

"Yeah, why don't you stick around for a while," said the longhaired boy. "Until things sort of chill out. Then maybe you could give us a ride home."

"You want me to be your getaway driver?" She giggled. It sounded like the sort of thing she might expect to do in this, her new reckless life.

"It'd just be giving us a ride."

"See," said Moron, "Ronnie, he's seventeen, that's still juvenile. But I'm eighteen so I'm an adult offender. I gotta be more careful."

"Did you guys actually steal anything?" Josie asked, beginning to take an interest.

Ronnie dug in his back pocket. "Just some bean inoculant they had up by the register. Little bags of it."

"That is so ridiculous."

"Hey, it's not like we had time to browse around."

"I wish the dumb cops would figure out the party's over."

"You don't think they had video cameras in there, do you?"

"Bean inoculant. You got a promising career in crime."

"Fuck you."

It was as hot as the inside of a black box. Even the blurred quarter moon was gassy and hot. Something like locusts, except louder and more metallic-sounding, were making a racket in the weeds at the side of the road. Josie tried to see what the police were doing. The squad cars hadn't moved. The red lights flared and pulsed over the empty lot. Mitchell Crook was there. She could just feel it. He was talking seriously into a radio, his dark eyebrows bent together in concentration. So close, no more than a hundred yards away. The one place she wanted to go and the one place she couldn't get to. Everything was hopeless, she was a hopeless fool. Of course he would have a girlfriend, it was ignorant to think he wouldn't. A grown-up girlfriend with a butterscotch tan and flippety hips and perfect fingernails, someone just as impossibly beautiful as he was. Moron and Ronnie were having an argument about corn.

"It's supposed to be 'Knee-high by the Fourth of July.'"

"That was before hybrids."

"So, Fourth of July was last week. It could have grown. It's like, 'As high as your fly.'"

"Clever. Maybe you could be a farmer. I always figured you for the 4-H type."

Josie said, "Hey, I think the cops are leaving." She watched forlornly as one car sped away, its flashers extinguished now. The other two squads loitered for a while longer, then car doors slammed. Their headlights were like spaceships turning and hurtling through a black void, speeding back into town.

"Boy are they dumb," Ronnie gloated. "I don't think they even looked around back."

"They were just too awestruck by the devastation we left behind us."

"Shaddup, OK?"

Josie straightened and tried to uncramp her legs. "So where do you guys live?"

"Oh, we don't have to go home right away. We could hang out for a while."

"Sure." She didn't care what she did anymore. None of it mattered. They piled in together, Moron in the passenger seat and Ronnie in the back, and they said nice car, just to be polite, although she could tell they didn't think much of it, a dinky little Toyota, a girl's car. They went through her CDs and they seemed to think she had at least a few decent ones. They blasted the air conditioner but put the windows down to feel the artificial breeze their motion made. Josie thought how bizarre it would be if Tammy or anybody else she knew saw her cruising around with these guys. She'd never live it down. Moron was about twice the size of any normal human being outside of the World Wrestling Federation. And Ronnie was just . . . Well, she'd rather be her fucked-up idiot self than poor pit-faced, skanky Ronnie on the very best day of his life.

But here they were, motoring along, all goofy and full of fun. Moron said they should stop at Ronnie's brother's so they could get a couple of six-packs. Yeah? said Josie. She already felt drunk on nothing at all. When they got the beer she drank one just for thirst and didn't feel a thing. It was long after eleven, too late for her to track down Mitchell Crook and do her usual twisted stalker thing, so she might as well enjoy herself some other sick way.

"This has to be the most boring-ass town in the world," said Ronnie. He was trying to light a cigarette but his lighter was empty and the little wheel ground itself dry.

Josie said, "I'm looking forward to Y2K. Everything either shutting down or blowing up."

Moron said, "You know all the Russian nuclear missiles? They could go off at midnight New Year's Eve. The government just about admitted it."

"Yeah, but Springfield's not important enough to have its own missile."

"My shit lighter just went Y2K." Ronnie threw it out the window. It skittered away, as insubstantial as tinfoil.

They were driving past St. John's Hospital, one of the few places in town with its lights still on. There was a row of corridor ends blazing away and the dimmer glow from the rooms themselves, their curtains mostly open, empty, since this was Springfield, after all, and few people even got sick in interesting ways. It was the same hospital where she had been born, although she didn't like to think about that. The doctor said, It's a girl, and her father said, Oh. If Abe had daughters instead of sons, would he still have loved them?

Josie wiggled one hand and Moron popped the top on a new beer and gave it to her. She said, "Seriously. What do you think's gonna happen when we hit good old Y2K? Anything?"

"God I hope so. I don't think I could stand another thousand years like these last ones."

"But what?" she persisted. "How? All right, the missiles, that's one thing."

Moron cranked the music up so loud the speakers buzzed. "Fiona Apple, totally great. If you figure—"

"I have to turn this down, OK?"

"—that everything has computer chips in it now, I mean, how many chips do you think are in this car? And those satellites that control phones and ATMs and the stock market and airplanes and television and weather and shit? They're gonna drop, splat. Burn big holes in the innocent bystanders. Civilization as we know it hits the tank. Then it's every man for himself. The strong will live and the weak will die. But don't worry. I'll be watching out for you."

"Thanks," said Josie, unsure what he meant, or if he was joking. He was giving her a strange look, as if there was something they'd already agreed about. Then Ronnie said, "Hey, pull over, would ya?"

She found a space at the curb and Ronnie got out to stand at the back of the car. "What's he doing?" she asked, and then, "Oh."

The taillights showed Ronnie's thin, nearly flat behind, his old slick jeans hanging in folds. Josie thought he could at least have found a bush or something. He hiked his jeans back up, but instead of getting into the car he took off running down the block.

"Now what?" She was getting a little tired of Ronnie.

"Oh, he's just goofing." Moron stretched out his arms in a big fake yawn, letting one of them come to rest, as casual as a felled tree, around her shoulders.

She wasn't imagining things. He was trying to hit on her. Oh no, icky. Ronnie opened the back door. "Miss me?"

"You mean you were gone?"

"Ha ha. I got eight, count em, eight."

"Eight what?" asked Josie. She was starting to feel the beer, all the little stupid-making bubbles in her head.

"Let's not hang around, huh? Step on it."

"What is he talking about?"

"He means he keyed a bunch of cars and we should probably not be here right now."

Josie tried to give Ronnie a meaningful stare but her eyes weren't following orders. "You scratched their paint? What did you do that for?"

"Is she for real?"

The two of them were yukking it up and high-fiving, like they'd accomplished something important, and she couldn't believe she'd ended up with two people even more pathetic than she was. "I have to go to the bathroom," she said. "And I'm not doing it in the street."

"We could go to Denny's," suggested Moron. "Yeah. Patty melts."

As much as she didn't want to be seen anyplace with them, it seemed like a good idea to get out of the car. Maybe she could ditch them at Denny's, then drive by Mitchell Crook's apartment so the night wouldn't be a total loss. Her bladder, once it had announced itself, was cresting dangerously. She had to put the car in reverse to get out of the space. "Excuse me," she said, waiting until Moron removed his arm. In the backseat Ronnie sniggered.

At Denny's she sat on the toilet and thought: This Is Your Life. Your life is a public bathroom. Sticky floor, smelly smells, ghosts of bodily fluids, yellow flourescent lights on yellow tile. She flushed. Down the tubes. It was too bad she wasn't serious puking drunk, just to top things off. As it was, she was stuck somewhere between sober and dry-mouthed fuzzy, with a little riff of headache playing at the back of her skull. In the yellow mirror she poked at her teeth and combed her hair. She looked hideous. She looked like Bride of Moron.

She was hoping to slink back to the car, but Moron, who'd

been using the pay phone, was waiting for her. He was parked right next to the ladies' room door like a dog tied up outside a grocery. "Hey, I'm sorry if Ronnie's being uncouth."

"No biggie."

"I'll beat his ass if you want."

"Look, I really have to get home now. My mom freaks if I'm not in by midnight." This was true, although it never kept her from staying out as late as she wanted.

"Yeah?" He actually drooped. His enormous shoulders lowered as much as his overdeveloped muscles would permit, and his chin fell. He wasn't such a bad-looking guy, he would have been normal-to-cute if he didn't do peculiar things to his hair and dress like a goon in all that camouflage stuff and the sleeveless flannel shirts. She didn't think he had many girlfriends. Everyone was too scared of him. "Well, stay and get something to eat. I'm buying."

"Thanks. Not hungry."

"A Coke or something. Besides"—he brightened, as if he'd found a compelling argument— "there's still all the beer in your car and we can't bring it in here."

That did seem sort of important, or maybe she was too addled to think it through. "All right, how about you get your food, then I drop you and Ronnie and the stupid beer off on my way home. Deal?"

"Sure." He was happy that he'd gotten her to agree. She was aware that he hoped to make her keep agreeing to things, like a salesman. Ronnie was slouched in a corner booth, stinking up the air with cigarettes. Josie did a quick reconnoiter. Nobody she knew in the place, thank God, just an old dried-up farm couple who looked like they'd been stranded there for the last week and a man in a cowboy hat who was studying yesterday's newspaper a page at a time. Not until two or three in the morning would it turn into the *Night of the Living Dead,* a ghastly overlit graveyard filled with all the after-closing drunks and the guys who'd just finished beating their wives.

Ronnie seemed almost pleased to see her. He blew a smoke ring in her direction. "Hey, what's your name?" he demanded, which she took as a sign of friendly interest.

"Josie."

"What kind of name is that? That's a name you give to a cow. Josie the Cow."

"And Ronnie's a name you'd give to a pile of bull."

He stared at her with his little cracked, red-rimmed eyes. In ten, twenty, thirty years he would never look like anything but the tragic result of inbreeding. He smacked his palm flat on the table and hooted. He had decided she was funny.

Josie drank two Cokes and swallowed an Advil she found at the bottom of her purse, and Moron and Ronnie worked their way through patty melts and fries with gravy. She was beginning to feel steadier, more cheerful, as if sometime in the future this would all make for an amusing anecdote. When they paid and walked out to the parking lot, the heat closed around them once more.

"This is really sucky weather," she complained. "It makes you hate having skin. OK. Where do you want to go?"

"To Podolsky's so we can beat his chicken ass," said Moron.

They directed her to one of the little blocky houses on that same western edge of town where they'd been before, a neighborhood that no one she knew lived in, a place where some portion of everyone's household goods ended up in the yard: kids' Big Wheels, plastic coolers, rugs hung over porch rails. They must think she was a spoiled little rich girl, which she guessed she was, actually. "End of the line," she said, pulling up in front of the Podolsky residence.

Ronnie got out. "Have to make sure he's home."

Josie sighed, because Moron wasn't budging and was this night of the giant fuckup ever going to end? "I really really have to go home," she said, politely fuming.

"Yeah, sure." Nothing short of a crane was going to get him out of the front seat. The bicep closest to her had a blue barbed wire tattoo around the meatiest part of the muscle, like it was holding a package together. He said, "I liked it when we worked together. You were always nice to me."

"I think I should tell you. I'm sort of going out with somebody."

"Yah?"

"You probably wouldn't know him. He's older. He works nights. What are you—"

Ronnie and another boy were getting into the backseat.

Moron said, "Podolsky, you are dead meat."

"I figured you'd be OK. And here you are OK, see?"

Ronnie said, "Podolsky, this is Josie the Cow. Josie the Driving Cow."

"So you guys up for this?"

"Yeah, you ready to squeal like a little piggie and run wee wee wee all the way home?"

"Sit on my face, would you?"

"Excuse me," said Josie. "Everyone should get out of my car now."

"We got to go see some guys," explained Ronnie.

"So call a cab."

"What's her problem?" asked Podolsky. He was older than the other two with his hair cut down to bristles and a hollow-looking face. He was wearing cheap wraparound sunglasses. He was creepy. "Let's step on it."

He was sitting directly behind her and she had to turn around to look at him. "Hey, this is my car. I don't even know you. So don't tell me what to do."

They ignored her. Ronnie said, "Unless you want to use Mo's truck."

"Everybody knows Mo's truck."

"What do you think, you want to drive?"

"No, let the cow do it."

Josie turned to Moron, trying to speak calmly. "What are you guys doing?"

"We just need the car for a little. It's cool." He put his hand on her bare knee and squeezed.

She tried to get out then, get out and walk away, but Podolsky said no no, in a mean-joking way, and pulled her back into the scat. For a moment her vision tilted and went flat, planes of black and white skating away. She kept thinking she hadn't explained herself well enough.

"Relax," said Moron. "It's just driving, you can do that. You're a good sport, you know? Most girls aren't." He turned around to the backseat and Podolsky handed him something.

"Is that a real gun?"

"Yeah, you want to hold it?"

"Say, Bonnie and Clyde, could we get this show on the road?"

Josie put the car in gear and started back to the highway. It didn't look like a real gun. Even when she had big red bullet holes in her it would not seem real, none of it. The only things she could think to do were dumb things you saw on TV, like wrestle the gun away from him or crash the car into a tree. They passed the FS Co-op where a hundred years ago she and Ronnie and Moron had hidden in the cornfield. She was so crazy tired and it was so hot. Maybe this was the end of the world. Maybe it snuck up on you.

They told her where to go, down all the normal streets where normal people lived, asleep in their normal boring beds. There was almost no one else out. Stoplights changed color at empty intersections. They were quiet, mostly, except for Ronnie bouncing up and down, babbling about somebody else she hoped she'd never meet who was also a chickenshit. Once she looked up to see Podolsky smirking at her in the rearview mirror. In spite of the sunglasses she could tell.

"Yo, big man. What you gonna do later?"

"Don't know."

"Gonna do some fucking?"

"Maybe." Moron shrugged. He wasn't looking at her, as if Podolsky had embarrassed him.

He still had the gun in his lap, an ugly gray stub of a thing, just laying there like it was nothing, like it could go off and shoot something, shoot her for no stupid reason at all, oh goddamn them. She was going to be raped and murdered and tomorrow night a local newscaster with bad hair would announce the discovery of her body in some very undignified place.

Get a *grip*, she told herself. "Who is it you're going to see?" she asked brightly. The advice of all the girl magazines. Be a good conversationalist. Take an interest in his hobbies.

"Just some guys that owe us money."

She wondered if they were a gang, if they qualified as one. They were driving up to one of the public housing complexes, barrackslike buildings set in dirt that just barely supported grass, superbright streetlights in the parking lot turning everything into hard-edged shadow. They told her to pull up on a side street.

"See anything?"

"You better hope they don't see us first. OK now, Elsie—"

"Josie."

"Whatever. You're gonna take a lap through the parking lot, real slow and normal-like. Pretend you're on your way home from cheerleading practice."

"I'm not a cheerleader," she muttered. The parking lot looked like a photographic negative, all that staring light and black shadow. Moron leaned forward. The gun leaned forward with him. The car moved, even though she had forgotten how to drive. There was something wrong with the parking lot. It was too bright, too easy to see things. Podolsky's breath rasped over the back of her neck. She tried to hold on to each thought in case it was her last, and it came to her that all this was happening because she had fallen in love, because she had wanted to burst out of her old life and so she had. You didn't know what that meant until you did it but now here it was.

Ronnie said, "Is that—" and Podolsky said, "Shit man!" and noise exploded all around her and she was dead but then she wasn't because things kept happening. Somebody was screaming, the way guys screamed, loud and hoarse. There was another car, a big Jeep-like thing coming at them head-on, and Moron grabbed the wheel and spun it and Josie floored the accelerator and they bumped over the curb into the street. It had not occurred to her that whoever they were shooting at might shoot back.

"Go, get out of here, shit!" The car was so full of them flailing around that it was hard to tell if they were moving at all but she guessed they were. The Jeep was right behind them, its headlights high and white and blinding in the rearview mirror. Something popped and cracked.

"Are they shooting at my car?" she demanded, incredulous.

"No, they're shooting at us and the car's in the way. Don't stop for stop signs. Christ, where did you find this stupid-ass bitch?"

Moron had the gun pointed out the window, trying to aim it, but he was having trouble getting turned around. It served them right for wanting her car; it was way too small. "What did you *do* to them anyway?"

"Just shut up."

"Oh fuck me. Fuck me to death."

The gun went off right in her ear and the car got away from her and she lost track of the deep lights back there somewhere.

"I think I got em."

"You got jack, man."

Something smelled horrible. It was her own sweat. Ronnie said, in an almost normal voice, "Hey, where did they go?"

They all looked. The street behind them was empty. "Those pussies," said Moron.

Now they were all laughing, like this was the funniest thing. Since they weren't dead, she wanted to kill them.

"Man, they couldn't shoot for shit."

"Niggers. What can you say."

"Sharp-looking ride, though. I like that real dark window tint. Very cool."

"Hey sugar britches, that was some lousy driving," said Podolsky, knocking her affectionately on the back of the head.

Josie said, "Are those flashers back there?"

Like she had to ask. They were three or four blocks away down the dark tunnel of the street, closing fast. Podolsky swore.

"Pull over at the alley."

When the car stopped they bailed. All three doors opened and out they flew. "Hey take your dumb beer," she called after them, and Ronnie doubled back to scoop it up.

"You guys really stink," she said, but by then they were gone, running lickety-split between two apartment buildings, Moron bringing up the rear, trying to get his big legs working.

Josie sat and waited for the flashers to reach her. She flipped the hazard lights switch to show that she was a law-abiding driver. She checked her mouth for beer-breath. She regarded her feet, surprisingly normal-looking in her old Nikes, as if they'd been off on their own, doing ordinary things all this while.

The squad car pulled up behind her and sat there, calling in her license plate, she guessed, her virgin car that had never even had a traffic ticket before. She put both her hands on the wheel where they could see them. The liked for people to do that, she remembered.

And when someone got out and tapped on the window and she opened it, the hot night poured back in. There was a flashlight shining on her and not until it was lowered and her eyes had adjusted could she see anything. Then, considering all the things that had already happened, not only that evening but in her mind for weeks and weeks, it was perhaps not so strange for her to say what she did, as if all their previous conversations had been real ones: "Oh, you grew a mustache."

Desperate Remedies

The lawyer, a younger, sleeker version of Ed Pauley, was explaining things with the practiced ease of a man who got paid for talking. His words shaped themselves as if he bit them off a bar of silver. His office had the same prosperous high gloss to it, everything substantial and well ordered. The carpeting yielded softly to the foot. The double-paned windows gleamed, holding back the blasting heat. The silent air-conditioning chilled the air so deliciously that Elaine could have drunk it.

This was Frank's lawyer, or one of them. Not the divorce guy but someone else. It almost felt as if they were getting divorced again, both of them sitting in upscale office chairs and wearing their game faces. Frank was looking especially unlovely these days, she couldn't help uncharitably noticing. Puffy and soft, like a very well-dressed stuffed animal. His jowls were piling up above his shirt collar. He listened to the lawyer with that expression of bland seriousness that men used for such occasions. Women always felt they had to keep making animated, interested faces. She had learned not to do that, thank God.

"Power of attorney," the lawyer was saying, "is the instrument people use to safeguard their interests in the event they become incapacitated. Of course, that assumes the individual is capable of making a rational decision to delegate that power."

"Rational," said Elaine. "I suppose there's room for interpretation there."

"Yes, fortunately, or we'd have to lock up all the Cubs fans."
The lawyer showed his expensive teeth. Lawyer humor. Elaine
and Frank bent their mouths politely. Elaine tried to catch
Frank's eye: *Is this guy any good?* Frank wouldn't look at her. "Now
you have two options here. The preferable one is to have your
uncle agree to sign over to you a durable power of attorney.
Durable means he can't change it. The alternative is a great deal
more expensive and time-consuming, and that's having a court
appoint you as his guardian of person and/or guardian of estate."

Elaine shifted uncomfortably in her comfortable chair and
waited for Frank to say something. She had a urinary-tract infec-
tion, something she thought you only got from sex. She couldn't
get over the unfairness of it. Honeymoonitis, they used to call it.
An unwelcome thought with Frank in the same room, or anywhere in the same county, for that matter. She was hoping the
meeting would be over before she had to humiliate herself by
running to the ladies room.

The lawyer was Frank's idea. It was the way he liked to resolve
things, it was that marble-in-the-maze process again. The law was
the maze, and you dropped people in the top and they came out
the right slot at the bottom. She was filled with foreboding as to
what this might mean for Harvey, but she had to keep reminding
herself that she was only here by Frank's negligible courtesy. She
had no standing in this. That was the legal word, *standing.*

Frank said, "Assuming he's too out of it to sign over power of
attorney, how does guardianship work?"

"You would file a petition to have a court hearing. There would
be a report on your uncle's condition by a physician who has examined him."

"Except the whole problem is he doesn't want to see a doctor."

The lawyer said that this could probably be arranged through
court order. "Well that seems like the way to go," announced
Frank. "Resolve the situation right then and there."

Elaine couldn't keep out of it any longer. "Unless you ever want him to see a doctor again."

"I'm sure the professionals know how to handle these guys."

"What, the sheriff shows up and holds him down while somebody injects him with elephant tranquilizers?"

"Who said anything about elephant tranquilizers?"

"You know what I mean." She addressed the lawyer. "There has to be some better way than coercing and traumatizing him."

"The court might view his refusal to seek medical care for a serious condition as prima facie evidence of incompetence."

"Unless he has a genuine phobia about doctors."

The lawyer tented his hands, beginning to get interested in the legal subtleties. "There's a great deal of interest these days in the legal rights of the mentally ill. Americans with Disabilities Act, you know."

Frank said to Elaine, "You want him to go blind, is that it?"

"Right, Frank. That's my secret agenda here."

"All of a sudden you're what, the Social Work Queen?"

Now they'd gone and done it. Dogfighting in public again. The lawyer gazed serenely out the window, blind and deaf to any unseemliness. Elaine decided to just let it go, resist the temptation to answer back. She tried once more to shift the pressure off her bladder. You couldn't hope to keep up your end of an argument when you had to pee so badly.

She had called in to her gynecologists's office for antibiotics. She couldn't remember having to do that before, she was always the picture of rude good health, she sailed through her visits to plague-ridden India without so much as a sniffle. The nurse had been almost too sympathetic. Ah well, you're at the age where you can expect that sort of thing to start happening.

Not what she wanted to hear at all. She wanted someone to tell her it was the fault of the hot weather and its attendant risks of dehydration, a simple climatological phenomenon. Instead she was at the age where you could expect all sorts of increasingly unpleasant things to start happening: wrinkles, softening teeth, the surgical removal of body parts. She tried to have a sense of humor about this whole getting old thing but she didn't, not really. She tried to arm herself with wisdom and serenity and common sense but none of it worked. She couldn't even take proper satisfaction in Frank's looking so lousy because it reminded her too clearly of a time when he (and she) had not, and was this what life would be from now on, a series of mean little triumphs based on vanity and fear?

By the time she returned her attention to the conversation, it had moved beyond her. "It's called a guardian ad litem," the lawyer was saying. "An attorney appointed by the court to represent your uncle during the proceeding. It's pro bono work; we usually get the younger people do to it." He turned his hands palms up, to indicate the negligible weight of young attorneys. "And that guardian ad litem is required by law to sit down and talk with the client and determine what they want and to represent their interests. So it's not your automatic slam-dunk type of situation."

Frank was busily taking notes, just to show her how firmly committed he was to following through on whatever awful legal procedure they had been talking about. If she kept objecting, it would only make him more determined. The lawyer said, "I should ask if there are any substantial financial assets involved here."

"Hardly. Unless he has bags of dimes hidden under his bed."

Elaine stood up. "I'm afraid my parking meter's just run out." She shook hands with the lawyer, who barely had time to rise out of his chair, and nodded to Frank. Baby steps to the door, then she practically galloped down the hallway. She didn't care what either of them thought of her.

When she came out of the restroom and headed for the exit, she was surprised to see Frank standing just inside the glass doors waiting for her. "So what do you think we ought to do about him?"

Was he actually asking her advice? "I don't know," she said warily. "There's probably no ideal solution."

"Maybe we could find a nursing home that would let him watch the Weather Channel."

"Could we not talk about nursing homes just yet?"

Frank gave her an unfriendly glance but subsided. He rubbed the back of his neck and squinted through the glass. The sun reflected off every surface: automobiles, street signs, glinting particles in the sidewalk, so that the light seemed to be in constant, hectic motion. "You believe this weather?"

"Yeah. It's like the planet's moving closer to the sun."

"I can't wait to get to Aspen. You know what they have there? Actual snow."

Elaine sighed. "I don't suppose you want to hear about your daughter."

"Go ahead. Make my day."

"She's not sure she wants to go with you. Actually she's sure she doesn't."

"Since when does she know what she wants about anything? The kid's got some kind of disorder. She doesn't talk, have you noticed that?"

"Now that you mention it."

"Everything's 'Yeah,' 'Unh-unh,' or 'I dunno.' What kind of future is she going to have if all she can do is make these retarded noises? Is she doing drugs?"

"She says she isn't. I don't know." Elaine felt the strangest sensation then. As if she was watching a movie she thought she already knew and suddenly the film wobbled or jumped and she and Frank were still married. None of the last five years or more had happened and they were having this conversation over breakfast coffee and she was going to have to remember to send his shirts out. They spoke of their daughter in voices that were exasperated but fond. They had aged so gradually, day by day, that they hardly took notice of it. In this other movie, other life, she would not have remarked upon what seemed to be a hair crisis on Frank's part, but then, it was probably Teeny's idea to have him get this peculiar stiff brush cut so you wouldn't notice all the encroaching pink scalp. She caught a whiff of something pungent and aromatic, some product probably designed to stimulate hair follicles, and took a hasty step back from him.

"Anyway," she said, "you'll have to talk to her. Maybe she's getting too old for family trips." Something about her words made her pause. The notion of Frank and Teeny as family? "So. Harvey."

"Believe it or not, Elaine, I want what's best for the guy."

"Then call off the attack lawyers."

"Tell me how else he's going to get medical help."

"I don't know, but you weren't there when I tried to talk to him about it. He howled. Curled up on the floor and howled and blubbered. It took me almost an hour to get him calmed down." It had frightened her to see him that way, his face stretched into an unrecognizable mask of dripping misery. "It was so pitiful," she said inadequately.

"Well for Christ's sake, Elaine, of course he's not going to like the idea. You can't just give in to him."

That was it, of course. He thought she was soft, when the situation called for stern, manly measures. She said, "Remember that woman downstate a couple years ago who refused to go in for a court-ordered psychiatric exam and the state police surrounded her house for three weeks and cut off her water and power and blared rock music over loudspeakers? And she shot a dog, I think, before they finally took her in."

"And your point is?"

"Just wondering if you really want to go that route."

"Nobody's calling the state police, why do you keep saying things like that? So what do you want me to do instead? You can feel as sorry for him as you want, you can be the ministering angel of mercy, but then what?"

"Just give it a little more time." The sunlight was nearly liquid in its brightness, it hurt her eyes even looking out at it. She poked around in her bag for her sunglasses. She felt sad, irritated, hopeless. Frank was right. Feeling sorry for Harvey didn't do him any good. Nothing would do him much good for very long. "Look, I have to go."

Frank reached for the door handle, paused. "So why are you so into this? He's not your responsibility. Are you just trying to prove to everybody what a big jerk I am?"

No, it's because there are times I feel like him, she stopped herself from saying. Alone and crazy and afraid of everything. She said instead, "His house needs some work. New roof, that sort of thing. Easy enough to do."

"Let's wait and see if he's really going to be living there first." Frank's face had shut down and there was an end to talking. She walked past him into the staggering heat. The sun seemed not to have moved, but to have been hung up on a nail in the middle of the no-color sky. She willed herself to endure getting into her car and starting it, trying not to breathe until the air conditioner had purged the worst of the murderous air.

Across the street at the edge of a gas station lot someone had set up a vending enterprise, a van bedecked with giant muddy canvases, the paint laid on in slabs, of animals in heroic poses: wolf howling at the moon, eagle in flight, lion rampant. Behind the van a number of American and Confederate flags were set out on tall poles. Along the sidewalk was a line of half a dozen tiny tricycles, customized with plastic handlebars and seats and streamers and plastic rosettes fastened to the spokes, all in combinations of the most painful plastic colors: flamingo, lime, orange, cerise, grape. There was something crazed and preternaturally ugly about the whole assemblage, as if it were a colonial outpost in the empire of the mad. It was so impossible to imagine people who would look on such things with admiration and consider placing them in their homes, or people who thought it reasonable to fabricate the things and expect a profit from them, who likely did earn a profit from them, that Elaine felt as if the world she had lived in up to now had cracked open in the heat and this twisted version had risen up in its place.

She blotted her face with a Kleenex and tried to bring herself around. She waited for some of her old energy to course back into her. But the heat was against her, or perhaps it was the weakness of the body, or the image of Harvey in his perfect loneliness reaching out to pass his hands over the glowing television screen. A wave of grief washed over her, filling her eyes with salt. The dashboard warning light was on, as it had been for days, a winking yellow. Yellow, the color of danger, fear, urine, heat. She knew what the light meant now: that everyone died.

Two days later, suitably medicated, Elaine drove to Harvey's house with the cleaning lady she had engaged sitting beside her in the front seat.

The cleaning lady's name was Rosa. She worked for some friends of Elaine's who pronounced her a "jewel." She was a small, bright brown woman whose gray-streaked hair was pulled into a bunch at the back of her neck. She wore a flowered smock and sweatpants and her tiny feet were encased in tennis shoes that might have been designed for a child, bright pink, the shoe laces printed with red hearts. She smiled often, in an agreeable, uncomprehending fashion.With the aid of her high school Spanish and a publication called *Inglés Esencial,* Elaine had tried to convey the differences between Harvey's house and the suburban palaces that Rosa was accustomed to working in: *La casa de mi tío está pequeño, pero muy sucio.* Small but very dirty. Rosa smiled and nodded. "You don't have to say much of anything, just show her what you want done," Elaine's friend had assured her, but this seemed like something that ought to be explained. Perhaps it made no difference to Rosa what she cleaned, as long as she was paid. Still, Elaine had decided that for any number of reasons it would be better to make an introductory visit to Harvey's before proceeding further.

Elaine parked in Harvey's driveway and took note that he had moved his little garden pots out of the sun's glare and into the partial shade of the porch. "Here we are," she sang, full of false cheer. Rosa climbed out of the car and Elaine, watching her, was relieved to see that she wasn't visibly distressed by anything before her.

Harvey's air conditioner was racketing full-blast in the corner window trying to make headway against the heavy air. Condensation dripped from one edge. With Rosa behind her Elaine knocked at the door, which was shut against the heat. When no one answered she opened it and stepped inside.

The temperature was barely comfortable, the little air conditioner laboring hard. After all, it was nearly a hundred degrees outside. The television was on, as usual, and as usual the Weather Channel was busy selling off-brand automobile insurance, chain saws, Magic Mops, Shoe Away, Zim's Crack Creme, other products she'd never heard of. Where did they get these commercials? "Harvey?"

He wasn't there. Elaine trooped through all the rooms, even down into the haunted house basement. The bedroom was stuffy, since not much of the air conditioning made it back that far. She roused the cat from its nest at the foot of the bed; it showed the pink inside of its mouth in a silent hiss and flopped onto the floor.

Should she worry about him? It was dangerous to be out in this kind of heat, everybody said so, God knows he must hear it often enough on television. Rosa was standing just as Elaine had left her in the center of the living room, like a polite museum visitor. *"No está aquí,"* Elaine said, trying to pantomime "not here." "I hope he gets back soon," she added foolishly.

As if she had been issued some order or permission, Rosa walked through to the kitchen, where she began opening and shutting cupboards, taking stock. From beneath the sink she brought out the new plastic scrub bucket and rubber gloves that Elaine herself had bought. *"No necesita,"* Elaine began, but Rosa only smiled, the way one might acknowledge a politeness, and went on measuring Lysol into the bucket. After all, why would you bring a housecleaner along unless you wanted her to clean, and she certainly agreed with Rosa's premise that you began with the kitchen in any house.

This might turn out to be one more in a series of her good intentions gone awry, she was prepared for that, but then, how could anything bad come of cleanliness? She supposed her foolish secret hope was that, once presented with his new, orderly, enlightened home environment, rationality would begin to seep into Harvey as inevitably as water trickling downhill, and he would agree to the doctor.

Elaine retreated to the living room so as not to hover and get in Rosa's way. The television was displaying, in a graphic reminiscent of old science class films, how much sunshine the Earth received at different seasons of the year. The sun was a yellow circle that emitted a red triangle. Pulsing lines, like death rays, rose from the Earth where the triangle touched it. Fascinating. She examined what there was to examine of Harvey's living room, aware that she was close to snooping, that it would be considered snooping with anyone normal. The room was more notable for the things it lacked than for anything in it. No family photographs, perhaps that wasn't so strange. Nothing that spoke of ornament of any kind, except a green milk glass vase, empty, with a cracked rim. No books, apart from an ancient volume titled *Abe Lincoln from Illinois,* and an old school yearbook. There was a pedestal clock, its face varnished with age, long since retired from keeping time. A propeller-bladed fan so old that it was once again fashionable.

Where did Harvey go when he needed household goods, a blanket, or a lamp? She'd never thought about it. Every Christmas they gave him things like flannel shirts and house slippers and underwear. She seemed to remember Frank once arranging to get Harvey's washing machine fixed, and he paid the real estate taxes on the little house. But none of them, it seemed, had paid attention. Twenty-some years ago when she first met Frank, Harvey had been a big shambling stoop-shouldered man who wouldn't meet your eye and carried on a constant murmuring conversation with the ground just beyond his left knee. Peculiar, certainly, but hardly frail. "He's in his own little world," Frank had explained. "He likes it that way." And they had liked it that way too, because they hadn't had to do anything.

Bleach smells wafted in from the kitchen, and a sound as of road construction started up. Rosa was tackling the stove. Elaine looked out the front windows, hoping to see Harvey, but the sidewalks were empty. She could hardly leave now to go look for him, not with Rosa going full-throttle in the kitchen. She didn't want to imagine the two of them encountering each other without some sort of interpreter present.

The Weather Channel was showing one of its innumerable pictures of creamy sky and dramatic, horizontal sun. For the life of her, she couldn't understand the appeal. The front door opened and Harvey stood there, blinking at her.

He was wearing a straw hat with a big floppy broken brim, and he was eating ice cream out of a half-gallon carton. Without seeming to avoid Elaine, he steered a meandering course around her and came to stand in front of the air conditioner, still spooning ice cream into his mouth. The flavor was strawberry swirl and the container was leaking pink milk from its bottom.

"Harvey, look, your ice cream's melting. Let me get you a towel." Elaine went to what passed for Harvey's linen closet and selected the most raglike of several rags. "Is that good ice cream? It looks good. No, I'm not trying to take it, I don't want any. Come here, I want you to meet somebody."

She guided him into the kitchen. At least he looked like a crazy man, in his ridiculous battered hat, mashing the ice cream carton protectively in the crook of one arm, a towel draped bib fashion around his neck. Whatever the language barrier, that much should be clear. "Harvey, this is Rosa. She's going to help you around the house. Rosa, Tío Harvey."

Rosa looked up from the sink, where she was doing battle with the broiler pan. Twenty years of pork chops and grilled-cheese sandwiches had turned it as black as an old steam locomotive. She gave Harvey a measuring, narrowed glance, and without warning reached over and plucked the ice cream carton from his grasp. A waterfall of Spanish followed, the first words Elaine had heard Rosa speak, and although they passed over her without comprehension, she caught the scolding in them. Rosa produced a bowl and portioned the ice cream into it, wiping the lip clean with a dish towel. That she had found such a thing as a dish towel in the wasteland of the kitchen was itself an accomplishment. She held the bowl out to him, then peered up at Harvey, a long, critical stare. She shook her head, popped the ice cream carton into the freezer, and went back to punishing the broiler pan.

Elaine looked at Harvey. Harvey looked back, or seemed to. In his cracked and cloudy eyes was a layer of buried light, something quizzical and alert, almost as if there were a different Harvey hiding down there behind the absurd hat and the rest of his foolishness. Elaine brushed past this notion and its oddness. "Well Harvey, what do you think? Wouldn't it be nice to have everything clean and tidy?"

He didn't answer, of course, nor did Rosa look up from her violent scrubbing. How peculiar to be carrying on a normal conversation, or trying to, in such circumstances. She might as well have been barking or braying. But now she was wondering what she ought to do. She had to get back to the shop, the girl who was at the register left at noon to go to her other job and she was expecting a phone call from her clients at the Chicago boutique, who required endless assurances that everything was humming along on track for the planned product line, it was enough to give you hives. Clearly she had to leave, but did it make any sense to interrupt Rosa in the middle of such splendid industry, might she not think it was one too many crazinesses, no matter how well the Señora paid?

"Yo—" What was the verb she needed, *regresar*, first person, future tense? "*Voy a regresar*," I will return, she told Rosa, who bobbed her head but didn't pause in her combat. She wielded the steel wool and scouring powder with furious concentration. Already a streak of shine was showing through. The woman was more than a jewel; she was an artist. Perhaps she looked on Harvey's house as a sort of measure of her powers.

Elaine got Harvey settled in his spot on the couch with his ice cream and a tumbler of drinking water, told him she'd be back soon, and drove downtown to Trade Winds. She was just in time to replace her assistant, and not long after that the Chicago call came through and she spent a good twenty minutes reassuring and flattering and promising, so that she hardly had time to worry about Harvey and Rosa and what she might have set in motion. Then the shop was unexpectedly busy with a vanload of Eastern Star ladies from Moweaqua who had picked exactly the wrong time to visit the state capital and were staggering around in the heat like parched turkey hens until they reached her refuge. Of course none of them bought anything, but they unfolded every length of cloth they touched and wanted to use the bathroom and tried on sundresses and blouses, stretching the fabric over their sweating backs. In between waiting for the indigo dye to rub off their damp underwear and agreeing that everything was much more expensive than it used to be, she tried to call Harvey. There was no answer, which was worrisome. Harvey always answered his phone in case anyone needed the forecast.

Once the Eastern Star ladies left, she grabbed the phone again. This time he answered. "Local Forecast."

"Harvey? It's Elaine, how is everything there?"

"Danger danger extreme heat and humidity will make for high levels of danger danger danger."

"Is Rosa still there? What's she doing?"

Something heavy fell down, bangboom, and in the stinging silence that followed she heard, faintly, the blowsy saxophone music that played whenever the current weather came on. Then the phone went dead.

She thought of the police but decided that she could get there quicker herself, flipped the CLOSED sign, no one sane would be out shopping in this heat anyway, even in India they would have stayed home, all the while thinking danger danger danger, and what had she done that she could not now undo?

Knocking on Harvey's door, then flinging it open. The television lay on its back, still placidly announcing record highs and heat advisories. The stand it had always rested on was upended like a bug, legs in the air. When Elaine rushed around the sofa to look for sprawled bodies there was nothing, no one. No one in the antiseptic kitchen, which, now stripped of its protective skin of dirt, looked merely small and mean.

She stood still, listening. Over the television noise came a different sound, of drumming water.

Christ, he'd strangled Rosa and now he was drowning her, or himself. Elaine ran back and pushed the bathroom door open. Steam veiled the air, hot water on a day like this, who would want such a thing, it made her sick and giddy. "Harvey? Rosa?"

Rosa was sitting, very primly, on the closed toilet seat, her little pink sneakers lined up exactly, heel to heel, toe to toe. She held a large towel; every so often she flapped it before her, as if shooing something away. Harvey was in the bathtub. His pink, boiled-looking back was to Elaine. Rosa issued some Iberian command, hopping up to flap and point, and Harvey scooped water over the rinds of his ears.

Neither of them took any notice of her, and after a moment Elaine retreated and closed the door.

She wished there was someone else in the house, someone normal who spoke English, so they could marvel together. Elaine had never thought of Harvey as particularly dirty, she knew he bathed, but then, she didn't have Rosa's professional standards about these things.

In the living room she righted the stand and stooped to lift the television back in place. What titanic struggle had landed Harvey in the bathtub? It was beyond imagining. She checked her watch, almost three. She had other things to do, even with the shop closed, and she was hoping there was a way to extricate Rosa before she began refinishing floors and painting walls.

She didn't have long to wait. The water stopped running and there was an interval of other, more muffled sounds, sloshings, openings, closings, and at length Rosa emerged, wiping her hands on a towel, pleased with herself. "Clean," she announced.

Harvey followed, walking soft-footed behind Rosa. The fringe of hair around his ears was water-dark and combed slick. His face was scraped and shaven, his fingernails shone like moons. He wore green pants and a thin clean ancient white shirt that Rosa must have excavated from some forgotten drawer; you could see the crease marks where the sleeves had been folded for the last hundred years. Mothball smells wafted from it.

"Well don't you look nice," Elaine said, finding her voice.

Rosa was toting a plastic bag that Elaine guessed contained Harvey's dirty clothes. She turned and pushed past him into the bathroom, intent on some new mission of purification. Harvey craned his neck after her, tilted his old, well-scrubbed head in such a way, smiled in such a way, the corners of his mouth twitching with happy secrets, that Elaine, watching, was made aware of an entirely new problem.

More Secrets

Officer Mitchell Crook's hand rose toward his mustache, then lowered. "Step out of the car please, Miss."

"Absolutely. No problem. Yes sir." Babbling idiot. Josie fumbled around for her various body parts. She wasn't drunk, she was something else, brimful of everything, the crazy night, the heat, fear still sweating out of her every pore, plus the way he looked, different, not just the mustache. People always looked like a mask of themselves in the dark. The sort-of dark. Red and blue lights were whirlygigging all over the place. Maybe she was a little drunk. She scrambled out of the car and kept her chin tucked down so he couldn't smell her breath. But she peeked up at him through her eyelashes, all trembly. It was either a miracle, or one more stupid Springfield small-town coincidence.

"Do I know you?"

She wobbled her head no. She was the one who knew him.

"Stand over here, please." He shined his flashlight inside the car, reached down and stirred the heap of empty beer cans, held one up. She'd forgotten about the empties. "What's this?"

The mustache was killer. It made him look like a movie star, no, better. She was trying to hold on to every second, every eyeful of him, but her head was full of fizz and her heart was a clanging gong and she couldn't slow anything down. It was as if he was already a memory, had already escaped her senses.

When she didn't answer, he said, "Maybe you could tell me where your buddies went."

Josie pointed down the alley, empty except for the streetlight, so white it was nearly purple.

"And who was it chasing you back there?"

"Bunchofguys."

"What guys? Look at me. Do you have any idea how much trouble you're in?"

"Oh yes." Wobble-nodding.

"Turn your pockets inside out."

It was harder than she would have expected. Her hands didn't fit inside the way they used to. She bet she looked like absolute shit, all sweaty, and she hadn't even worn anything nice. "Sorry," she said, giving up.

"Driver's license?"

Josie pointed to her string bag on the front seat of the car. She watched Mitchell Crook retrieve it, bending because he was tall. Why was he a cop, she wanted to ask him, what put that idea in his head? Was it dangerous? Meaning the real criminals, not little punks like her. This was probably totally boring for him.

"All right, Josephine—"

"Josie." A great blessing settled over her. Whatever else happened, he would know her name.

"—let's have you take a seat back here." He opened the rear door of the squad car. "Watch your head." She wanted to point out the strangeness of all this to him, how it had happened before, or almost had, all the times she'd imagined it, but of course he didn't know that. She sank into the vinyl seat, which felt a little sticky under her bare legs. She was inside the whirlygig lights now. They stabbed through her head, redblue, redblue. Her little car stood with all its doors flung open, something unseemly about it, as if it was being undressed in public. She wondered about

Moron and Ronnie and that jerk Podolsky. She hoped they had to walk miles and miles to get home. She was just beginning to take hold of the thought that very bad things had almost happened to her, and that other bad things might still happen.

Where was Mitchell Crook? She'd lost sight of him and had to shift around to get a better view. He was kneeling in the front seat of her car, where there was probably something illegal in the ashtray or ground into the carpet. His beautiful head was visible just above the seat back. He was actually inside her car. A little of her breath came out in a moan. She reached up and touched the metal grate between her and the front seat. Locked in a cage, with all her heart on the other side. What sadness that there were always two halves of her, the stupid kid who did everything wrong and her true, feeling self.

He came back around to the front of the squad car, got in, and without turning around to look at her, switched on the dome light and began writing on a clipboard. Between his dark blue collar and the dark clipped edge of his hair was half a hand's width of skin, marble swirled with pink. She reached one fingertip toward it, resting on the metal screen. In the rearview mirror she saw her own eyes, yearning like a saint's in an old holy picture, and his eyes looking back at her.

"You sure I don't know you from someplace?"

"No place you'd remember." *Saints, God, heaven:* What was any of that, only words people shook in your face and told you were important? None of it was real or meant anything compared to this very minute, his perfect skin and the space her finger could not travel.

The radio squawked and he spoke into it, something private and businesslike, then he did turn around to look at her. His eyebrows were two perfect dark velvet strokes. "Suppose you tell me what happened tonight."

"I saw this guy I know at Denny's and I gave him and his friends a ride home, but then they made me drive over here and all of a sudden this other car, a Jeep or a Blazer or something, was shooting at us. Then they split, I guess because you showed up, and those guys made me pull over and ran off and left me here."

Josie blinked, trying to look as stupid as she sounded. Well, that was pretty much what had happened. Mitchell Crook gave her a guilty-till-proven-innocent look. "And the friend you met at Denny's, what's his name?"

"Brian." There was no particular reason for her to protect them, but she figured the less anyone knew, the better.

"Brian what?"

"I don't know, he's not really a friend. I just see him at school."

"Him and how many friends?"

"Two," she said promptly. The truth.

"And while you were making the run from Denny's over to these parts, they had time to drink nine beers?"

Sullen now, she scuffed at the back of the seat. She felt injured that he didn't believe her.

"And the guys that were shooting at you, any idea who they were, why they were so unhappy with your pals?"

"They're all a bunch of creeps and I hope they do get shot." In spite of herself she was sniveling, she was so tired, and someone really had pointed a gun at her, and now she'd ruined everything by being an idiot. A boo-hooing idiot with a crust of snot and dirt underneath her nose because she didn't even have a stupid Kleenex. She was really crying now. It was like vomiting, the way a little got you started. She was bawling. Josie the Crying Cow.

"Hey," Mitchell Crook said. "Hey, come on, you're OK." No she wasn't. What did he know. Even his sympathy was professional and impersonal. There was a metal grate between everything she had imagined and the way it was really happening,

between Mitchell Crook as she had cast him in a hundred different dramas and the fact of him who was not in love back with
her.

It was too bad, really, that you couldn't go on crying. Sooner or
later it trailed off into runny sniffs and whimpering and you were
right back where you started. She didn't even want to look at him
now. She folded her arms and glowered.

"You know, you're actually a very lucky girl."

She shrugged, to indicate just how lucky she didn't feel.

"For one thing, you didn't get hurt tonight. But if you keep
hanging out with creeps, you will."

"I didn't even—"

"—know those guys, right. So don't get into a car with guys you
don't know."

She slit her eyes and mumbled.

"What's that?"

"Yeah, OK, whatever. Right."

"Now what I'm going to do is file a report. And if you turn up
again riding around with lowlifes or some other monkey business, then we'll let the juvenile authorities sort it out."

Important cop voice. Like she was just a little kid.

He sighed and plucked his shirt collar away from his neck, as if
the heat was getting to him. "You listening back there?"

Total power trip. Nya nya. Josie tried her Tough Girl sneer,
couldn't get the proper lift to it. Couldn't even pretend to be
angry at him. Every time she looked at him she felt the cheap
crockery in her chest break all over again.

"OK, we're leaving your car here and I'm going to take you
home."

She gaped at him. "Really?"

"Like I said, you're lucky. This time, at least."

His eyes flicked over her in the mirror, then he turned off the dome light, had another conversation with the radio, shut off the flashers—she sighed at the welcome dark—and put the car in gear. Josie watched the streets glide past, familiar landmarks and intersections, everything small, dull, dopey, ugly in unspectacular ways. She'd have to tell her mother the car had broken down, she'd have to get a ride from Tammy and lie her way through it all, but that would be just more same old same old in the endlessly stupid story of her life. She wondered a little about Mitchell Crook's working the night shift; it was apparent that she had lost track of something, but it didn't matter because all that was over now.

"Is this you?" he asked, gliding up to her house, which was, mercifully dark. Her mother not sitting up to see her inglorious return. Josie said yes it was, and waited while he got out to let her out of the backseat. He opened the door and stepped aside. The night was still not cool, but it was as if the heat held its breath. Everything was silent, a flat, black, outer-space silence. A burnt smell, the neighborhood's overfertilized grass going down to defeat. What had happened to the moon? A lightbulb switched off. "I need my bag," she told him.

He retrieved it from the front seat and held it out to her. And because she would never see him again, and because no one in the whole blind dark world was watching, she reached up on her toes and kissed him on the mouth.

It didn't last long. She released him before he had a chance to struggle and pull back, which would be the final humiliation. She tasted the inside of his mouth, a strong taste, not unpleasant, but full of currents of history and possibility, his lips a little apart in surprise or shock, his skin full of heat and salt, the column of his neck beneath her hands—all this she held, then let go.

Sprinting away without looking back, she prayed that her key would work without fumbling and it did, and she was able to get inside and put the door between them. Standing just at the edge of the window curtain, she saw the squad car sitting at the curb, its engine muttering. She wanted to think it looked perplexed, although that was foolish, almost as foolish as what she had done, and yet her blood raced like electricity and once more she felt reckless and triumphant. Whatever else happened or never happened, she had for one moment made the world take the shape she wanted.

When Josie woke up the next day—really woke up, because earlier her mother had pounded on her door, alarmed about the car, but she'd gone back to sleep—she had to convince herself again and again that everything was real, not just last night, but herself this morning, here in her own bed, like always. Her real self could not have done those things. She kept holding up the night before her memory and shaking her head, and sometimes she grinned a randy little grin and sometimes she groaned and threw her head against the pillow.

The phone rang from somewhere beneath the bed. The bottom dropped out of her stomach. Two three four rings, then it stopped just before the machine clicked on. Josie broke out in a rolling sweat. Whatever, whoever it was, it had to be bad. The phone started up again and this time she dived for it. "H'lo."

"God, what's it take to get you to answer?"

Tammy. She flopped back on the bed, unstrung. "Give me a break."

"What, don't tell me you're still asleep. You slut."

"Time sit?"

"Almost two, loser. What did you do last night?"

Her scalp itched furiously. She clawed at it. "Last night?"

"Yeah, or is it one of the ones you don't remember?" Tammy

laughed. Ha ha. Bitch. "Because, what's your car doing over by the post office?"

"Everybody's always so interested in my car."

"What?"

Josie said never mind, and she told Tammy the sequence of lies that she had already rehearsed, or maybe she had already spoken them, or maybe things had actually happened that way, since what she remembered was so much more improbable: her car had broken down and she'd had to call her mother for a ride home, and could Tammy pick her up in an hour to go deal with it?

She hung up the phone and squeezed her eyes shut so that only a little smeared daylight came through. After a while she got up and went into the bathroom and splashed cold water over her face. And although her head felt like it was full of sand and her mouth was puffy, as if she'd taken a sting along with the kiss, she was struck by her own shining image. Her mussed hair looked weirdly all right, good, even, like a model's when they mussed it on purpose. The light from the window filtered through it in a sunny tangle. Her skin, through some trick of the same light, was perfect, like the inside of a summer fruit, and her eyes were full of liquid depths and her eyebrows shadowed them with mystery. She was beautiful. Who would have thought it.

Four days later, she was hopelessly sunk back in her same old life. Her shift at Beefeater's was sagging to its close. There were only three diners in the place and usually she'd be off by now, but the pimp manager was in an evil mood and said she could goddamn well earn her pay for once. Josie might have said something sarcastic back to him except it wouldn't change anything, wouldn't make him any less of a pimp. She listened to the thin, annoying music that squeezed out of the speakers in the ceiling. It must be computer generated, because surely no human being could make a conscious decision to produce that kind of noise. At least it masked the sound of people chewing, very thoroughly, their stringy meat. She'd stopped stalking Mitchell Crook. She'd given up on being anything but ordinary.

After the first surge of glee at her own daring had worn off, she'd felt shame, then more shame, and a kind of angry hopelessness. What a stupid stunt, little kid stuff, really, something they used to do at recess, pretend to kiss the boys so they'd run away. She actually remembered doing that. Kisserbug, they'd called it. Cute, if you were in the second grade. And so gradually, the physical memory of him, his taste and feel and hot smell, were erased by the sneering inner voice that always knew the very worst thing to say.

It was after ten o'clock when she left work and paused just outside the door. Behind her the restaurant's lights were dimmed so that they looked more lonesome than complete darkness would have. She hesitated because she had absolutely nowhere to go except back home. Maybe that's what she should do. Except her mother was probably still awake, and these days it was just as hard to explain why she was home early as why she stayed out late.

Josie dug her keys out, took three steps across the parking lot, and stopped. A black Acura with a sunroof was pulled up next to her car. The driver's window was open and someone's arm was resting along the door, the fingers keeping time to the radio music she could only just hear, the thread of an old Beatles song, the one about Sexy Sadie: *you know you turned on every wu-un, you know you turned on everyone.*

Not knowing what to think, Josie crossed the lot and bent down to stick her head in the window. "Hey."

Mitchell Crook wasn't smiling, wasn't even really looking at her. Was she in some new kind of trouble? "You work here?"

"Yeah."

"I saw your car," he explained after a moment.

"Oh."

"Beefeater's," he said reflectively. "I don't think I've ever eaten here."

She shrugged, looking back at the restaurant. "Well, it kind of sucks."

The Beatles song ended and a commercial came on, nothing he could pretend to pay attention to, so he fiddled with the tuner until he found another music station. God, he was acting weird, like a cop who'd forgotten how to arrest people. He wasn't wearing his uniform, but a green T-shirt and jeans. The neck of the shirt fell below one side of his collar bone. A new territory for her greedy eyes. Since he wasn't saying anything, she prompted, "Do you have to work tonight?"

"Yeah, in a little while. So, you want to tell me what all that was about the other night?"

"What all what was about?" But in that instant *she knew*, both what he meant and everything that would follow.

"Maybe you should get in the car."

"Front or back seat?" Josie asked, and he looked as if he wasn't sure it was supposed to be funny, as she'd meant it to be, then he reached over and unlatched the passenger door. She took her time walking around the front of the car where he could see her, because this time she was wearing something really good. Her pink sundress that was low and bare on top. As she walked she tried to rearrange herself without being obvious.

Once she was in the car she was glad for the music. Neither of them knew what to say or even how to look at each other. Josie crossed her legs carefully at the ankle. She especially wanted him to notice her legs. Mitchell Crook pretended not to be watching them. He turned around with his back against the door so he was facing her. "OK, so where do you know me from?"

"You really don't remember?"

"Remember what?"

She shook her head, mourning. "And here I thought it was so special."

He finally figured out she was teasing. "Jeez."

"Boy, you must have a guilty conscience."

"Come on, where did I meet you?"

"Just around." Josie ruffled the air with her fingers and smiled. The words *Taco Bell* were not going to pass her lips. She shifted her weight delicately on the car seat. His car was so classy. A real grown-up car, very new and clean-looking, with one of those leather covers on the steering wheel.

Mitchell Crook narrowed his eyes at her, thinking. "You know Tom Cook?"

"Nope."

"Bobby Cook? Kim Burlingame?"

She shook her head. She wondered how long she could keep up her Mystery Girl act, before he figured out she was nobody. To change the subject she said, "Thanks for being so nice to me the other night."

"Well, I wasn't that nice."

"Sure you were. You could have thrown my little punk ass in jail. It was such a totally messed-up situation."

"It was a drug dealers' gunfight and you're lucky you didn't get hurt."

Josie tried to look chastened at this. But in fact nothing had happened, her heart was beating as if it would live forever, and joy was something she could almost hold in her hands. He was only sounding stern because he felt obliged to, the cop part of him that had to keep making cop noises, or perhaps it just came easier to him. She thought about how she had drawn his face down to hers, the shock to her senses. She thought about doing it again. She said, "So you changed your mind and you came back to bust me." "No, just to make sure you're staying out of trouble."

Now there was a flirting note in his voice that she recognized and knew how to answer. "Trouble? Me?"

"Yeah, you." He smiled, his first real all-out smile. It just about finished her. The wild bad thing between her legs was making itself known, agitating, putting crazy pictures in her head, and again she had the sensation of wanting to slow things down, make sure they were really happening. She missed a beat and didn't smile back the way she should have. When she finally got her face working, it must have twitched or blanched, because his smile lowered a notch.

She felt she had to apologize. "I'm sorry, I was just thinking how weird this is."

"You think I'm weird?"

"No, it's weird that you're talking to me and you're an actual human being." Could she have said anything stupider? "I mean you being a cop and, all. How do you like it, ah, police work? Was it something you always wanted to do?" Lame. Conversation 101. But Mitchell Crook appeared to give it serious thought.

"I used to want to play ball."

"Ball, like basketball?"

"Baseball. I played semipro for a while. In Texas."

"Really?" Weak. But she couldn't think of one thing to say about semipro baseball. Not one.

"Yeah. Pitcher. I had a fastball that clocked at eighty-fve miles an hour." She knew to be impressed with that, although she didn't want him to keep going on about baseball. It made her anxious, it was nothing he should be thinking about right now.

"Yeah. Then I blew out my arm. So much for that idea." He shrugged as if to shake himself loose from the memory. "My Dad's a cop. My uncle too. I kind of grew up with it. You know."

Josie nodded seriously, to indicate the depth of her understanding. Then he said, "So you're what, still in school?"

It killed her to admit it. She tried to make it sound as if school was something she only did in her spare time.

"I would have figured you for older."

"Really?"

"Yeah. A year or two, maybe."

The radio filled the silence. Josie knew what he was thinking about. Her stupid driver's license that said she wasn't eighteen yet, wouldn't be until next April. That made her some kind of illegal, so that if he ever God . . . God. She couldn't even think it. But it was what she wanted most in this world.

She said, "I bet girls lie about that stuff all the time. I bet nobody ever blames the guys." That sounded like she was desperate, begging. She tried again. "Age is just a number. It's nothing you should let define you as a person."

Mitchell Crook said Sure, in an absent way, gazing out the windshield at nothing at all. That earlier joy was turning slippery and liquid and dense, like the mercury in a thermometer, falling away. She willed herself to keep silent, not to make things even worse. He leaned forward and turned off the radio. The only sounds were the engine and the air-conditioning whoosh that had been there all along. Was she supposed to leave now?

Then he said, "You still aren't going to tell me where you know me from?" Josie shook her head. "You're something else, you know?"

"Something good or something bad?"

"Oh, very good," he murmured, and that heavy, silvery joy began to crest in her once more.

"You mean you don't have girls throwing themselves at you all the time?"

"Not such pretty ones."

Lord God Almighty.

She said, "I guess I just wanted to . . ."

She didn't get any further than that, and Mitchell Crook didn't find anything to say for a time either. Then he spoke up, sounding almost angry. "Look, I don't want to get you in trouble. Or me in trouble."

For once in her life, she was inspired to say exactly the right thing. "I can keep a secret."

" . . . or hurt you. Take advantage."

"You wouldn't. I know you wouldn't."

"I'm twenty-five," he said moodily.

"That's nothing. That's not even ten years more than me."

"I don't know why, I just can't stop thinking about you."

Their voices had dropped, as if they were already telling secrets.

They bent forward. Josie wondered if she would ever see his face in daylight again, or he hers. The darkness was so perfect. Everything had slowed way down. She could count her breaths in heavy beats. He shook his head. "What am I supposed to do with you?"

She raised a finger to her mouth, meaning he was not to talk, and he wrapped her hand in his and that was how they began touching. She let him pull her toward him. Her bare shoulders shivered from something other than cold, she even shrank back because she was almost afraid, he was so clumsy and so strong. But she made herself be fearless, she wanted to meet him at least halfway and she did. She took a step in her mind and her body followed.

They were all tangled up in each other, kissing and touching as if their hands were mouths also, when a car door slammed nearby. Josie broke loose and twisted around to see the pimp manager grinning at her from the front seat of his own car. "Oh Christ."

"Who's that?"

"Nobody. Arrest him, OK?"

The pimp raced his engine, then pulled out, tires squealing. Mitch said, "He was jealous. I can tell from the way he was driving."

"Oh screw him." Josie sat back, exasperated. She knew that now she'd be in for all the idiocies he could think to inflict on her. "Did you change over to working nights?"

"Yeah, I used to work second shift. You knew that. How did you know that?"

Josie did Mystery Girl again. Smiled. "I was just thinking, I probably won't work here much longer. So I'll have my evenings free." She was about to quit her second cruddy job because of him. Good.

"Oh wow, it's late. I gotta go. Fight crime and/or evil." He reached out and tousled her hair and they kissed again, more practiced this time, with something serious and knowing behind it.

Josie said, "So I guess . . ."

"Hey, I'll be around."

He really was waiting for her to go, so she smiled in a way that she tried to make carefree, and walked to her car just as cool and slow as she could manage. He waited for her to start her engine, then he waved and pulled into the street.

Unreal. Unfuckingreal.

She drove around for a while, thinking about everything, but she didn't want to run into him again while he was being Officer Cop, so she gave up and headed home. There was no one in the world she could tell. Not Tammy, God knows. And not her mother, who, when she parked her car in the garage and tried to creep up the stairs, called out to her from the den.

"Just a minute." Josie checked herself in the powder-room mirror for any visible signs of depravity, then went to stand at the open door of the den. "What?"

"Come in and sit down, please." Her mother motioned her over. Oh shit, did she have some kind of instant sex radar? But no. Her mother was absorbed in one of her shows, one of the hospital shows. She followed the screen for a moment, then turned back to Josie. "Sit, honey. How was work?"

Josie perched on the arm of an overstuffed chair and stared the television down. "OK."

"You're home early."

"Yeah, it was kind of slow." Sometimes she thought that she and her mother hadn't said anything new to each other in years. Meanwhile, her real life was going on all around, it lit up the sky like neon, it sang out loud. Her mother's wineglass was empty, and she had her hand in a bowl of crackers, just resting there, ready to resume the automatic cracker-feed. She was wearing her glasses and the lenses were all smudged and fingerprinty, from the crackers, Josie supposed. She made a move to get up but her mother waved her back down.

"Just a sec, this is almost over." The television music reached its swelling, roll-credits conclusion and her mother turned her smudged glasses in Josie's direction. "You ever watch this?"

"No."

"It's so good. It's enough to make you go into medicine. Of course you'd have to be gorgeous like all of them."

"Was there something you wanted?"

"Your father has to make airline reservations for Aspen."

"Who's stopping him?"

"If you still don't want to go, you need to call and tell him."

Josie waited. "That's it?"

"Well, nobody's going to tie you in a sack and make you go. I think it would be nice if you could bring yourself to appreciate the things he tries to do for you. But you're getting old enough to make your own decisions. Live with the consequences."

"Gee, thanks." She was sarcastic, because of course her mother was trying to make her feel guilty, but her stomach went hollow as she thought about Mitchell Crook and everything she had already decided. It was as if she stood once more on that cliff edge, or no, she had already jumped, and it was a lonely feeling, all that empty air.

"Are you going to tell me what it is?"

"What what is?"

"You just have this funny look on your face."

Josie could have kicked herself. She knew better than to be caught with her face showing anything at all. "I'm just kind of tired."

"It's not Jeff, is it?"

"Jeff? Excuse me while I vomit."

"Then who is it?"

"God, Mom, give me a break." Was she drunk? Sometimes her mother drank a lot of wine and fell asleep in front of the television with her mouth open. Sometimes she got the idea she was very funny and made remarks that were supposed to be clever. But she was never nosy like this; she'd been trained too well. Josie gave her a look of polite indignation and her mother stared blandly back. "How would you like it if I started asking you a lot of personal questions?"

"I don't know, I might like it. Something new and different."

"Well, I'll try to come up with some." There had to be a way to get out of this room.

"Just because you walk around in your own little world and you don't pay attention to anyone else, that doesn't mean you're invisible."

Josie stood up, really alarmed now. This was creepy. "I'll talk to you sometime when you're sober."

She headed up the stairs but her mother was following her. "A word to the wise. To the wiseass."

"All right, Mom. Sleep it off."

"Go ahead, make fun. I'm not drunk. I'm just in a ruminative mood. Wondering what illicit activity my only child is up to. Insurance fraud? Product tampering? I ask myself. *Je me demande.*"

"Good night, OK?"

She closed her bedroom door. But her mother stood outside it. "I was thinking, maybe we could do something together sometime."

"Do something?"

Beneath the bottom edge of the door was a crack of light, and in its center was the dark space that was her mother. "Lunch. Shopping. Or you could come to India with me next time."

This last was so unexpected that Josie laughed a little barking laugh. "India? What would I do there?"

"Oh, I don't know." Her mother seemed to abandon the idea as soon as she voiced it. "You could meet some of the people I know there. Well, good night, honey."

"*Good night.*" The space beneath the door lightened, then almost immediately she was back.

"Jose? Sweetie? I'm sorry to keep bothering you. It just makes me sad that we don't like each other more."

Josie put her fingers to the door. Her mother sounded as if she was breathing through the cracks in the door frame, it was as if the wood itself was breathing. "What are you saying, Mom, you don't like me?"

"Baby, how could you even think such a thing? I love you more than anything in the whole big blue-eyed world."

The blue-eyed world? Where did that come from? "Yeah, but you just said you didn't *like* me."

"I love you more than this boy whoever he is that you won't tell me about. Open the door."

"No. Go to bed. I hope you don't remember any of this in the morning."

"I just want to give you a hug."

Josie opened the door. Her mother had a fixed, sorrowful expression, and her eyes were small and red. "Don't be mad at me, Sunshine."

"I'm not mad, Mom. I just think you're a little out of it."

"Whoever this boy is, he doesn't deserve you."

"Mo-om."

"Come here."

Josie allowed herself to be hugged. It was awful. She and her mother were exactly the same height, and her mother's hair caught her full in the face. It smelled perfumey and it made her nose itch. "All right," said Josie, trying to get loose from her mother's sagging weight, the soft insistence of her breasts. "All right."

Her mother kissed her on the neck in one of the places Mitchell Crook had kissed her. "You've just go so much to learn, baby."

"Yeah, well. I'm trying."

"Don't let anybody ever tell you you're less than absolutely precious."

Josie promised she wouldn't, and her mother retreated down the hall to bed. It was probably some menopause thing.

Just when she thought things couldn't get any stranger.

Why hadn't Mitch told her when she'd see him again? Why had she let him get away without making plans? If she thought she was crazy before, now she was worse, remembering all their greedy touching and wanting more. Maybe he was afraid to call her at home, she could understand that. Or maybe there was some kind of police/crime emergency, except there wasn't anything in the papers, or maybe he'd just been playing her, but no, he wouldn't do that. Most likely she was supposed to wait, be patient, which was of course the adult thing to do. But she had gone to her odious job for the last three nights, had endured the pimp calling her Parking Lot Peg, had loitered around afterward as long as she dared, and there was still no sign of him. Didn't he want to see her, didn't he want it as much as she did? Everything that she'd thought was so certain was now in doubt. And yet it could be restored in an instant.

She was going to call him. She'd call some morning when she was sure he was home, wake him up if she had to. She would think of some good excuse, except she didn't have one. She felt how she could hate him, truly hate him if she had to, and how she could love him again in spite of it. Meanwhile the world went on and on about its stupid yakking business, and each day was as hot as a year of fever.

Was it possible to take some kind of amnesia pill and go back to the way she was before, when she was only unhappy? No, you had to remember everything you ever knew or felt or saw. Everything stayed with you forever and marked you like blobs of paint on a canvas, so that by the end of your life you were one big blobby mess.

On the fourth night he came into Beefeater's. She saw him the instant he walked in. He wore a short-sleeved white shirt and he smiled straight at her and the pimp manager sneered and swaggered and Mitch was right, he was jealous, which seemed to her both sad and awful, but she was too blissed out to care.

"Hey."

"Hey yourself."

"Would you like to see a menu?" Josie asked, playing it serious.

"I don't know. Is there anything good here?"

"Ooh, I'm not sure I want to touch that one," she teased, and he rested an elbow on the counter and leaned back to survey the restaurant and it didn't matter that they were talking like total flakes, he was perfect, everything was perfect.

"You have to work?" she murmured, because of course everybody, the line cook and the waitresses, were gawking at them, even the dishwasher was peeking around the corner with his child-molester leer.

"Not unless they call me in because of civil insurrection or something.

He had to move to one side so a man could pay his bill. Josie rang up the customer and gave him change and told him to have a good evening. Then she reached beneath the cashier's stand for her bag and hooked it over her shoulder. "Let's go."

It was like in *An Officer and a Gentleman* where Richard Gere comes into the factory and carries Debra Winger away. Well, not quite like that but almost as good.

Now they were drifting out over the hot black asphalt. The night sky was enormous and blazing with lights. Even the pink streetlights that always reminded her of the sun on some ghastly planet had a shimmering look to them. Josie said, "You would not believe how glad I am to get out of that place." And she laughed, out of nervousness. They hadn't touched yet, but she felt him walking beside her, that zone of almost-touching.

When they reached his car he kissed her, stooping just enough to graze her mouth. "You didn't tell anybody who I was, did you?"

"Of course not."

"I could get into some big-time trouble. Seriously."

Was he changing his mind? "I haven't told anybody. I won't. It's nobody else's business. I'm a sphinx. A repository for secrets."

"What's a repository?"

"It's a . . . place you keep things. Could we leave my car here for now and take yours?"

"OK, but where are we going?"

Josie had assumed he'd have a plan of some sort, know what to do. And maybe he did but wouldn't let on, maybe it was a test. She didn't want to pipe up and say "your place," although she assumed that was where they were going, for fear of sounding cheap or overeager, so she said, "Let's just drive around for a while."

"Sure."

Josie couldn't tell if it had been the right thing to say or not, since he didn't look particularly disappointed. She wished she was old enough so they could go to a bar, the right kind of bar, and flirt with each other over drinks, but the car was fine. Even though it was only the second time she'd sat across from him in it, there was a familiar and settled feel to being there. They looked over at each other at the same time, and smiled.

He said, "It's great not to have to go in tonight. I'm still trying to get used to the schedule."

"Yeah, I bet." Josie was a little disappointed, she might have wished him to say something more personal or intense, by which she supposed she meant something about herself. Oh well.

"Coffee. I must drink six, eight cups a night. Maybe ten."

"Oh yeah, I love coffee." Small talk. Meanwhile she had a fistful of condoms in her purse, she'd been carrying them all week, just in case. And she was on birth control-pills; she didn't know if she should come out and tell him that. She'd only been on them a few months but she guessed they worked, considering Jeff and all. Some nights she woke from a dead sleep with the breath yanked out of her and her heart racing, thinking she'd missed taking a pill, although she hadn't once missed. She wondered if she'd ever be able to tell him about that.

"So what do you like to do for fun?" Mitch asked her. They were driving toward his apartment, although she wasn't supposed to know that.

"Fun." She was desperately trying to remember if she'd ever had any. "Just hang out, mostly. I used to dance, ballet. Do concerts and recitals, but I don't any more." Hi, I'm a ballet dork. My other hobbies are brushing my teeth and picking up rocks. She made a last grim effort to find something interesting about herself. "I play acoustic guitar sort of, but I'm not that good."

Her poor little offering of conversation trailed off into silence. Well maybe talking didn't matter right now. Josie focused instead on the arm nearest to her, its knots of muscle, the white shirt making his skin look almost tan, the way his wrist bone jutted, funny, how men's hands were built like that. Her stomach was squeezing itself into peculiar shapes, nerves, she supposed. It wasn't like she'd never done it before. Plenty of times with Jeff and once she sort of did it with Rick Conrad except they were both drunk and it probably didn't count. God, she wished it was already over and they were lying next to each other in bed, all peaceful and close. She turned her face away from him because she couldn't be looking at him while she thought such things. She had to remind herself that he was a policeman and nothing bad would happen.

The night and the speed of the car were turning everything on the other side of the glass into a quick-jumping blur of fence and tree shadow and triangles of lamp-lit sidewalk. So that by the time Josie said, "Oh," they were already a block past, and she had to ask him to turn around.

"What is it?"

"Just turn around, OK?"

Mitch pulled into a driveway, his hand poised on the gear shift. "Something wrong?" She might have been gratified to see how polite and tense and annoyed he was at having to stop, but she was too distracted.

"That's my uncle back there. My great-uncle, really. He shouldn't be out walking around, we have to go get him."

"Get him?"

"Hurry up, he was heading the other way. He's like miles away from home."

Mitch put the car into reverse. Josie craned her neck to see past him. Across the road was the Knights of Columbus and their softball field and she was afraid Harvey might have wandered off into its darkness. But no, he was even farther along the sidewalk. He was moving fast in spite of the heat. He wore a broken-crowned straw hat, his shirttails flapped, and his arms swung loose-jointed from his shoulders. He looked like an escaped scarecrow.

"Hey Uncle Harvey!" Josie hopped out and waved him down. "Hey, it's me. Where are you going?"

Harvey stopped and turned in her direction, although they were out of the zone of lamplight and she couldn't read his face, couldn't tell if he recognized her or not. He was half-blind anyway, he was the last person who ought to be wandering around in the dark. "Come on, we'll give you a ride home."

Josie opened the backdoor invitingly. "You don't mind, do you?" she asked Mitch, who only shrugged. He didn't have to be such a pill; it wasn't like she could do anything else. "Come on, aren't you tired of walking?"

Harvey looked at her sideways, swaying a little, then began to creep forward. But he stopped at the grass that edged the sidewalk.

"Har-vey. Don't you want to go home?" The hat shook, shedding straw, no. "Well where do you want to go, are you hungry?"

Sidling forward half a step. His foot curled over the curb, hesitating. "How about a cheeseburger? Fries?" The foot retreated. "Well, there's Wienershnitzel. We could get corn dogs."

Mitch said, "Looks like he's not hungry."

"Just give me a minute, OK?"

"Not much of a talker, is he?"

"Do you mind? My uncle is not a well guy."

"No kidding."

She ignored him. "Here's another idea. Dairy Queen. I'll get you any kind of ice cream you want."

Finally he stepped off the curb and shambled toward them in the dark. "Attaboy. Uncle Harvey, this is my friend Mitch. Oh don't worry, he's not gonna tell on us, are you, Uncle H.?"

"What's that in his hand?"

The car's dome light showed Harvey clutching a cellophane sleeve that contained a single dark red rose. His hand had already mashed the cellophane so that it was chewed and unfresh, the rose itself broken somewhere along its stem, the blossom hanging at a fatal angle.

"What a beautiful flower. Is it for me?"

"Ne, ne." Harvey clutched the flower tighter, a death grip, trying to shield it from her. "Oh, it's all right, I was just teasing." Josie turned back around, a false and sprightly smile on her face. Mitch was looking straight ahead, like a cab driver. "Dairy Queen, anyone?"

He didn't answer, but accelerated, the way guys did when they were mad. In the backseat Harvey shrank into a corner. Josie imagined she could smell the rose, its bruised and darkened perfume. So now everything was all screwed up. She wished she could be angry at Harvey but what was the point of that, or at Mitch, but it was hard to blame him either. So that left only her stupid self, and at least she was on familiar ground there. But she held her smile, turned the radio up, and sang along to some sucky Britney song, like she was having the time of her life.

At least she got Harvey to take his hat off before they went into the DQ, although he wouldn't give over the wreckage of the rose.

She didn't even want to think what that was about. The three of them stood in line at the counter and with any luck people would think they were just a nice young couple taking their slightly addled grandpa out for ice cream.

Josie coaxed Harvey through the menu and determined that he wanted a Dixie Belle sundae with caramel and fudge and pecans. That sounded good, but as punishment for being such a loser she ordered herself a virtuous plain vanilla cone. Mitch got a chocolate cone and he paid for all of it even though Josie got her own money out. "It's OK," he said, and at least he didn't look mad anymore, just sort of detached and bored, well sure. The big first date, an ice cream social with her barmy uncle.

They found a booth and sat down and Josie tried to get Harvey to tell her what he was doing walking the streets, but Harvey was giving all his attention to the ice cream. Harvey eating ice cream wasn't a thing you wanted to watch up close anyway.

Josie was sitting next to Harvey, and Mitch was across from them. She thought dismally that he hadn't even wanted to sit next to her. Harvey lapped and slurped. Mitch studied the ceiling tile with minute attention. He was as beautiful as ever, and as far away.

Josie reached into her bag, fished out a small blue notebook with its cover fraying away. All she found to write with was an eraserless pencil:

I'm sorry you're mad. I didn't know what else to do with him.

She pushed it across to Mitch, who read it without changing expression. Then he picked up the pencil.

I'm not mad.

Josie wrote back,

Sure.

Mitch studied this, still not looking at her. Wrote:

I'm not. I just don't know what's going on here. It's like all
of a sudden you changed your mind and didn't want to do
anything. What's wrong with him anyway, is he some kind
of mental?

I don't know, my mom helps take care of him. What do
you mean, do anything?

Whatever you wanted to do tonight.

You mean, go back to your place so you can ravish me?

He scribbled and flipped pages one-handed, his ice cream cone
melting down.

Thanks. That makes me feel like a complete creep. Maybe I
just don't understand girls. I had this one girlfriend who

Here a line was scratched out.

never mind but she was really weird. I don't want to get involved in anything weird again. So don't talk like, I know
you don't know me real well but I am not some kind of

He shook his head, couldn't come up with the word, pushed the
notebook away. Josie took the pencil, still warm from his hand,
and bore down hard enough to make grooves in the soft paper:

SORRY. I was trying to be funny. I really really want to be with you but this is all kind of SCARY.

Mitch read this, then closed the notebook's cover and handed it back to her, and she wasn't sure if she'd made things better or worse. Harvey had finished his ice cream and was blinking at the brightness of the ceiling lights, one eye weeping a little. Josie felt bad that she'd made him take the hat off just so she wouldn't be embarrassed. She was the most selfish useless bitch in the world.

"Come on, Harvey, let me clean you up." She swabbed at his face with a paper napkin, which he permitted. He was docile, pre-occupied with sending his tongue around the corners of his mouth to catch the last of the ice cream taste. She felt Mitch watching her.

"He's really just a big sweetie."

"Yeah, he seems pretty . . ." Again he struggled for a word, gave up.

"And he's a weather expert, aren't you, Harvey? Ask him a weather question."

"Weather question?"

"Yeah, like how hot it's going to be tomorrow." Josie widened her eyes at him, "Come on, play along."

Mitch did so, a little stiffly. Harvey addressed the tabletop. "Fair, highs in the mid to upper nineties, less humid. Southwest winds, five to fifteen miles per hour."

"It's his thing," Josie explained. "He's always got the Weather Channel on."

"Jeez. You'd think . . ."

"What?" Josie prompted him.

"Wouldn't that drive you crazy?"

They both sniggered, trying not to. Harvey ignored them and petted his rose. They were awful. But at least they were laughing together. In another minute they would have to get up and leave and they'd be back to nerves and silence and the whole slippery future, or maybe they didn't have one. Why couldn't she just enjoy this moment without dread or regret, why couldn't you make your whole life up out of those moments, why weren't they enough? That was all she ever wanted. To make one perfect moment count for everything.

They were outside again in the black, dreaming night, Harvey shuffling between them. "Let's take him home, OK?" Josie swallowed a yawn. It was late, or at least it felt late. She got Harvey into the car and settled the straw hat on his head.

She gave Mitch directions to Harvey's house. "Thanks for the ice cream," she said, formally.

"You're welcome."

"And for helping me with him."

"To serve and protect. That's our motto." He didn't take his eyes off the road but he smiled, and she began to think, in an anxious way, that maybe things weren't yet over between them.

She walked Harvey to his door. Between the gaps in the curtains she saw the TV screen's deep blue, the Weather Channel doing its thing in the darkened room. "Now promise me you won't go wandering around anymore at night," she scolded uselessly. She should probably tell her mother about Harvey's nocturnal activities, except it would inevitably lead to a discussion of her own. She was aware of the car's headlights on her, and of Mitch watching her, and of having to walk back to him in the lights' glare and maneuver her way through all the hazards of her own wild hopes.

Harvey's rose still held its petals, although the stem was now in three pieces. It must have been some tough variety grown especially for supermarkets, like tomatoes. Josie opened his front door, sighed. "Turn on a light so you don't hurt yourself."

"I'm getting married."

He'd only whispered it, and the next minute he'd closed the door behind him, and Josie was left blinking at it, wondering if she'd heard him right. He was nuts. Absofuckinglutely. It probably ran in the family, this was probably how she'd end up some day, walking the streets in a crazy lady's hat, flagging down police cars and declaring her undying love.

She walked carefully back to the car, got in. "Well . . ."

"Yeah."

"I was thinking, maybe we could try this again some other time."

"If you're sure . . ."

"Yes," Josie said, and once the word was out there in the air it seemed to grow round, hang in the air like an inflated balloon. She said again, stronger now, "Yes."

"Yes not tonight, or yes later?"

"Both." She liked the sound of herself saying it, the boldness of it. "Tonight got all screwed up. But I still want to." She let the back of her hand rest, almost carelessly, against his crotch.

He drew a long breath and they started in kissing and she thought maybe she'd change her mind and they'd do it anyway, right there in Uncle Harvey's driveway. But he disengaged himself. "Boy."

"I'll say."

"Do you like the mustache? You never said."

"It's totally great."

"You think so?" He tilted his head to catch his reflection in the rearview mirror. "You don't think it looks faggy?"

"Absolutely not. You should keep it."

"One of the guys at the station was giving me a hard time about it being faggy. But I think he's full of it."

They drove back to the restaurant and her car, which sat in the empty parking lot like a reproach, and she kissed him again, almost impatient to get the good-bye part over with. When she'd already gotten out of the car she turned around to tap on his window.

"I'm not gonna be working here anymore. So if you need to find me . . ."

"Give me that notebook." He scribbled on the inside cover. "That's me."

"So I should just call you?"

"Let your fingers do the walking."

When he'd gone she looked down at the number she already knew by heart. It seemed he ought to know she'd called him dozens of times, even though she'd been careful not to give herself away. He should have just figured it out. She kept shoving back down the thought that maybe he was a guy who didn't figure out a lot of things you might expect.

Roadkill

Somewhere out in the desert, after he'd long since lost track of the days, the tape began talking back to him.

God, Rolando hated the desert. If there were any desert guys back there in his ancestral soup, they'd been elbowed out by guys who came from jungles or the tops of big snowy mountains. He wasn't built for this place, he had no use for it. Zero. The sun, his friend, betrayed him here, became a horrible swollen ball of pain. He kept driving east, speeding to get through to something else, because you knew as a true fact the desert didn't go on forever. But it had a way of fucking with your mind so you started thinking maybe it was everything and everywhere, had swallowed the rest of the world into its big blank self.

He'd never been here before. He'd never been much of anywhere. But he'd liked the idea of the desert, which he must have put in his head from some old cowboy movie and never got around to changing. He had imagined stars as thick as silver stitching in a deep blue night, cactus flowers, painted cliffs. Thunderstorms riding in twenty miles ahead of you, so that you watched chains of lightning, yellow and red, ignite the horizon. Room enough to walk for days (somehow he had pictured himself walking), until your soul rose right up into your skin and then into air and left you pure.

He had thought there would be more out here somehow. More

of anything. There wasn't even sand. Just bare scrub dirt with some kind of tough ground plant poking up here and there like a half-grown beard. There were probably rattlesnakes—he would have liked to see a rattlesnake—but you couldn't tell from the car. Every so often there would be some butt-ugly little town strung out along the highway, trailers and sheet-metal roofs and giant antennas and maybe a corral with a heat-stupefied old horse in the middle of it, and then Rolando would feel a shuddering relief that whatever else was wrong with his life, at least he didn't live here.

That first night he drove almost to Palm Springs, then pulled over at a rest stop to sleep. When he woke up it was cold, and the first white morning light was cold also, and he slapped at his wallet and his duffle bag in reflexive panic. The money still there. At the bottom of his pocket, the flattened pebble welcomed his fingers. But some other dread held him as if below the surface of water while he struggled to get free, and it was more than waking from his muzzy sleep in a strange place with a thick taste in his mouth and a crust in his eyes. Something else was missing and it wasn't his gun or his money, it was himself. As if he'd been emptied out by anger and motion and darkness and fear. He was weighed down by absolutely nothing. He was free to go anywhere, be anyone, and maybe later that would feel good but not yet.

So he drove on into Palm Springs, past irrigated fields as green as Easter grass, and a line of distant powdery mountains. Palm Springs. A place where rich people played golf and tennis in clothes bought only for those purposes, and everyone had a swimming pool, and everything was air-conditioned and easeful. It was summer now and the rich would be elsewhere he knew. Still, ideas, speculations, possibilities began to tumble and click in his head, in a recreational sort of way.

He found a gas station with a minimart and breakfasted on coffee and packaged doughnuts. He brushed his teeth in the john and tried to clean himself with the soap in the dispenser and paper towels but that was so unsatisfactory he decided he'd rather stay funky. He bought cigarettes and an orange soda for later when it got hot. He leaned back against the car and let the smoke draw into his lungs and along with it there was the sensation of heart and nerve and will returning. Some of whatever had drained away in the night was filling again.

The morning, the day, was like money in his pocket, his to waste or spend. He drove past suburbs of large and undoubtedly well-guarded homes, condo villages, streets lined with palm trees, the useless-looking downtown with stores where the rich could pretend to need things like ski jackets and fancy dog food and expensive furniture painted to look beat-up. It was still early, the sun was tangled in the shadow of buildings, the air was clear but with a glowing edge of heat. How all-out weird it was to be in a place you'd never seen before, where you couldn't take anything for granted, weather, streets, faces. It was part of being his brand-new, This Space-Available self, he figured.

Next to him at a stoplight a Latino guy was driving a step van, half-blue and half-green with a wavy squiggle in between. The guy looked over and Rolando nodded. He was dressed all in white, like he worked in a hospital. The light changed and they scooted along together for another few blocks, stopping and accelerating in unison. After the second light they struck up a shouted conversation.

"Que onda, ese?"

"Que onda, vato? You following me?"

"Naw man, just cruising. Where you goin?"

"Work, where else?"

"Yeah? Where you work?"

He shouted something Rolando couldn't hear. "What?" he mouthed back and the driver reached up and slapped the roof of the van. Rolando craned his neck and saw that the blue-green was supposed to be water, and the letters on the side read OASIS POOL SERVICE.

The van signaled for a left turn and the driver waved goodbye. But Rolando dropped behind him and turned also. They passed into a district of winding roads, big houses set on lawns, if you could still call them lawns, arranged with cactus and boulders, brick-colored gravel raked into designs, clay pots at the front doors filled with blazing pink or red flowers. The van turned at an alley and parked and Rolando pulled up behind it. The driver got out and stood waiting for him, a little warily. He was a young guy with a broad, square face and burnt-brown skin.

Rolando, all casual, pulled out a cigarette. "Smoke? Hey, I just wanted to ask is it a good job, you like it OK?"

The driver reached for a cigarette, accepted Rolando's light. "It's not bad. Boss is a jackass."

"Jackass, that's just another name for boss."

"You got that right." The driver opened the back of the van, began unloading nets and hoses and jugs of chemicals. "Look, I need to get started before people call the office complaining cause there's a dead dog or something in their pool."

"Dead dog, you find that kind of stuff?"

"Brother, you don't want to hear about all the things you can find floating in water."

Rolando put out his cigarette half-smoked and pinched it carefully back into the pack. "See, I just got into town. I'm looking around for work."

"They're not hiring."

"Yeah, just got in, trying to get to Phoenix but I got a bearing going out. Garage says it wants three-fifty. Man!"

"Try the Chicken Shack."

"No, I got to earn more than that. How much you get, seven,

eight an hour? That's what I need. Cleaning pools, I bet that's big here. I bet I could get on somewhere. Maybe I could hang with you today, help you out, learn the ropes."

"What, I'm supposed to pay you?"

"No, man, I'd be like, your apprentice. Just for today. If I get in your way, kick me out."

Rolando planted himself square and easy while the driver, who he judged was not an automatically friendly person, made up his mind. His heartbeat clock keeping perfect time. He wished he had another cup of coffee. He wished he was floating on his back down a big cool green river, looking up at these same clouds, smoking weed. And probably because he wasn't anxious about asking his favor, was willing to let it go either way, the driver shrugged and said, "So where you from?"

Rolando said he was from San Ysidro and his name was Javier, lying out of habit and policy, and the driver introduced himself as Nacio. Rolando hopped right to it, loaded himself up with equipment and enthusiasm. Nacio unlocked a back gate and opened it onto a high-walled patio with a sort of desert-style garden and big lounge chairs, all real nice. There was a pool in one of those blob shapes and a trickle of waterfall coming out of a fake rock on the wall. Everything here was still in shadow and almost cold, so that he was glad to exert himself wielding the skim net and the vacuum as Nacio directed. He pushed a broom this way and that, made everything spiffy. What a trip. He was Javier from San Ysidro, and for all anybody knew, Javier was a hell of a guy. "This is like some easy shit."

"Wait till you do another fifteen."

"I can do fifteen standing on my head."

"Yeah, let's see you stand on your head once it heats up to one-hundred twenty. It's dry heat, everybody says. So's the inside of an oven dry."

They had been speaking in Spanish, but when the white man

came out of the house, Nacio switched to English. "Good morning, Mr. Buchanan."

"Morning." Buchanan was a smallish man in a blue terry bathrobe with a bit of mouse-colored hair all rumpled from sleep. He retreated back into the house then almost immediately reappeared.

"Don't worry, Mr. B., we'll be out of here in a jiff." Nacio motioned to Rolando to gather up the equipment. When they were back in the alley Nacio said, "He likes to swim naked."

"What, you hang around watching?"

"Walked in on him one day. Man, if I had a body like that, I wouldn't even shower naked."

They worked through the morning, cleaning, draining, scrubbing, and Rolando busted his ass being a good little pool boy and entertaining Nacio with stories he made up or misappropriated about his life as Javier, wild stories about racing cars and knife fights and fucking two girls at once, and Nacio told him he was full of shit up to here. By eight o'clock it was already what he would have called hot back home, and by nine he was sweated dry, a rock had more juice in it than he did. He went through the orange soda right away and Nacio laughed at him because he was drinking water from the cooler every five minutes. The sky was all sun: yellow, hateful, flat.

There was a whole block of condos where nobody seemed to live—time-shares, Nacio said, but the management company kept the pools up, and Roland jumped into one of the pools, clothes and all. That felt good, it almost felt like being clean, and his clothes dried in about ten minutes and he was ready to do it again. Because he was helping they were getting things done fast, and Nacio said if they pushed it for another hour they could quit for the day. Another hour would probably kill him, and they'd put on his tombstone: Here lies a sorry fuck who died busting his hump for free. But he kept going out of stubbornness, and when Nacio pounded him on the back and said, "We got to toughen you up, boy," he said, "Yeah, your mother don't have no complaints." He'd done his share of muscle work, he lifted free weights and shit. It was just the bastard heat.

All the houses they worked at had lots of glass in back, you could see right into them, and even as he was making a mental list, which places seemed more or less accessible, more or less inhabited, he was imagining himself inside looking out. They probably had giant refrigerators in there, stocked with orange juice and beer and iced tea. At one condo where the air conditioner cranked as loud as a jet engine, a woman sat at the kitchen table wearing a wool coat that looked like an Indian blanket. A blanket! She was writing something on a piece of paper, a grocery list? Needing more stuff for that holy big-ass refrigerator. And she looked up once and stared right through him, which was about what you'd expect from people who let somebody else do their sweating for them. Rolando wrapped a water-soaked bandanna around his head to keep his brain from frying. The sun turned the cement as bright as pain made visible. When he was the guy on the other side of the glass, he was going to invite everybody in for lemonade and beer.

Nacio was in a good mood about getting done early and bought him lunch. They sat at a back table with an older guy named Victor and drank beer and watched the races from Hollywood Park on the bar's little television. God bless walls and roofs and floors, he was never going to take them for granted again. Victor was a big bull-chested guy with gray showing up in his chin whiskers. He worked for Caltrans and he said nothing was hot compared to tarring roads out on I–10. The crews mostly worked at night but once in a while they sent them out to burn in hell. He could handle it, heat never bothered him, he was a goddamn armadillo.

Rolando figured this was the way they bragged around here, who could boil his balls off and not feel it. It was a small town, he'd already taken the measure of it, and there probably wasn't much to talk about besides how hot it was and who got to carry Bob Hope's golf clubs last week. He felt a lot better now that he was out of the sun and had a beer to take his thirst away. There was nothing for him to do until night and he was content to sit back and listen to the other two talk. They were easy not to pay much attention to. Nacio had a girlfriend who was giving him a hard time and Victor had a wife and three kids and a girlfriend who was giving him a hell of a good time, if you could believe even half of his noise. Rolando let a moment of sweet sleep take over behind his closed eyes, jerking awake when Victor said, "So what are you, Puerto Rican?"

All the ease inside him vanished. Even before he opened his eyes he felt Victor's belligerent curiosity beating down on him like another kind of sun. He said, keeping his face frozen, "Yeah, the old man was. My ma, she's from Jalisco."

"I figured. I knew a Rican guy once who was damn near black."

Rolando said nothing. The words stayed out there long enough for everybody to walk around and look at them from all sides. Then Victor said, "No offense, man. It's kind of a hobby of mine, figuring people out. Like when you can see a dog's got shepherd and beagle and maybe a little coyote thrown in. I just find that interesting."

"Yeah. Interesting." On the table before him, a five-dollar bill, that ugly bad-luck face staring up at him.

"Me, I got some Apache. The warrior bands that outfought the U.S. Cavalry for five years."

The other two were waiting to see how big a deal he'd make of it, no offense, man, he was going to find Victor's hot girlfriend and make her do things this ignorant piece of stink never imagined and then he was going to do the same to his wife and she'd put out a litter Victor wouldn't know what to make of and then he was going to find Victor out on that highway and see how he liked the taste of boiling tar, no offense. He said, "Apache? I thought they killed all of them."

"Naw, there's lots left. The Mescalero, those were Geronimo's people. That was my one great-grandmother, a pure-blood Mescalero."

"So what's the other seven-eights, those Bullshit Indians?"

Victor decided this was funny. Ha ha, he laughed, and Rolando smile and asked what his girlfriend's name was.

"Angela. Sweet Angelina. She's wild for it, she wants to do it in all these crazy places. Once we did it in the truck, practically right out on the street. Last time we did it in the shower."

"The shower," scoffed Nacio. "Very tame."

"Yeah? How about, she wants to do it in a earthquake."

The other two whooped at this. "What, you got her hooked up to an earthquake machine? 'Honey, get on over here and catch a little five point two action.'"

"No, but you do it enough, you got better odds of catching the next big one."

"Explain to me why you want to have your dick out when the damn roof comes down on you."

"I don't. It's just this idea she got, she thinks we could put it in the *Guiness Book of World Records* or something, that we were screwing in the biggest earthquake in history. Hey, I don't mind humoring her."

Nacio said, "I got no use for earthquakes. Times I can't sleep, that's what I think about. The Big One."

"Funny, that's Angelina's name for me. The Big One."

"There's no Big One coming, that's bull," put in Rolando, just because he didn't want to hear any more of that talk from Victor. "Don't tell the girl. Break her horny little heart."

Rolando said he'd left his cigarettes in the truck and Nacio gave him the keys. Rolando reentered the heat, which was enough to stagger you, slow-walked to the van, opened it and retrieved his cigarettes, slow-walking and quick-fingered, his heartbeat dead level, detaching two of the keys from the ring and pocketing them, and when he got back to the table they were still talking about earthquakes.

Nacio said when he was a kid in Sonora there was a big earthquake, an evil time. If Victor's girlfriend didn't have all her brains between her legs she wouldn't think earthquakes were some kind of fuckfest opportunity. He was just a little guy, barely walking, his nose and his ass always running but he'd never forget it. Sky everywhere there was supposed to be buildings. Stinking smoke in the air. People dead, dogs pawing through the ruins, use your imagination. They laid some of the bodies out on the beach because there was no other place for them and the tide came in and washed them out to sea. He'd never stopped thinking about those lonely dead, the shame of it, how the living had failed them. Not even a cross raised over their heads. They'd gone to sleep in their own beds and then they were dead in the ocean where they never thought to be. He was glad he lived in a hot place where those water ghosts couldn't follow.

"Ghosts," said Victor. "You ever see one?"

"Just because you can't see something don't mean it's not out there. Can you see gravity?"

They watched the television and the horses flying round and round and money being won and lost. Then Victor said For Christ's sake, you couldn't worry about earthquakes because there wasn't one thing you could do about them. If one had your name on it, so long. Besides, the Big One was going to hit up north, everybody knew that. Rolando reminded him of the

Northridge quake, and there was some useless discussion about fault lines, a topic none of them knew anything about but each of them had an opinion on. Rolando thought Nacio was right, earthquakes were nothing to mess with, and bigmouth Victor was right, if they happened, they happened. In places like Japan and Hawaii they had earthquakes in the ocean. Giant walls of water rose up and swept everything away. Like something in the Bible, one of those times God smote people down. Smote. A word you didn't hear too often.

People used to believe that, the smoting stuff, people like his mother still did. Get Him pissed off enough and he trashed the place. Everytime there was anything fucked up, fire or flood or hurricane, his mother said it was a punishment. Now that she was too old to have any normal fun, she'd gotten religious. She was always trying to get a better deal out of the Virgin with her little altars or the time she spent on her knees. A bunch of crap. Racehorses didn't pray to win races, they just ran harder when the whip came down, and that was life.

The sun was as red as a torch when they came out of the bar. Victor was on the loud side of drunk. "Ange-lina," he called. "Light that fire, baby, I'm coming!"

Nacio said, "Yeah, she probably appreciates the warning."

"Funny guy. Very funny. Guy."

Nacio told Rolando he hoped he got his car fixed and see you around, which he wouldn't, waved, and drove off. Victor and Rolando were left out on the quiet street. There was dust in the air and the sun turned it to lurid pink.

"Hey, Angela wouldn't have a friend, would she?"

Victor stared at him, squinting through the sunlit glare to get the idea straight in his head. "You mean for you?"

"Yeah, or maybe, she likes new and different things, she wants to try some black Rican dick herself."

That was all the warning he gave him, and Victor was as drunk as the pig he talked like, but he was a big man and wasn't going down easy. He just swayed when Rolando caught him under the chin, swayed and got his arms working, but he was slow and among the many things he knew nothing about was boxing, using his hands. Rolando drove his knuckles right up into Victor's nose. Victor screamed and the blood looked almost black in the inflamed light. He tried to get Rolando in a bear hug but Rolando danced away and got in another head shot, forget about trying to hurt these big sacks of shit in the body, it didn't work. "Come on, chief, over here!" Got him right over the ear and then he tried to kick the legs out from underneath him, except Victor's legs were like fucking trees, he'd need an ax to drop him.

Victor had a mouth full of blood but he was still talking, spitting through it. Did nothing ever shut this guy up? "Crazy fuck, what's a matter with you culero, I kill your nigger ass." He was bent over trying to protect himself and still taking blind swings when Rolando tripped him up and finally put him on the ground, yanked Victor's arm and used it like a handle while he stomped his ribs, heard bone crack, the air leaving Victor's chest in one leaky whoosh.

Someone was coming out of the bar then so he walked away fast without looking back. Victor hadn't touched him but he was shaking from letting everything out and his hands hurt and were going to keep on hurting for a while and he'd been a fool to think there would be any such thing as a new start or a new skin for him and next time he was just going to drink alone.

Although Victor didn't know what his car looked like and it would probably be a while before he was saying much, Rolando decided it would be better not to be driving right now. He checked his clothes for blood, didn't see any, walked four blocks, still didn't hear sirens. One Mexican beats another one up, it wasn't like anybody much cared.

He squatted in a drainage ditch behind a tract of houses until it was dark. The ground was still as hot as bread crust but it felt almost good, he was so tired, he could have stretched right out on the ground and slept. He should have felt good about whipping Victor's sorry ass but he was back to empty again where none of it mattered.

He took a roundabout way back to his car, past a park with kids playing softball, he guessed they did most things at night here, league play with regular teams, red-and-white against blue-and-white. Parents in the bleachers rooting them on. Him and his draggy-ass clothes didn't fit with this scene but he kept it cool, just sauntered past, stopped and drank from a water fountain, smelled his own nasty smell when he bent over. The car was just where he'd left it. One of the keys he'd lifted was to the back of the time-share condos and that's what he needed right now, a rabbit hole.

He drove past the condos, didn't see lights. One master fit all the back gates. He picked an end unit, let himself in all slick and smooth. The pool was dark and glassy and when he leaned over it he saw reflected stars and only then did he look up to see the sky the way he'd always imagined it here, blue like the first and only color in creation, stars blasting away like crazy.

Rolando knew the feel of an empty house. He worked on the sliding-glass patio door with a thin, flexible metal blade he had found useful for such purposes. The lock snicked open and he stepped inside, listening. The air was stale, thin, unbreathed, nobody home. One of those metal lollipops in the front yard advertised security, but nothing was wired so he paid it no mind. A field of pale carpeting stretched out before him, with other looming pale shapes that were furniture. He had to wait for his eyes to adjust, then he soft-footed into the room, trying to get a sense of the place. All set up with lamps and glass coffee tables and pictures on the walls and beyond a kitchen stocked with everything you'd need except food. Not even ice cubes.

Finally he found a box of crackers in a cupboard and washed them down with tap water. The tap groaned as if no one had used it for a time, but the water ran cold. Upstairs, two bedrooms with the same stripped-down hotel look to them. He didn't want to use the lights so he bumped around in the dark, running his hands through drawers and closets and underneath mattresses. All the places you might expect to find something left behind, some spilled crumb of wealth. Nothing. Not even a radio you could walk off with. The place was useless, every brick and board of it spoke of money but they made it so an ordinary person couldn't touch it, you had to be a bank or at least somebody bankers shook hands with. He was so tired his mind kept shorting out, he should blow the whole place up except once you started thinking that way, you might as well blow up the world.

There was a bar of pink soap in the bathroom, so he stripped down in the dark and stood under the running shower. His knuckles were all bruised and torn and they stung where the water hit. The soap was full of perfume, by God he was going to smell rich if nothing else. He dried himself with his shirt and lay down naked on one of the bare beds, with the streetlight shining through a crack in the curtains.

He fell asleep once without really meaning to and then he woke halfway fighting Victor all over again, his own hoarse shout in his ears. Then he lay awake for a long time.

He remembered where he was but when he tried to put together how he came to be there he couldn't follow one *because* with another. Because he had driven east instead of north or south and because he had seen Nacio on the street but he was leaving something out. Because he had come away from what passed for his home and that was because of a lot of things. Or maybe he had it wrong and there was no *because,* even if you went back to the very beginnings of his befucked life and you might as well enjoy yourself by raising hell.

Because was everything you couldn't see, the world going about its business that had nothing to do with you, who were you anyway, empty man in an empty house. The world had its important work of. Of. Something. Getting the sun up and down on time. The bastard sun so hot here, cooked you like bacon, but how cold the water in the pool when he jumped in. Cold and silent. Once you got beneath the surface you couldn't hear a thing. Fish lived in silence, silent bubbles rising up, circles in the water.

Then he was awake and it was bright day, light falling across the room in a yellow stripe, but it wasn't light that woke him. It was the sound of a door closing downstairs.

Stupid ass fuck shit Christ. Trying to get his pants on at least. Somebody down there making leisurely rummaging noises. Tap of shoes on the kitchen floor. It came to him that they didn't know he was in the house. Out in front there was a red car at the curb. Whoever it was, they thought they belonged here, driving right up to the front door.

If they went around back, he could get out through the front, but the bedroom didn't face the patio and he couldn't see. How many were there, more than one? Hide or run? They might not come upstairs but if they did it was too small, he'd have his back in a corner, and if he ran, the weight of the duffel would slow him. Why had he left the gun in the car, *mother fuck.* Downstairs the air conditioner came on, whoosh and push of machinery. Nothing else. They might be gone. Barefoot, quiet as quiet, except for the sound of his heart jumping through his ears, a clock gone crazy.

At the top of the stairs he listened, nothing, started down one creeping step at a time. Three more steps and then the door, the goddamned door. He reached the landing and swung around and she was right in his face, the woman, and she screamed, a ripping sound.

She was square in the way, blocking everything, he couldn't get out back or front except through her. Even scared like this she held her ground, a tall woman no longer young, dressed in red, red mouth, red fingernails, everything about her fancy, her twisted-up yellow hair and the gold at her wrists, fancy and loud. "Who are you, what do you think you're doing here?"

You had to admire the way she came back at him after her first fright. He might have tried to shove her aside or even hit her but she was only a woman so he opened his mouth instead, tried to look sheepish. "Ah, sorry, I was working out back, came in to take a little rest, you know?"

"Working where? How did you get in here?" Cold-eyed, like a witch. She had a handbag the same leather as her narrow shoes and she clutched at it, he wanted to tell her he didn't care about her stupid money, she should just back off and he'd be on his way. But she was used to bossing people, you could tell. "Do you work for Carpetmaster? Answer me. Is that how you got in here? They are *supposed* to be bonded."

"No, lady, I clean the pool"—the moment he said it he regretted it—"and the door was just open."

"What's in the bag? What did you take?"

"Nothing, it's just my stuff." He shrugged and shifted his weight. He couldn't believe his bad luck in this town. The woman tightened her red mouth.

"And what if I had been the Kirbys? Do you think they would appreciate your roaming around upstairs? Using the toilet? I don't think so."

"All right, sorry, I go now."

She had a little phone in her hand and was punching in numbers. "You stay right there."

"No, *hey,* be cool—"

Rolando reached out, tried to grab the phone, but she held it behind her. "Don't come any closer or I'll scream."

He would have laughed at her if he hadn't been so exasperated. She was so full of righteous meannness and up close he could see where her red mouth was leaching away into powdery wrinkles and her eyes were blinking ninety miles an hour, like being mad at people was her job and she loved the work. When he took a step toward her he saw alarm in her face for the first time, like it was just occurring to her that there might be people in the world who didn't give a shit about her and her orders. She backed up into the living room and the front door was clear but he had to get that phone. She was making noise now, shrieking like some kind of bird, a big red bird with flapping wings.

"Sshh," Rolando told her, as if keeping his own voice low would quiet her. She kept on hollering. "Shut up, Christ!" She had the phone held up to her face and was screaming into it. He hadn't laid hands on her but she wouldn't stop her racket. He caught her by the wrist. "Give me the damn phone!"

She hauled off with her free hand and raked him across the face with those long red nails. It hurt like poison and the anger rolled through him and he was on her in an instant, stupid bitch, cracked her flat-handed across the jaw.

She staggered but didn't fall. Her yellow hair had come undone and a part of it was sticking out wild on her neck, making her look more than ever like a witch, bruja. She wobbled around on her stupid shoes then they broke or something and she got the sofa between them and was hobbling out the backdoor, her big red ass rolling away.

Cursing, he ran after her, hauling his duffel. She was screaming again and now he was crazy to shut her up, she was calling like there was somebody out there who could hear her. But instead of running for the back gate she turned around and leveled her big hand with its rattling gold, pointing at him. "You're not going to get away with this, Mister! You are going to lose your job *and* go to jail!"

All he'd done was sleep, since when was that a crime? You couldn't argue with people like this, ignorant of everything, taking it for granted that she could order him around, dress herself up like a whore and spend her days being useless, and so it was not entirely surprising that he should run at her and push her the few feet to the pool's edge, where she fell in like a rock.

He had to laugh. She rose up all dripping and wrecked and she was still making her noise but it was full of water now. "You dirty little—hoodlum!"

"Hava nice swim!" He waved and shouldered the duffle but once his back was turned she lunged after him and caught him by the ankle. He tried to kick loose. The duffel made him top heavy and it pulled him over and he landed hard, half-in and half-out of the water. Hit his tailbone on the cement deck, it hurt like hell, while his duffel rolled into the water. The woman laughed and splashed away from him to the pool's far end.

"You think that's funny?" Rolando screamed. "You playing some kind of stupid bitch game here?" He felt crippled. He had to crab-walk along the edge of the pool to reach the duffel. It was floating but its bottom half was soaking through, all his money washing away, *stupid whoring cunt.* He flopped into the water after it, which made the woman begin screeching once more.

He reached the duffel and hauled it out and then he started after her, not wasting words this time. The water here was waist-deep and he had to slosh through it, it was taking a long while to cover the little distance between them. She was half-swimming, half-running as best she could, so that they did a kind of cartoon, slow-motion chase, at least until she reached the ladder and tried to climb out. That was when he caught up to her and grabbed her by her wet hair and dragged her back down.

She kept making noise even underwater, you could hear it. Her throat opened and let out a stream of noisy bubbles. The color had mostly washed off her lips. Strings of sticky red trailed away from the corners of her mouth. Her hands slapped at him. His own hands were reflected crooked through the water and it wasn't until then that he saw he was choking her. He had not thought to do it but now that he was he hung on like he was some kind of machine built only for this purpose. He sent the pain in his spine traveling through his arms and hands and fed it into her skin so that she would be nothing but a bloated bag of pain. Her clothes were weighing her down. She kept trying to kick or struggle or scratch him again but she couldn't get to him. The anger was burning through him in a crackling wave, filling his head with jumpy light. It blew out everything but the holding on so that it might have been a long time before he realized she had stopped moving.

Her face was the color of bad meat, a dark mottled red, and her eyes had rolled back so they were almost all white and some of her yellow hair was caught in her mouth, like something thick she had spewn up.

It made him sick, touching something so ugly. He tried to wipe his hands on his wet pants. Turned his face to stare up at the sky, which was as bright and evil hot as ever. He heard a buzz of traffic, neither very near or far away.

The pain in his back gripped him. He couldn't even run, just hitched along, looked back once before he got out of the gate but his eyes weren't working right either because all he saw was a mess, a kind of floating mess in the water. The wet duffel was heavy, he had to half-drag it, *bad, very bad shit, a dead bruja.*

The car was where he left it and down the street an old lady in a pink bathrobe was walking an even older poodle dog and she gave him a curdled look. With any luck she couldn't tell one Mexican from another, couldn't see the flapping wetness of his clothes. He threw his duffel in the trunk, didn't even allow himself to think the car wouldn't start right up and it did.

Then he was on the highway with the bastard sun in his eyes and his back on fire but at least he was out of there. He kept flicking glances in the rearview mirror but there was nobody and nothing in the world behind him and not much ahead. Once he got past the first few highway signs it was bone bare. Every so often a car passed him going the other way, and a couple of times he caught up to trucks or some old couple in a slow-moving van plastered with stupid tourist stickers. Other than that it was as if the road was unspooling new before him as he drove. His wet clothes rubbed and scraped until his skin felt wormy cold. The rest of him was turned inside out with shaking and thirst. He felt for the pebble in his pocket but it was gone, washed away.

He woke up without being aware he had slept, and found he was still driving, that some part of him had kept the car pointed on the road while the rest of him went far away. It swerved as if only now that he had come back to himself would things go wrong. He wrenched the wheel the other direction. He was going way too fast, the speedometer needle said red, red, red, and the land and sky flew by in strips and patches. For another moment he was not driving the car but riding it until he remembered to remove his foot from the accelerator.

From then on he kept more of his mind anchored, enough to do the work of driving, although not enough to think about anything that happened back there. He had to stop once in the middle of an empty stretch of road to let the engine cool and to take a piss. Amazing that he still had enough water in him for that. The ground was so bare and hard-packed that nothing of his stream soaked in. Overhead, the thinnest scrim of clouds was outlined against the impossible sun, not enough to shade anything, while the only object on the endpoint of the horizon was a line of accidental-looking brown hills. A car passed without slowing, leaving a stinging sound in the air. Aside from that, there was nothing to show that anything in the world was alive. His dull brain considered this. If the Big One hit out here, or say it already had, how would you know it?

He stopped once more for gas in one of those mean little desert towns but wasn't paying attention to distance and so Phoenix surprised him, creeping up on him with its snarl of freeways and traffic. He bore down on the wheel and once more rode the car through it until there was highway again. And then his mind spun away into the pale sky and somewhere he must have gotten food because there was a food taste in his mouth, bits of beef and salt, but for his life he couldn't have said how he had come by it.

Then it was dark and he stopped the car until it was light again because he thought if he drove in the dark, he might lose even the horizon. When the sun came up he aimed toward it but he had gotten on some different, smaller road now that wasn't going straight in any direction. He would have been lost except *lost* meant there was somewhere in particular you were going.

The radio didn't work. Or else he was somewhere the radio didn't go. He played the tape because it was noise, and because those angels sang Ohh like it was a whole entire language. He tried to sing along with them, beating time on the steering wheel, and laughed because he sounded like a damn goat. Then the dude came on, the one that wanted to be his best friend, and his voice was like chocolate syrup pouring over clean snow.

"Weary? Confused? Anxious? The chaos of our times affects us all. The barriers in the mind reflect the barriers we place between ourselves. Imagine instead, one self that contains all selves. One will that joins the forces of all wills together. All our energies focused on the great work before us. I'm talking about nothing less than the physical manifestation of that which we call God."

More angels. He tried another chorus with them. His voice spiraled away like water going down a drain. He was beginning to smell again and his mouth tasted like sin. He figured he must look pretty funky too, because he stopped once for gas, falling out of the car practically bent double because of his back, with a cracked grin on his face from those fine fine angels. And a woman standing at a pop machine saw him coming and double-timed it back to her car, rolled up the windows and locked the door. The grin wasn't even for her; he had forgotten there was anybody on the other side of his face. Just to see what she'd do, he sauntered toward her. She couldn't peel out of there fast enough. Adios, darlin! He jumped up and down waving, then turned around to see two men watching him from inside the gas station, arms folded across their chests. At that moment he also became aware that he was not wearing shoes and had not been for some time and his feet were as tough and battered as hooves.

Well, screw these guys. But he shrank into himself, pumped his gas, and paid with his head down, not looking at them as he pushed his money across the counter. When he went back out to the car he saw that it was all beat to shit as well, coated with dust from the wheels to the windows, the paint faded in patches. It looked like some kind of ugly lizard. He felt bad about that and made a point of checking the oil and coolant and pumping the tires.

He was driving as fast as he could but he wasn't really getting anywhere. He seemed to have lost the deciding part of his mind. The sun went down behind him again, or maybe a couple of times. He liked the nights out here. They were righteous. If you could just hide in a hole all day, you could stand to live here. He thought he was in New Mexico now, or at least he remembered a sign for New Mexico, but he was embarrassed to admit he forgot where New Mexico was. His beard was growing in all itchy. The food he ate he ate with his hands. There were times he saw cops, state troopers who might pull him over just for being dark and solitary and worthy of suspicion, He kept his hand on the gun shoved between the seats and rallied some of his old cool self to glide past them and it worked, they let him be. He tried to take stock. His money was still damp, the bills limp and curling. The clothes in the duffel had turned sour from the water the witch oh kill him back oh my Christ so he went as fast as he could until he raced the dust that billowed up behind him and he was almost flying, floating in that hot blue sky.

He knew every bit of the tape by now, although he didn't listen to the bullshit words. But he had the rest of it so cold. He could keep one hand on the wheel and with the other direct the chorus of harps and tweedling birds and his angel girls, like a conductor. Times it was hottest, he pulled over and stopped in whatever shade he could find, beneath an overpass or a concrete slab on stilts that passed for a rest stop. He was getting more used to the heat but still he found it best to stop and let the sun take charge now and then. He had just started the car up again after one such interval and the afternoon glare was as thick as if it had been laid on with a brush when something wrenched and jolted beneath him, not the car, because that kept on going, but the road itself. "Jesus Christ, what was that?"

"You know. The Big One."

Rolando had talked to the tape so often that he didn't find it surprising to hear it talking back. He lit a cigarette, tasted smoke. "Oh wow."

"Right. Kaboom. There went California. Into the drink."

"You're kidding."

"Yeah. Had you going there, didn't I?" It was the man's chocolate-on-snow voice, but whispery, as if he was telling dirty jokes.

"Very funny," said Rolando sarcastically. "Yeah, you're a damn stitch."

"I didn't mean I was kidding about all of it. Just the California part. There's definitely something going down."

"So what are you saying?"

There were gaps and flares of hissing static, as if the tape was going bad. "It's the end of the world."

"Right. Prove it."

"Prove I'm wrong."

"Road's still here. Car's still here. I'm still here."

"Naw, man. Not really. You're just in the habit of being alive and you haven't noticed the difference yet."

"You are so unfunny."

"Like that lady. She's busy fixing her hair, putting bread in the toaster, watching *Good Morning America*. She's got no idea she's really swallowing a swimming pool."

"Shut up, why you want to talk about her?"

"Did I say it's the end of the world? I meant it's just the end of you."

"Go fuck yourself. Quit messing with me."

"Have it your way."

The tape spewed out of the deck in big loops, and there was a mechanical garbled sound, and the cassette ejected, covered with its own insides, like a trick. Rolando reached for it to see if he could rewind it somehow, push everything back. Then his heartbeat clock stopped. Hung suspended. The smoke from his cigarette didn't dissipate but stayed in its lazy curling vine shape, which seemed the more remarkable thing at that moment. When he looked through the windshield it was like it had become a kaleidoscope, everything fractured into a million needles of light, or maybe he was on a spaceship where you went so fast that time itself grew rubbery, elastic. Then his mind stopped making thoughts.

The physical manifestation of God was a yellow school bus. Rolando watched it take shape and color in a gradual, unhasty fashion, or maybe it was just the process of words trickling back into his head, *yellow* and *school bus*. It filled the entire windshield, its oversize grill staring him down, unmoving. "I didn't mean for her to die," Rolando said. "There was no *because* to it."

"Hey, buddy?"

It wasn't the tape talking, but a white man in a cowboy hat, peering in at his open window. "You broke down or what? You aiming to move anytime in the near future so somebody else can get by?"

Rolando saw that the car was stopped at one end of a narrow bridge over a concrete-lined ditch with a little brown water in it. The road was laid down straight as tape in a landscape of fenced and dusty acreage, pastureland, maybe, although he could see nothing grazing. He coughed to get the dust out of his throat and said, "Sorry. Let me see if I can get it to start." He tried the ignition and the engine balked, then caught.

"Hey!" The man in the cowboy hat, already walking away, stopped and turned back to him. "Where's this road take you?"

"In that direction? Fifteen miles to the interstate, then another sixty to Amarillo." The man didn't much like the look of him or the idea of him, Rolando could tell. He steered carefully around the bus, stared at by a row of curious children lining the bus windows.

In Amarillo he found the kind of motel where no one cared what you looked like.

He showered and washed his hair and shaved in the cloudy

bathroom mirror. He selected the best of the clothes in the duffel and threw the rest out. He slept on the floor to try and ease his back, then got up before it was light and, leaving the blue car where it was, found another vehicle that better suited his purposes. He headed north on the freeway with a warm wind at his back, wondering just how far you had to go to leave a water ghost behind you.

Part Three   August

The Light of the World

Rosy rosy rose. Rosa rose. Local Forecast had trouble keeping names in his head, so he practiced. Row row row of rosy Rosas. He wanted to be ready for Rosa day. He never knew exactly when that was coming, because most of the time he mixed up his days something awful.

The worst of the heat broke exactly on August the First. He knew because he marked it special on the calendar. He wanted to be able to remember it. New weather on a new, first day. It was ten twelve fifteen degrees cooler, down where it ought to be in the eighties and bottom nineties. Still hot, but normal hot. There was even some pattering rain from time to time. He could take his coffee out onto the front porch and watch his plants green up and think about Rosa.

Rosarosarosa. She had little hands, as small as brown mice. They were quick like mice too. He watched them scurry in and out of dishwater. They wrapped themselves in snowy clothes and made gleaming tracks all along the floorboards. She had a brown face. He had to get up close to it to see how it worked, the sly folds of her eyelids and the star folds at each eye's corner. If he got too close she slapped him away. She said: Ya ya ya ya ya ya.

Local Forecast let her noise roll around in his head. He wondered if it was a game he was meant to play. So he worked his mouth: Ya ya ya ya ya. She slapped at him again, but in a way that was not meant to hurt. She was kneeling in front of the bathtub and scrubbing. Local Forecast admired the way she flung up clouds of bleach smell. He was behind the shower curtain, pretending to hide. She knew he was watching her and he thought there was something prideful in the arch of her back and the way her chin pointed out ahead of her, as if she liked being watched. Encouraged, he said, very softly: Ya ya ya.

She giggled and rushed at the shower curtain so it wrapped around him. Local Forecast pretended he couldn't get out. The shower curtain was filmy-colored. It made everything look underwater. He poked at where the giggles came from. There was a squawking sound. He froze.

It was a sin. Unless you were married. And even then, you couldn't get all carried away.

Everything was quiet. The shower curtain crinkled when he took a careful breath. Little by little, he unwrapped himself and stepped out of the shower curtain. The bathroom was empty except for the bleach smell. Local Forecast went galloping out the door, his heart in a rush. When ever things got too clean, she went away.

But she was still here. She was in the bedroom, rooting around in the closet. Local Forecast was always embarrassed to have her fooling with his clothes. Without him inside them, they were just saggy baggy things of no distinction. Rosa hurled them into the laundry basket as if she didn't think much of them either. Local Forecast hung back at the door. Fat Cat stalked past him and gave him a look as if Rosa was all his fault. Local Forecast wished he could get Rosa to stop and pay attention to him again. Maybe she didn't like him anymore. It was such a desolating thought that a sound came out of him, a bleating sound.

Rosa looked up from the laundry basket. She muttered to herself, ya ya ya, led him back to the kitchen and fixed him a tuna fish sandwich and iced tea. That made him feel better, although it wasn't as good as the slapping and giggling.

Once he tried to follow her when she left the house but she only went as far as two corners and stood there until a bus roared up. She got on and waved him away, shoo. The bus scared him. It smelled bad. He watched it cough its way down the street and that night he tried to follow where it had gone but it didn't leave any tracks. There had to be a street you took to get to Rosa and a street you took to get back but he hadn't found them yet.

When they were married she could stay here all the time.

He was still eating his sandwich when the phone rang. He got up all in a hurry and answered it with his mouth still full: "Oca fucust."

"Harvey? Do you have a cold? This is Elaine, how are you?"

He managed to swallow, though there was still some fish taste stuck behind one tooth. "Fair, light south winds, highs mid-eighties—"

"Yes, well, never mind about all that. I'm going to come see you and I'm bringing a friend who wants to meet you. So I hope you won't get upset about it, OK?"

He put the phone up next to the television, where Man In A Suit was talking about isobars. He let it stay there for a while. When he brought it back to his ear, he could hear the listening sounds on the other end of the line. Then she said everything all over again, twice as slow and loud.

He hung up and went back into the kitchen, leaving Man In A Suit talking to himself. Rosa was in the basement, making the laundry machines run. He wasn't hungry anymore. He didn't see why people couldn't just leave him alone.

Rosa went away. Then Yoo Hoo came. He sat on the couch with his hat pulled over his eyes, sulking. This day was not turning out so good. He heard Yoo Hoo come in and exclaim in her loud voice about how clean the house was. "And this is my friend Robert. Would you like to say hello to him? I've been telling him all about you."

Robert said, "Hello, Harvey. Very nice to meet you."

No it wasn't. Local Forecast spied on them through his hat, where they couldn't see him looking. Robert had red hair and a red mustache. He had something in his hands, a light that went on and off. He held it up to his face, one eye at a time. Robert seemed to see him watching. "Here, do you want to see it?"

Local Forecast took it in his hand. It was some kind of metal stick. He couldn't get the light to go on. Robert said, "You have to look into it. Take your hat off and I'll show you. Now hold very still."

The light shone straight into his brain and held him there. He said "A-aah." Robert was on the other side of the light, looking in.

"That's very good," he said encouragingly. Local Forecast felt Robert's cool fingertips on his forehead and at the back of his neck, steadying him. "Now the other eye."

Obediently, he let his other eye open and flood with light. The light of the world.

"What's that, Harvey?"

"Daddy said He who follows me will not walk in darkness, but will have the light of life."

The light shut off and he blinked. Robert said, "I didn't quite catch it."

"He can be a little hard to understand. He doesn't get much practice talking."

He still saw the white, even when he closed his eyes. Then when he opened them, everything had a ring of rainbow around it. "There now," said Yoo Hoo, from somewhere inside the rainbow. "That wasn't so bad, was it?"

He wasn't sure yet. Robert said, "Harvey, is this where you sit to watch television? Can you see it from here?"

"No hazardous weather is expected today or tonight in central Illinois."

"All right. How about the newspaper? Can you see to read the newspaper?"

Local Forecast waved it away. He didn't like newspapers. He was never in them.

"And you don't wear glasses. That's really unusual. I've had to wear glasses ever since I was a kid."

He hadn't noticed Robert's glasses before. They were the small kind and didn't reflect much.

Yoo Hoo said, "I think he compensates. You know, gets used to seeing things a certain way."

"As we all do, to some extent," said Robert, with a smile in his voice. He liked Robert. "Harvey, I have to wonder if you used to have to sit this close to the television. You couldn't get much closer, could you? Now I don't want to scare you, but what if you got so you couldn't see it at all?"

Local Forecast tried to put his hat on but they'd taken it away.

"Sometimes that happens when people get older. It's like your eyes are windows and the glass gets clouded."

Yoo Hoo said, "You should listen to Robert. He's an expert."

At windows? But he knew there was something serious that he was trying not to understand.

Robert said, "I want you to think about letting me help you. It's not an easy thing. It's an operation. And we'd have to go to my office and talk some more. But after everything's over, I feel certain that you'll see at least some improvement."

Green Woman came on. She was talking about hurricanes. They hadn't had any yet, but it was still early. Hurricanes were Big Weather. He was going to learn everything about them, the statistics. They came all the way across the ocean, ninety, a hundred miles an hour.

"Serious. Important."

"I can assure you."

"operation?"

"doctor."

Hurricane Harvey roared and roared. Nothing could withstand him. He blew trees into toothpicks, blew the shoes right off of people's feet, the eggs out of chickens before they'd been laid. He was merciless. Noisy too. Hrhaaahaa. The window curtains fell in a heap. A lamp went smash. Yoo Hoo and Robert ran for the door. Yoo Hoo kept trying to talk. She said, "Now, Harvey." He roared at them and they skedaddled.

After they left him alone, he had to sit down for a while. The glass thingamajig on the lamp was broken. And he'd have to put the curtains back up before it got too bright. His eyes were his own business. They couldn't make you do anything unless you were in the no no no hospital no no no no humidity dewpoint precipitation.

They could put you in there without you even knowing. One day you just woke up and there you were. On the inside with the outside a million miles away. He made himself sit very still and remember. His tongue fluttered around his mouth, looking for a place to hide. Your mouth was always dry in the hospital. That was how you knew they came around with the medicine. They were sneaky about it, they did it when you weren't paying attention.

There was a chair he used to like because it held you down when you might otherwise go floating off. The chair was in front of a wall and the wall stayed put right where you wanted it. The nurse said, Now Harvey. If you don't eat your soup, you can't have more milk. He didn't know why you couldn't have one and not the other. It was how they let you know who was boss.

Mamma and Daddy sent him new slippers and a Christmas card. The card said Christ and his love shall redeem us all. Christ had holy light shooting out of his fingertips. The slippers were too small.

The doctor said, That's a mighty fine card, Harvey. Now don't you feel bad about tearing it up? Because he had. He'd called Mamma and Daddy names out loud and he'd torn up the Lord God and now the doctor was going to tell on him. The doctor would put him in the cold bath and God would make him burn in hell and Daddy there was no telling.

The doctor said Calm down. We can't have you acting up like that, you understand? It upsets the other patients. And it's not good for you to get yourself so worked up. You don't want another Treatment do you? I didn't think so.

Mamma said, Your father has something to ask you. Stand up straight and look ye forthright. Daddy sat at the table in his big chair. In front of him on the table was the white bowl Mamma used for mixing. There was a crack like a dark hair down the front, turned so that there was no way not to see it.

Come here, boy.

He was already right there, so he didn't know where he was supposed to go. He moved his feet up and down, trying to stay forthright.

Tell me what you see on this bowl.

Crack.

I can't hear you.

A crack, sir.

That's right. It's cracked. Now tell me how the crack got there.

I don't know, sir.

Well, I'll tell you what I do know. I didn't break it. Your mother didn't break it. Frank says he didn't break it. So that leaves you. What do you have to say about that?

His knees went cold. There was something he was supposed to

say. Only one something in the whole universe, and everthing else was fatal. He imagined that one right thing like the Holy Ghost, a bird circling away overhead out of reach. Daddy was waiting. He tried to think pure thoughts. He prayed that the bird would descend and light on his head and show him the way but his tongue couldn't come up with even the taste of a right word. He didn't break the bowl. At least he didn't think he did. But he knew that wasn't the right thing to say. If he said Yes, he did it, he could just take his punishment and get it over with.

But wouldn't that be a lie? And what if that was the trap that was waiting for him, telling a lie because it came out of your mouth so soft? Mamma looked at Daddy and Daddy hitched his pants up, getting impatient. Then the Holy Ghost flapped right down on him and he knew the answer was to convince himself he really and truly broke the bowl.

It wasn't that hard. He thought of all the ways it could have happened. He was trying to reach the raisin box and the bowl was in the way. Mamma told him to stay out of the raisins. Once he sneaked some when nobody was watching. And there were times he opened the cupboard doors and *looked* at the raisins, and plenty more times when he *thought* about looking at them. So it was easy to imagine how it might have happened, and from there to how it had happened. He saw the bowl from underneath, its smoothness and the lip or shelf that marked its rim. It looked a little like a flying saucer, if you were to see one from upside down. Then it wobbled and grew larger and slowly vibrated itself into the waiting air.

I did it.

What's that, boy?

I broke the bowl. I went to eat the raisins and I broke it. I'm very sorry, sir.

He felt himself shining with white truth. He was dazzling. For just that one moment, he shone. There had to be a punishment now. But he was unafraid, clothed as he was in his new righteousness.

Daddy spoke. So you disobeyed your mother.

He didn't like to think of it that way but he had to nod, yes.

This bowl will never be whole again. It's broken, just like your immortal soul.

He sniveled a little imagining his poor soul, all sad and cracked.

Now the difference between this bowl and you is that Jesus Christ has the power to restore you. If you let him. If you cast out pride and humbly repent. Do you want Jesus Christ to heal and cleanse you?

Oh, he did. The bowl of his soul. He saw it rise up on white wings.

Are you willing to sacrifice for Christ's sake?

Frank came in the front door from school, whistling. He looked around, the air went out of his whistling, and he went back out.

It was a new question. Another something out there in the universe. But this time he knew what to say: Yes!

So Daddy led him down to the basement. Mamma sang Bring Forth the Royal Diadem. They stretched him out on a long table and Daddy prayed as he drove the spikes through his hands. They raised him up on the cross and he looked into the whitest light. It made his head split with pain. He screamed and tried to get away from it. A hot thread burned from ear to ear and the water poured from him so his skin wept and his teeth melted. Daddy said Oh hallelujah hallelujah and heaven was descending

But no. That was just the Treatment. It turned the inside of his head into blank whiteness and he knew he was leaving something out. There wasn't one thing he could know for certain. Except the Weather, which was always there. So he sat in his usual place on the couch, hunched forward to watch the words scroll by like perfect clouds.

What Went Ye Out into
the Wilderness to See?

Most of my work is with people who want to quit smoking or lose weight. That's the bread and butter. Then there's your compulsive habits: counting floor tiles, cracking knuckles, hair pulling. Plus a few more you don't want to hear about. I do stutterers. And agoraphobics, folks who get nervous about leaving the house."

Elaine said, "How do you get the agoraphobics to come to your office?"

"Well, the really serious cases, I'll go see them. And we use tapes a lot."

She was somewhat distracted by the agoraphobics, the thought of them peering out from behind their shy curtains, but she soldiered on. "How about, ah, less specific problems?"

The hypnotist—hypnotherapist, she reminded herself, he preferred that—was ready for the question. "Low self-esteem and assertiveness issues. Lack of focus. Goal-setting. Grieving."

Elaine stopped herself from nodding, and got down to business. "I want to be happy."

"Of course." Waiting, visibly, for her to say more.

"No, that's really it. I want you to hypnotize me into being happy."

He was doing his professional best to understand. "What be-haviors are preventing you from achieving happiness?"

"None. There's nothing in the world keeping me from being happy except me."

The hypnotist guy—she decided that was how she would think of him—considered this. He was a neat, slim young man, prema-turely balding. There was something reassuring about the pale dome of his forehead. It was reminiscent of laboratories and op-erating rooms, of scientific industry and verifiable knowledge. Al-though his pleasant office was a marvel of indirect lighting, earth tones, and framed landscape photographs, wheat fields and ocean waves, chosen for their pretty, restfully vapid effect, Elaine supposed, she wasn't ready to be lulled into any peaceful, pre-hypnotic mood. She felt anxious, and more than a little silly. She said, "I know you don't dangle a gold watch in my face, at least I think I know that, but I hope you don't mind my asking, what is it exactly that you do?"

"I gradually relax you so that you lose that layer of conscious attitudes, defenses, and anxieties. Then I can speak directly to your mind. Don't worry, you'll be entirely aware the whole time. I won't make you cluck like a chicken or anything."

"Thank you."

"But let me try and clarify. How do we define happiness, how do we quantify it? Say we undertake a course of therapy. How do we know if it's been successful?"

"I'm not sure," Elaine admitted. "I don't know if happiness is just the absence of unhappiness, or if it's something more posi-tive. And I suppose there's a kind of continuum, from content-ment through happiness to ecstasy. I'd settle for the middle of the spread. You know?" The hypnotist guy's bald head stayed immo-bile. She tried again. "By any rational, objective standards, I have a good life. There are things I might wish were different, but honestly, I have nothing to complain about. I just want to turn some knob in my brain so that I can appreciate it without worrying that it's not enough, or that some disaster's going to come along and punish me for enjoying myself."

"If you feel you might be clinically depressed . . ."

Elaine shook her head. "No. I'm discontented. I'm apprehensive. There's a difference."

"All right. How does being discontented and apprehensive feel? Physically, I mean."

She considered this. "Dense. Slow. Droopy."

"So we need to speed you up some."

"You could throw in a little weight loss too, if you wanted," said Elaine, trying to make a joke out of it. She was never going to admit to anyone that she was doing this.

The hypnotist guy laughed. "Why don't you close your eyes."

"What, right now?" She thought there should be more prelude or preparation or something. It was alarming.

"Sure, right now. Give it a whirl."

With her eyes shut she felt even more ill at ease and unhypnotizable, on guard against whatever she irrationally imagined was about to attack. There was a space of silence filled with her own cautious breathing. Then another silence. Elaine was tempted to cheat and sneak a look. Then his voice crept into the silence and took everything over. She hadn't remarked his voice as anything special before, but now it seemed enormous, as full of growling power as a car engine yet subtle as smoke.

"I want you to lean back until your head rests against the cushion. Yes. Now some deep breaths, each one starting as far down as you can reach. And every time you let one out, I want you to feel yourself getting a little lighter. A little freer. Each breath a little slower. That's good. And Elaine?"

"Yes?"

"Don't try so hard."

From there he asked her to imagine herself walking down a long flight of stairs, and at every step she was to relax a little more. That was fine, that was the sort of thing Elaine expected. Nothing flashy. Relax her toes, her ankles, her knees, and so on. She kept thinking how normal she felt, how she was probably one of those people who couldn't be hypnotized. Pelvis, ribcage, shoulders. The stairs led down through a kind of tunnel, arched with brick or stone, and at its end was a floating, green-gold light, indistinct but promising the rarest sort of beauty, a garden, perhaps. Or something less contained than a garden, some impossible storybook landscape whose forms and colors were as delicate and improbable as if they were made of blown glass. The colors washed into paler and paler shades, into white. That floating light was joy, and each step on the staircase brought you a little closer. The important thing was to realize that the staircase went on forever.

"Elaine? You can open your eyes now."

She couldn't at first. She had forgotten how. When she did open them there was a moment of disappointment so pure she could have wept, at being back in the normal world. The pretty office seemed harsh and wrong, or she herself was wrong, until some lens slipped back into place and she saw things as she always had.

"How do you feel?"

Elaine raised both hands and touched her face with her fingers. It felt cool. "All right. I guess I'm all right. Was that it? Was I hypnotized?"

"Yes ma'am. I'd say you were." His pale forehead nodded. He seemed pleased.

"It wasn't exactly what I expected. It was . . . Was that you talking the whole time? I wasn't sure."

"That depends on what you heard."

The hypnotist guy smiled and picked up a brochure from his desk. "If you'd like to consider a complete course of treatments, this will give you information about fees and payment options."

She walked out into the ordinary afternoon, which either was no longer ordinary or else it never had been. Surely he couldn't have hypnotized the whole world? There was an edge of almost fluorescent green to the trees where the late sunlight hit them. Since the heat had broken, it was now possible to stand outside without making immediate plans to get under cover. An invisible bird called from a tree, its voice a liquid question. An airplane passed overhead, as slow as any bee, arcing downward to land.

When she started the car and attended to all its mechanical demands, gear shift, parking brake, accelerator, she had to do so consciously, as if she had been stripped of some bodily habit that allowed her to do such things without thinking. The Service Engine Soon light went on, winking at her like a joke she'd heard a dozen times and was still supposed to laugh at. Right then and there she decided she was going to trade the car in.

Teeny had left a message on Elaine's answering machine. This in itself was an unheard-of thing. And Teeny's voice was strained and hesitant, even filtered through electricity: Would Elaine mind calling her? Soon?

Perhaps something had happened to Frank, but no, she wouldn't be on the A-list even for drastic news. She tried to think if she'd inadvertently offended them. There was always the Harvey situation, but that was hardly the sort of thing Teeny would get audibly distressed over.

Teeny must have been expecting her because even her hello

was abrupt. "Elaine, thank God. I was hoping you could stop by for a little while this afternoon."

"Is something wrong?" Elaine asked, concerned, but annoyed at all the drama.

"Is Josie there?"

"Yes, she's in the shower. What about Josie?"

"Oh, I'd really prefer to sit down with you. Just a little heart-to-heart. How's two o'clock?"

"You and Frank and me?"

"Frank's playing golf. This is just girl talk."

Teeny must have had one of her soap operas in mind, where people had nothing better to do than trek around having heavy conversations. What in the world had Josie done anyway, and why would Teeny care? Josie wasn't going with them to Aspen, but they'd settled all that, hadn't they? Had there been some kind of flare-up?

As soon as Elaine agreed to see Teeny, she regretted it. It was Sunday and she'd planned on catching up on her bookkeeping. When Josie came slouching downstairs later, her hair sleek and wet, Elaine tried to gauge the chances of getting any information out of her. Josie responded to Elaine's good morning with a noise that did not require her to open her mouth. She communed with the refrigerator for a time, snared an orange soda, and headed back upstairs.

So Elaine dressed in her smartest black linen jacket and pants, hating that she was dressing up for Teeny, hating even more that Teeny would be decked out in something preposterous but four sizes smaller. She wondered if the hypnotist guy could help her with Teeny, like make her invisible. Simple posthypnotic suggestion.

One hour, she told herself, backing out of the driveway. No, forty-five minutes, and she begrudged even that much. Frank and

Teeny lived in Panther Hills, in the new house Frank had built to go along with his new life. Elaine would have liked to say the house was vulgar but in fact it was a very nice house, she would have liked to live there herself if there weren't places like India in the world, or, more to the point, if she were someone who could ignore the existence of places like India.

Frank employed a landscaping service so that laborers came out to plant and water and tend to the weeping cherry and daylilies and ornamental grasses. The house itself was low and expansive. The front door was a marvel of inlaid wood and asymmetrical glass. The doorbell had a sound like a Buddhist temple gong. Elaine listened to it echo through the vasty corridors of the game room, sunroom, master suite with full-size fireplace, and so on. Elaine had only come here to deposit Josie or pick her up, back when Josie was making her increasingly reluctant weekend visits. Once, when Frank wasn't home, Teeny had given her a tour, and Elaine had admired the hand-painted Portuguese tile, granite slab kitchen countertops, had even been granted a peek at the enormous, pilow-decked, salmon-and-cream California king bed where Teeny and Frank disported themselves. She had liked Teeny better for showing her the bed, for not even thinking there was anything indelicate about doing so.

Elaine rang the bell again and the echoes died away. Just as she was about to leave, annoyed, the door opened and Teeny, already talking before she was visible, said, "Sorry sorry sorry, I was all the way back in the laundry room," as if that was a reasonable place to be when you were expecting guests, then poked her head around the door and waved Elaine inside.

"Thanks so much for coming." Teeny's tone was serious, even hushed. Some of her tawny hair was clipped into two peculiar, asymmetrical tufts, one over her left eyebrow, one over her right ear. She was wearing a lime green tank top and a short white pleated skirt, red-and-green-striped jute sandals. She resembled something Elaine couldn't quite put a name to. A tennis-playing parrot, maybe. "Would you like a drink? I've got stuff for margaritas."

Elaine said No thank you, and Teeny offered iced tea, white wine, Kahlúa, milk, diet Sprite. "Iced tea," said Elaine, resigning herself to raising a glass with Teeny. Teeny led her to one of the rooms they'd run out of names for. Gallery? Porchette? Garden nook? It was furnished with pale green wicker and glass-topped tables and Elaine took a seat opposite one of Frank's discarded beige polo shirts, which she eyed mistrustfully, as if it might be capable of speech. Beyond the French doors was the pool, with its hallucinatory blue water, and Frank's enormous gas grill, suitable for preparing haunches of beef. Elaine wondered if they entertained much. Frank had never been the entertaining type.

Teeny returned with the iced tea on a tray, whisked the shirt away with an apologetic fuss, and waited until Elaine had raised her drink to say, "You know Josie was over here last night."

Elaine said she wasn't aware of that. Goddamn the girl.

"Oh, yes. She asked if there was a time she and a couple of her girlfriends could use the pool without disturbing us. And since we were going to Joliet with the Rhineharts to the riverboat casino, we said sure, come on over. Although Frank would appreciate it if Josie wanted to spend some time *with* him."

"Of course," Elaine murmured, bracing herself for whatever was to come. But Josie was safe at home. The house was still standing. What, then?

"So she came over to get the house key and the security code and she was as sweet as pie, and promised they wouldn't make any sort of mess, or get into the liquor, and I have to say she was as good as her word. We'd left some Cokes and chips out for them, and they washed the glasses and put the garbage away and hung up the towels. But when we got home, and were getting ready for bed, I turned the covers down and there was no bottom sheet on the mattress."

"Oh, dear," said Elaine, feeling grateful, mostly. She'd been expecting something like stolen jewelry.

"I found the sheet in the dryer, And I know if it was my daughter having some kind of lesbian affair, I would definitely want to hear about it."

Elaine didn't laugh because there wasn't anyone to laugh along with her. One-on-one against Teeny's belligerent seriousness, she wasn't sure she'd prevail. "Did you tell Frank any of this?"

"Oh Lord no. I had to pretend the housekeeper messed up."

"You know it's possible it wasn't a girl she had over here, but some boy. In fact it's more than likely. I'm sorry about the sheets."

Teeny's face pulled in two directions, like her sprouting hair, relief and indignation. "A boy?"

"I agree, it's still distressing. Just in a different way."

"She said Jennifer and Tammy. I distinctly remember."

"Yes, they're the usual alibi. If you'd like me to talk to her . . ."

Teeny shook her head. "You'd think they could just do it in a *car* like everybody else."

"It was the pool. They wanted the pool. Aren't you glad you don't have a teenager?"

Teeny said, "Well, even if it was a boy . . ."

"I still would have wanted to know. Thank you." Teeny had some apricot-colored makeup coating her face and throat. Elaine hadn't noticed it at first, but now she was fascinated by the way it floated over Teeny's features like a mask. There were orangy deposits at the corners of her eyes and mouth. Something stretched and frayed about the flesh beneath her chin. Teeny was twelve years younger than Elaine. Frank's frisky filly. Teeny hadn't caused the breakup of the marriage; she'd been more of a coup de grace. Now she was already showing signs of high mileage. But it was too easy to make fun of Teeny. It always had been. Besides, she had Josie to worry about. Josie and her new mystery swain. Elaine had no clue as to who he might be and that in itself meant trouble. Whoever he was, she'd gone to a lot of elaborate care to play house with him. Elaine only wished she could be there to watch when Josie finally remembered the sheet in the dryer.

"I didn't know Josie had a boyfriend," said Teeny, in a new, sugary tone. "Do they spend much time over at your house?"

Elaine stood up. "I'm glad we got to talk. And it would probably be just as well not to mention it to Frank. If you wouldn't mind."

Teeny batted at the air, dismissing the thought. "Frank would have himself a cat fit. He doesn't know how girls are these days. He thinks everything's the boy's fault, and the girls are just innocent victims."

"They're just young. Part of being young is having bad judgment."

"Call it that if you want to." Teeny stood also. She came up to the level of Elaine's shoulder. "Good thing she's not coming to Aspen with us. I wouldn't want to try and keep track of her."

Takes one to know one, Elaine thought nastily. From some distant precinct of the house came the mechanical whine of a garage door ratcheting up.

Frank home early from golf. The two women looked at each other. "Crap," said Teeny.

He would have already seen Elaine's car, so there was no point in trying to escape. She decided she'd let Teeny handle it. They heard Frank in the kitchen, rattling ice cubes, then water running. "We're in here, honey," Teeny caroled. His feet padded along the corridor outside. He stopped at the doorway and peered in at them with the cautious distaste of a man lifting the lid of a diaper pail. He wore khaki shorts and another polo shirt, red this time.

The sun of the golf course had newly boiled him. His nose, forehead, the upper surfaces of his arms and legs were a burnished, flourescent pink. Teeny said, "How was your game, dear?"

The same thing Elaine would have said herself in years past, the same wifely, pretending-to-take-an-interest tone. She found it unnerving. Frank must have thought so too. He glanced narrowly from one of them to the other and said that the game had been not bad.

"Elaine just stopped by to drop off the key Josie borrowed."

"Oh."

"Yes. Thanks for letting her have her pool party. It was nice of you both."

Frank said, "I figure, all the money you put into a pool, you might as well get all the use you can out of it." Delivering an opinion seemed to steady him. He stretched luxuriously, rotated one shoulder, then the other, testing the muscles.

Teeny said, "You didn't strain your back, did you? Do you want me to walk on it? I do that sometimes," she explained. "It works better than those electric massagers."

"Well," said Elaine, trying to remember the way to the door.

She was already getting into her car when Frank came out to the front porch and waved her down. "Hold up a minute."

Elaine pointedly checked her watch. Frank said, "It's about Harvey."

"What about him?" *Crap.*

"I was talking with George Ebersole today at the club."

Elaine made a "who's George Ebersole?" face.

"He's one of the partners at the opthamology practice. Works with Bob Worthy."

She was busted. Goddamn this town, everyone always knew everybody else's business. "I was going to tell you."

"Yeah, sure."

"Just not right away," she admitted.

Frank stood there, visibly blistering, staring her down. He must have worn a golf cap out on the course because there was a line of demarcation just above his eyebrows, as if he had been dipped by his ears into some furious dye. Elaine wished he'd hurry up and get it over with. "That wasn't a very good idea, was it, trying to sneak up on him with the eye charts and all?"

"He didn't bring an eye chart. It would have been a great idea, if it had worked."

"Well, since it didn't, do you think maybe it's time we let the professionals handle it?"

Absurd as he looked, he had her on his own turf. And her knowledge of Josie's indiscretion, or more accurately her withholding of that knowledge, made her feel guilty, at some further disadvantage. She said, "I suppose so," resisting even as she gave way, not wanting to admit she had failed Harvey, lost the fight. But had he ever been hers to lose or save?

"I'll talk to Dave again"—Dave was the lawyer—"and get everything set up for when we get back from Aspen. Don't worry. He's going to get first-rate care."

First-rate sedation. Lots of nursies. Lights that were never turned off, doors that never shut. She would go visit Harvey in the hospital, bring him flowers and talk about the weather. She would take care of his smelly cat. There would be a further series of alarming and painful events, the surgery. Harvey would wear gauze patches on his eyes and when the patches came off, who knows what he would find to see?

Maybe it would turn out all right. Maybe eventually he could go back home and live out the rest of his small life in peace. All he had ever wanted. Of course, she didn't really know that.

"Frank? Do you remember, did Harvey ever talk about anything like his plans, the kind of work he wanted to do, that sort of thing?"

"He used to drive a cab."

"I know that. But nobody ever *dreams* of driving a cab. I mean things like goals, interests, ambitions."

Frank gazed up at the sky, which was becoming thinly overcast, its color draining away. "He used to run track," he offered. "Back in school."

"Harvey? That's wild."

"Track and field," Frank amended. "You know, high jump, broad jump, discus and all. I remember my dad talking about it. Why?"

"Just curious." Oh *run Harvey, run.* "If I don't see you before you go, have fun in Aspen."

"Yeah. Rocky Mountain high." Even as Frank spoke he seemed bored by the idea of Aspen, as if he'd already gone there and come back. Unexpectedly he said, "I've been watching that Weather Channel. Just once in a while when there's nothing else on. It's kind of—not interesting, exactly. More like they give you all this information."

"That so," said Elaine, her eyebrows held at neutral.

"Yeah, you could see somebody like old Harvey, somebody who didn't have anything better to do, really getting into it."

"But you're not. Into it. You just watch it."

"I said once in a while, OK? I don't know. Maybe I'm finally getting the wackos. The family wacko syndrome."

"What syndrome?"

"Well, there's Harvey. And granddad, when he got real old he used to sit in his big chair and wait until somebody got close enough. Then he'd spit at you and laugh like the devil if he hit you. Nice, huh? Even my dad had what he called his 'low-down days.' Times he wouldn't get out of bed or talk."

"You never told me any of this."

"I didn't ever think much about it. Then you read stuff on brain chemistry and genetics. Like there could be some kind of hereditary time bomb that goes off when you reach a certain age. So what do you think, am I gonna end up being another crazy old man?"

He was trying to keep his tone light, but there was a layer of anxious bravado that she didn't know what to make of. Why was he telling her this anyway? Wasn't it Teeny's job? She said, "I think you'll probably die of skin cancer before you get the chance to find out."

Frank looked down at his blazing forearms. "Yeah, I know, sunscreen. They talk about that a lot on the Weather Channel."

"I don't think you're going to go crazy, Frank. If it matters what I think. Maybe you should talk to somebody, it might make you feel better. Maybe the professionals you want to turn Harvey over to."

She drove away, leaving neither of them satisfied with the conversation. But she had to shift focus, she had Josie to worry about now. She needed to get back to the house and decide what to do about her. Lecture? Scream? Confiscate the car keys? Refuse to pay for college? Had she really believed she'd get away with such a brazen stunt?

Of course, she almost had gotten away with it. Elaine supposed she should be glad that she'd found out what Josie was up to, but truthfully, she would have been just as happy *not* to know, since it seemed there was no way she could prevent or control anything the girl did. It frightened her to think of Josie out there in the vastness of the world, thinking she could take it on, make it do her bidding, escape not only unharmed but triumphant. Elaine remembered feeling that way herself. Years and years and years ago. Not invincible; any number of things had made her suffer profoundly. But she'd felt as if anything she did would come right in the end, no matter how reckless or foolhardy, because life was meant to be lived, seized, met head-on. Like the time she and her girlfriend had gotten into the car with the Italian men they hadn't known for two minutes, strange men, strange car, strange country, motoring off into the hills outside of Florence on some forgotten excursion. And in fact it had turned out all right. The men had not been rapists or murderers. They'd treated them to Oranginas and bolted upright from their seats the instant Elaine and her friend had said they wanted to go back. Which proved exactly nothing, except that whatever bad luck was floating around that day had settled on different people.

She had done other things she liked remembering less. Risky, histrionic, self-destructive things—even before AIDS there were such things. Wild oats, people called them. She'd taken a kind of pride in them. They had been her credentials, her merit badges, her proof of citizenship in life. Now she would rather not dwell on them. Was that the difference between youth and not-youth, the difference between pride and shame? Why was shame supposed to be better for you?

So it was with some confusion of feelings that Elaine reached home and went to look for her daughter. Josie wasn't in her room nor was she parked in front of the television. Elaine found her out in the backyard, sunbathing.

She was sprawled in a lounge chair, face up, her knees raised and lolling apart. She wore a pair of cutoffs and a pink halter top and a new pair of red plastic sunglasses with squared lenses, a fashion that made anyone wearing them look like a robot from an old sci-fi movie. Elaine let herself noiselessly out the screen door and stood watching her from a few yards away.

Josie had not, thankfully, inherited her father's skin. Her tan had deepened layer by layer over the summer, gold on gold. Where she had oiled herself there were patches of brightness that glinted like mirrors. The secret places of her body, the soft folds at the bends of knees and elbows, slope of her breasts, rise of thigh, were damp with sweat.

Elaine watched her silently for a few moments, then Josie became aware of her, jerking her head and knocking her sunglasses loose. "Jesus *Christ.*"

Elaine said nothing. Josie reached for her sunglasses, but they had fallen beneath her chair. "You know, if you're going to sneak up on me, you could at least warn me."

Still Elaine didn't speak, couldn't. Some mix of anger and yearning was lodged in her throat. Josie resettled herself. "Was there something you wanted? Or are you just going to stand there looking weird?"

It was as if an electric current had her paralyzed, staring down. If electricity were cold.

"Mom?" Josie sat up in her chair and wrapped her arms around her elbows. "Mom, you're creeping me out."

She stared and stared. Her brave beautiful idiotic lying damn-fool daughter.

"I'm going in, OK? You can stay out here and be all spastic." But Josie made no move to go. Her gaze met Elaine's and locked there. "What?" She waved a hand before her face. "Quit looking at me!"

Josie's mouth began to shake. Then her face went rigid, trying to keep the tears back. "What do you want? What did I . . ." She stopped and her eyes flickered upward, caught. "All right, I'm sorry. OK? I'm . . ." She hunched over and hugged herself tighter, weeping in high-pitched bursts.

Elaine waited out the crying. Josie tried to mop at her eyes with the strap of her top, gave up. Elaine said, "Who is he?"

Josie shook her head. "Can't."

"I want you to tell me."

"I can't talk about him. You can't make me."

"Come on, Jose. You know I'm going to find out sooner or later."

"No." The tears had only softened her partway. "I just can't. I just can't. I wish you'd accept that."

"Why, is he black or something you think I'd object to?"

"God, Mom." Instantly she was back to being scornful. "What a jerky thing to say."

"Then at least tell me what questions I should be asking." Elaine had a terrible thought. "My God, is he married?"

Josie sniggered, though there was a thickness in it, a residue of tears. "No. Quit asking, OK?"

"I'm glad to hear you have some standards."

"It's not standards. He's just not married. If you really want to be with somebody, being married doesn't stop it."

Elaine felt a headache crawling through her brain like a neon worm. Pain strobed red and bitter blue behind her eyes. She told herself it was a good thing they were talking frankly, or with some approximation of frankness. She said, trying to shape the words to push them past the horrid colors, "You forgot about the sheet."

Josie didn't get it at first. Then she flung her legs over the side of the chair so fast it nearly capsized. "Shit." She shook her head and kept shaking it. "Shitshitshit."

It didn't please Elaine as much as she'd imagined, catching her dead to rights this way. It only made her think with despair how childish the girl was still, how hopeless it was to expect of her any sort of clearheadedness or restraint. The worm in her brain throbbed.

Josie looked up. "Does Dad know?"

"Teeny covered for you. She told me instead. There's no excuse for treating their house that way. Since you don't even like them to begin with. That's really crass."

"So what are you gonna do, kill me?"

"I don't think it matters what I do anymore. It matters what you do. You're the only one who's going to kill you."

Josie's mouth flattened, ready to turn down. "God, Mom. You

wouldn't want to be happy for me, would you? No, that would be way too radical."

Elaine tried to shake her head but it was made of glass. The pain was going to drop her where she stood.

"Because I've got somebody and I'm happy. I'm really really happy."

Elaine saw her own hand rise before her face; it blurred and flopped away. She stumbled to the backdoor.

"You can't stand that, can you? Are you jealous? Huh? I bet you don't even remember the last time you—"

The house enveloped her with its own sounds, air-conditioning, refrigerator rattle. In the bathroom upstairs she swallowed three Tylenol and wrung out a washcloth in cold water. Her reflection floated in the mirror but she resolutely kept her eyes from it because that would be the final defeat, to see all the ways her face had become that of an old woman.

In bed she tried to relax her toes, ankles, knees, bleeding heart, exploding brain. It must be a migraine, she never had them but she thought this was the way they were supposed to feel. One more bodily failure. She was coming apart like a cheap doll. Who needed sex when you had such a fascinating new hobby, dying by pieces? She wasn't as wounded by Josie's taunts as she might have been because she couldn't hold the concept of sex in the same skin as her writhing pain. She couldn't even remember the last time she did. That part of her life was probably over anyway. There were times she mourned this and other times she simply forgot to be mournful. Josie or anyone else young couldn't be expected to understand.

A rolling wave of sweat and nausea seized her and even though she was lying down, the room revolved in a whizbang spin like a planet torn loose from its orbit. Josie was at the door, pushing it open. "Mom?"

She stood in the doorway, pulling the room even further off balance. Its edges threatened to flip, exchange places. "I'm sorry I said some of that stuff. It was really vile. There's some of it I meant but not the stuff about you, all right? Mom?

"Go away."

Josie closed the door behind her.

Elaine got out of bed once to throw up. A long string of filth that left her empty and shaking. Migraine. Had to be. Some kind of negative biofeedback, her hapless life trying to squeeze out through her ears. She rinsed her mouth and went back to bed and slept somehow and by the time she woke up and was able to move about the house it was already dark and Josie's car was gone.

In the backroom of Trade Winds, Elaine sat on the floor leaning against the wall. All around her she had unfurled a dozen bolts of fabric and was trying to empty her mind of everything except their patterns and colors. There was a pale green paisley with a border of pink. Next to it, a crimson and blue batik. A yellow sunburst print. A turquoise and sky blue scroll. Stars of deep orange stitched together with silver. She took those holy deep-down breaths. She breathed in red and orange, breathed out blue and green.

For migraines the doctor said you should avoid chocolate, alcohol, smoking, and stress. The same thing doctors said about everything. The hypnotist guy suggested relaxation therapy. Apparently you could train your mind to fill itself with nothing, like a balloon, watch it float away on a current of pure spiritual ether. Elaine shifted her eyes out of focus so that the colors swam together. The fabric smelled of India, of sun and fruit and jungle and smoke and city sidewalks as dense as rivers.

She let the cloth drift over her head like a veil. Behind her closed eyes she saw the faces of the villagers, her villagers. Their dark walnut skins and white white smiles, both shy and excited, their slim brown hands and feet that kept endlessly busy with the most ancient and primitive sorts of labor. Planting millet seeds, tending cooking fires, making bricks out of mud, carrying bundles of sticks. It drove you mad that people were still made to live this way, that girl children were routinely given less food than their brothers, that you might spend entire days without meeting one literate person, that none of the villagers would be likely to ever travel fifty miles from the place where they were born, that such a country possessed nuclear weapons. And still they smiled, smiled and sang for her. She loved them, she knew that, of course, but she was not prepared for how much she could miss them at any given moment, half a world away, a longing that felt like a migraine of the heart.

So much for achieving nothingness. Elaine gave up the effort but remained where she was, the turquoise-and-sky cloth draped over her face. Josie. She didn't want to think about her, but there she was.

These days they were being extremely polite with each other. Elaine didn't try to make conversation except for the barest necessary minimum. Josie didn't talk any more than she ever did. That meant they passed whole days like cloistered nuns, maneuvering around each other in contemplative silence. Josie came and went as she pleased. Elaine never asked questions anymore. She felt how thoroughly she had failed and was continuing to fail. She thought about talking to Frank, enlisting him in an effort to beat some sense into the girl. She congratulated herself on recognizing a truly bad idea when she had one. Besides, Frank was leaving on vacation, or maybe they'd already gone, she'd lost track. Right this minute Frank and Teeny were probably splashing around in a hot tub, toasting the mountain peaks with vodka and tonics.

She'd lost track of things at work as well. There were payroll taxes, bank deposits, advertising deadlines waiting for her. She was going to have to get up, regroup, care about such things once more. But she couldn't bring herself to do so just yet, which was why she was still sitting on the floor with a bolt of fabric tented over her face when Lyla, the part-time girl, walked in looking for her at the beginning of her shift.

Lyla emitted a faint, dismal shriek. Elaine tried to whip the fabric off her head but her hands snagged and she had to fight her way free. "Oh, hi," she said blandly. "Is it two o'clock already?"

"I thought somebody tied you up and killed you or something."

"Nope, just resting. Forty winks." Elaine got to her feet.

Lyla's look of alarm was turning to suspicion, as if she'd been left out of a joke. She was a short, heavyset girl, a year behind Josie in school. She had close-set eyes and light brown hair that she wore in lumps. Her mother worked in one of the grade school cafeterias and her father kept retiring from various small enterprises. They were the kind of household that always had a sign in the front yard advertising saw sharpening or small engine repair.

Josie and Lyla were not friends. Girls like Josie were not friends with girls like Lyla. Even if they had been in the same class at school, they would have had no use for each other. It was probably just as well that Lyla was not more appealing, that Elaine felt no temptation to make her a kind of substitute daughter. Once Elaine had made the mistake of suggesting that a particular blouse would look pretty on her. Lyla, who wore dreary polyester turtlenecks winter and summer, thrust her jaw out and glowered mightily as if she'd been insulted, which she had, Elaine supposed. Lyla was sullen and stolid, but at least she was a reliable worker. She did as she was told. Not one inch more. If Elaine said she should clean, she cleaned. If not, she could ignore smeared glass, muddy footprints, worse. Stolid, even grudging at times. The kind of girl who would just as soon stab you in the back as look at you.

So that when Lyla asked, "Is something going on with Josie?" Elaine jumped.

"What do you mean?"

Lyla shrugged and kept on unpacking a box of wooden hangers. "I was just wondering about her. If she was in trouble or anything. Did you want all these out? I don't know if there's room for them."

"Lyla."

She stooped to pick up a bit of the packaging material, and when she straightened up Elaine saw the spiteful, ugly step-sister gleam in her eye, the triumph of the despised and lowly. "Oh, it's probably nothing. Just that the other night I was out at the Big Lots, kind of late, it was just closing, and I thought I saw her drive past in this police car."

City of Glass Towers

Josie and Mitch met at his place most afternoons around four, and hung out until it was dark, when they started feeling restless. They'd go get something to eat and drive around listening to music and not talking much, because they would have done most of that earlier. They were better at talking, Josie thought, when their skins could help. Once it was time for Mitch to go to work, he would drop her off at her car. Josie would wait around to see if it was a slow shift, because then he might come back to see her again. She loved it when he did that, when they could sit together in the squad car with the radio sending out its messages of vigilance and danger, Mitch, as always, looked handsome and severe in his uniform. Even now when she'd seen him put it on piece by piece, she marveled. His service revolver was holstered on his right hip. She could reach out and touch it where she sat. She wanted to shoot it but so far he hadn't let her.

At any moment the radio might break in to send him in pursuit of the drunk and disorderlies or traffic accidents or whatever else her fellow citizens were amusing themselves with that evening. He'd kiss her, in a distracted fashion, and tell her to keep the car doors locked on her way home. She worried about him all the time. Even in Springfield there were plenty of guns and plenty of fools who might not have the ambition to be serious criminals but who could sure as hell pull a trigger. She knew that the odds were against this, and besides, it was not the kind of town where anyone died tragically. But as she drove through the quiet streets she couldn't help feeling a tide of grief building in her, the nerve she plucked when she imagined him dead, gone, murdered, the deep pleasurable shameful wrench she could give herself whenever she chose.

Some nights it was almost chilly, a reminder that before too long summer would give itself a nudge and start its long slow decline toward winter and school and everything else that was normal and hideous and inescapable. She wondered what would happen then with her and Mitch. It was so hard to imagine the two of them in winter coats, scraping ice off the windshield. It was hard to imagine them anywhere except on these summer streets with the hot roiling smells of asphalt and cigarettes and something cherry-sweet, like candy left out all day in the sun.

There were times she was brave enough to think about the future, what she would get him for Christmas and Valentine's Day. When she was eighteen they could move in together because she'd be old enough and no one could stop her. They wouldn't have to stay in Springfield. They'd be so gone. Everybody would talk about them the way you talked about famous people from dull places, trying to believe they'd ever lived there.

When she was alone, when she was forced to return to her own uninteresting bed for the few hours that remained of the night, she wavered. That persistent mutinous, sneering voice started up again in her head. He would get tired of her. Of course he would. It didn't matter how much he liked her now, or said he liked her, or how many tricks she could do in bed. There might be a perfect moment between them, even a series of such moments strung together like a necklace, but that proved nothing, it was not a promise or a future or anything else. This was a fool's paradise. A dream she happened to be walking through with her clothes off, a sealed bubble of heat and delirium, a perverse fairy tale, a city of glass that would shatter whenever she took one step beyond its boundaries.

She asked him about his old girlfriends. Mitch groaned. "Why do we have to talk about this?"

"Because I'm a crazy jealous woman."

"No kidding."

"So?" Josie sent her finger traveling from his chin down the center of his chest, then further south. She was fascinated at having this wealth of body to explore. She couldn't get over how hairy he was. Not in any disgusting way, just how a man was constructed. The nests of dark hair beneath his arms, the hair down his belly and around his penis, like it was grass planted from seed. Jeff had been blond. It made a difference. "Tell me how many there were."

"Before you? There was really only one."

"One. Sure."

"Yeah, but she was really big and fat, so she counts for three or—"

She clobbered him with a pillow. They wrestled some. Wrestling just about always turned into having sex. He wound up on top. He raised himself up on his forearms so he could push into her harder. She was always sore these days. She wondered if men ever got sore, wore themselves out, or if they could just keep going until it fell off. There was some kind of bug that did it that way, she remembered, screwed itself to death, left its little bug part inside its mate. Mitch was using his fingers on her down there and she knew some girl had taught him that. Christ God. They were stuck together, slick and rocking. She was only a writhing pulse, everything in her balanced on a high shelf where she sweated and shivered and her vision turned blank, furious white, then she broke and fell down with him, their two hearts finally slowing, each pulling back into its own skin.

Josie waited until they reached a place where they were able to talk again. "Are you gonna tell me about them?"

"About who?"

"You know. Those fat girls."

"I can't believe you even want to hear about them."

"I do. I want to know everything about you. I want to suck your brain and know everything you know. That didn't come out right." She'd already told him about Jeff. That had been embarrassing only because there was so little to tell. The dorky high school guy she used to sleep with. "Just tell me this one time and I promise I won't ever pester you about it again."

Mitch yawned. "They were just normal girlfriends, OK? I don't know what to say about them. What you want to hear."

"Were they pretty?" Josie asked languidly. And held her breath.

"Yeah, I guess so."

She waited, but he didn't say any more. She sighed. "What, you don't remember?"

"You want me to tell you they were gorgeous or something?"

"No-oo." Josie sighed again at his obstinacy and looked around the bedroom she used to try so hard and so hopelessly to imagine. Now she knew it as well as her own. The closet with some of his clothes, dress shirts and other stuff he never wore, on hangers, the rest in stacks on the floor. The bed was two mattresses piled one on top of the other so you had to roll yourself in and out of it. Magazines, *GQ* and *Sports Illustrated* and some weird martial arts kind, within arm's reach. A plain pine dresser—she'd already sneaked a look through the drawers—with the usual jumble of keys and coins and matchbooks and gum wrappers and receipts on top. His sheets were a bamboo pattern and he didn't use fabric softener. A weight bench in one corner of the room. A trail of sweat socks across the floor. His whole apartment was like that, neither dirty nor clean in any interesting way, nothing in it that you couldn't buy at a Wal-Mart. At the same time it was precious to her, because it was his.

Josie swam up the length of his body and licked at his ear. "I just would like it better if you remembered something special about them. If they were" —she hesitated— "passions."

"You're funny, you know?" Mitch reached over, his eyes still closed, until his hand found something friendly to light on, her left breast. "You don't have to worry about them. They're history. Finito."

"What about the weird one?"

"The what?"

"You said you had this really weird girlfriend once."

"Do you remember everything I say? Jeez. She was the one who always wanted to do stuff with the handcuffs."

Josie would have liked to ask more about this, but thought better of it. "Who was the last one? Why did you break up with her?"

"She kept asking me questions, in bed. All right, all right." Josie was prying his hand loose. "Her name was Marilyn and she works for the Department of Revenue and I met her in a club and we went up to Chicago a few times to see a ballgame. Enough?"

"What did you like about her?"

"I don't know, lots of things. She had great teeth."

"That's how you talk about a horse. God."

"She was a good dancer. She had a sense of humor."

"This is really hard for you, isn't it? Trying to come up with reasons you liked to fool around with somebody."

"Why do I need reasons? She was a nice girl. Is a nice girl."

"So why did you break up with her, really?"

Mitch stretched out on his back and examined the ceiling for a long, thoughtful time. "We didn't actually break up. More like we tapered off."

Josie rolled over on her stomach, tangling herself in the sheet.

Her hair fell over her face like a tent, so that even with her eyes open she couldn't see him, didn't have to look any farther than the intricate dark gold tangle. "I don't want to be just another nice girl."

She felt the sheet being peeled away, very gently, fold by fold. "But you're the absolute absolute nicest."

She wished they could go places together. At first it was thrilling to have a secret, to hide from everybody and laugh at how they were putting one over on the rest of the world, people who would never have anything worth hiding in their whole dull lives. Then as time went on and no one discovered them, they began to feel a little foolish, even irritable.

She had thought maybe they could go to the State Fair, just walk around together, no big deal. But even that hadn't worked out. Of course Mitch had to work extra shifts to help with the crowds. He stood at an intersection right outside the fair entrance, directing traffic and giving directions to all the senior citizens and other lame types. Officer Friendly. It was annoying sometimes, the way he could be such a perfect cop. Like it was easier for him, a relief, when he could put on that badge and a serious face.

Josie brought him a lemon shake-up and hung around waiting for him to take a break, which he kept saying he was going to do but never did. She'd worn a new white blouse that rode up above her navel and her favorite red shorts and she knew she looked good, too good to spend all night sitting on the curb in the dark. Finally she told Mitch she was going to walk around the fairgrounds by herself and he said OK, sure, when he should have told her to wait, he'd find a way to come with her. Josie stomped off in a mean mood.

The fair was pathetic. It was so Springfield. You only went to it in the first place for laughs. All the 4-H kids hit town with their stock trailers full of sheep and hogs and goats and champion steers. They brought electric fans and cots and coolers and radios, like they were going camping, like this was what they lived for the rest of the year. And it probably was. It told you something about the place when you saw people spritzing hair spray on a hog. She'd seen them do it.

Then there were the country kids her age from Pana or Tallula or Mt. Pulaski. They were either totally into farming, clumping around in their work boots to appraise the new combines, or else they were the hoodiest things. The girls always looked like they were trying to win the blue ribbon for sluttiness. But Josie was almost jealous of them, the couples who lurched along the midway arm-in-arm, those hood boys and the girls with their punked-out orange or purple hair, their tacky black nail polish and black leather that they wore in spite of the soupy heat. At least they weren't alone.

She'd wanted to do all the corny fair stuff with Mitch, the Ferris wheel and the Tilt-A-Whirl and the grandstand with its awful yee-haw country music show. She would have made him buy her a steak-on-a-stick and vinegar fries and elephant ears and all the other sinful greasy food you craved because you could only get it once a year. They would have strolled through the carny games as she was doing now, and the disgusting criminal guys who ran them wouldn't dare leer at her, but would be intimidated into allowing Mitch to win—they had it all rigged, everybody knew that—and for laughs he'd get her a prize, an ugly flourescent-colored teddy bear that they would give away to an appropriate small child.

Josie bought a corn dog, just to have something to do. She was already tired of walking around by herself, but she wanted Mitch to think she was having a good time without him, maybe even make him worry a little. There was a big carved wooden statue of

Abe near the main entrance, fifty feet tall, Abe the Railsplitter, she guessed he was supposed to be, in painted wooden coveralls and suspenders. It wasn't one of her favorite Abes; the face was carved in big flat ax strokes so he looked like some kind of distorted caricature, Abe as rendered by the Japanese, perhaps. Still, she thought she could go hang with him for a while, commiserate about the unfairness of the fair and everything else.

"Hey, loser!"

In spite of herself she turned her head.

"Yeah, you, Sloan! You're the only loser I see."

It was Tammy and another girl from school named Lauren, and a boy Josie didn't know, a tall skinny kid with hair that looked like he combed it with a SaladShooter. Josie couldn't decide if she was glad to see them or not.

"So what's your loser self doing?"

"Same as you guys. Taking a walk on the wild side."

Tammy gave her a funny look, like she was about to make one of her sideways remarks, but she just said, "Hey, this is Evan. He's from Arizona."

"Yeah?" asked Josie, mildly interested.

"We're gonna show him the butter cow. He thinks we're making it up."

Evan said, "Butter cow," like even saying it was supposed to be funny. He shook his head so that his hair seemed to be taking off in all directions.

"Come on," said Tammy. "You aren't doing anything else are you?" Like she had to be reminded. They trudged off together, back up the hill to the Dairy Building. Lauren and Tammy had their heads together and were giggling about something, probably her. She didn't trust Tammy anymore. It wasn't that they'd had a fight, more like they'd forgotten why they were ever friends in the first place.

Evan wrinkled his nose. "What's that smell?"

"Manure," said Josie, not bothering to sound shocked or apologetic. She didn't think she liked Evan very much. But then, at the moment she didn't much like anyone. There was a crowd in front of the Dairy Building. They had to stand around swatting mosquitoes and listening to two old women complain about how the fair had gone steadily downhill every year of their whole dissatisfied lives. Tammy and Lauren were still carrying on and Josie almost walked away then, left everybody to snigger and gossip and bitch about the same things forever and ever, but she was already in line and you couldn't go to the fair without seeing the butter cow.

It stood in one of the glass cases in the big chilly room, a lifesize, pale yellow, sculpted cow, perfect in every detail. It had butter hooves and a butter tail, pointed butter ears and a baglike udder with butter teats. Its expression was one of perfect tranquil buttery stupidity.

The crowd stood at a respectful distance, like they were art critics and this was Michaelangelo's *David*. "Wow," said Evan. "You guys weren't kidding."

"We don't have that much imagination," said Tammy.

"Yeah, but why do this? How did they get the idea in the first place?"

"God, I don't know. They've just always had one. It's what makes the fair the fair."

"The origins of the butter cow are lost in the mists of history," Josie intoned. "We worship it because our ancestors did. We need no other reason."

They all looked at her like she was an old-time comedian telling jokes in a stupid accent. Evan said, "So what do they do with it once the fair's over? Does somebody get to eat it?"

She should have left right then. They weren't her friends, not really, they were going to make a game out of ignoring her or worse, but screw them, she wasn't going to be run off. She followed them out of the Dairy Building and back through the midway to the Beer Tent where they hung around pretending they might get served. Josie wished she had a beer, a lot of beer. It was getting to be that kind of piss-on-everything night.

Evan said he had somebody's Arizona ID, but it didn't much look like him. Tammy said forget it, the whole place was narked, probably every third guy was a cop. She rolled her eyes Josie's way and traded amused mouths with Lauren. So Tammy had probably told everybody in the world. Not that she knew the half of it. None of them would ever know anything real about her.

They wound up sitting on some picnic tables at the edge of the grounds, just beyond the hokey Ethnic Village, where you could try and pretend you were in Greece or Mexico or Nigeria, assuming they all used the same brand of paper plates. Evan said, "So this is where the action is. How happening." He was from Phoenix and was here visiting some relative and he was just too cool.

"You should come back for the hog-calling contest." Tammy yawned.

"Or Senior Citizen Day. Or Republican Day."

"That's just about every day here."

Evan kicked at the splintered edge of the seat, trying to knock a chunk of it loose. "We got these great clubs in Phoenix. This guy I know gets us in. He's a dealer, so he gets in everywhere. I saw the Frantic Flattops last month."

"Totally awesome, dude," said Josie, meaning to be sarcastic, but as usual nobody got it.

Lauren said, "Seriously. My brother's got some pot. We could get a little."

"Yeah, maybe later. It's too hot to even move."

As if talking about the heat made it crowd in closer, the air seemed to resist their breathing. Josie wondered if Mitch was worried about her yet, or if he was even thinking about her at all. Probably not. He was too busy serving and protecting the whole entire town.

Evan said, "What's that over there? Through the trees."

"Oh, that's another stupid Abe Lincoln statue. We've only got about a hundred."

"He is one ugly honky."

"Why are you saying 'honky'?" Josie asked him. "It's not like you're black."

Evan gave her an indifferent look. "That's just something you say, honky."

"Then it doesn't mean anything."

"It means he's still ugly."

"Yeah, like anybody important ever lived in Arizona."

"What's with you, Sloan?" asked Tammy. "You PMS-ing?"

"God, that is so ignorant. Whenever somebody wants to be superclever, they say you're PMS-ing."

"Well, excuse me. I guess you're just being a jerk."

Josie saw the three of them shifting their weight, sharing private smiles, getting ready to have some fun. She said, "What most people don't realize about Abe Lincoln is, he was a soldier. In Black Hawk's War, the Indian war, of 1832. He joined the militia and was elected captain. One day some poor old Indian wandered into camp. And the soldiers were ready to shoot the guy when Abe got in front of the guns and told them not to. He never could stand people ganging up on somebody."

After a moment Tammy said, "You were always weird, Sloan. I mean that sincerely."

"Thank you."

"And you have a sense of humor like an alien."

"I am an alien. I'm from Planet Arizona."

Lauren hopped down from the picnic table. "You guys, I want some ice cream. Let's try and do one fun thing, OK?"

The others got down too. Josie stayed where she was. "You coming, alien?"

"I like it fine right here."

As they were walking away, beneath the strings of pink and yellow lights, she heard laughter floating back and one of them saying, "totally spastic."

Josie sat there a while longer, communing with her sore heart. She walked back to the intersection where she'd left Mitch but another cop was there, an old guy who looked at her cross-eyed. She didn't dare ask him anything.

She went on home and the next day Mitch said, "Yeah, they called me to help out on a traffic stop. So how was the fair?"

That's when she got the idea about her father's house. It had a pool and a hot tub and a killer stereo system that was totally wasted on her father and Teeny. They could watch the big-screen TV and eat all her father's mail-order cashews and do it in about ten different beds. It was pathetically easy to fool Teeny. You could sell her tickets to home movies.

Mitch took some convincing. "What do you want to go over there for?"

"Because it's something different. Because it's not the car or your place."

"And they don't mind if you bring guys over?"

"Well, I didn't tell them that. Come on. Wait till you see their house, it's like a resort or something."

"So they must be rich."

"I don't know. I guess." Josie shrugged. She didn't like thinking about her father's money, and here Mitch thought she was trying to impress him. Maybe she was, in some sick way she hadn't realized. "I don't live with them. I don't even see them real often. It's not like they give me anything."

"Yeah, but I bet there's a stock portfolio somewhere with your name on it."

Finally she got him to say he'd do it. Her father and Teeny left around five. Josie spied on them from the corner, just to make sure. Even hunched down as she was in the front seat, she got a good look at them, Teeny decked out in one of her peculiar metallic dresses, like she was going to the Academy Awards instead of some tugboat in Joliet, her father unsmiling in a coat and tie. Why did it always take people so much work to have any fun?

When Josie picked Mitch up he had his swimsuit rolled in a towel. She thought that was so cute.

"Ready to get wet?"

Mitch smiled a twitching smile. "Sure."

He didn't have to be a total killjoy. He was probably only acting that way because this was her idea. When they stood at the front door and she was having trouble working the key, Mitch kept looking around like he expected some neighbor to start photographing him. Exasperated, she jiggled the latch back and forth.

"Maybe they gave you the wrong key."

"Maybe I just need two seconds where I'm not being totally hassled."

Finally she got it open. Mitch perked up a little when she was entering the security code on the keypad. "That's a state-of-the-art system."

"Oh yeah. Nothing's too good for Daddy. So whaddya think?" Josie led him down a passageway and made a sweeping gesture.

Mitch whistled. There was a fireplace made of enormous boulders with an oversize beam for a mantel. A red-felt pool table with a rack of balls set out at one end. An old-fashioned jukebox in one corner glowed with ribbons of flamingo and violet light.

"Daddy's playroom."

"Not too shabby."

Encouraged, she presented him with further wonders. The big saltwater aquarium with its blood-colored coral and nervous fish, the library, the built-in cedar closet, the twin leather sofas, and finally the pool, liquid turquoise, the water ruffling in the warm breeze.

They floated and splashed and dried off with Teeny's fluffy towels and fixed themselves ice cream and Kahlúa from the bottle they didn't know she knew they kept in the pantry. She could have sneaked them a real drink but Mitch was always very serious about not drinking before he went on duty. They played hide-and-seek through the bedrooms and landed finally in the expanse of pillows in the master suite. Here they made love, although Josie was conscious of a certain distraction. It felt obligatory, rushed, even smutty, as if they'd come here for the wrong reasons. Lying there afterward, watching the evening shadows creep over the ceiling of the strange room, she was nearly melancholy. She was unprepared to feel this way, it seemed unfair that after working everything out, all the planning and coaxing and anticipating, her own self would ambush her like this. Wanting different from having. Longing from loving. Nothing ever what you expected. But thinking this way only made her restless and confused so she reached out and buried her hands and mouth in his warmth.

She did cheer up once they went back out and had another swim and were relaxing on the lounge chairs. It was dusk and the line of lights beneath the water's surface had a filmy, moonlike glow. The horizon was still streaked with orange and burning pink. If she looked only at a certain slice of sky and water, she could imagine herself somewhere else, anywhere in the world that was not Springfield. As they watched, a pair of swallows came wheeling and skimming low over the pool, incredibly agile, startling, alive.

"This is heaven." Josie sighed. And it was. The stereo was going, playing something bluesy. They were holding hands across the space between their chairs. And Mitch wasn't acting mad or gloomy or some other way she couldn't understand. He was just being normal and she loved him and it was a beautiful shining evening, yes, heaven. This moment. If you didn't think about the moment before or all the moments that would follow when it would not be heaven.

As if all it took was one bad thought to trigger the next, Josie exhaled and said, "I can't believe school starts in what, three weeks."

"Well, I can't believe I have a girlfriend who's still in high school."

She swatted him with a towel for that, although she was secretly delighted to hear him say it. Girlfriend.

"Well, if you're nice to me, maybe I'll take you to the prom."

Her tone had been the heavy teasing that she fell back on when she didn't trust herself to say anything else. Josie waited for him to tease her back. Instead he worked his forehead around into a serious shape.

"Hey, there's something I need to talk to you about."

Her heart went to her knees. "Yeah?"

"There's this thing I have to go to. A police thing."

"Yeah?"

"It's sort of a banquet. They make awards and have speeches and stuff. It's coming up at the end of the month and I already made the plans. I can't get out of it, I set it up a long time ago."

"Well if you have to . . ."

"I really do. It's kind of a big deal. Like I said, it's been on the books a long time."

"Are you getting an award?"

"Naw, you have to stop a bullet or drag a kid out of a burning house, you know, hero stuff. But I have to be there in the dress blues and the shiny badge. I'm real sorry you can't come with me. It's just the way it worked out."

"No biggie," Josie said cheerfully. Like she really wanted to hang out with a bunch of cops making cop speeches. But it was sweet of him to worry about her. It was completely dark by now and the pool lights made tunnels of glow in the quiet water. She stood up and drew him out of his chair, standing on her tiptoes to breathe in his ear, feeling him through his swimsuit and pulling him toward the water.

So of course they lost track of time and it was late and they had to rush to get everything cleaned up and that was why she forgot about the stupid sheet and all hell broke loose with her mother. She didn't tell Mitch about that part. It was so little kid to complain about your mother. And besides, some cautious instinct told her that if she let on to him about being under suspicion, he might grow alarmed, veer away, or chicken out entirely. She had to wonder if he really would get into any kind of trouble about her, if it was a big deal to anybody besides her mother. So it was illegal, she knew that, but a lot of things people did were. Most likely it was only a big deal if somebody made it one. Most likely the rest of the police guys would just give him an elbow in the ribs and make dirty comments. That would just kill him. He was so into his truth, justice, and the American way of life notions.

Of course, there were any number of things she thought it best they not talk about. Anything that reminded him she was a jail-bait kid, of course. Which meant anything that made her sound ignorant or naïve. That covered a lot of ground and resulted in her nodding along a lot and pretending to know about car insurance or limited warranties or fly fishing or whatever else he was talking about. Anything having to do with the infamous night she'd been riding around with Moron and Ronnie and that slime devil Podolsky, anything about her career as a stalker. She still hadn't owned up to seeing him for the first time in the Taco Bell. She wondered if she ever would.

Whenever Mitch tried to get her to say where she knew him from, Josie smiled and told him she'd spotted him on radar. It wouldn't hurt to keep on being Mystery Girl for a little longer.

"Once we've been together for a while, maybe I'll let on," Josie told Abe. "Love at first sight at the Taco Bell. How we met. What a hoot."

Abe was noncommittal. He stared serenely past his polished nose, past the empty parking lot and the exhausted, late-summer grass, into some region of history and disinterestedness that only descended on you once you'd been dead for a hundred years or more. It was just before sunrise; Josie had stayed at Mitch's all night, or at least as much of it as she dared, enough, she hoped, for it to count as spending the night. She liked watching him sleep. He said he never remembered his dreams and maybe he didn't have any. Josie said no way. Everybody dreamed, even dogs dreamed about chasing rabbits, you could watch them twitching and woofing. Mitch said that was probably what he dreamed about. Chasing speeders. Oh you are so funny, Josie told him. Not.

She hung over his sleeping face, watching. He breathed in and out with perfect unchanging ease. That beautiful line of his mouth, the white edge of his teeth just visible below his raised lip. His eyelashes were curled up and dampish. His dark level eyebrows, she thought she must have fallen in love with his eyebrows before anything else. She watched him so hard and so long, she imagined she could see the whiskers surfacing in his jaw. She could watch over him every night of his life and still not be able to tell what sort of movie was playing inside his head.

She had to admit that not only was he a man, and older, and a cop, but that he was unlike her in some other important way. He lived just inside his perfect skin as if it was another uniform. There wasn't that much space inside him for a lot of other things.

"I really do love him," Josie said. Abe didn't disagree; he just let her words float out into the air by themselves, until they had a lonely sound. "I do. So he's different from what you'd expect. Like anybody would be. He probably thinks I'm different too." Why was she talking to some dead guy anyway, it wasn't like she was going to hear anything she didn't already know.

School started next week, one more dismal thought. Maybe she could drop out, get a GED. There were lots of people who'd done the same thing, and nobody cared once they were famous. She knew dropping out wasn't really an option, not unless she wanted to declare outright war with her parents, but high school seemed so, well, high school to her now. The cliques, the tiny gossip, the droning teachers. It would be like doing prison time. Josie yawned and headed back to her car. She was just tired and cranky. "My hair hurts, my feet stink, and I don't love Jesus," she announced.

Josie crept into her house and into her unmade and rather stale bed and if she dreamed she didn't remember it either. She woke up after noon and showered and did her nails and tried not to think about how this time next week she'd be taking an American History quiz or watching kids play gross-out with the fetal pigs in biology lab or some other dreariness.

She was up in her room when she heard her mother come home. Early, though Josie didn't think much about it. She was reading a fashion magazine and wondering if anyone was really going to wear those stupid little head-scarf things when the door to her room pushed open.

"You want to knock next time?"

Her mother's face had a cracked, off-balance look. "What did you get arrested for?"

"What?"

"You heard me. What did you do? And don't say 'nothing.'"

"Do when? What are you talking about?"

"Don't lie to me for one more minute. I absolutely have a right to know this. If you won't tell me, I'll call the police."

"Call the . . ."

"I assume they keep a record of these things. They should have notified me. I shouldn't have to hear it from someone else."

"Hear what from who? God, Mom, slow down."

"I already called the restaurant. You haven't been there for weeks. So don't tell me you get all dressed up and stay out all night going to work."

Caught, unable to come up with words, Josie shrugged. A mistake. You had to deny everything, not just parts.

"Are you pregnant?"

"No!"

"I hope not, but I'm not sure I can believe you anymore."

"Oh, sure, but you believe some bullshit from I don't even know who."

"You're saying if I contact the police department right now and ask them to look up your name, there's nothing?"

When Josie didn't answer, her mother's face narrowed, hardened. "It's drugs, isn't it? This boyfriend of yours is making you do things for drugs."

Josie gaped at her. Then she laughed, a barking noise cut short. Her face felt numb.

Her mother nodded. "All right, then. At least I know."

"You don't know anything. I don't believe this, you are so out of it."

"Then explain to me what you got arrested for."

"I didn't! Besides, it's none of your—"

"I'm sorry, but it is very much my business. I suppose it's my fault for not taking a firm hand. Wanting to be a pal. Well, those days are over."

"You're making this whole thing up. But entirely. You are going to feel so stupid later, I promise."

"I'm going to have to ask you for your car keys."

Her mother waited, hand outstretched. "Now, unless you want me to call the police this minute."

She didn't want that. And her mother had this spooky look on her face, like she might do anything, like she was almost glad to believe her daughter was a drug-crazed hooker. Josie fished in her purse and tossed the key ring over. She said, "I'm going to expect an apology later."

"Once I've had a chance to think things through, we're going to have a talk. I just want to understand how this happened. I want to get you the help you need. In the meantime I'm going to have to ask you not to leave the house. Excuse me, I need a little time alone."

She left, but was back in an instant. "Unplug your phone and give it to me."

"What is this, jail?"

"I'm sure we can arrange jail, if you'd prefer it."

Josie handed over her phone. The door closed and she was alone in the room.

Good God.

She was sweating and the sweat was turning cold on her. Carefully, she went to her bedroom door and cracked it open. The house was quiet. Her mother had gone crazy, it was some kind of hormonal thing, she'd always been jealous of her. Somebody must have seen her with Mitch and her mother took it from there and came up with something she'd seen on last week's lurid TV special. It was so nuts, she was going to have to talk to Mitch and warn him, except he was already so paranoid about people finding out. And if her mother actually did call the police . . . There might be some record of when he'd stopped her that first night. They might even call Mitch in, ask him about her, oh shit, why hadn't she ever told him to take it out of the computer or whatever you did? It was the only thing keeping her from laughing in her mother's face.

She stayed in her room until sunset, then crept down to the kitchen. The house was still quiet. Her mother was probably up in her room, chewing Valium. The kitchen phone was mounted on the wall and her mother couldn't have ripped it out.

But the handset was gone, unplugged. The hook where the spare car keys were kept, empty.

This was just ridiculous. Enough was enough. She started back upstairs to try to talk some sense into her mother. She wouldn't tell her about Mitch, of course, but she would come up with something . . .

A noise from the den made her turn and soft-foot back down the stairs. Her mother's voice, low and rapid. Josie snaked around the corner and flattened against the wall.

At first she didn't hear much through the closed door. Her mother's side of a phone conversation, syllables. Yes and yes, scraps of sentences, I see, and Not exactly. Even her mother's secrets were boring. Then she said, "I would want to make sure it's the right place for her before we made any final arrangements."

Space of silence, her mother listening. "That sounds a little . . . You seem to put a lot of emphasis on the physical conditioning."

"I'd have to talk to her father first. I'm the custodial parent, but . . ."

"No, I actually like the idea that it's so isolated, it's just that Utah is such a long way away . . ."

Murder blazed up in Josie's heart. Her mother was going to have her shipped off to some goddamn desert *boot camp* where they made you wear an orange jumpsuit and have encounter sessions about your issues. Expensive place for parents to dump their problem children. There was a kid last year who got sent, *hijacked,* to one of those camps. They came and got him out of bed in the middle of the night and threw him in the back of a van and he spent the next two months living in a barracks and doing calisthenics.

Back upstairs, quick and quiet. The door to her mother's room was open and her mother was so simpleminded she'd put the keys in her purse and the purse was open on the bed. Josie unclipped her car key, then went for the emergency money, two hundred dollars, that her mother kept in the bottom of her jewelry box. She glided back to her own room, shut and locked the door.

A while later her mother knocked on it. "Go away."

"I'm fixing sandwiches, if you want one. Chicken salad on bagels."

"No thanks, just bread and water."

"There's no need to be sarcastic."

Josie said nothing, and after a moment her mother went back downstairs.

She would go to Mitch's, she'd tell him her mother had gotten drunk and threatened her or something else that would make him let her stay. It was getting so she couldn't tell anybody anything true. Maybe she'd talk him into leaving town, running off, why not, she hated everyone and everything here except him. She began to gather things up from the closet and the bathroom shelves. It occurred to her, with a kind of nervous excitement, that this might be the last time she would ever stand in this room, in this house.

She settled herself to wait. All she needed was a clear path to the garage and a ninety-second head start. Any goons from Utah wouldn't be here for a few days. Her mother would have to talk to her father, for the money if nothing else, Josie figured, and her father and Teeny had decided to stay in Aspen for another week. But mostly she wanted to leave because she knew that sooner or later her mother would soften, relent, change her mind, just as she knew her mother didn't really believe the worst of her, had only found it necessary to accuse her of the worst so she could yell at her about every single part of her life. As Josie herself wanted to seize this moment of high indignation and grievance, propel herself out the door in a passion of glorious bad feeling.

Finally she heard the shower running, all she needed to cover the noise of the garage door opening. Josie shouldered her backpack and the carry-on bag. Thank God her mother hadn't put a Denver boot on her car or anything. The damn garage door took forever rolling up and down again and Josie half-expected to see her mother screeching after her wrapped in a towel, but there was nothing, only the steady lights of the house, including the one in her bedroom window that stared straight past her like a blind eye and then she put the car in gear and was gone.

Because she was hungry, starving, really, and because it was such a smart-ass, spiteful thing to do, Josie spent the first of her mother's money at McDonald's. She was thinking about what she was going to tell Mitch when in the middle of a french fry she remembered. Shit! His cop dinner was tonight. He'd reminded her, she'd just been such a head case since her mother went off on her, she'd forgotten all about it.

Why hadn't she ever gotten a cell phone? She'd only asked her mother for one about a hundred times. Josie scattered food and food mess and peeled out. It was almost eight o'clock and if she didn't catch him before he left, she'd have to wait in the parking lot until he got back. Well, she didn't want that, she wanted to bust in on him all urgency and tears, which she didn't think she could manage if she had to hang around for two or three hours.

His car was parked in its usual spot so he hadn't left yet, and she was just bounding up the walkway when the entrance door opened and Mitch and the girl came out.

There was a moment when he didn't see her even though she was only twenty paces away and so she had to scorch her vision with the sight of them. Mitch, tall and handsome in his darkest blue uniform with his collar hitched up by a tie and his face burnished from shaving. He was holding the door open for the girl and smiling down at her. She smiled back. She had great teeth, and a smile shaped like a heart. Her hair was dark red and cut in a bell that swung from one shoulder to the other. She wore a white dress with little straps and a glittery necklace and white sandals that showed her toenails, painted like pink mirrors.

The next moment Mitch raised his head and looked straight at her. His face went slack. The girl didn't notice anything, just kept talking away in her fake, excited voice.

Josie couldn't move. They kept walking toward her. Mitch didn't seem to be able to do anything except slouch along, keeping up his end of the conversation with mumbles. He didn't look at Josie; the girl glanced at her, but Josie meant nothing to her, that was clear enough. Josie actually stepped out of their way, while coward Mitch said Uh-huh, Yeah; she wasn't even worth making a scene over.

She didn't have anything in her hands she could break or throw, so she watched them get into his car, and Mitch adjusted the mirror like he always did and made sure the seat belts were fastened and then they drove off.

She felt how completely her own vanity and foolishness had betrayed her.

By the time she reached her own car, each breath was bringing up sobs. She thought about killing herself but how were you supposed to do that, it was probably a lot harder than you thought. She could drive anywhere she wanted, but there was nowhere to go, not one friend she could trust, and even now her mother was probably calling all the police who weren't at that horrible dinner, telling them to arrest her on sight for general depravity.

Was there any place she could go where no one would find her? Only one, so that's where she went, pulling up into Harvey's driveway, prying open the doors to the little swaybacked garage. Pushing aside the lawnmower and ancient mess of flowerpots and milk crates and cardboard boxes until she could fit her car inside. Then she and her make-shift luggage stood at Harvey's front door, her hand raised to knock.

North South East West

The tape had got into his brain somehow. It made him itch where he couldn't scratch. When it talked to him, he shouted it down. He didn't take no shit. He was *Porque,* he was *Because.* Things happened when he made them happen. He told the car go, it went. Stop, it stopped. Goddamn magic.

He was higher than high, faster than fast. His head hummed with power. In Oklahoma City he set a house on fire. *Because* he felt like it. It wasn't much of a house. People hadn't lived there for a long time, he could tell when he crept inside and found a space for himself on its sour floorboards. No one lived there, but others like himself had visited. They'd left piles of things that were no longer of use, things halfway between junk and nothingness. When he was tired of the house he took up a tire iron and turned all the glass into sparkling dust. He poured gasoline on the piles of filth and set them alight. Running flames twisted and looped and popped. A furious orange mouth opened and spoke the word Fire. The heat of it drove him outside and across the street where he squatted in the shadow of a fence and watched the show. Big chunks of blazing wood hurled up in the air and came down as ash. Something inside, some pocket of grease or gas, ignited and sent up a pillar of blue sparks.

Then it wasn't a house anymore and the tape said: Oh congratulations, *perfecto,* my man. Now let's see you do something hard, like build it back up. Or raise the dead.

Shut up, he told it, and got in the car and made it go fast to drown out the rest of the nasty whispers. The tape gave him no peace. It put dreams in his head that were all screwed up, like they belonged to someone else. Songs he didn't remember knowing, faces he didn't recognize. Like everywhere in the air there were mysterious messages, and he was some giant antenna picking up all of it and he couldn't shut it off. And this too was a power.

He was *Porque,* he was *Because.* He used the gun to get the things he needed. People took one look at it, at him, and handed over food, money, whatever. They could tell who he was.

In Wichita he decided he had a taste for something sweet. Not candy out of a wrapper this time, but a real bakery, the air gritty with sugar. He wanted to see pretty frosted cakes and dough made into knots and rosettes and fans. He remembered all the tastes—lemon, coconut, almond, cherry. And pineapple, although that had never been his favorite. But now he wanted that too, he wanted all the tastes in his mouth at once. He wanted it now. He drove up and down the bastard streets, getting madder and madder. What was the matter with this town, that it didn't have a bakery? It wasn't too much to ask.

Finally he found what he wanted, a big window with a white white wedding cake on display. The little bride and groom dolls on top reminded him of something vague and disquieting. *Voodoo? Did he really remember that? Darkness and the dark fingers stirring pieces of bone?* He shook his head to clear it. Pink cupcakes, macaroons, a jolly bell that sounded when he opened the door.

The girl behind the counter had this attitude. She pinched up her face and fussed with something so she could ignore him. There was an old party in there too, getting ready to leave with her coffee cake, and the old party also had an attitude. She looked at him and rustled her paper bag and sucked on her teeth.

He could have knocked her flat, but instead he moved up close to the old party and gave her his best greasy smile. That got her out the door in a hurry. The clerk took a step back from him. This was annoying, seriously. He was hungry, was that such a crime?

"Can I help you?"

Prissy little voice. He didn't like her face either, skinny and grudging, like everything in the glass case was her pussy and she wasn't giving out any. The gun, riding easy in his waistband beneath his shirt, bumped up against him then, like a reminder. But then he forgot about it, his fingers tracking and smudging on the glass. "Whassat?"

"Those are the cream-filled horns." Boy, she was mean. It was a wonder the place was still in business. "What's that one?"

"Brioche."

He tried the word in his mouth, spit it out. "Those."

"Shortbread. Eclairs."

She was getting impatient. But there was a lot more he had to look over. Cookies shaped like chocolate leaves and cakes swirled with nuts in pinwheel patterns. Angel food. You could die of hunger before you even got all the names straight. Then he thought the hell with it, and vaulted right over the counter, scattering doilies and toothpicks and whatnot, the girl saying, "Hey—" Just that, Hey, and she flailed against the wall and he paid no more attention to her.

Then he couldn't get the stupid glass open so he struggled and cursed it and finally wrestled it free and scooped up everything he could lay hands on. He filled his mouth, oh, heaven! Everything was so good! He squooshed it all together in one big creamy marshmallowy buttery nougaty taste. He'd always wanted to do this. And now he could.

Some of the messy stuff was getting caught in his beard and his face was sticky. He had a thirst, he looked around for the girl but she was gone, well screw her. She didn't take the coffee machine with her.

He poured himself a cup, it was thin, not even hot, but he filled his throat with it, looked around, the place was a mess, seriously, they should get somebody in here to take care of things. The sun came out from behind a cloud and lit the cake in the window so you could see every bit of the white sugar filigree and ribbon, hard and sparkling, like you could break a tooth on it. Something about that damn cake kept bugging him. On his way out the door he grabbed the bride and groom, licked the frosting from their feet, and shoved them into his pocket.

In no particular hurry, he drove in a lazy track around and around the city's red brick downtown, through a meandering park and across a narrow, uninteresting river channel. He felt sleepy but jumped-up from all that sugar. A hot day, muggy, with a sky full of sweating gray clouds that reflected light in a way that made you squint. He pulled the car off the roadway and into a patch of scrubby brush. Yawning, he settled himself in the front seat with a newspaper over his face.

But he couldn't sleep. The air was too full of headachy heat and he was too full of sugar nerves, plus this monster fly kept trying to light on his face through the newspaper. It planted its filthy fly feet on his lip or his nose, and anytime he went to smack it the thing lumbered away just out of reach. He couldn't even relax because he knew the next minute it would be back, making its stupid noise.

There were still crumbs and icing on his face, that was probably what was drawing it. The tape laughed at him. Somebody's sweet on you, big boy.

Fuck you. He made another lunge at the fly, clobbered it but only managed to wing it. It landed upside down on the dashboard, zzzzz, tiny and furious, but he wasn't paying attention anymore. The newspaper in his hand was all wadded and wrinkled, but one headline unscrolled before his eyes:

WOMAN FOUND MURD

The edge was torn, the words below it were all in a mess: *night floating spokesman unknown dead Tuesday.* He turned it round and round, sweating and scrabbling, he couldn't make it make sense, like he'd forgotten what reading, or even words, were for. He didn't remember getting a paper, it could have been in the car for a day or a week, it could have been from anywhere. Somebody was running a game on him and he could guess who so he reached out and SLAM, the fly crumpled and lay still.

Just to mock him, the tape said, Zzzz.

What do you want? I need to get some sleep, OK?

Go ahead. What's stopping you.

Look, I never did nothing to you.

Ya, I know. You wouldn't hurt a fly. ZZZZZ.

His head spun with noise. He screamed and screamed. Hurt himself flailing around, blood in his eyes. He battered his way out of the car and rolled around on the ground. His hands hurt, how did he hurt his hands? Gravel dust in his mouth, coating his sugar tongue.

He was *Porque,* he was *Because.* And he could do anything except sleep.

In Kansas City he fired the gun. Bang bang bang. Or maybe he had fired it before, he couldn't remember. He was tired of the car so he was walking, in no particular direction, northsoutheastwest. It was night but he couldn't see stars, moon, nothing. Maybe it was his eyes. They didn't work so good these days, like there was a film or screen before them, something he couldn't rub away. Since he no longer slept, not really, he dreamed all the time. He dreamed he was in Kansas City, walking under a smeared sky with a smell of rain. Every darkened house held sleep. It leaked out the windows and under the cracks of doors. He could almost see it, touch it. It was like the air, all around you but nothing you could lay your hands on.

The sleep was inside the houses. He thought he could follow it there, sneak up on it somehow. So he looked for a house that would let him inside. The sky growled as if there was a storm coming and the rain smell thickened. A window had been left open a crack for the sleep to escape. Curtains whipped and knotted in the sudden wind. He crouched beneath the window, listening. Did sleep have a sound? He thought he heard it, faint and silvery. Soft as pillows. He used his knife to loosen the screen. It scraped and rasped and he froze, but nothing changed. He raised the sill an inch at a time, smooth as his heartbeat.

He had to hoist himself up to look inside. The blowsy curtain drifted across his face. The thunder edged closer. The whole world was asleep except for him.

His eyes didn't work for shit. The inside was just lumpy darkness. Then, gradually, things took shape. White bedsheets unfurled before his vision like a rose blooming. He actually thought this, a rose. Such things kept sneaking into his head the way they never would have before he had his powers. In the bedsheets, arms and legs.

You wouldn't want to wake them and scare the sleep away. So very soft, very careful, feeling his way, head and hands first, he got himself through the window. He landed upside down. Carpet rubbed his back through his shirt. His back hurt but that wasn't his fault, *bitch,* she should only stay dead, it was probably messed up forever like his scrambled head that couldn't stay focused on the very important thing he was doing right now. Something on the bed moved, making the mattress bounce. Quickly he turned himself right-side-up in case he had to move, take them on. The sheets rustled. The bed only a few feet away. He flexed his hands. But the sleep held, and it was quiet again.

There were two of them. When he got to his feet and stared down, he saw their two heads clearly. Close together, like melons on a shelf. Man and woman. He could have reached out and touched them. In the window behind him the sky filled with edgy light, startling him, and the thunder rolled and the first rain scattered against the window. He almost cried out. The light rippled across the surface of something that he did not at first recognize as a mirror. Because his reflection showed his hair and beard so wild and matted that he looked like a goat, his eyes also the eyes of a beast, a goat, maybe, if the goat were also the devil and the devil hadn't slept for a hundred years. He raised his hands to the crusted edges of his hair. So this was him now. It was going to take some getting used go.

For a while he just watched the people in the bed. They didn't seem to move but if you looked close, you could see a slow, continual shifting, one body aligning itself toward or away from the other. They were old, he realized. Creaky old. The man's hair was thin and seedy. The woman's pale bare arm was fatty dough. The sleep came out of their mouths in little puffs and snores. He bent close to them, breathing it in. If only there was some way he could lay down between them, soak it up. Old people's sleep was probably good stuff. Peaceful. Everything worn smooth.

The tape said, in a voice that was like a nudge in the ribs: A guy could have some fun in here.

You are a total pig, you know?

Seriously. How long's it been? So she's old. You can just keep your eyes closed.

I'm gonna pretend I didn't hear that.

Like you never even thought of it. Right.

The rain was coming on harder now and the tape's voice blurred and went quiet. Good riddance. Honestly, it hadn't occurred to him. But now he couldn't help sneaking looks at the rest of her. You couldn't tell much. She was all humped up under the covers, sea-monster style. He wondered if her and the guy still did it, in some disgusting old-timer's way.

The sheets were white like the wedding cake. The bed was like the cake all sliced up. Now that was a weird thing to think. But it was how his crazy head worked.

He dug in his pants pocket and fished out the little bride and groom. They were stuck together and they'd picked up a layer of grit and crud, as if they'd gotten into a hell of a fight once the wedding was over. He pried them apart and tried to clean them up some. *Voodoo?* His father was the one who had known that, and he had never known his father. But his new extraordinary kick-ass weird-looking self was picking up on all manner of previously unimaginable things. It really shouldn't surprise him anymore. And what was voodoo except trying to get all the good and bad luck in the world to answer when you called its name?

He set the bride and groom in front of the mirror, on a tabletop that held some old-lady stuff, pictures in frames, hairbrushes, perfume. He turned the figures so they faced the mirror, so that everything was reflected in it, them, his goat-self, the sleepers in the bed. *Sleep,* he said, but not out loud, and leaned forward to fog the mirror with his breath. Then he crouched down and wiggled himself underneath the bed. There was more room than you'd think. Lots of dustballs, like the old lady's housecleaning had fallen off some. But he could stretch out, prop his head on the crook of his arm and look up into the complications of the bed frame. The mattress sagged in the center. Years and years of sleep weighing it down.

There had to be two dreams. A his and a hers. Bride and

groom. Like two different TV channels coming through the static. He closed his eyes. There was such a thing as trying too hard. With his eyes shut he was more aware of the ebb and flow of their breathing. The old guy didn't breathe so good, there was a hitch or a catch in it. He was dreaming about . . . digging in a garden. Digging with a spade in black earth that had its own good smell, like you could eat handfuls of it. Digging and digging until the hole was so deep the earth closed in around you. The old lady's breathing was a song, a little snoring song with trills and flutes in it. Her dream was mixed up with the rain falling outside and dripping on the carpet where the window had been left open and with the water running in the gutters. She was singing to the rain. Hush hush hush. Thunder gone under. Rain brain. Heap of sleep. Night good night.

A toilet flushed. Even that didn't fully wake him. He tried to roll over and caught himself on the bed frame. What the shit? There was a gray light in the room, a morning-after-rain light. But even the panicky swell in his head didn't change the ease in the rest of his body, knowing that he must have finally slept.

A sink tap turned on and off. Somebody up. Then slow, padding footsteps, and a pair of feet in quilted house slippers appeared next to the bed on a level with his eyes.

Reach out and grab them feet. Tickle them, even. She'd scream, but that wouldn't last long. Even if the old man pitched in, you couldn't regard an old man as a serious concern. Then the slippers lifted clean away and the mattress groaned with her weight and the old woman groaned along with it and he could have goddamned laughed at the three of them all tucked in and cozy. Now he had to think about what to do, either wait them out or make some boring scene, and why couldn't anything ever be easy?

Hack ack ack. The old man coughing. His lungs sounded no

good, rubbishy. There was a noise of flesh smacking flesh, like one fatty leg heaving on top of the other. Somebody moaned. The old man? The woman said, "Is it another bad one, Jim?"

"Oh blessed Jesus."

"Just bear down on it. Thrust it from you."

"It won't leave me be."

"Do you want your pills?"

"Pills don't help none."

"It's only the body, Jim. It's not intended to last."

The bed cried along with the old man. Its springs drooped. The old woman murmured to him, "Just say the word, I'll grab them pills for you."

"I can feel it eating on me."

"Now that's no way to talk. Think about something happy, like rainbows."

He was starting to feel that under this bed was not a good place to be. These people were just too messed up and sad. And here he'd stolen sleep from them. He could trade them the gun, so the old man would have a way to end his suffering. Or he could just shoot them. They were old and sick and tired. Do them a favor. Quick, so he wouldn't scare them. Hell, just the sight of him would probably be enough to finish them off. If they fell back to sleep, he could do it easy. But he wasn't going to wait too long because he had to piss like a racehorse, not to mention getting hungry.

He must have made some noise. The old woman sucked in her breath. "What was that?"

"Help me, Jesus."

"Hush up a minute."

He heard her listening. He must have been careless, had been thinking inside his head too hard to pay attention to what the outside of him was doing. The bed sagged as the old woman struggled out of it. Her feet in those ugly slippers scuttled past his face.

The old man coughed and asked her what was it and she said, "Nothing, Jim," and by her voice he knew that she had seen something, either the window screen or else the little bride and groom, all dressed up in crumbs and spit. "Jim? Let's get up now."

"Oh I don't know."

"Come on, honey. Let's get up and go to the IHOP."

"Oh I don't want no pancakes."

"Well, I do. I want us both to go. Come on."

Coughing. "What's the big—"

"Come on, Jim. Please please please."

He felt for the gun, squirmed around to work it free.

"I can't—"

"I'm just starving. Oh my."

The old man groaned and hacked and lurched upright and his knobby bare feet appeared at the edge of the bed. It didn't seem right to shoot someone in the feet so he waited for the old man to stand up and walk away, which was taking him a very long time. Why did there have to be such a thing as sickness anyway? Why couldn't you just fall down dead when it was your time, like a bird dropped out of the sky? There had to be an end to this suffering shit, his and everybody else's, and perhaps he was meant to shoot every limping leaking coughing body in the world, cleanse and purge it, which would give him a great deal of personal satisfaction, the world being the screwed up place that it was. He would look them all in the eye, straight on. Why should he have to hide himself? He had spent too much of his life seeking out corners and doorways and empty streets. There would be an end to that now, an end to caution and camouflage and all the devices of shame. He drew air into his chest and readied himself for the bellowing cry that would be the last thing they'd ever hear, squeezed himself free of the bed frame, rolled out, and sprang to his feet into the center of an empty room. Stone empty.

It gave him the creeps because here he had been trying to pay very particular attention and instead his thought had wandered off somewhere and left him looking very foolish. His warrior's cry slipping back down his throat, gun pointing at nothing. He took a look around the room. In daylight it was just ordinary. Small and overcrowded, a miracle he didn't break his neck on all their stupid fusty old people's furniture.

Enough of this scene. He gave a salute to the bride and groom. They could hang out here, keep tabs on things. He slung one leg over the windowsill. And looked up to see the old woman's face at the door.

Her mouth was open. You could have popped a lightbulb in it. People kept sneaking in and out on him, it was so rude. He raised his gun hand, just to see what she'd do. Her face went all rubbery, like every bone in it had been broken. He would have liked to ask her just what was the matter with the old man, and if they had been happy together, and if they were ready to be shot now. He wanted to know if he'd gotten their dreams right. But it occurred to him with some embarrassment that he had forgotten how to say any of this in either English or Spanish. It was all turning into too much hassle anyway. So he put a finger to his lips, silencio, the gun still leveled at her rubber face as he hoisted his other leg over the sill and dropped to the ground.

He felt some urgency, not just wanting to get away before the old woman began flapping around and screeching and making phone calls, but an anxiousness and pressure, a need to catch up with the day, as if it had moved on without him. He would need another car, on top of all the other needs. He didn't see any cars around here. People must keep them locked up. He'd come to a wide bare intersection. Not even a friendly wall he could stand against to relieve himself. Incredible.

But *because* he needed a car most of all, one appeared, sidling and idling up to the stoplight. A hot-looking ride, red and low-slung and sparkly. The driver, a kid, leaning his arm out the open window, radio playing some loud crud with the bass turned all the way up. Oh yes.

Strolling alongside the open window, like he wanted to ask for a light or directions. The kid either not noticing him or not paying attention, not until he was right on top of him. When he stooped and poked his head into the window—"Hey, man"—the kid looked up at him with his face a perfect blank. The next instant the gun was under his chin and the door was yanked open.

"Out of the damn car."

The kid still looked like he didn't get it. The cruddy music was so loud, he probably hadn't even heard him, hadn't yet figured out that there was something going on besides the noise in his ears, that he was about to lose his pretty car, not until his ass was kicked out on the street. Eat cement, white boy! But he fumbled around trying to get the car in gear and then the radio turned out not to be a radio but a CD player, which was excellent but how did you turn it off? Then the music became sirens and the rearview mirror filled up with cop lights, ah shit.

Except now the kid on the sidewalk was yelling Don't shoot!, his hands paddling in the air, because here was a laugh, a cop jumping out of his squad and reaching for his gun but distracted by the kid, hesitating for an instant so that it was possible to step out and aim his own gun, all the while the little asswipe on the ground crying like a girl. The gun popped and did something to the cop's hand, like it exploded from the inside out. Blood sprayed from it and the cop was rolling on the ground but still trying to get his unhurt hand on his holstered gun and then instead of putting the car in drive and getting away clean, he hit reverse. Smashed into the squad car and maybe the cop and the kid too, he couldn't tell because of the music noise, BOOM BOOM BOOM, finally getting the whore ass gear into drive and hauling out of there. BANGBOOM. The cop might have been firing, or else it was just the bass on the speakers that kept up its noise for blocks and blocks until he finally figured out how to shut it off.

Not wanting to slow down, he got on some freeway and kept going. It was a hell of a car, truly, the best he'd had so far, but there was no time to appreciate that now because everything had happened so fast and was still happening. He kept finding himself on bridges. He was either crossing three or four different rivers or the same one many times. The tires hummed on the steel plating, the sky above was crosshatched by girders, the river below surprising him with its bigness, its toy boats kicking up foam, its distant misty green-brown curves, what a ride he was having! A song came into his head, *Across the wi-ide Missouri,* was that where he was? He didn't know the rest of it, so he sang it over and over again, *Across the wi-ide, across the wi-ide,* and then he forgot that too.

He was a little sorry when the rivers went away but he had a pleased sense of really covering ground now. Seeing things he had not been able to imagine, he was cooking, he was damn near *flying,* and for everything his useless brain forgot there was a new thing to take its place. All day he drove in directions he did not think anyone would look for him, and when he reached the Mississippi it was night and the water was dark, lit by beautiful red and green and white lights. He was *Porque,* he was *Because,* his own reason for doing what he did. And so he passed on into Illinois, looking for the next place he had never been before.

Part Four   **September**

Eye of the Storm

Arlene never got past Tropical Storm. Bert was a hurricane. He made landfall along the south Texas coast and pooped out. Cindy stayed out in the Atlantic, past Bermuda. None of them anything to write home about. But low-pressure masses kept firing themselves from the Cape Verde Islands, from the coast of Africa, like baseballs. An ocean full of storms. Dennis was lumbering toward Florida. Emily was a whirling blob somewhere east of the Windward Islands. Floyd was stacked up behind them, a giant saucer of wind and rain. Floyd was the one everyone at the Weather was keeping an eye on, the one getting all the attention. If there was going to be a Harvey, it would simply have to wait its turn.

Local Forecast had a lot to keep track of. Winds coiling up and then unraveling, all the watches and warnings, storm surges, rainfall totals, evacuations. Most nights he sat up late, waiting for updates. It took a lot of concentration to keep it all straight in his head. Especially since now there was this girl sleeping on the couch. He had to scooch around her just so he could see.

He woke her up when Dennis's winds jumped to seventy-five miles per hour, official hurricane strength. All the lights were off except the television, and the weather was turned down low so as not to disturb her. She had her face buried in the cushion and her hair was every which way. Local Forecast coughed experimentally. She didn't move. Then he fiddled with the television volume. It got away from him and went loud, right in the middle of a Slim-Fast commercial.

She rolled over with a fuzzy look on her face. "Wha?"

"Dennis is a hurricane now."

"Dennis who?"

"He's a hurricane."

"God," said the girl. She sat up and rubbed her eyes. On the television a lady was dancing around in front of a mirror, happy about losing a hundred pounds. "There's a hurricane here?"

"Nananana. In the ocean."

"Well that's exciting. That's a news flash." She rolled off the couch and went into the bathroom and Local Forecast tried not to listen to her in there. The toilet flushed and she came back out. "God, Harvey. It's two in the morning. Oh, well. It's not like I have to get up for anything."

She sat down on the couch and wrapped the blanket around her knees. "So Harvey, look, if my mom calls, you haven't seen me. It's sort of a game I'm playing with her. Like hide-and-seek."

"Hidenseek."

"Or anybody else. Even the police. Especially the police. I just need to hang out here a little while longer, okay?"

They were showing the ocean from yesterday. It had a bumpy, bulging look to it. He'd never been to the ocean. It wasn't fair. Somebody should have taken him. Then when it was on the television, he could point to it and say: You see that there? That's an ocean, don't let anybody tell you different.

Then maybe they wouldn't make fun of him. He wasn't dumb, he could tell when they pitched their voices up a notch, pretending they liked him more than they did. A stupid game he played along with because that's what people expected. (Hidenseek?) Sometimes he wanted to tell them: Listen, I know what you're doing. I'm not some born-yesterday kid. But they talked so fast, by the time he got it worked out what he was going to say, they'd either gone away or they were pestering him about something different that needed different words.

Nobody made fun of hurricane experts. You could go on television. The thought grabbed him by the top of the head and spun him around. He just had to figure out how it was done, where you had to stand so you ended up on the screen. He figured they had people who were in charge of those things. So how expert was expert? Did you have to take a test?

"Uncle Harvey?"

She yawned it out, Har-vee. The Weather's blue screen was quiet, giving temperatures. "Why don't you want to get your eyes fixed?"

He shook his head and kept shaking it. The girl reached up and held his chin to make him stop. "Really. Why not?"

"Scairt."

"What are you scared of? People get it done all the time. It turns out fine. They just take off the cataract part. It doesn't hurt. I don't even think they knock you out anymore. It's lasers or something."

Local Forecast put his hand in front of his face and wiggled his fingers. His eyes were fine.

"You could seriously go blind if you don't get it done. You understand?"

Oh doctor doctor. No thanks no doctor.

"They're plotting something. My mom and dad. I think they want to have you declared crazy."

Because everything had to stay the same. Always the Weather, the Forecast, and him here to watch it. Or else it was The End. Sky falling down nobody everybody alive and dead.

The girl said, "All right. I'm going back to sleep. But I'm worried about you. You could end up in some boot camp too. Crazy boot camp. I wouldn't put it past my mom."

The girl wrapped herself up in the blankets but kept talking.

"So don't tell her anything if she comes around. Zero. I don't trust her. We'll both just have to lay low."

She had pretty hair. It was all goldy. He touched the ends of it, just a fingertip touch. One of her bare feet stuck out of the blankets. Even her feet were pretty. The toenails were shiny red. Fat Cat, who was inclined to jealousy, jumped into his lap just then, which was lucky because he was getting a little you-know down there.

"I don't suppose . . . I asked my mom once why you went into the hospital and she didn't know. So is it anything you can talk about?"

"Hospital schmospital."

"Yeah. I guess not."

There was a floating space in his head right there. Like a cloud you couldn't see past. It made him feel stupid not to remember things. Cloudy clouds. He lived with Mamma and Daddy before the hospital. Frank had up and got married. It was after the war. He had the taxi job. He didn't remember remembering that. It was like he'd that minute pulled it right out of the cloud. He wanted to tell the girl but she was asleep again.

After the war it was boom times. America, which was the country, flexed its muscles. Everybody had new jobs and cars and houses. Frank had a job in a bank, selling money. He wore a tie to work. America had showed its enemies what was what. Of course, there were still communists on the loose. Communists were the Red Menace. Daddy said they were Godless. Communists were sneaky. They could be anybody.

Maybe they had sent him to the hospital for being a communist. The idea that he had been something dangerous excited him. Maybe they had sent all the communists to hospitals, cured them somehow. You sure didn't hear a lot about them anymore.

Frank said the next war would be with the communists. They were practicing with bombs. Airplanes would drop them. When he drove the taxi, he watched out for airplanes. You wouldn't want a bomb landing on you. All this was before the Weather, so there wasn't any good way to warn people.

Nononono, he was getting confused. The Weather wasn't for bombs anyway. What they had were sirens, just like for storms. When he thought about sirens he got all shivery. Did they have sirens in the hospital? Or bombs?

He knew there was something important here, but he was too tired to keep squeezing his head. He went to sleep and when he woke up there was a new problem because it was Rosa day and Rosa was knocking on the front door. And here was the girl, still asleep on the couch.

Oh boy. Rosa was going to be so mad. She hated a mess. Local Forecast ran back and forth between the couch and the front door. Get up, get up, he fretted. The girl just waved him away. She still had the blankets over her head. Rosa kept knocking. He didn't want her to leave. Rosa!

He peered through the glass at the top of the door. Rosa saw him and wagged her finger. It was a rainy day and she had a big umbrella with pictures of fish on it. The fish were blowing bubbles. Rosa was mad because she was out in the rain. Local Forecast opened the door and tried to hide behind it.

Rosa set her umbrella to drip on the mat. Her feet in their little sneakers went swipe swipe swipe. Then stopped. He couldn't bear to watch.

Sound of blankets thrashing around. The girl said, "Oh, hello. Are you a friend of Harvey's? I'm Josie."

Rosa didn't answer. It was even harder to understand the things she didn't say than the things she did. Local Forecast sneaked a peek. Rosa had her arms tucked up. She looked the way she did when she saw a mess. The girl said, "Oh, I get it. Spanish, huh? I'm taking French. Sorry."

Rosa swept past her and into the kitchen. There was the sound of her shoving dishes in and out of the sink. The girl sat up. "Jeez. Is it always so busy around here?"

On Rosa days, she made him breakfast. So Local Forecast felt better when he smelled coffee. He ran outside and looked in through the backdoor to make sure. The kitchen table had two places set instead of his just one. Two mugs, two glasses, two plates on dinky embroidered cloths. He had new plates now. Rosa had brought them from home. They had gold edges. Rosa saw him hanging around the door and crooked her finger, so he had to shuffle inside, dripping rain and embarrassed at himself.

The girl came in with her hair in a towel from the shower. She smelled like steam and soap. "Wow, corn muffins." She sat down and loaded up a plate and poured coffee. "So is she, what, your girlfriend?"

Local Forecast cleared his throat. Rosa was making a racket with the breakfast things. She wouldn't look at him. But he knew she was listening. He felt the kitchen light shining right down on top of his head, filling him with giddy heat. "Yes," he said.

"Really? That's great."

"She's Rosa."

"Rosa, huh?" The girl looked into her coffee mug, like it was part of the conversation. "Well, that's terrific, but . . . do you speak Spanish? I don't guess she speaks English. Isn't that kind of weird?"

Rosa put a plate of little pig sausages on the table. She had not said one word. Local Forecast stuffed sausages into his mouth and smacked them around. He wanted her to know they were good. She still wouldn't look at him. It was all about the girl. She didn't like the girl being here. She must be thinking . . .

Coffee sloshed in the mugs as Local Forecast stomped to his feet. Rosa and the girl looked up at him with their mouths unhinged. Local Forecast made his voice loud. He said, "This girl is just here to be lying low. Nobody has to get sniffy about it."

Then he sat back down. He felt grand. He blew a kiss to Rosa. Something he'd never done before but he'd seen it on TV. Rosa must have seen it too, because she giggled and did that finger-wagging thing.

The girl said, "Well, I guess the two of you have everything worked out." She took her coffee and went and sat on the back porch to watch the rain. Local Forecast sneaked up behind Rosa and tickled her until she shrieked.

Later the girl helped Rosa move furniture so she could do the floors. The girl said, "She doesn't mess around, does she? She's like samurai cleaning lady. If you can be that and still be Mexican."

They sat in the kitchen to keep out of Rosa's way. "I'm glad the two of you are in love and all. I'm glad somebody is."

Local Forecast figured the girl just liked talking. He didn't mind. It was what company was supposed to do.

"You remember that night we went for ice cream? You remember that guy? Well, he's a world-class bullshitter. Love sucks."

"Loveydovey."

"Maybe it's easier to be with somebody if you have, no offense, diminished capacities. Your expectations would naturally be lower. You could just ignore some of the rancid behavior."

The rain outside was actual hurricane rain. That was something. The edge of the same storms hundreds of miles away reached as far as You Are Here. Out on the ocean it was raining sideways, in great sheets and torrents. Low-pressure systems were sucking everything into them, boats, palm trees, swordfish spinning out of the water in terror, their wet blue sails gleaming. He felt restless, like he should be getting ready for something.

The girl started crying. "I can't stand it, I want to be with him so bad. Why am I calling you crazy? The craziest thing in the world is when you still want to be with somebody who . . . Promise me if I even reach for the phone, you'll slap my hand."

If there was a siren for storms, you were supposed to go down in the basement. It was the same for bombs. But he didn't like the basement. It had a bad smell. Mamma kept her jars and home canning down there and sometimes they broke and the juices leaked out, runny and spoiled. Something in the basement was making his eyes go blind. Nononono, that was now.

Where was Moses when the lights went out?

Down in the cellar with his shirttail out

Rosa saw the girl crying. She came in and petted her on the back, which made the girl cry harder. "Is anybody ever happy? Are you even supposed to be?"

Rosa made them all tea with lemon and they sat around the kitchen table, watching the girl be sad. She said, "I'm missing school right now. So I guess that makes me truant. An official juvenile delinquent. A wayward girl." She stopped crying long enough to drink some tea. "You know what the funny thing is? I could still get him in so much trouble. Like enormously. I hope he's thinking about that right now. I hope he's sweating bullets. Ha ha. The reason that's funny is . . . never mind. It's not that funny."

Rosa said ya ya, and shook her head in sympathy. The girl blew her nose into a Kleenex and said, "She's really kind of cute, Harvey. And she's not that old. I mean, I don't think she's any older than you are. I should get you a Spanish dictionary. In case you decide you want to have a regular conversation."

Local Forecast never had a girlfriend before. He wasn't sure why. He guessed it was a scairdy thing. Back in School all the girls moved in a kind of flock or herd. They put their heads together and whispered secrets and laughed at things that amused them. It was hard to focus on any one girl, cut one out of the herd, although he liked them all in general, the general look of them. Girls wore petticoats and charm bracelets and stockings and hair bows and there was always a lot of fuss about these items, their color, fit, and shape.

In the hospital, it had been a surprise when girls had none of these things.

All the fuss was meant to distract you, you were supposed to think that this was what was important or different about girls, clothes, and not what was underneath the clothes.

If there was a hurricane here, it might blow your clothes right off. It wouldn't be anybody's fault.

The girl said, "I'm going to lie down for a while. Maybe sleep. Watch the Weather Channel, sure."

When she was gone, Local Forecast and Rosa were shy again. It was like they needed somebody else to help them be lovey-dovey.

The girl stayed on the couch most of the time. Even days, she slept a lot. When she was awake, she watched the hurricane news with him. Floyd was a monster. He was getting ready to dump the whole ocean on North Carolina. He was a dirty white blur on the map, a pinwheel of cloud arms with the calm space, the eye, a darkness in the center. Every day he nudged farther inland. Local Forecast worried some about his eyes. When he looked away from the television, there was still a cloud. If there was a cloud in your eyes, did you cry rain? If you saw something you should not have seen in the basement, would your eyes be punished?

Where was Moses when the lights went out?

The girl was asleep again. It was dark, it got dark earlier now and the crickets were back. Some stayed outside, some turned up in the closets where Fat Cat pounced on them. The cricket song rose and shrilled, like a siren, almost. It made him fretful, out of sorts, he'd been like that all day. Rosa had been here but she was gone. He should water his garden. He should pay the power and light. In North Carolina, Floyd was drowning pigs. They had acres of pigs in North Carolina and they were all underwater. It was terrible. But that wasn't what was worrying him, nor anything else he could put a name to. When the red car pulled up in the driveway, it was almost a relief that whatever he'd been waiting for was finally here.

Wit's End

Josie?

Elaine sat up. Every light in the house was on. She thought she'd heard something. But the room stared her down. No one was there. Josie had been gone for three days and three nights.

Gone wasn't a word that stayed put. It kept time. Josie was gone for every minute of every hour of those three days. She was still gone, still gone, still gone. *Gone* kept happening.

There were times Elaine was furious, her anger spiking through everything else, so that she could have shaken the girl hard enough to make her teeth chatter in her head, if only, if only, if only she were here to be shaken! The anger didn't last. What lasted was *gone*.

She had lost everything. All the years of motherhood, the skin she'd grown into through long habit, birthing and tending, dispensing bedtime stories and punishments, yes you may, no you may not, because I said so, because I'm your mother, because I love you entirely and absolutely—all that she had played false and lost in an instant. She never should have pushed things to this point. Or maybe Josie was the one who'd pushed, but Elaine should not have pushed back. It didn't matter now. When Josie was small, Elaine had the nightmares common to all parents, of her child being abducted, lost, stolen from school or stores or from her own bed. But what if the child stole herself?

The morning after Josie escaped and didn't come home, Elaine went to see Josie's friend Tammy. Tammy was at work, she worked in the library. Elaine found her trundling a cart of books through the aisles, emitting that total lack of energy that seemed to accompany her every movement. "Oh, hi, Mrs. Lindstrom," she said, rearranging her bad posture. "How ya doin?"

Elaine wasn't in the mood to waste time on her. "I need to know about this boy Josie's been seeing. I need to know where she is."

"Haven't seen her. Sorry."

"Tell me about the boy."

Tammy hefted a book and put it down again. "She has some kind of new boyfriend?"

Not that Elaine expected the truth out of her. Tammy had one of those horrid eyebrow piercings, which gave her whole face a skewed, piratical look. Elaine said, "I really need to find her, Tammy. I'm afraid this boy, whoever he is, is dangerous."

Tammy's eyebrow took a different, smirking twist. "Oh, I wouldn't worry about that."

"Why's that, Tammy? Huh? Who is he?"

Tammy's expression went back to sullen neutral. She was a girl with rather coarse, staring features who got herself up so provocatively you didn't at first notice. Did the library allow glitter eyeshadow? Apparently it did. Tammy said, "Look, we don't really hang out anymore. I don't know what she's doing. Is she in trouble or something?"

Elaine, aware that anything she might say would be gossip fodder, and that she'd probably already said too much, shook her head. "I can't find her and I need to talk to her. If you see her, please tell her that."

"I bet she's fine, Mrs. Lindstrom. She's probably just out partying. Hey, Tuesday's the first day of school. Is she going to be there or what?"

Elaine left and drove the streets for a time, thinking that Springfield wasn't so big you could hide for very long, sooner or later she'd be bound to find her. But Josie could be anywhere by now. Kids ran off all the time, to Chicago or New York or the rest of the world. She was beginning to realize it wasn't so much a matter of finding Josie as waiting for her to come home.

Still, she called the police, who told her it was too soon to file a missing person's report, and that most kids came home after a day or two, especially if there's been an argument. She should call back in a few days if she hadn't heard anything. Elaine wasn't about to settle for that. She was accustomed to not settling for answers she didn't like. She simply persisted, saying the same thing over and over again in different ways, until people gave ground. By the time she got off the phone, the police had agreed to flag Josie's car on their computer, and Elaine had an appointment with the department's youth officer.

She decided it would be better to call Frank sooner rather than later, so he couldn't accuse her of withholding things. Elaine reached him in Aspen the morning after Josie's second night gone. "We had an argument. I took her keys and told her she was grounded. She found them and sneaked out while I was in the shower."

Frank seemed to have trouble comprehending this. "So where is she now?"

"I don't know, Frank. That's why I'm calling."

"You can't exert enough basic control to keep her off the street?"

"Don't start. You can't keep teenagers under lock and key." Although she had been considering doing exactly that.

"Well, what do you want me to do? I'm fifteen hundred miles away, Elaine. Can't I leave for a simple vacation without some damn catastrophe?"

"You're right, Frank. I'm sorry to disturb you. If she ever does come home, I'll drop you a line."

Sound of Frank being annoyed in silence. Then he said, "What did you argue about?"

"She's been lying to me about some boy she's been seeing. She wouldn't tell me who he is."

"Lying? What, she said he was somebody else?"

"She was just very evasive." Elaine decided she would spare him her darkest suspicions. Frank would think she was nuts, maybe she was by now. "I was trying to get her away from a bad influence." How far away was another thing she wouldn't tell him. She never should have called that place, what was its name, something smarmy and deceptively encouraging, Horizons or Challenges. She hadn't been thinking straight, she'd been angry and frustrated and she'd wanted to get Josie's attention. She had wanted not to be ignored anymore.

"Bad influence," said Frank. "You ask me, everybody under twenty-five's a bad influence these days."

"I'm trying to find the boyfriend. I expect that's where she's staying, with him."

Frank swore off to the side of the receiver. Elaine had a horrible thought. If Josie had . . . She couldn't have overhead her on the phone. But if she had . . . "How's Aspen?" she asked idiotically.

"The damn time-share people screwed up the drain in the tub. It's a total mess. I think they were grooming dogs in there. Look, shouldn't you be doing something? Shouldn't the police?"

"They are." She was trying to convince herself there was no possible way Josie could have been listening. "When are you coming back?"

"Thursday. Unless you think we should get there sooner."

"No, I guess you can't really . . . do anything." It would be just like Josie to overreact in some grandiose and spiteful way. Make some rash gesture she didn't even mean, out of pride and wounded feelings. Just like her mother.

"Harvey's going into the hospital the day after we get back. I'm telling you now so there won't be any carrying on."

Oh God, Harvey. "Does he have any clue? Have you told him?"

"The less he hears about it the better. You know I'm right."

No she didn't, but there was only room in her for one crisis at a time, and Harvey would have to wait. "I'll call you if there's anything."

"You sound whipped."

"That's me."

"She'll turn up. Then I'll beat the crap out of her."

"Don't even joke like that. We're going to have to do some serious, serious . . . Do you really think she's all right?"

"She better be or I'll kill her."

She must be really far gone if talking to Frank was actually making her feel better. She hung up the phone and went back to waiting.

School had already begun. The start of Josie's senior year. Elaine met with the principal and the assistant principal and the guidance counselor. They were all very sympathetic and supportive and kept assuring her of what a good, an excellent, student Josie was, and how unlike her this behavior was, a minor episode, a peccadillo that would not interfere with her completing her coursework and graduating on schedule. Assuming, it went without saying, that she came back sometime soon. Meanwhile, if there was anything they could do, anything at all . . . There wasn't, really, but it calmed her to talk to people who treated her as if she was in fact a good and responsible parent.

Even as she was consoled and buoyed up by the helpful principal and his staff, Elaine couldn't help thinking if this was so unlike Josie, did that mean Josie had been someone else all along?

Elaine assumed that the usual rumors, pregnancy and the like, were making their way through the school hallways. She wanted to get on the intercom, scream at them all to shut up.

There were times she imagined Josie was dead. She let the unspeakable idea come to rest in her mind. There were plenty of people out there who did horrible, brutal things. You didn't have to look very hard to find them, in fact you could hardly get away from them. Elaine had seen a news show once about a murdered girl, and the girl's mother who had gone to the crime scene some months later, just to witness it. To some people it had seemed morbid or crazy, but Elaine had understood completely. She would have done the same. Would do the same if she had to. Was already seeing, in her vision, the reeking stairwell, or the sidewalk with its pattern of crazy cracks, or the floor from which the stained mattress had already been removed. Then she asked why she was doing this to herself, and called a friend who had become a Baha'i and was famous for her optimism.

This was the way things went on for most of a week.

Elaine went to her appointment with the police youth officer. She gathered that this was someone who usually dealt with gangs. Walking into police headquarters felt unreal, like innumerable bad movies in which she was the somewhat overdressed lady whose role it was to clutch at her handbag and snivel. She sat in a plastic chair in the lobby. There didn't seem to be much going on, in terms of crime. A fattish man in a coat and tie walked past, drinking coffee from a styrofoam cup. A woman came in to complain about a neighbor who was either cutting down trees or refusing to cut trees, Elaine couldn't tell. She listened to the two desk clerks talk about their weekend.

"We got the subfloor done. And two of the cabinets. Then we

went to the Spaghetti Shop for dinner because you couldn't even get to the refrigerator."

"What did you have, the Bucket of Meatballs?"

"No, the Chicken Alfredo."

"Oh, that's good too."

Elaine had arrived there early, she was always early for things. It was a bad idea because it assumed that other people took your business as seriously as you did.

"Mrs. Lindstrom?"

One of the clerks led her back behind a half-gate and directed her to another chair, wooden this time. It wasn't a proper office, only a semipartitioned desk in a room full of desks occupied by unbusy-looking men. One of them was very carefully unwrapping a large sandwich. A fly circled him. She had expected a little more privacy. She couldn't imagine anyone here being any help.

"Sorry to keep you waiting." A man came up behind her and Elaine revolved in her chair trying to keep track of him and to catch up with the hand he offered. "I'm Bob Kellerman. Why don't you tell me about your daughter."

Elaine recited the meager list of known facts, thinking that Bob Kellerman did not look much like a cop. He had curly black hair, the type that was impermeable to brushes or combs, cut short. A woolly goatee. He wore a suit and one of those skinny, rumpled ties that was either very trendy or very much not so. She didn't even pretend to keep track of these things anymore. Big black-rimmed glasses, the same thing. The suit fit as if it was borrowed.

"I'm really a social worker," he said, when Elaine finished talking.

"Beg pardon?"

"People are always trying to get me figured. My background is social work, then I did advanced courses in criminology. I don't have a gun or handcuffs or any of that."

"Well, what do you have?"

"A tape recorder and a cell phone. OK. All we were able to find in the computer was a curfew stop a couple of months ago. Your daughter had no other record of police involvement."

"Oh."

"That's usually good news."

"It is. But I thought . . . I know she's been hiding things from me. I was sure it was drugs, or worse. I was afraid she might be . . . being exploited."

Kellerman shoved his clunky glasses to the top of his nose, considering. "Do you have a picture of her?"

Elaine handed it across the desk. Josie's class picture from last year. Josie hadn't liked it. In it she wore a white sweater and her hair was fluffed over her shoulders. She was smiling in a way that she had complained was "sappy."

"Pretty girl."

He probably said that about all the runaways. "Thank you."

"Can I keep this for a while?"

Elaine realized this would be the picture on the Missing poster, if there was going to be such a thing. Josie was going to be furious.

Kellerman asked if there was any particular evidence of drug use. Alcohol? Scholastic problems?

No and no and no. He rubbed at his goatee as if it itched. "Well, she's certainly not your usual at-risk kid. Believe me, I see enough of those to say."

"Then where is she?"

"The odds are she's fine. She's mad and she's making sure you know it."

"Odds," said Elaine unhappily.

"Does her father live with you?"

"We're divorced but he's here in town." Elaine felt she had to make some explanation. "That is, he's not here right now. He's on vacation." That didn't sound right either. "I've talked to him and he's coming back in a few days."

Elaine gave up. She honestly hadn't intended to make Frank sound like an absentee slob of a parent.

Kellerman asked her about Josie's friends, anyplace she might have gone. Older kids who might have their own apartments. Elaine said she had called everyone she could think of. "They either don't know anything or they won't tell me. It's the boyfriend, I'm sure. You hear about these things all the time. Young, impressionable girls taking up with criminals because they're able to exert an influence over them." She hoped that Kellerman would know she was talking about sex without her having to come out and say it.

"You know, you're just making it harder on yourself. You don't know any of this for sure."

"Being hard on myself isn't the problem right now."

"Would you say you have a generally good relationship with your daughter, at least until this episode, or have there always been problems?"

"Is any of this going to help you find her?"

"It's a family situation. So I'm asking."

She hadn't come here for counseling, especially from some bad-suit semi-hipster. He was younger than she was, but still too old to be dressing like a comedy-show host. She couldn't see his feet, but she would bet money he was wearing tennis shoes. "We argue over the usual things. Curfew, schoolwork, boys. She's never run away before. Please tell me what you're going to do."

"I'll pass her description and photo on to the patrol units. They won't start an investigation without some evidence of coercion or foul play."

"You mean, finding her body?"

Kellerman said, evenly, "It's not a criminal matter yet. That's all I'm saying."

"Fine." Elaine began to get up.

"I know the most urgent thing is finding her, but you might want to think about what you're going to do once she gets back. How you want to address the issues."

Elaine sat down again. "I want to be able to talk to her. We can't have a conversation now that doesn't explode in our faces. I want her to stop being so angry at me just because I'm there to be angry at. I don't want her to be so unhappy."

"What is she unhappy about?"

"Her father and me divorcing. Him remarrying. I'm not sure what else. That she can't grow up and move out in the next fifteen minutes."

"That all sounds pretty normal."

"It's not a normal world anymore."

"How so?"

"There are too many sick, crazed people out there who make meanness their life. Everyday you read some new depraved thing in the headlines. I can't not imagine the worst. I can't not worry about her. Even when she was sitting in the same room with me I worried. Kids think they can handle everything. They don't have a clue."

"Maybe not, but most of them get by. Turn out just fine."

"Do they?" Elaine was aware she was being shrill, her voice spiraling up into some region of fatigue and grievance. "Fine. None of us are fine."

"Why's that?"

"We're sick at heart. Everybody. More or less. Nobody knows how they're supposed to live. Or even if there is a supposed to. Never mind. God, I hate it when I get like this. I want my daughter back."

"You'll get her back. I'm betting on it. And maybe it'll turn out to be a good thing. A chance to put your relationship on a different basis."

"Yes," said Elaine. She felt as if she had emptied herself out in a heap on the desk, in front of a strange stranger.

"I hope you'll do some things for yourself in the meantime. Be with family, friends, whatever support group you have."

Elaine had a brother in Denver, but he was not the kind of brother you called to make yourself feel better. "I've told some of my friends, certainly, but I haven't wanted to broadcast it. People start feeling they ought to do something. People you don't especially like show up at your door with pound cakes."

"Of course, the more people who know about it, the more out there looking for her."

Elaine acknowledged that this was so. She supposed she felt reluctant about telling people. Josie's running away some kind of disreputable event. Bullshit, Josie would have said. Would she ever stop making mistakes, marching off smartly in all the wrong directions? She had to admit, Kellerman was good. He'd gotten her to consider any number of things, say aloud any number of things she had not intended. She had not taken him seriously. She supposed people often did not. He was contemplating his hands, which he had tented together on the desk, as if he knew what she was thinking and was modestly avoiding her gaze.

Elaine said, "Thank you. I guess I needed to unload some of that."

"You really feel that way? About the world being rotten and everybody's miserable? Something like that?"

"I don't know. Sometimes. When I'm feeling low. When I haven't slept for three days and my only child runs off to show how much she despises me, yeah, I do. Other times I think that being alive is what paradise is. Or that's how it should be. Listen to me. Have you ever heard such blathering?" She was glad no one else in the room was really close enough to hear.

"It's interesting blather," said Kellerman. "High-minded. Gives the joint some class. What about people who walk around saying, 'It's the Lord's will,' or 'Everything happens for a reason.' Aren't they happy? They've got a system. They're covered."

Elaine was beginning to enjoy the conversation in a way she would not have expected. "It must be a wonderful way to live. Thinking that your every action is fraught with significance. Finding a parking place. Not finding a parking place. Everything part of the infinite plan."

"Well, maybe everything is. Just not the way people think. I was reading this article about something called 'cellular automatons.'"

"Cellular . . ."

"It's a computer simulation that tries to mirror the way the laws of nature work. It has to do with how complex results derive from simple beginnings. Seemingly random events are actually predictable. The result of repeating a sequence of possible combinations."

Elaine shook her head. "Sorry. Not a computer person."

"It's not really about computers. I'm not explaining it very well. Imagine water vapor freezing into snowflakes. The flakes can take any number of shapes, an infinite number. But you start with just a few basic combinations of crystals. Think of a horizontal row of three squares. Then one square beneath it. Some of the squares are empty, some of them are filled in. All solid or all blank or something inbetween. A sequence. Replicate the sequence according to a regular set of rules, over and over and over, like a computer would, and you get, guess what?"

"No two snowflakes alike."

Kellerman nodded, pleased. "So let's say you wake up on an

ordinary day and you make a series of choices. Coffee or tea. Shower or bath. Read the paper starting with the front page or the funnies. Every one of those choices is a sequence. A simple beginning that generates a potentially complex result. Something in the paper alarms you and you spill the coffeepot on yourself so you have to go to the emergency room where you're given either the right or the wrong treatment; if it's the right kind you get to go home and that sequence of your life continues, but if it's the wrong kind you're admitted to the hospital or maybe you die, and each of those events generates its own set of results. Just like the snowflakes, except the rules get more complicated. All the big and little events of your life. Everyone's life. All part of some original, infinitely repeating sequence. The same enormous pattern."

Kellerman leaned back in his chair, looking a little self-conscious, the way people did when they finished a long speech. "Blather." He shrugged.

Elaine said, tentatively, "Well. That's a different way to look at things. Instead of the will of God, we have the Universal Computer. I guess it makes sense. But as an explanation for life itself, it seems a little . . . mechanical."

"Depends, I guess, on what you think is programming the computer to start with."

They smiled at each other and Elaine was aware of a current of personal interest between them, not sexual, exactly—not with those silly glasses—but something on its borders. Then she remembered Josie, and her heart flattened, and the engine of worry started up again in her head. "Well, thank you," she said again. Stood up and shook hands with him. "I hope you're right about this being just normal teenage acting out."

"Call me if there's anything I can do."

Another smile with that edge of acknowledgment in it, then Elaine got herself out to the parking lot, thinking that life couldn't get much stranger, except that it usually did, and maybe that was part of the Cosmic Computer Program. Infinitely multiplying weirdness.

She no longer slept in her own bed. Instead she lay on the couch in the den all night, half-dozing, the television on but the sound turned off. She clicked through channel after channel, watching the hectic shapes and colors succeed one another on the screen. Here was an old sci-fi movie of the sort that used cheesy models for spaceships. You could almost see the wires dangling against the cardboard firmament. Here were three ladies from a psychic hotline, all of them wearing wigs. They were taking calls and turning over tarot cards and, Elaine knew from previous viewings, giving the callers the bad news about the fidelity of their spouses and sweethearts. She wondered if the Cosmic Computer programmed the tarot cards as well, the Magician, the High Priestess, the Fool. On the Weather Channel, a woman was standing in front of the map, wielding a pointer and moving her mouth earnestly. Red and yellow hurricanes were spinning through the South Atlantic. Green rain-shapes were nudging into Illinois. And in India, she knew, it was monsoon season.

She was supposed to go to India early next month, a two-week trip. Of course she'd have to cancel. Even if Josie came home unharmed, how could she pick up and leave? Always before on such trips Josie had stayed at Frank and Teeny's, an arrangement that nobody was ever very happy with. Now it would be pure poison. Then again, she and Josie would have to get a lot of things worked out before they could stand to live under the same roof again. That would be a different, normal sort of problem, along with all the business complications that canceling her trip would bring. She supposed she should wish for a return to normal problems. But right now, in the middle of another numb and haunted night, it seemed as if she was burdened with the entire universe of bad possibilities.

You weren't supposed to go to India during the monsoons. Everyone said so. There was the rain itself. Torrents of it. Roads washed away and sewers failed. Telephone lines went down. People caught agues and fevers and funguses. Best to stay home until the skies dried up. But of course, the Indians *were* home. Elaine thought she should go there some time in the rainy season, just to avoid feeling like a dilettante tourist. She tried to imagine that much rain. The air gray with it. Steam rising from the forests, from the backs of patient cows. What happened to people who had nowhere to go, the street vendors and the barefoot children squatting on sidewalks and the fishermen in their cockleshell boats? She didn't know, it seemed negligent of her not to know.

Perhaps she should move to India. Make a new start. People liked her there. She could lead a useful, harmless life. Spend her days in simple tasks. Make offerings of food and flowers at the local shrines. Ganesh, the lucky elephant god. Shiva of the graceful arms. Blue-skinned Krishna. Gods who had been around for long enough to offer the consolations of ancient wisdom. In this vision she walked barefoot over the cool wood floor of a quiet room. Birds with names she did not yet know sang in the branches of a many-trunked banyan tree. Elaine drank a perfect cup of tea and lay back on a scented cushion and she was not aware she was asleep until the doorbell rang.

Morning. The bell chimed again. When Elaine hurried to the door, her blood stopped cold. A uniformed policeman stood on the front step.

"Mrs. Lindstrom? I'm here about your daughter."

She moaned, a deep, animal sound.

"Ma'am? It's nothing bad. I'm just here to ask you some questions."

She moaned again.

"If that's OK. Or maybe right now isn't a good time for you."

Elaine backed into the living room and sat down on the couch.

She waved a hand in front of her face. A swarm of small black insects had materialized in her vision.

"Can I get you something? Glass of water?"

She nodded. His footsteps crossed the hall and she heard him opening cupboards and running water. Then he was back, presenting her with a not-quite-cold glass of tap water. Elaine drank it. "Thank you."

"I apologize, ma'am. I should have called first."

"No, it's nice they sent someone." He was a very serious-looking young policeman with a sunburn and a little black mustache. "What questions, what did you say?"

"Just some routine . . . some routine follow-up matters."

She told him to sit down and he cleared his throat formally. "I really am sorry for alarming you like that."

"I'm a little on edge these days."

"Of course. Understandably. When did you last see your daughter?"

"Friday night around seven. I already reported this. Twice. Officer—"

"Crook. I know, ma'am. This is just . . ."

"Routine. All right. Aren't you going to write anything down?"

Elaine waited while he produced a notebook and balanced it on one knee to write. He was making it all look very difficult. Meanwhile her hair was a rat's nest and she needed to brush her teeth. He asked her for Josie's age, description, license plate number of her car. Friends and associates. Who what when where. All of which she had provided before. She was beginning to feel a kind of dismal foreboding about the police, any rapport with Kellerman notwithstanding. And she was ready to be disappointed in him also if he was the one who'd sent this polite but desperately laboring young man. She couldn't help feeling that he was here as part of some training exercise.

"And the two of you had an argument. About . . ."

"She has a boyfriend I don't approve of. Excuse me." Elaine got up and fled to the bathroom before young Sergeant Friday could fumble himself out of his chair. Behind the closed door she tried to get as much of her head as possible under the cold water faucet. At this point she looked better wet. She toweled off and returned to the living room. "Don't get up, please." With lessening patience she resumed her seat across from him.

He was flipping through his notebook as if there was something important there, although all he was doing was going back and forth between the same two pages. "So this boyfriend . . ." he began again.

"Yes, *cherchez* the boyfriend."

He looked at her without any change of expression. Maybe it wasn't that funny. "And what did she say about him?"

"Not much. I don't even have a name." Elaine had decided not to go into the details. "Look, I don't mean to be rude, but I really have reported all this before."

"Always a chance that going over the same ground again will yield some new information," he said stolidly. Elaine wanted to ask him if he was new to the force. She wanted to shower and go in to her neglected store. She wondered what it would take to get him to leave.

"Let me see now. OK. What items did she take with her from the home? As in. Belongings. Clothing."

He was such a nice-looking young man. It was a shame he had so much difficulty putting two words together.

"Some clothes. Not a lot. Her purse, wallet. A little money." Not her own, Elaine could have told him, but she didn't see the point of that. "She left most of her things. She didn't have to run away like some . . ." Elaine couldn't think what it was like. "She's very impetuous. Emotional. Once she gets mad or worked up about something, she gets all carried away."

"Yes ma'am."

"Anyway, I didn't see or hear her go."

"She leave any sort of note, letter? Anything that might be helpful?"

As if she wouldn't have noticed. "I don't think so, but perhaps you'd like to look around." Glad to have an excuse to dislodge him, Elaine led him up the stairs and waved him into Josie's white-carpeted bedroom. "The scene of the crime," she said, and left him standing irresolutely in the center of Josie's guitar books and dinky jewelry and the heart-shaped pillow she'd had since sixth grade and the shoes scattered where Josie had kicked them off. Elaine couldn't go in there any more. It was like the home of a messy ghost. She went off to take her shower, not caring what he thought of her.

He wasn't upstairs when she finished dressing and came out. He was back in the living room, looking dour and twitchy. He didn't seem to have found anything in Josie's room, at least he didn't have any evidence bags or fingerprint stuff or whatever the police toted around. "Are we finished?" Elaine said. "Shouldn't you be out investigating now?"

"She must be very intelligent, your daughter. All those books."

"I suppose so," said Elaine, wondering at this.

"She's going to college, I bet. I mean, she could if she wanted to."

"If she plans on coming back to finish high school first."

"I'm sorry to have disturbed you."

"I was already disturbed."

She put a hand on the doorknob and he ducked his head and sidled toward it. "Is someone going to call me?" Elaine asked. "Updates and so on? Because I have to be honest with you, I haven't been knocked out so far by the police effort."

"I promise you, I will personally be doing everything possible to correct the situation."

He was so odd. Did they train them not to smile?

On his way out his gaze was caught by a framed photograph on the wall, Josie at age seven, an age when she still beamed for photographs. Her hair was silky and daffodil-colored and she was wearing her favorite pink velvet dress. Elaine thought of all the photographs of missing children, the pictures on milk cartons and such, how they aged the pictures to approximate what the child would look like now that time had passed. What if you started with this happy little girl, then added ten years of sullen growing up? Would you get a good likeness?

"That's the best time," said Elaine. "When they're little and it hasn't occurred to them not to love you. Do you have any children, Officer?"

An easy question, she would have thought, but he didn't seem to want to answer. Shook his head, no.

"She's all I have," said Elaine. Behind her in the house the telephone rang. She nodded, embarrassed because she could never keep from saying things, exhausting herself with words, then shut the door on him and went to pick up the phone.

It was Frank, back in town and wanting to hear the news. Of which there was none. She was glad he'd returned because now there was someone else to deal with the school and the police and whoever else. Frank knew people, people he made money for. Surely he would know who to call to find her. He would organize a posse, offer a reward. But he sounded just as aggravated and unsure as she was. "I can't believe nobody's seen her. What is this, *Unsolved Mysteries*? *Alien Abductions*?"

"Will you please not talk like that?"

Frank said he was sorry. "I don't believe in that stuff anyway," he apologized.

Elaine let some silence tick by, to show him she was still upset. Frank's disappointing her was such a familiar sensation, such a well-established injury, her anger at him so well rehearsed, she could tune into it as easily as if it were a preset radio station in her car. Punch the button, sing the song. Would she ever be free of it? She said, "Maybe we'll get a postcard from Hawaii or Buenos Aires or somewhere. I'm almost beginning to hope so."

"How could she get that far without money?" said Frank, then they were both forced to think about all the ways a pretty young girl might be conveyed to distant places. To change the subject, Elaine asked him if he was still going to take Harvey to the hospital tomorrow.

"I'm not the one who's going to be there, but it's all set up. And don't worry, it's a group of trained professionals."

People who came to your house and sprayed for termites advertised themselves the same way. But Elaine only said that she would try to find time to go see Harvey today, just because somebody had to start worrying about his cat and his clothes and such. Fine, said Frank, not paying particular attention. This new crisis was turning Harvey into nothing more than a piece of unfinished business.

After Elaine got off the phone, she tried to call Harvey. No answer. At Trade Winds she tackled the pile of work waiting for her, but she kept forgetting what she was doing. Paper was only something inexplicably attached to her hand. Numbers were in code. People came in and she spoke to them and they spoke back. Once she put her head down on the counter and slept so hard that she drooled. When she woke, her fingernails were clenched tightly into her palms.

In this same muzzy, unfocused state Elaine left the store and drove to Harvey's house. All his shades were drawn, as usual. Nobody really used window shades anymore, it occurred to her. They'd gone out of fashion when she wasn't paying attention. Harvey's grass needed mowing. It was still warm enough for it to have grown shaggy. The elm tree in the front yard—trust Harvey to still have an undiseased elm, maybe the last in town—was dropping its leaves in a shiftless fashion. The last rains had clumped them together and they stuck to the bottom of her shoes as she crossed the yard to the porch. Knocking. "Harvey?"

The glass at the top of the door had a little curtain over it. Rosa's doing, she imagined. "Harvey?" When she tried the doorknob it was locked. Another something different. Because she could not think of what else to do she simply stood there for a time. The house across the street was currently occupied by a black family or families with a tribe of little kids who played in the yard or rode their bikes in taunting orbits around one another. People were always coming and going, coming and going there. Car doors slammed, tires kicked up the gravel in the driveway, morning and night. Maybe they were drug dealers. Maybe they only had complicated social relationships. Elaine decided it didn't really matter. There was something heartening about a house with so many people in it, so much human commotion. She had never lived that way. Both the family she had grown up in and the one she had started were small and getting smaller. Frank long gone. Josie missing. For someone with a reasonable number of friends—a support group, Kellerman called it—a retail business, a chamber of commerce membership, and a book club, she seemed to spend a lot of time alone. Now she was getting maudlin, self-pitying. When Harvey was taken away she would lose one more connection, one more path to something outside of herself. How strange and sad that she should feel that way about him. She knocked on the front door one more time, then left.

Back at the house there were three messages on her answering machine, none of them from Josie. Lyla had called from the store to say that the credit card machine wasn't working so was it all right if she just took people's names and phone numbers and they could come back later to pay? A neighbor Elaine was not particularly fond of had called to ask about the police car she'd seen in the driveway, wondering what exciting misfortune was in progress. And Bob Kellerman left a message saying that he just wanted to check in with her, assure her that steps were being taken. She should feel free to call him anytime.

Elaine listened to this last message a second time. Then poured herself a glass of wine—she hadn't been drinking at all lately, for fear of losing whatever control she had left—and went upstairs to lie down in her own bed. There she dozed, woke up to fix herself some dinner, went back to bed and slept dreamlessly until the phone woke her the next morning.

"You won't believe this."

"Frank? Is that you?" She was having too many conversations like this, with her brain still stuck in park.

" . . . most bizarre . . . You'd better get over to Harvey's. This is incredible."

"What is? Frank!"

He took a long, whistling breath. "Harvey has a gun and he's barricaded himself in the house and he's holding Josie hostage."

Bandido

Could her life suck any more? Were the bookies in Las Vegas giving odds? Fifty to one, hundred to one, it didn't matter. She'd bet money that somehow things were going to get even worse.

Josie cried and cried. Buried her face in those funky dusty couch cushions and leaked tears. Whenever she thought she was finally going dry, she remembered Mitch's craven face turned away from her, or the girl's gauzy, perfumed shoulders, or her mother accusing her of hateful, unspeakable things, and she started in all over again. Her face was always puffy now from crying, and she was getting a backache from the crack in the cushions you could never avoid. It would serve everybody right if she ended up with a deformed spine.

Then there was the cat. It kept stalking her as she lay there, swishing its tail in a low, angry arc. It would stop, gather its feet beneath it, and launch itself on top of her. Sometimes this happened when Josie was awake, but more often she was asleep when Fat Cat clobbered her, scrambling to find purchase on her legs or back, digging in with its claws, landing with a hiss and a thump when she finally dislodged it. Like her biggest problem right now was a cat.

She couldn't stay at Harvey's forever. She couldn't go home. It wasn't home anymore. It was time to quit sulking and leave. For somewhere. Her new life was waiting for her, starting just outside the city limits. All she had to do was get off the couch.

Of course it was scary. She had never imagined leaving alone.

She wanted to call Mitchell Crook and tell him she would never talk to him again. She wanted something horrible to happen to her so that he would feel very bad. She was aware that these were childish imaginings, and that she was just hanging around brooding and rehearsing her pitiful fantasies because she was too cowardly to do anything for real.

She even thought about calling her mother, pretending she was somewhere else, telling her she knew about her underhanded Utah scheme. In this fantasy her mother was alternately heartless and scornful or else abject, begging forgiveness that Josie did not grant. Josie tried on both versions, one and then the other, until even her anger felt flabby. There was something about lying on a couch for a week that took the edge off of it.

Meanwhile, the Weather Channel cycled through its own boring routine: forecast, ads, forecast, ads, interspersed with the hurricane stuff. Footage of galloping surf, people sleeping on cots in gymnasiums, rooftops poking out of floodwaters. She supposed she should feel a lot worse about the eroded beaches and homeless pets and million billion dollars washed away, get as excited as Harvey did about the whole thing, but as sad as it was, it was still only television.

It wasn't so bad at Harvey's. Just slow. They watched the Weather Channel and ate things like Raisin Bran and lunchmeat sandwiches and pork chops and canned corn and a very good chicken casserole that Rosa had made for them. Rosa! Harvey's girlfriend! Now that was a surprise. Josie wished she'd taken Spanish instead of French. Who could you talk to in French, waiters? She would have liked to ask Rosa just how the two of them, her and Harvey, got started.

She was discovering other things about Harvey. He talked to himself, he was always talking to himself, she came to realize. You just couldn't hear him most of the time. Little breath sounds, clicking of tongue and teeth, head-shakings. A private conversation that only once in a while surfaced into speech. Just yesterday morning he had come in from the backyard, stomping and blowing and muttering. "What is it, Harvey?"

He had one of his homegrown plants in one hand, a coffee can with a sprouting carrot top. But something had uprooted it, dug a trench in one side and broken off some of its green hair. "Backwards world"? Was that what he was saying? No, "bad word squirrels."

Was he crazy? She didn't think so, if you meant crazy like people who thought they were Jesus Christ or the CIA was poisoning their drinking water. He just lived in Backwards World. A place where you didn't have to worry about the stock market or AIDS or cheating boyfriends or anything else crummy. Every day was a new sky and a new start.

But she was alarmed about his eyes. She could tell they were bad and probably getting worse. He bumped into door frames and cupboards. When he reached to pet Fat Cat, he stroked the air around it before the creature arched its back to meet his hand. Sometimes, if she stayed quiet and didn't move, Josie thought he forgot she was in the room. To see the television screen he practically knelt in front of it, cocking his head from side to side, as if trying to work some remnant of vision around the cloudy lens of his eye. Did he not care he was going blind, did he just pretend it wasn't happening? She wanted to grab him by the shirt buttons, get right in his face, tell him she didn't know what.

Josie found herself almost wanting to call her mother, just to have somebody she could share these worries with. Of course, her mother's solutions sometimes made things worse, as witness the Utah fiasco. Her mother couldn't stand the thought of problems, the way some women couldn't stand a messy kitchen. She got the urge to Do Something. Her face took on this dauntless, enterprising expression, like she was the submarine commander in an old war movie, giving an order to ram the battleship head-on. But then her mother hadn't figured out what to do about Harvey either.

The next time Rosa came back, Josie tried to talk to her about Harvey's eyes. Rosa seemed to be there a lot, more than you'd expect a cleaning lady with a regular day. Maybe she was just keeping watch on Josie, although she didn't seem to be holding a grudge about it anymore. She showed up bright and early, as always, her little pink sneakers making time across the wooden floor. Josie peered over the back of the couch. *"Buenos días,"* She knew that much of the lingo.

"Buenos días," responded Rosa, pronouncing it like a real Spanish person would. She went straight into the kitchen and put on the big coverall apron she kept hanging by the stove. Harvey was already there and Josie joined him at the kitchen table, waiting for Rosa to make them coffee. He had this goofy expression on his face, like Rosa was a Weather Channel celebrity who had come by to sign autographs.

It was actually a little embarrassing, having somebody wait on her like this. You weren't used to it. Her mother hadn't done anything of the sort for years, except once in a while when Josie was sick. The whole idea of having a servant was so snobby. But Rosa didn't seem to find it demeaning or anything. She even made you feel like there was something feeble and useless about you for just sitting there while she managed everything so splendidly.

She wondered if Rosa had lived a hard life, the way she imagined Mexican people did. Not that she really knew that much about them. But they had a different standard of living down there, she was pretty certain. They were all Catholics so they had big families they couldn't support, which was why they all came

here. Sometimes Josie wished she was Mexican or black or somebody else who had a more interesting background and a legiti-
mate reason to be pissed off about life. Anyway, Rosa didn't look
like she was actively suffering or being oppressed. She had wrinkles, sure, but her skin was shiny brown and her hands weren't
knotted up like a lot of old people's, and of course you couldn't
keep up with her once she got it in gear.

Rosa served up coffee and ham steak and some kind of cinna-
mon pastry she must have brought with her. Harvey ate it all
down with his usual enthusiasm and lack of table manners. If it
bothered Rosa, you couldn't tell. Maybe she liked seeing her
cooking appreciated. Josie drank coffee and nibbled on a pastry.
The one good thing about being miserable was that she never had
much of an appetite. She hoped she was at least losing weight.

She waited for Harvey to finish eating and for Rosa to scrub his
face with a dishrag, the two of them giggling and carrying on.
They were shameless! Then Harvey went gallumphing off to the
bathroom with his stumpy flapping comical walk, and she and
Rosa were left alone.

"How about I help you with the dishes?" Josie asked, stacking
plates. Sometimes she talked even though Rosa couldn't understand, because it seemed less dumb than pointing and making
faces. Rosa said something that had *señorita* in it and shooed her
away from the sink, like maybe she did get it. "Say, Rosa?"

Rosa looked up without stopping her serious battering of the
dishes. Josie cleared her throat. "Harvey," she said, pointing first
at his empty chair, then in the direction he had gone. "Harvey,
OK?"

So far so good. Next Josie put her fingers up to her eyes and
looked through them, spectacle-style. Swiveled her head back
and forth, like she was hunting blindly for something.

Rosa had paused over the sink and was watching her the way

you did a movie when you weren't sure if it was supposed to be funny.

Now what? She really needed verbs. "He has cataracts and if he doesn't get them taken care of, he could go blind," Josie said, basically giving up.

Rosa said something in Spanish, like she was trying to meet her halfway. Maybe if the two of them kept jabbering at each other for the next ten years they could eventually batter down the language barrier. "Well, I'm just glad you like him so much. They say there's somebody out there for everybody. That's kind of a scary thought."

Josie retreated to the couch and spent the day in her usual weepy lethargy. Mitch probably hadn't even noticed she was gone. He was a total pig. She was in love with a pig. At lunchtime Rosa brought her a mug of chicken noodle soup and an egg salad sandwich. She could get used to this servant thing, she guessed. Rosa cleaned the floorboards you wouldn't have thought needed cleaning. Harvey did some strange calisthenics routine in front of the television, pumping his arms up and down and bending to wiggle his fingers at his toes. The cat declared a one-sided truce and perched on the back of the couch with its tail tickling Josie's feet. Rosa sang a Mexican song while she cleaned and Harvey joined in, making his sounds instead of the words, and Rosa pretended to hit him with the broom. It was like visiting your grandma and grandpa, sort of, if they were both a little wacked.

Josie didn't have much experience with grandparents. The ones on her mother's side had expired in a nursing home in Kansas City, and she'd only been to see them once or twice when she was little. She retained a brief impression of their twin wheelchairs and unhinged jaws and fretful questions, and her mother speaking very loudly, as if she could bully them into better health.

Her father's mother had died before Josie was born, and her other grandfather—Harvey's brother, of course—had long since succumbed to some old war wound. It was strange that a war could take so long to kill you. They gave Grandpa Frank a big send-off with a bugle and flags. The VFW was there, standing at attention in their blue peaked caps, and even though Josie had been only nine years old she knew there was something very sad about it. Not just that Grandpa Frank had died, because after all everyone had expected that, but because these old men trying to keep their faces fierce, his comrades-in-arms, were now the only ones who remembered him the way he was when he was young. Oh, and Harvey. He must have been there, hadn't he?

Josie tried to recollect. Her mother and father, taller than they used to be. Her mother wearing black and shushing her, which had to do with showing respect even if you didn't particularly like the dead person. It was harder to tell how her father felt. Except for when he was angry, his lid was always on tight. Like it would be such a terrible thing for him to cry at his own father's funeral. If she was in charge of the world, she'd fix it so men cried the same way women did, then they couldn't go around acting like you were this weak inferior creature. Anyway, she honestly couldn't remember Harvey being there. Had they kept him away, been afraid he'd embarrass them?

Grandpa Frank was always too sick to be a real grandfather. He was strapped to an oxygen tank and when he spoke his voice was all air. He looked sort of like Harvey did now, except Grandpa Frank's face was more caved-in. He slept in a hospital bed so he could crank it up and drain the fluid out of his collapsing lungs. You were not allowed to play with his medals or with the German helmet with the dark stain that was supposed to be blood or the brass uniform buttons with the German eagles or the rose-colored German money or the eyeglasses that folded so cunningly in half and fit into the soft leather case. Josie was not sure why it had been necessary to take so many things from the Germans. She understood it was good they had lost the war, but collecting souvenirs made it seem more like some big dumb football game.

Later that day she asked Harvey about the funeral. A little nervously, in case it was a painful memory. "Uncle Harvey? You know when your brother, Frank, died? My grandfather?" She thought it was a good idea to remind him who she was from time to time. "Did you go to the church and the cemetery?"

"Frank whupped the Germans."

"Yeah, that's right. Were you there when they buried him? They played taps and they gave my dad a flag."

"Mycountrytisofthee."

Well, it had been worth a try. But Harvey wasn't through with the train of thought that had been set in motion. "Frank was Daddy's favorite because he wasn't weak in the head."

They were sitting on the back porch watching the blue jays dive bomb the bird feeder. Behind them in the house, Rosa was winding down her day, putting the finishing touches on Harvey's laundry. Josie waited to see if Harvey was going to say anything else. He looked his usual placid self, except his eyebrows were rounded in mild surprise, as if what had come out of him was an unexpected belch. Josie said, "They told you that, didn't they. The weak in the head part."

"Said head dead. Red bed fed jed med zed."

"No, come on, Harvey, talk to me. I really want to know what it was like. Growing up. Were they mean to you?"

"Daddy was mean."

Again, the surprised eyebrows. Josie said, "What did he do, how was he mean?"

"I was ornery bad. I had it coming."

"Bad? You? I don't believe it. Was Frank bad?"

"Frank didn't go in the basement."

"What was in the basement, Harvey?"

He put his hand up to his mouth and pinched his bottom lip. "Don't remember."

"It's OK, Harvey. You can say whatever you want, they're all gone. They can't hurt you."

"Badbadbad." He was doing the head-shaking thing again. "Cold front warm front pressure pressure pressure."

"All right, shh, never mind. Just relax. I'm sorry." She felt rotten about persisting as she had. She wondered about people who did this for a living, doctors and therapists who were always asking questions and trying to pry your mind loose. There was something unfair and dishonest about it. The stuff inside your head should just stay there. People deserved their privacy. Except, it went without saying, Mitchell Crook, who deserved to be subjected to some exquisitely painful Vulcan mind-meld or government experiment.

Rosa was getting ready to leave. She'd made them a ham salad from the breakfast leftovers and boiled potatoes and lima beans to go with it. Everything neatly laid out in foil-covered dishes. Josie went into the bathroom so the two oldsters could smooch farewell. They were so cute. Where did Rosa live, who did she go home to? Josie had a feeling that whoever it was, Rosa walked in the door and started in all over again cooking and cleaning.

Nighttime. She and Harvey were left alone. Harvey went out on the front porch probably to moon about Rosa. Josie watched a square of window turn from royal blue to black. It got dark so much earlier now. You went along thinking it was still summer, with acres of daylight. Then you took a look around and here it was September. Josie felt a chill. Time was gathering speed, leaping and bounding along with or without her. Her life and everyone in it going on without her.

She knew now that she wasn't going to embark on any fabulous grand adventure, wasn't going to run away from home any farther than she'd already gone. She was too young, too broke, too chicken. If she had been serious, she would have left right away, vamoosed, not kept hanging around waiting for people to find her and apologize, entreat, arrest, or whatever they were going to do to her. It was time to give it up.

She supposed she'd have to call her mother. Get some assurance she wasn't going to get packed off to some desert juvie prison. Not that Utah was such a bad idea, compared to going back to school and facing everybody's cheap gossip. Her mother was going to put her through hell. Cry at her. Josie would probably cry too, why not. After that, she didn't know. They probably still loved each other because you couldn't help that, but they didn't trust each other. Now that was screwed.

As for Mitchell Crook, she had no idea. She was either going to have to do something truly horrible to him, or else get used to the idea of the two of them walking the same streets, ignoring each other.

Maybe in the morning she'd call her mother. Right now it was too late, and in spite of lying around all day she was tired and she felt too low to decide if calling was a good idea or a bad one. The Weather Channel was still talking about Floyd, which was turning into the world's biggest hurricane, or at least the longest. It seemed like the Floyd show had been on all week. More than fifty people had died. Whole towns were underwater. Floyd was a Category Four hurricane. If you watched enough of the Weather Channel, you learned these things. There was a Hurricane Gert, but she was out in the ocean. Harvey would be the next one, if they didn't run out of hurricanes.

There was some kind of commotion outside. Josie assumed it was the neighbors, who were always carrying on in some excess of good or bad feelings. But then she heard Harvey's voice in the middle of it, stuttering and protesting.

What in the—

Things started happening. The door flew open with a whump and Harvey backed in with this *expression.* Josie said, "Hey—"

She never got the rest of it out. A man's head appeared in the door, with a face that might have been a mask, it was so smudged and wild. She didn't scream until the rest of him was inside and even then it was more of a yelp, just surprised.

Oh, he had a gun. He waved it around in an irritated fashion. Josie was still on the couch, Harvey was flat against the wall. Zero time had elapsed. It was like when you stub your toe and it takes a moment for the pain to travel up your nerves to whatever actually felt it. Waiting for the import of whatever this was to hit.

Then it did, and she screamed again and got her legs moving underneath her but the man with the gun was way ahead of her. He pushed Harvey toward the couch and Harvey fell on top of her.

Harvey's knee was in her face. She said, "Uff," and tried to get untangled, but Harvey was making sounds like he couldn't breathe and the man with the gun was yelling, "Shut up, shut up!" Funny since he was the one making all the noise, not funny, she finally got herself out from under Harvey and tried to see if he was hurt. She realized that she was still screaming and that was why her ears hurt.

"Shut up!" the man yelled again. So she did. Josie and Harvey sat side by side and stared. She had never seen anything like him. He had a misshapen pillar of nappy red-brown hair, a greasy shirt unbuttoned on his dark, greasy chest. His teeth were bared, on display in the middle of his wildman's beard. His eyes strobed. He looked nasty mean. Josie realized she had wet her pants.

Harvey was still clutching on to her, but at least he was breathing again. The front door was still open. The man with the gun didn't seem to notice. He was rubbing at his scalp with the hand that held the gun, like he was scratching an itch with the gun barrel.

Josie cleared her throat. "So what do you . . ." Her voice sounded geeky. "What do you want?"

"I can't sleep!" he shouted.

Josie and Harvey held hands. She was too afraid to look at him, she might even laugh. The sound of the television reached her ears, the jingle for the car dealership you heard fifty times a day, *You've got a fri-e-end at Feeny's.* It had been playing all along. She said, "Well, that must feel terrible. That must—"

"Shut up!"

At least Harvey was quiet, wasn't screeching or blubbering or losing it. She clutched his hand harder to steady him or maybe herself. She had to stop herself from running straight out the door like a deer jumping through a window. Deer did that because they always went toward darkness. Someone had told her that. The door was a perfect dark oblong of night. She would run and run with her heart bursting and then the shot would bring her down, bleeding out in clean snow. Stop that.

The gunman noticed the door then, as if he had heard her thinking. He slammed it shut. "Your money or your life!" he shouted, waving the gun around. Then he stopped and looked confused. None of them seemed to know what to do next.

"We don't have a lot of money," Josie said. "Of course, you're welcome to it." Aiming for a soothing, reasonable tone. "It's in my bag. I forget where I put it. Oh, and I gave my uncle some for groceries. I don't know if there's any change. Probably. Is that thing loaded?"

Then she ran out of everything at once: air, wits, words. It was like exhaling and not breathing in.

The gunman kicked the pile of her clothes and other belongings on the floor next to the couch. A lipstick shot out and rolled lopsidedly across the room. "What money, where's the goddamn money?"

"Oh . . ." Josie had to think. "Over there." He began dumping out her backpack, which was sort of embarrassing, chewing gum and tampons scattering all over the place, not to mention the Kleenex farm she kept in there. Then he found her wallet and instead of opening it like a normal person, he shook it by one corner so that bills and coins sprayed out of it. He was undersize and scrawny, no taller than herself, and if he wasn't armed and crazy there would have been no reason to be afraid of him. She could smell him, a burnt smell, hot and corrosive, like metal with an underlay of stink. Every so often he reached out and clawed at his own skin, his ribs under his shirt or the back of his neck, as if a rash were eating him alive. He stooped to gather up the money, all the while keeping his eyes on the two of them, Josie and Harvey, and showing his teeth as his lip twitched and curled. He was small and itchy and confused, but Josie knew that here was a face you could match to all the meanness of the world, all the newspaper headlines of cruelty and vicious ignorance: the nail bomb piercing the baby's skull, the slaughtered cattle, the beaten child, the poisoned river, the mass grave. All the things you kept in the nightmare part of your brain. The stranger's hands on your skin, your body reduced to its liquid parts.

With an effort she managed to lasso her mind back where it belonged, right here right now, sitting on the couch and holding Harvey's hand. The upholstery was so beaten-down and slick and the springs so overwhelmed that she had to brace herself to keep from jackknifing into the folds of the cushions. Harvey, incredibly, seemed intent on the television, where a happy family, Moms and Pops and Sis and Bobby, basked in the sunshine of full insurance coverage. Then the gunman's strutting legs appeared, blocking the screen. He was screaming something she couldn't understand, like her brain had so many holes in it right now that words slipped through. But no, it was some other language he was being mad in.

Josie managed to shout over him. "Slow down! I can't understand you. U-N-D-E-R-S-T-A-N-D?"

He stopped his noise and gave her the funniest look, like he was the one scared of her, or of something that was sitting right behind her. Then he growled. Actually growled. She'd never heard such a thing before. This guy was stone crazy. The gun flapped around in his hand like a live thing he barely had control of, oh if she was going to be shot let it be for some reason! Not just because all the evil of the world was busting out through the seams. She closed her eyes and waited for what would come next.

In the Red Car

Nobody could catch him because he was moving beyond the speed of superinvisibility. All he had to do was touch his foot to the pedal and he was instantly disappeared. This was on account of electricity, the red electricity of his mind. He was *Porque,* he was *Because.* He carried a universe of boiling possibilities in the box of his skull, he *was* the universe, vast and charged and shooting off sparks in all directions. Even on those occasions when he left the car, no one could see him unless he allowed them to, unless he slowed himself down. Jam those brakes! It amused him when mere people gave him the big-eye stare, or hollered, or wanted to fight. Then he was gone again, zipwhip! like electricity, which could jump in and out of wires whenever it wanted.

It was night. It was always night. Something had happened to day that he couldn't figure out. There would come a time when his mind would be wired hot enough to bring the sun up as easy as one of these fancy push button windows. It was night and the road was dark, with dark air rushing over and around him. Darkness held him so smooth and slick, he hardly felt himself moving. Through the windshield, he saw ropes of greasy lightning drop from the sky. Or no. It was just the hair hanging in his eyes.

He felt silly when he got things mixed up like that. And his hair smelled bad. When he tried to push it aside, his fingers were confused by the woolly feel of it. Now that he was turning into pure brain power, a lot of stupid body stuff wasn't working right. His eyes played tricks on him. His skin crawled with rashes and terrible burning sensations; he rubbed and scratched and scraped like he was a snake trying to shed. Sometimes everything inside him squeezed up tight, and he had to force his breath through the metal in his chest. Sometimes he threw up blood, which was what the electricity looked like when it came out. It was the price he paid for being what he was. The electricity whispered to him that soon he would be able to leave this itchy, funky shell of himself behind and live in his own exalted air.

The road was dark, but the headlights stayed straight. The red car always found the road. He loved this goddamn car. It should have a name, like a horse, Diablo, or maybe just Red. Horses were smart fuckers. Loyal too. When you were wounded, parched with thirst, they nudged you toward the water hole. They rode into battle with you, they made tracks up and down mountains just to reach your side.

And wouldn't you know it, all he had to do was think *horse*, and here one was.

Or at least a picture of one. It was a black horse and it was standing on three legs with the other leg pawing the air and its neck rearing back and its eyes blazing and its whole righteous self ready to kick ass. He supposed it was possible that he was thinking about horses because of the picture, which might have been there all along although he just now noticed. It really didn't matter which, it just went to show you that there was a plan, an enormous, elegant, glittering design in everything he thought and saw and did.

He stopped the car to stare at the horse. The picture was way up in the air, a billboard. It was selling something in a bottle, whiskey maybe. Letters he couldn't read. Reading was one of those things he had decided would take up too much brain space.

Floodlights shone down on the picture. Now that he was out of the car he could see the metal scaffolding that held it up, all looming and dark beyond the circles of light. It stood in a field full of whatever it was that grew in fields. There was a noise teasing his ears, little chips of sound. Ears one more majorly fucked-up body part. But no, it was a real noise, although it took him a moment to put a name to it. Crickets! Such an incredible thing for his mind to provide him with crickets, not to mention this soft night with its swarm of stars overhead, and the amazing horse.

There had to be a way to get up there. He walked around the base of the scaffolding and flexed the muscles of his mind. They'd made it difficult, it was plain they didn't want anybody up there grooving with the horse, but they also had not reckoned with the likes of *Porque.* He took a running start at the metal pole, bounced off, owowowow, tried again, wrapped one arm around the pole and hung there, balanced the tip of the tip of one toe on the smallest bump of metal, not much more than a hinge, holding on, scrabbling around, inching his way up to another toehold. High overhead was the metal grid they must use for a platform, and half a ladder hanging down, just out of reach. He closed his eyes and went for it.

Then he must have hurt his head because a wind was blowing through it and his mind felt quiet. His eyes opened to darkness. He thought he was falling, he flailed and kicked and braced himself for the impact. But he was only sprawled on his knees on the metal platform, his hands wrapped around its edges. Once his eyes cleared, he saw the horse stretched above him, enormous and silent.

Up close like this he could see the glossy paint on the horse's hind legs, its imperfections, the places where the color bled out a little, and from here it was hard to recall that vision of power and beauty that had made him go to all this trouble in the first place.

So he sat on the edge of the platform and let his legs dangle out in the air, and everything below him was small and remote and he felt cold, which surprised him, *cold* not being one of those things he had thought about lately. He had to wonder where in the hell he was. He was riding a paper horse forty feet up in the air, he was in the country of night, he was entirely lost.

If he scootched around on the platform, he could see in all directions. There was a lip of brightness on one horizon, something he connected with possibilities both hopeful and dangerous. Empty paved road below him, crisscrossing with another road some distance ahead, and another road beyond that, and on this farther road a car no larger than a speck was traveling, a grain of light burrowing into darkness. It occurred to him that someone must be driving that car, and maybe they were alone like he was, and at this very moment they might be looking up at him, at the black horse. But could they see him from so far away? He hollered at them—"Hey!"—but the sound fell away into the dead night air. As he watched, the headlights traveled over the edge of the world and vanished.

It was all so quiet. Even the crickets had stopped. He couldn't remember *quiet.* Was it a place you had to go, somewhere he hadn't been in a while, like daytime?

He didn't like the quiet in his head so he started humming, just sounds that came when you pushed your voice through your open mouth. If he didn't keep the electricity going, other things would try and screw with him, and he had forgotten why he was sitting here with his ass hanging out on this dizzy ledge. What was the deal? Too many things too weird. A bad taste was crawling up his throat. The horse was no help. And here he'd had such a good feeling about it. Its mouth opened just wide enough to say, *You fucked up big-time, bato.* Which he knew was the truth, straight from the horse's mouth ha ha. He was pretty sure he had been driving a long time, he thought something must have been chasing him although he couldn't see it now but he tasted it in the back of his throat and the horse said *You are one messed-up moreno.* He looked down at his wrists and hands and yes, it looked black, moreno skin all right, which was probably why it was trying to itch itself off.

The only song he could remember was *Las Mañanitas,* the birthday song, so he sang it loud enough to drown out the horse's sly whisperings and the pictures that came along with the whisperings. Was it his birthday? His birthday was in June July August one of those, it was dangerous to open his mind in that way so anything could get in. But here he was, a child, hardly able to reach the table when he sat at one of the chairs. It was his birthday and he was crying because the cupcakes his mother bought at the store were frosted pink and his brothers were making fun of that. Pink was for fags, he was such a little fag. I am *not,* he said, but he didn't know what a fag was or how not to be one, and he couldn't stop crying. Oh look, fag baby's crying, what a little snot nose. His mother hollered at them and chased them outside to play their swaggering games.

Why did he have to remember anything, why that scrap of himself? It only told him that he had been unhappy. He hummed and sang louder now because the horse was pointing out to him that he was small and ugly and filthy and of no consequence, a moreno fag, an accidental man, a world-class loser, a joke, a fool. Singing, was he? Right now they were making up songs about him, the kind you got a good laugh from. Here they were, a chorus of ghosts. Here was a face the color of bad meat with snakes of yellow hair. Its rotten mouth opened to sing to him, *oh, feliz, feliz cumpleaños, happy happy happy.*

He screamed and held on tight to the metal grid as if a strong wind was trying to blow him off. And indeed, the horse that had turned out not to be his friend after all was telling him he might as well jump. What was the point of sticking around for more of this bad shit? Jump and let the mess inside of his head spill out. But it was only more ghost-talk, designed to make him weak and confused, and he knew where it was coming from so he took the gun and shot the horse four times through its painted eyes.

Then he climbed down the ladder and dangled by one arm until he worked up the nerve to drop to the ground.

Back in the car he felt tired, the way you did after a fight, and he was conscious of all the places in him that had bruised or torn. Why did he have to bust himself up so bad? Was there a way to make the electricity stop or no just for his head not to hurt his life not to run away from him?

He drove toward the lights, which were now close enough to start unraveling into separate lights. He thought there was a good chance that day was in this direction, maybe sleep too, he never slept anymore, unless you considered the times he must have slept as he drove, but he didn't count those because they were not truly restful. And it must have happened again, because one second he was only thinking about this town and what he might find there, food, he hoped, and now here he was admiring the sidewalks and grassy lawns—

and then once again, because the next *instant* a woman was screaming like an alarm, scared the shit out of him, where was he? The racket was so loud he couldn't see. His hands had a grip on something. Cellophane? It made a crinkling noise and damned if it wasn't a package of pink cupcakes. How amazing was that? He broke off a piece of the frosting and put it in his mouth. It tasted pink, it made his tongue curl up all sugar sick. The woman—girl? a girl's face—was hollering "Don't shoot! Don't shoot me!" What a thing to say, she must be some nervous type, until he noticed that he had the cupcakes in one hand, the gun in the other.

Well, maybe he should shoot her. There was no good reason to do so, but there was no good reason not to. The smallest movement or not movement of one finger. How much holy power lived in this one muscle, how easy it was for his enormous brain to direct it one way or the other. Shoot not shoot. It was turning into one of those aggravating things. What was this place anyway? He looked around and saw rows and rows of cellophane food, lots of lights and mirrors and trashy stuff in the aisles and big refrigerator cases full of beer and shit—did he want a beer? No, he wanted orange juice! He didn't see any, so he asked the girl, nicely, he thought, if she would just stop her noise long enough to help him find some. She had short red hair and a sort of piggy face and she was blubbering, squeezing out little tears. It was a simple question, where was the orange juice, didn't she work here, hey! She was deliberately not understanding him or not paying attention.

He got right up next to her with the gun but he'd forgotten the cupcakes, now wasn't that silly, so he shoved them into his mouth one-handed and all that sugar exploded inside him in a wave of shaking energy. His stomach cramped and threads of sugar nerves ran up and down his body. He was going to throw up no yes no. The girl's mouth was open but no sound was coming out because of the roaring in his ears? because she'd used up all her screams? She wasn't pretty, not really, but up closer to her like this his body couldn't help but get the way you did around a woman, which was a different kind of electricity.

She wasn't looking at him. Her eyes were closed and she breathed huff huff huff. Because he felt the need to make conversation he said, "You have pretty hair." It was, it looked like copper feathers. When he reached out to touch it, it sifted through his fingers. Her eyelashes were the same color, little pale spikes. She had drawn blue crayon lines around their edges. All her crying and carrying on had smeared them so they looked, oddly, like an extra pair of eyes.

Just to see what it felt like, he put his hand on her skin where it met the top button of her shirt, wiggled his fingers around underneath. Her skin was cold. He walked his hand down to the cold nipple at the end of her breast then stopped, curious. There was something jumping around under his hand. Her heart trying to squeeze through the skin. He squeezed back. A sound came out of the girl, eeee, like she was one of those toys you had to press in the right spot.

They were standing up and then all of a sudden they were toppling over, knocking down the racks of cigarettes and small things breaking. What the fucking hell? She must have fallen, pulled him down. It took them a long time to get to the floor. She was underneath him and her arms were around his neck which surprised him because she had not seemed like a friendly person and then her eyes inside their ragged blue lines opened.

They were blue too though not as much and they weren't crying now. They blinked once, slowly. She said, "You got to promise not to shoot me."

He searched around in his head for something to say. He didn't even have the gun in his hand anymore, it had landed down somewhere by his foot and he had to kick to reach it.

"Promise. Come on."

He pretended to say something but he was just stalling, because he was worried about the sequence of things you had to do in order to be with a woman in that way, and here he'd thought he was hard but he wasn't anymore, shit! Well that was just great.

"I bet you like scaring people. You do stuff like this a lot? Rob places and stuff? Is it exciting?"

All the while she was talking he kept trying to get a better grip on her, the pillowy parts that yielded to his hands and the unexpected hard parts like her knees. "Hurry up before somebody comes in," she whispered, and what did she think he was trying to do? It was like the thing between his legs had been electrocuted dead. Her face from this close up was pink and bumpy and her nostrils were like caves.

"What's the matter, huh? Are you shy or something? I didn't think you were but maybe you are. What's your name anyway?"

His name was out there somewhere with the rest of him. He was *Porque,* no he was someone else who did not want to be remembered and all he wanted to do now was get loose from her but her hands kept pestering him. The electricity was pouring out of him as sweat—

then the door opened and the girl started up screaming again and he had to dive for the gun and wave it in the face of an old white man with a very surprised look—

then he was back in the car again not driving. The car had brought him on its own to water, a flat gray lake with the sun rising over it. The actual sun. So here's where it had been all along. The sky was gray cloud and the sun behind it was small and red. He was thirsty so he got out and bent down at the edge of the lake to scoop up water with his hands. It tasted gray. He thought he had a fever, he was burning up from the inside. It was burning through his skin, it was making his thing shrivel up not to worry about that now. He just needed sleep. That was the ticket. He could sleep like crazy.

So he got back in the car and reclined the seat and waited, okeydokey for sleep.

It wasn't happening. His eyes were white hot because the sun was burning holes in them. And he couldn't keep his hands from tearing up his skin and he'd hurt his back again and there was fever deep down in his bones where he couldn't scratch. He heard traffic starting up somewhere in the distance. Time was slowing down and moving in an ordinary way just when he would have liked it to speed up and forget a lot of new things like how he had shamed himself with that girl and wasn't even a man anymore. He needed not to be thinking these thoughts hurting these hurts every minute his head was getting fuller and fuller of negative power like electricity gone bad. Was there no place either inside or outside his head that he could go to make it stop?

He gave up on sleep and sat behind the wheel of the car going nowhere. Once he got out and walked along the edge of the lake to stretch his legs but he didn't feel invisible without the darkness. There was a man fishing on the other side of the lake who seemed to be looking straight at him. He thought about going to talk to him, ask him if he'd caught anything, just a friendly conversation, except right then the man packed up and left in a hurry, well screw him.

God, he was hungry. He could eat a fish raw not really. Almost that bad. He found some corn chips on the floor of the backseat and he ate them even all mixed up with backseat fuzz. Then he walked around some more because his bones felt restless and he needed to calm himself because you had to remember the way the plan worked the plan the plan everything in the world fitting together like a great turning wheel that depended on him.

But his eyes still burned like he'd never see sleep again and his head had begun to feel lopsided from thinking too many of the wrong kind of thoughts and he didn't trust this lake. It was too quiet, not even a bubble breaking its surface. Was something hiding down there, holding its breath? Water was always dangerous in that way, it came in under doors and through the cracks in your head, reminding you of things, and if he turned his back to it, would slimy arms reach out to strangle him? Now wasn't that foolish, but just to make sure he waded into the lake and put his head beneath the water to look around.

Everything was murky mud. The light was thick, brown, so he saw only lumps and shadows. Something broke loose and floated past him, which was creepy. You weren't supposed to smell things underwater but he could swear he did, something foul down here that wouldn't let him drown his fever, a floating dead ghost filling his ears with moaning. He panicked and tried to breathe before he remembered that water choked you and he thrashed his way to the surface—

then he was driving in the dark, he was *Porque*, he was and everything else had been a dream. He was just this minute born. He was faster than the eye could imagine and if only he didn't have to keep tearing up his skin so bad his fingernails were bloody, if only he could get a little real sleep, everything would be perfect forever. Here were streets, houses, lights, things he hadn't seen for the longest time. The houses were like enormous toys. Big soft dolls lived inside.

He flickered past them like electricity in a red tube. Here were trees and chimneys and dollhouse lamps. Here was an old man doll, watching him from his front porch. Watching?

Something wrong about that, as if he could be seen. He stopped the car with a lurch, got out and walked on tiptoes, just to make sure, all the way up to where the old man stood. "Can you see me?" he demanded. The old man just yapped and paddled his arms in the air. "Can you see me, huh, answer quick!" Gurgly sounds came from the old man's mouth. Was he the old man from the store? He had the same scared, hollow look about him and was shame going to follow him around forever?

Just in case it was, he said, "You didn't see me there either, understand? And what you thought it was, it wasn't. That girl was too ugly so I changed my mind."

But the old man kept mewling like he didn't believe him or maybe he was trying to give him an argument, which made him so goddamn mad he went chasing after him. Who was some old man to tell him how to get his stuff working right? Like he was supposed to be some expert on taking it out of his pants. He kicked the bastard door and broke his foot, howled and kicked it again just to make it hurt more.

What was the girl doing in here? No, it was a different girl but they'd taken screaming lessons together SHUT UP SHUT UP what was it about these bitches? They were all in on things together, gossiping and making things up and probably the girl in the store had told this one everything just for a laugh SHUT UP.

finally they quit their noise and were just giving him the big-eye stare. He didn't like them doing that either but how to get them to stop? This girl was prettier than the other. Just look at those chiches, the sight of them was enough to get you hard but no he wasn't. What was she, one more bruja trying to mess him over? The old man was talking about rain, floods, storms, what did that have to do with anything? no it was something else, television. The television must be wired up to his brain like a kind of generator. He would have liked to shut it up also but he was too tired and the electricity was leaking out of him in ways it was getting difficult to control. Why couldn't he sleep? He must have forgotten how.

He heard his own voice. It echoed in the air. The two of them were looking at him like he had left something unanswered and then the girl began talking, trying to tell him what to do in her know-it-all voice and why couldn't everybody just SHUT UP. The girl went quiet but her mind was still talking. He could hear it like he heard everything in the world, all the voices that filled his electric head like a cloud of insects swarming around a light. Well of course she wanted to run away, everybody ran from him but he was the one in charge here so he made the door slam BANG and put an end to that.

Except now he could not remember clearly why he was here, which embarrassed him and seemed like the sort of mistake you shouldn't be making at such a time, and since the gun never forgot he held it up and tried to think of some words it might say.

"Your money or your life!"

What were you supposed to do with words anyway? There were so many of them and they piled up one on top of the other so fast that by the time you heard the last one you forgot the first. The girl was talking again, trying to confuse him with words that were meant to coax or tickle or persuade him to do or not do something. Give me all your words no he meant money, he was getting the two of them hopelessly mixed up so he kicked the son of a whore mess at his feet. Nothing in it. "Over there," the girl said, pointing, and when he held up the SHIT what did you call this thing this thing held it up and shook it, words came tumbling out no it was money. Coins spattered across the floor and the bills floated.

He bent down to pick it up and here was that fucking bad luck money, the face on it bearded like a goat, staring him down. The very feel of the paper scalded his hands GODDAMN GOD-DAMN a witch's trick, what were they trying to do, kill him? This girl who was so sneaky, her and every other witch woman who laughed at his shame. Everywhere he went they planted their bad magic. He made the noise in his head come out of his mouth. It felt good to have the stream of noise burning through him, the way vomiting out a sickness could feel good. The noise he made was red like electricity and blood and the mouth of the dead woman, the ghost who kept sending him the bad times.

Then he saw her. It scorched the breath right out of him. She was waving to him from the television with that same slit-eyed look, red smile and yellow hair. Prancing around in a tight red dress and shaking her ass like the whore she was. Somehow she'd gotten better-looking dead, which was just to taunt him. She had followed him all the way here, riding the electricity that he could not shut off. Get out of here, he said uselessly. Her giant head and face filled the screen. Her teeth were as big as piano keys. She laughed and sang a little song. She was pretending to be one of the angel girls, mocking the last pure memory that remained to him. Ohhh, she sang, turning it into something low and nasty, turning her beauty into something rotten dead. He gathered what was left of his courage and showed his own teeth—

and then she was gone and some other shit came on, so quick that he almost mistrusted his eyes but no it had been here, and she could come back anytime to play him, wear him down, steal his sleep, wilt the thing between his legs, burn up his skin. Sleep he could sleep for a week a month a year he was so hollow and fevered. If he could just lay down but not with this girl and this old man watching him. He had almost forgotten them as well as the gun in his hand that said things in its own language.

In his other hand was this pile of of he was determined to get it right money, and the girl was saying, "We seriously don't have a lot of cash. I think you must have the wrong house."

Was she making fun of him? He couldn't tell. She was giving him the big-eye stare but even scared she looked pretty, her face and the way she was put together just right, not too skinny, he didn't like that, he liked to lose his hands in softness. He wanted to explain to her that only out of necessity was he behaving impolitely, because everything was so uncertain, and the girl said, "Just take the money and go, OK? This really isn't good for my uncle, he's old and he's sick and"

He sure was old. And he had spooky eyes that didn't seem to be looking in the same direction they pointed. Which was maybe how he came to see him even when he was invisible except he wasn't anymore. How had that happened? The girl in the store must have stolen that from him along with his manhood BITCH. She'd slowed him down and now he couldn't get going again, not with these two following him with their eyes and their nervous thoughts. He wanted to holler at them and make them stop thinking but just then his insides twisted up on him so bad that he doubled over, his emptiness tying itself in knots and the electricity zooming into his head like it was on an elevator and his brain was the top floor. His mouth shook in an *Ohhh,* an electrocuted angel, and at first he thought he was finally dead but no he was just hungry.

Well, that was a surprise. He wanted to goddamn laugh except it hurt too much. He got himself straightened up and pretended he had just been coughing, because it was foolish, getting yourself so worked up over an ordinary thing like that. "Comida," he said, both by way of explanation and demand, but they just sat there, what was it with them, were they deaf or simple? He said it again, shaking his face in theirs, and when they still didn't understand he ran through the rooms, making them scream and dive behind the furniture and here was the place they kept it but all they had was SHIT little puny odds and ends and he wanted some FOOD, why were they hiding it from him?

The girl said, "If you would just not point that thing at us, OK? You can go buy food or whatever you want, there's nothing stopping you, I promise we won't even tell anybody you were here. In case you're a fugitive or something."

She was peeping over the edge of where they had been sitting except they were mostly on the floor now and the old man had his hands over his ears like he didn't want his thoughts to leak out. "Come on," he told them, sighing, because of course they didn't understand, and he would have yelled some more except what good would it do and also he was afraid he'd fall over from his bunched-up insides. "Come on," he said again, and they didn't want to come on but the gun made them do it as he held his stomach with one arm, out the door and into the night under the swarming stars.

Then he put them in the car because they were damn well going to help him find food and get it right this time. The girl was up front and the old man was in back. He couldn't keep from looking in the mirror to make sure the old man wasn't doing anything tricky. Something about him was hard to figure, the way he kept moving his mouth without anything coming out like he was working spells, the way his eyes wouldn't look at you straight on, and when he tried to read his thoughts there was only a fizzing blankness, like a television screen when the station goes off the air. Then the old man said *I will deliver them out of the hands of the Egyptians,* what was that shit, well, screw him, he wasn't going to worry about some old party. This girl now, he had to say she looked very fine in the front seat of the car. It occurred to him that never before had he possessed a car of his own into which he could put a girl. He liked how her legs stretched a long ways from top to bottom and how her hair caught the light from the streetlamps and just maybe she wouldn't be like all the other bitches in the world although she wasn't looking at him, like she was stuck up or something. So he said, "Nice car, yes?" just to be making conversation and besides it was a very excellent car and he wanted to make sure she was aware of that.

But she only said, "There's a McDonald's up there, is McDonald's all right?" Was he supposed to know what she was talking about? And then his hunger remembered itself to him with another violent squeeze of his midsection, like it was angry he'd forgotten it.

If he didn't get some food into his stomach in the next TEN SECONDS he was going to going to he couldn't think of what new and terrible thing would be bad enough but then the girl said, "Here, right here," and he saw those big yellow shapes lit up in the black sky, *pillar of cloud by day, pillar of fire by night,* the old man's whispery voice talking more shit but no matter because he knew this place meant food.

The girl said, "How about if I go in? That would be the easiest thing, just tell me what you want. You know I'd come right back because of my uncle," and boy she must think he was really dumb. He had the gun lying between them and he gave it a little pat, letting it speak for him. The girl slumped down in her seat and he didn't worry about her but here was a new problem, how to get at the food he knew was inside. There was a way you were supposed to do it but it was like making love to a woman, he might get it wrong in some embarrassing fashion. "Are you going to the drive-through window or what?" the girl asked, and of course that was the deal.

Now he had to concentrate because there were all these people and cars around and he couldn't shoot them all, but when he got up to the place where you told them what you wanted, he couldn't think and the old man was whispering *plague of locusts, plague of boils,* SHUT UP who wanted to hear that shit when they were eating? He didn't care what food they gave him as long as it was NOW and that's when the girl leaned over him to speak into the box. Then she asked him if he was going to pay for the food or just commit armed robbery? He thought she was making fun of him but already they were at the window with a fat man's face leaning out at him wanting money, so he shoved some at him and FINALLY here was food. He tore through the wad of paper and clogged his mouth with hot bread and God he'd forgotten about cheeseburgers but he never would again.

Cars were honking. The fat man in the window was pointing him out to somebody else, what was his fucking problem? He didn't want to stop eating to shoot them so he moved the car to one side and the girl said, "I ordered a lot of stuff so we could have some too since it's like, our money." And because his stomach was now in an agreeable mood, he shoved the paper bag at her and she gave some food to the old man and they all sat there under the yellow lights having themselves a swell little picnic, *a land flowing with milk and honey,* the old man whispered in between mouthfuls and he got that part exactly right.

His stomach felt warm and drowsy, like a purring cat. He bet he could sleep now. Little sleep bubbles were percolating in his blood. He licked the inside of his mouth for the memory of taste. He liked the big yellow arcs overhead. They never changed, they radiated holy peace and love and FOOD. The girl was scrubbing at her fingers with a paper napkin. He approved of her tidiness, he liked that in a girl. The old man in the backseat was rummaging through the bag for the last of the french fry ends. He guessed the guy was all right, for an old party. The three of them could drive around to places together. They could take turns driving. They could eat cheeseburgers. It would be nice to have company for a change. And he wanted to tell them both, the girl especially, that he was not a bad person, or at least he had never intended to do bad things that were not entirely his fault or maybe they were but none of it had been planned, none of it had made him happy. People were meant to be happy, weren't they? Even if they weren't he was going to damn well try because he couldn't think of why except he liked it better, the way he liked food better than no food.

He got the car going again and was only slightly annoyed when other cars were in his way, something that had seldom happened when he was invisible. The girl said, "You can let us off anywhere, we'll walk home. I have an ATM card I can give you. I'll write down the code and you can get, well, it isn't much but . . ." He wasn't listening to her, he figured she just liked to talk, and he was going to have to get used to it if they rode together. He wondered if he could ask her to drive so he could sleep. He wanted to be asleep inside the car with the darkness streaming past and the old man whispering dreams.

First, though, there was the matter of gas for the car, which he had learned must be attended to, and it was simple, you just went to the gas place and gave the car a drink and sometimes people came out and made noise but the gun always shut them up. Here was a place, not too busy, the way he preferred it in order to avoid complications. "Stay put," he told the others. There was still a cheeseburger smell in the car. It was making him yawn. When he got out and leaned against the pump with the hose in his hands, he almost fell asleep. It was lucky the car knew how to do this part and he could just stand here drowsy with the gas rushing smoothly through his fingers.

The old man's head turned toward him behind the glass and his eyes or maybe the glass reflected a chip of light back at him. The old man's mouth was moving as usual with nothing coming out, couldn't he ever talk normal so you could understand him? What the hell was he looking at, something behind him—

then the gas was spraying everywhere because he had it confused with the gun, trying to shoot that evil bad-luck face hanging over him, except it wasn't even money now, it was huge, a giant's face in the sky, swimming in colors to confuse his eyes and where was the damn gun? The gas smell was eating up his nose and the electricity howled through him and the girl was screeching, "What? What? It's a stupid chamber of commerce billboard," no, it was a curse laid on him that he would never sleep, that the food in his belly would turn to boiling stone. There was no escape for him nor any use in running because the ghost would always be a step ahead. He asked the car for one last ride and it carried them away.

Harvey's Catechism

Somehow they'd ended up back inside the house.

Josie despaired; in her mind she had worked it out that once the gunman had whatever he wanted, money or food or enough screaming, he would leave them alone, vanish. Instead it might go on and on and get worse and worse. Where were the police anyway? He'd only committed about ninety-five traffic violations. Mitchell Crook was out here somewhere, as well as the rest of the Springfield cops, and was it too much to hope that someone was looking for her? The gunman was behind the wheel, doing his psycho brooding thing, while Josie tried to think of what she would do if she was in a movie. Grab the wheel and steer the car off a cliff, if they had such things as cliffs in Springfield. But since they didn't, she could only sit there like a twerp. An idiotic random act of violence. That's what this was. All those times she had done wild and stupid things, practically begged for disaster, and nothing had happened. Now this. She hated being an innocent bystander. It was so insipid.

"Look," she said, "just take us back to my uncle's house, let us go, no hard feelings, OK?" Because they were in fact only a few blocks away, and he seemed to be listening to her as she gave him directions. He pulled up in front of the house and her heart was like a bird struggling to break loose from a trap, almost free. "Come on, Harvey," keeping her voice light and calm, she hoped, waiting for Harvey to fumble himself forward in the seat; once they were out of the car they would be safe.

But just as she set foot on the sidewalk, the gunman was at her side, muttering and herding her with the gun, Harvey too, all of them shuffling up the walkway and nothing was over yet.

Inside, something seemed to set him off again. He raged and stomped through the rooms, scratched up bloody welts on his arms, made them turn out the lights and lock the doors and windows. Lucky for Harvey, he left the television on. Josie decided that even if she got shot for it she was going to change her wet pants, such a nasty feeling, and scuttled into the bathroom. When she came out she asked the gunman, "Would you like some ice cream?" Thinking she could get on his good side. If he actually had one. He only snarled. He looked like he hadn't been eating regularly for about five years, which was probably the last time he'd seen the inside of a bathtub.

She and Harvey sat on the couch, as before, while Mr. Nasty kept lifting the corners of the window shades, all freaky nervous. What was he so afraid of, what was out there that was worse than his own horrible self? Now he was carrying on in whatever language it was he used for the purposes of insanity, was it Spanish? Earlier in the summer they had finally caught the infamous Railroad Killer, the Mexican man who had traveled the country murdering people near train tracks. At least they said they'd caught him but what if they hadn't, or if there was more than one of them? You could practically *see* railroad tracks from the back porch.

It got late, and later. Midnight. Josie was in some beaten-down state of mind, too tired and numb to care very much what might happen next. At least Harvey, now that he was back in his old spot on the couch, seemed fine. The blue reflected light of the television made him glow, and Josie thought, with a kind of holy exhaustion, that she loved him, and if she died before morning she would do so with love in her heart. Anyone might walk into Harvey's house, into his life, and take up residence there, herself, Rosa, or a madman, and he let them. He had no more self-importance than a trout in a stream. If only you could empty yourself of yourself. You got too full silly that was so tired.

She kept dozing off and jerking awake, dry-mouthed, to find Harvey pitched sideways and snoring next to her, the Weather Channel's tiny voice droning on, and the gunman staring her down from his perch on the windowsill. Josie always pretended she was still asleep, but she had the uneasy feeling that he knew she was awake, and that he knew she knew he did. It made her cold afraid. What would it be like to be dead? Would it be anything? Did it hurt?

Toward dawn she must have slept more soundly, because the next time she woke she felt almost rested. The first thing she saw was an enormous field of white cloud, shaped like a saucer. It took her a moment to realize it was on television. The cloud was circling around itself, slowly, it seemed, although Josie knew it was actually moving at terrific speed. Ridges, arms, spirals of cloud, hundreds of miles wide. The sky around it serene and sun-drenched blue. It was a hurricane the way no one ever saw it, from above.

The top of her head must have unhinged because the sight of it was pouring straight into her brain. It was so beautiful. It was where she wanted to be right now. Above all the weather and the mess of thinking and being scared.

The next minute it was gone and there was a commercial for of all things Taco Bell. The sun on the drawn shades filled the room with somber light. Harvey began to stir. She hadn't seen the gunman move, but somehow he'd wrapped himself in the curtains, twisted them like they were a rope ladder he was trying to climb.

Josie asked, "Would it be all right if I got up to make some coffee? Coff-ee? You want some?"

He showed her his teeth, but he didn't seem to mind her being in the kitchen. Josie put food down for Fat Cat, although she hadn't seen it since last night. Maybe it was smart enough to be hiding. She started the coffee and made a plate of toast and strawberry jam. When she offered it to the gunman, he grabbed the plate and stuffed all four slices into his mouth. "Sure, go ahead, I can make more." She was encouraged that he was doing something as normal as eating breakfast, although she'd seen dogs with better manners.

She made another batch of toast for herself and Harvey, then brought the coffee out in mugs. The gunman watched her, his face a shadowy blur. Lord, but he smelled. "Coffee," she said, holding one out to him, aware that she was being a brave, plucky girl. "This is black, but if you want milk or—"

He knocked it out of her hand and Josie screamed as the coffee burned her throat and arm. It hurt like sin. The mug rolled away at her feet. She crumpled onto the couch. He aimed the gun at the mug, like nothing was broken enough to suit him, and pulled the trigger three times. Harvey had his hands over his ears. The mug was all lumps and powder. Smithereens. A silly word. The skin on her arm was reddening, beginning to blister along one edge. Her throat was probably just as bad. She wondered if she would live long enough to have scars.

Her ears were still hollow from the noise of the gun. Other people must have heard it too. They would call the police. Mitchell Crook would show up and finally do something brave.

She wanted some ice for the burns but she didn't dare move. Where were the police? The phone rang and he swore and knocked it over and it made a dull, metallic sound and landed on the floor belly-up like a dead animal. The police kept not coming.

What was the matter with the neighbors? She hated them. They were selfish, stupid people. She hated them sincerely and with conviction. The gunman was reloading. Harvey said, "Daddy had his pecker out."

What? Josie moaned. Her arm hurt. She could see the muzzle of the gun, the small black hole that could fit so much death in it. Harvey said, "It was all red and skinned-looking."

"Harvey, not now."

The muzzle of the gun drifted down, away from her line of sight.

"Daddy said kneel and pray."

Josie moaned again. She was through being brave, she only wanted to hide and shut her eyes against death. What was Harvey talking about anyway, if she heard one more crazy thing she was going to jump out of herself like a jack-in-the-box. On the Weather Channel, trees were whipsawing back and forth in the wind, which was probably howling but you couldn't tell.

"Down in the cellar with his shirttail out."

Josie saw Fat Cat behind the gunman, yellow eyes taking everything in. All he'd have to do was turn to see it.

"Daddy was mean."

"Harvey, shh." The cat's tail whisked around the corner, disappearing into the bedroom.

The gun dangled from his wrist. The curtain, torn loose, was wrapped around him like a cape, like he was some demented superhero. "Bang bang," he said.

Was he making a joke? He was grinning, as if he had said something very funny. Josie nodded and tried to smile. He strutted around looking pleased with himself. At least he wasn't shooting anything. Her arm still hurt but she was getting used to it, the way she guessed you could get used to anything, because you didn't have a choice. He laughed and said something in Spanish.

"Who are you anyway?" she asked wearily. "Are you the Railroad . . . Are you from around here?"

More Spanish. Oh God, Rosa. Josie hadn't even thought of her, but what if she showed up? Walked in expecting nothing worse than dirty dishes and instead had to clean up their dead bodies? Maybe she wasn't coming. It was getting later minute by minute, she could tell from the pinholes in the shades that let in sunlight. Minute by minute. That was how you got through things like this. Shut down your mind. Let thought in a pinhole at a time.

Harvey was quiet, tired, probably. Josie worried that he wouldn't be able to take much more of this. All the hinges of her body ached. She got to go to the bathroom, finally. Her throat wasn't as bad as she'd feared, but the rest of her was all pasty and hollow-eyed. She looked like a refugee.

Just as she was flushing, the door creaked open and the gunman put one eye up to the gap. Josie screamed. He made a kissing noise, then closed the door again.

If he touched her, she would find some way to kill him.

The bathroom window was too small to climb out of. It held a rectangle of the perfectly normal world, the back fence and the orange trumpet vine and honeysuckle that grew so heavy they were pulling down the boards. If she got through this alive, she was going to go out there and smell that honeysuckle, hug that fence, splinters and all.

Later Josie had fallen back asleep, or what passed for sleep, when somebody knocked on the front door. The gunman was coming back in from the kitchen, his mouth filled with more bread. Another knock, and a hand trying the knob.

Rosa? The police? She couldn't think. The gunman froze. His eyes were all red and cracked from not sleeping and whatever else was wrong with him. The half-chewed bread bulged from his mouth. Another knock. Josie held on to Harvey's shoulders and waited for the shooting to begin but it never did and the knocking stopped. Whoever it was had gone away. The gunman hissed and cursed and Josie understood that he was afraid. And that he was no longer here because he wanted something, like money, which they might have been able to give him. Now he was simply hiding.

Toward evening Josie tried talking to him again. "If you want to, you can lie down in the bedroom. Give it a try. You know, sleep." She wasn't sure he understood her. He had found Harvey's collection of dull knives in the kitchen and was attempting, disquietingly, to sharpen the largest one on his leather belt. Josie put her palms together and rested her head on them, pillow-style. "Sleep."

"No sleep," he said, not looking up from his work with the knife. He spit on the leather and drew the blade across it.

"Why not?"

"Because," he said. A snarl of an answer. His hands were shaking. The whites of his eyes looked ready to sizzle.

Harvey tugged at her sleeve. "Is he staying?"

"I guess so."

"He should put that thing down."

"Yes, he probably should."

"He makes a lot of racket."

At least the gunman didn't seem to be paying much attention to them. "That's because he's . . . Look, Harvey, there's more hurricane on."

But Harvey didn't want to let it go, as if he'd been working up a head of steam all this while. "Is he a communist?"

Oh Harvey. "I don't know, honey. I suppose he could be. Don't be scared, OK? We're going to be fine."

"Why are people bad?"

"That's a very good question. I don't know the answer."

"Is he bad?"

"Well, he's acting bad."

"Does everybody die? Good and bad?"

"Yes," Josie said. "But people don't like to talk about it."

"No talking alking alking."

"Nobody's going to die here, Harvey." The kind of thing chumps like her said as their famous last words.

"Does everybody have a mortal soul?"

Where was he getting all this? "I can't say, Harvey. If I knew, I would tell you. I think we should just be quiet now."

"If Daddy does, then I don't want one."

"Shh."

This night was worse than the last one because the gunman kept up a steady muttering noise so that even when she did manage to sleep, her dreams had a crazy soundtrack, a voice whispering unintelligible words in the language of malice. And she started to itch. It was so embarrassing. She wondered if she'd caught the gunman's cooties, or if it had something to do with wearing the same clothes for two days. All the tender places, behind her knees and elbows, under her arms, crotch territory, developed excruciating sensations that could only be soothed by digging in with her fingernails. Her mother always said that was how scratches got infected. Her mother was telling her to get up, she was late for something, school, probably. Josie tried to pry her eyes unstuck. Because her hair needed washing, it hung over her face and she could smell its muskiness, which was so gross. She swam her way out of sleep, already scratching her scalp. The gunman was sitting on the floor with his back to the wall. He had the knife in one hand and the gun in the other. Every time Josie opened her eyes he was planted there, his voice turned down low like the television volume. Harvey's knees dug into her back. There was no way to get comfortable. She knew every torture spot on this couch, every place the bare bones of the frame poked through the upholstery. Josie dreamed that the Weather Channel was broadcasting in Spanish. Now that is strange, she told herself in her dream, and then she woke up.

It was morning, bright day. The gunman was asleep. It took her a minute of staring at him to realize this. His mouth was open; his tongue gleamed wetly. His hands were still curled around his weapons.

Josie couldn't move. She was only a few feet away from him. Harvey was gone. His spot on the couch sagged empty. Had he escaped? Gotten out the back door? Josie moved her neck in a narrow arc. No sign of him. And just as she was beginning to test the springs of the couch, negotiate how much of her weight she could shift before they creaked, she saw the shadow behind her. Harvey crept in from the kitchen, holding Rosa's favorite coated aluminum frying pan with both hands, like a club.

There was just enough time for Josie and Harvey to look at each other, and for Josie to shape her mouth into a silent question. The gunman stirred and Harvey brought the frying pan down on his head, WHUMPCRUNCH.

They stood over him. He looked like nothing so much as a heap of dirty laundry. Josie couldn't decide if she was afraid he was dead or afraid he wasn't. She kicked the knife away from him and his hands twitched. "Get his gun, get his gun!"

Harvey held it all wrong, by the barrel. "Careful," warned Josie.

"Ain't scaird."

The gunman flopped over to one side and moaned and Josie dived for the frying pan; it seemed an easier weapon than the others. "Come on, Harvey."

She grabbed his hand and pulled him toward the front door. But stopped short when someone began pounding on it. "Who's there?" she cried.

"Mr. Sloan?" A man's voice. Polite, or pretending to be. "Mr. Harvey Sloan?"

"Who is it?"

"We just want to talk to Mr. Sloan."

"Who's we?"

"Is Mr. Sloan there?" A little less polite. The doorknob turned, then the lock caught.

Josie led Harvey back to the couch, signed him to be quiet, and stepped over the gunman, who was still feebly twitching, to raise a corner of the window shade. Three men stood on the front porch, two of them state troopers in brown uniforms and Smokey bear hats. The third a civilian, in shirtsleeves. Although the window was shut, she could tell they were conferring, debating.

" . . . door," said one of the troopers, but the civilian shook his head. "Let me . . ."

"Mr. Sloan?" Different voice, chummier, professionally friendly. "My name's Randy. How are you today?"

Josie and Harvey looked at each other. Harvey whispered, "Do I have to tell him?"

"Mr. Sloan, how about you come for a ride with us? Frank sent us. What do you say?"

Her bastard father. He'd really gone and done it.

"Mr. Sloan?" The first voice. "We've got a court order here."

The gunman was attempting to get to his knees. Josie hit him with the frying pan, one-handed, and he went down again. It was like stepping on a particularly large bug when you could feel the shell crack. Then she screamed, convincingly, she hoped. "Don't come in here! He's got a gun!"

Law Enforcement

Elaine flew. Got herself to Harvey's in nanoseconds. There was already a squad car blocking traffic, and two more pulled up across the street from the house. Frank was there, surrounded by walkie-talkies and flashing lights. Harvey's place looked as fusty and tranquil as it always did. The shades were drawn. The elm tree in the front yard sent a stray brown leaf drifting to the ground. It seemed to be the only quiet place in the carnival of police and excited neighbor children. Frank saw Elaine coming toward him and met her eye without stopping the sour conversation he was having with some police type. She had to wait on the edge of the milling group until he was finished talking.

"What in the world is going on?"

The police type started in explaining, but Frank waved him off. "I got it, Joe." He steered Elaine a few steps down the sidewalk. "Look, it's going to be all right."

"Where's Josie?"

"Inside with Harvey. I'm sure she's fine. OK, it's like this. When my team got here—"

"Team? Please."

"You want to hear this or not? I told you he was going into the hospital today. They were supposed to do intake, evaluation, physical, the works. It's all legal. I got a judge to go for it."

"Legal. Try screwed-up."

"Well, how was I supposed to know he'd flip out? He's got himself and Josie locked inside, and he won't open the door."

"How do you know it's Josie, did you talk to her?"

"The phone's not working. But she came to the window and waved."

Waved? "What is she doing there in the first place?"

Frank shrugged. "Hiding from you, I guess." He was dressed for the office, freshly shaven and smelling powerfully of premium aftershave. Elaine was wearing the pants and shirt she'd had on yesterday. She didn't feel well-groomed enough to say hurtful things back at him.

"I want to see her."

"Well, you can't yet. Nobody's getting in. We're waiting for the negotiators."

"Negotiators," Elaine echoed. "Don't tell me they really do that."

"Yeah, I guess it's standard in a hostage situation. I've been talking to these guys; it's actually pretty interesting. They have a procedures manual, training film. Impressive." Frank nodded. He wasn't trying to be crass. He just was.

"I want to know what they're going to do," she said, keeping her voice stern. She was determined not to cry in front of him and give him one more reason not to take her seriously.

"Make sure nobody gets hurt. Address his demands."

"What demands? What do you think this is, one of your action movies? Harvey just wants to be left alone. He wouldn't hurt anybody. Especially not Josie."

"Then what's this gun business?"

"I don't know." Elaine, exasperated, turned back toward the house. "These people should all just go away, they're making everything worse. Let me see Harvey for five minutes. I guarantee I'll talk some sense into him. Josie too. After I strangle her."

"Getting hysterical doesn't help anything."

"I am not hysterical. I'm emotional. It's an appropriate response."

The police had come up with a bullhorn and were taking turns talking through it, testing one two three, one two three. At least they'd stopped short of a SWAT team. Elaine didn't like the enthusiastic way they were pitching. in. A chance to practice procedures. She kept waiting for someone to realize how ridiculous it all was. This was Harvey, for God's sake. A slingshot was enough firepower to deal with him.

Elaine recognized the young, glum policeman who had come to the house, even though he was out of uniform. He stood under a tree, talking to another cop. She walked away from Frank and approached him. "Hello again," she said. She realized that she had forgotten his name. "What a big production," she said idiotically.

He turned toward her, his face puckering into a frown. "Oh, hi." The other officer excused himself, giving Elaine a brief, noncommittal look that nevertheless made her feel he knew exactly who she was. Frank had probably made a general announcement. Expect my hysterical pushy ex-wife to show up at some point.

She was being paranoid. Although now that they were alone, the young man seemed reluctant or embarrassed to be seen with her, as if without his uniform he didn't quite know how to behave. Still, she didn't want to go running after Frank just yet, so she said, "Maybe you heard. My daughter's in that house."

"Yes ma'am. They told me."

"She turns up right in the middle of a huge mess. Typical. I don't really mean that. I'm just so worried."

"Of course, ma'am. It's a serious situation."

"I wonder if she can see me. I wonder if she's watching right now." Elaine shaded her eyes and looked down the street. "Maybe

I should hold up a sign or something." She was talking too much, like always.

"That's what they use the bullhorn for, ma'am. Communicating with the subject."

"Oh. Sure." He looked as if he was about to bolt, so she said, quickly, "I'm afraid somebody's going to get all Ramboed up and do something that'll only make everything worse. Harvey, the old man who lives there, is not . . . dangerous. He's the most undangerous guy in the world. Can you help me make them understand that?"

It was hard to tell if she was making any headway with him. He was handsome in an almost cartoon fashion, all jaw and eyebrows. They hadn't drawn in enough lines, his face wasn't capable of doing certain things. "Please." Elaine said. "If there's anything you can do." Wondering if she could get her crusted eyelashes to flutter appealingly.

"I could go in as part of a hostage exchange. Me for your daughter." She's not really a hostage, Elaine wanted to tell him, but he was already squaring his shoulders and looking resolute, obviously taken with the idea. "Well, if you think that would work," she murmured.

"We'll need to establish communications first. Gain his trust. Set up some ground rules."

"You really don't have to . . ."

"I feel it's my duty, ma'am. Following through on the case."

He did seem energized by his own words. Elaine had to admire his nearly classic profile. He could be on one of those television shows featuring Hollywood policemen.

"I'll go talk to my lieutenant," he told her, and Elaine thanked him, then promptly forgot about him. She stood by herself beneath the tree. It was one of those maples that turned so gold you wanted to put a leaf in your mouth. The sky was blue enamel and the sun was bright. Entirely the wrong kind of weather for guns and cops.

Two little boys on bicycles rode up and skidded to a stop, making sound effects as if they were . . . eighteen-wheelers? Urban desperadoes? She had no idea what little boys pretended to be these days. One of them said, "They gone shoot that ol man. Boom-o." More sound effects.

"Nobody's going to shoot anyone," Elaine told them. "That's just foolish talk."

"We got this machine gun at our house," offered the other boy.

Elaine said that she hoped he didn't really.

"Big ol machine gun. Supersonic laser death ray."

"You so full of it."

"Shup, man."

"Shouldn't you be in school?" Elaine asked.

"Naw, it's a teacher day," said the older boy, who looked to be around eight or nine. Elaine thought she recognized them as part of the family who lived across the street from Harvey. "We goin to Super-K with my mamma. When they shoot that man so she can drive us."

"I wish you'd stop saying that."

"They been shootin over there already."

"What are you talking about?"

But the boys were already darting off on their bikes, as quick as dragonflies, calling to each other in their high, excited voices. The police were clearing people away and stretching yellow plastic tape around trees. Elaine looked for Frank and found him huddled with his new police buddies. "I want to talk to Josie."

Frank intercepted her. "Let's just let the professionals handle it, shall we?"

"What is the matter with you that you're not worried about her?"

"Just because I'm not jumping up and down and screaming doesn't mean I'm not concerned."

"We don't need the police here. Especially not a lot of police. They're going to overreact, somebody's going to get hurt."

"Elaine, they're going to make certain tactical decisions. They've got it under control, OK? Sometimes I think you just like worrying."

She could have smacked him. Him and every other man you were supposed to believe when they told you not to worry about the world they were in charge of. Don't worry about the DDT, the Agent Orange, the acceptable levels of strontium 90 in milk. The oil pipeline that would never rupture in the caribou breeding ground. The aging jetliner that was perfectly safe right up until the moment it went cartwheeling down the runway in flaming chunks. You couldn't tell them anything because nothing bad had happened yet and when it did it was probably your fault anyway. The child wasn't hurt, he was only crying because he was spoiled, and why were you making such a big deal out of a little blood, or a cough, or a rash, or a touch of food poisoning? What was it about men that they marched straight into disasters they swore would never happen, invincible in their arrogance? They needed women around so that they could make fun of them for reflecting their own fears.

She said, "Frank, I think you should leave me alone right now," and there was something in her tone that made him turn without argument and walk away.

There were more people than ever on the street, in spite of the police trying to shoo them off. Everyone in the neighborhood with nothing better to do seemed to be congregating behind the yellow tape, even though most of them had no idea what the excitement was about. A few had even brought lawn chairs and were setting them up on the grass as if they were watching a parade. Elaine was startled to see Rosa there, a small figure pressed up against the tape by the herd of larger bodies.

"Rosa!" Elaine waved and headed toward her, and just then one of the police officers appeared in her path, telling her she was going to have to clear the area. "I want to talk to whoever's in charge," Elaine said. "I need that woman to come too. And you can stop calling me 'ma'am,' I've got a name."

It took a little while for Elaine to argue him aside, then Rosa was escorted from behind the tape. There was some commotion; another, younger woman ducked under the tape and began protesting. Elaine hurried over. She must think Rosa was being arrested or deported or something.

It's OK, it's OK, she told them. *Está bien.* The younger one spoke English. Rosa's granddaughter. Her name was Lorena and she was small and bright brown like Rosa and she had a pretty, scared, indignant face. "Can you help us?" Elaine asked them. "Come with me."

It seemed that Rosa had been here earlier, trying to get into Harvey's, had become alarmed at all the commotion, and had gone home to bring Lorena back with her. "Good, good," murmured Elaine. She steered them over to where Frank and the police lieutenant were conferring. "This is Harvey's friend," she told them. "She can talk to him."

They were not persuaded. They weren't men who were inclined to take Mexican cleaning ladies seriously. Rosa kept a firm grip on her big embroidered purse. She looked a little frightened, but determined to hold her ground, and every so often she whispered urgently to Lorena. Frank said, "This is a joke, right?"

"Who do you think he's going to listen to, you?"

"I didn't know Harvey spoke Spanish."

Elaine gave him a hateful look. "They're close," she told him. "They have a rapport, they communicate. Nothing you'd understand."

The lieutenant had heard about enough. "Folks, I need you to step back and let us do our job. For your own safety. I'll let you know if you can assist." They were left by themselves, off to one side behind the protective barrier of a police van. Its doors were open and Elaine regarded the jumble of baleful-looking gear—helmets, vests, plastic shields, batons—on its floor. At least she didn't see anything like tear gas, although she supposed they had that somewhere.

"Tell me she's going to be all right," Elaine said to Frank.

"I've been telling you that all along."

"Convince me."

Lorena touched Elaine's elbow. "Maybe we shouldn't have come."

She wasn't that much older than Josie, and she was dressed as Josie might be if she had more flair for jewelry: black jeans and a pink tank top with a collection of thin gold necklaces and three jeweled studs outlining the curve of her pretty ear. She had a trace of an accent that tilted her i's into e's and was serious about r's. Elaine said, "No, I'm glad you're here. I want you to ask your grandmother if she knows anything about a gun in the house, if she ever saw such a thing."

The Spanish word for gun, Elaine gathered, was *pistola*. Rosa went on for some time. Lorena translated. "She says your uncle is a gentleman and an honest person and he would not hurt even an insect with a gun. And if she herself had a gun, she would use it to shoot his enemies."

Frank and Elaine looked at each other and shrugged. Something lost in the translation. Elaine said, "Please tell her she's done a terrific job taking care of the house. We really appreciate it."

Frank walked away, bored by such domestic matters. Lorena conveyed the message, then told Elaine, "Yeah, she's nuts about clean. Her and my mom both. You can't walk across a floor without one of them tracking you with a broom. You should see our house. Between the two of them, they keep it so clean it hurts your eyes."

"She's very thorough," Elaine offered.

"We're always telling her, slow down, take it easy. But she says she likes working. She's so stubborn, she's like a truck, you see her coming you better get out of the way." She patted Rosa's arm. "So what's happening, why are all the police here?"

Elaine said that her daughter was inside, without going into the messy details of Josie's situation. And that her uncle needed a cataract operation but he was afraid to have it. There had been a misunderstanding. Things had gotten way out of hand. It was all because they were concerned he could no longer take care of himself. "He's been on his own for so long," Elaine said vaguely, feeling, as usual, guilty. Lorena, with three generations under one roof, would think all their arrangements especially coldhearted. "But sometimes, when people get older, the best place for them is . . ." She trailed off. "The dementia ward of a nursing home" wasn't something she wanted in her mouth just now.

Lorena spoke to Rosa again and conveyed Rosa's response. "She says your uncle needs new eyes and your daughter needs a new heart because she is sick with love. And that she has been saying special prayers for them and soon they will be answered."

"Well, that's nice of her." Elaine was unsure of the etiquette of thanking people for prayers. "But what does she know about my daughter?"

Another conference. Lorena shook her head. "She won't tell, she just says she has received signs of good luck. She's superstitious like that, all the old people are. They all believe in fortune-telling and blood-sucking ghosts and the Virgin appearing in your dreams. I don't even try to make sense of it."

"Excuse me, ladies." One of the policemen got into the driver's seat of the van and spoke into the radio, his voice too low to make out. When he was finished, the bullhorn was left behind on the dashboard. It was white plastic, sleek and functional. It always amazed Elaine to realize there must be companies out there in the business of making things you never thought about. She reached into the van for it and held it up to her ear, as if it were a shell and you could hear the ocean, as if all the things she ought to say to Josie were somewhere inside. Then, embarrassed, she set it down again.

"My grandmother wants to know what that is."

"It's like a loudspeaker, they'll use it to talk to the people in the house."

"That's what I told her. She wants to know 'if it makes your voice important.' Don't ask me."

"I suppose you could say that."

Lorena said, "They're probably scared to come out now. I would be, with all these people."

"Harvey's really not used to crowds." The house was still as silent as a closed mouth. If there were any signs of good fortune, she couldn't read them. She turned back to Lorena and, reduced to small talk, asked, "Are you in school? Working?"

"I go part-time at the U. And I work at County Market."

"Oh, what are you studying?"

"Advertising. I figure it's creative and you can still earn a living. Is your daughter in college?"

"She still has a year of high school." Elaine wondered what Josie wanted to study, or do, or be. She had no real idea.

"Actually I'm in general business right now. Later you get to sign up for the advanced courses. I'm taking marketing, finance, your basic money-grubbing."

"I'm in retail myself. It's not the easiest way to earn a living."

"Neither is cleaning other people's houses."

"Of course. I'm sorry."

"You don't have to be sorry. It's just the way it is. My grand-mother had eight children. My mother had five. I don't have any yet. I guess that's progress."

Elaine opened her mouth to ask some other question and kept it open. Rosa, who had been standing right next to them, was now across the street. She passed over the neighbor's lawn, not running, but moving with purpose. She still carried her embroi-dered purse, and in the other hand, the bullhorn.

No one seemed to see her until that very moment. The police were shouting at her, and at one another, and while they were trying to decide what to do, run after her or open fire, Harvey's front door was opened by someone invisible. Rosa stepped in-side, and the door closed again.

Lorena said, "Oh my God. Tell me she didn't do that."

Frank was trying to get Elaine's attention from down the street, mouthing something she was sure she would rather not under-stand. She turned away hastily. "I hope they have another one of those bullhorn things."

Now the waiting had a different, more uncertain quality. The police appeared to be stalled. No one was talking about hostage exchanges or anything else. One of the local television stations had dispatched a camera crew, which set up its equipment and busied itself with filming all the things that weren't happening. Some of the crowd drifted away. Elaine wondered if it might be possible for her to leave and find a bathroom, and maybe a cup of coffee. Lorena had already gone to call her mother. Was it good or bad fortune that Rosa was now inside? A portent, an answered prayer? A wrench in the works? Or just another permutation in the infinite sequence of repeating combinations, resulting in the formation of a new, previously unimaginable but mathematically predictable snowflake?

Harvey's front door opened a crack. Look, the first ones to notice it said. Look, and all the permutations of Look, until the air was full of them. The police walkie-talkies crackled. In a panic, Elaine craned her neck, trying to see if they were ordering some sort of charge, or worse. She caught sight of the young, absurdly handsome policeman standing off by himself, his gaze, like everyone else's, forming a plumb line to the front door, his expression . . . It was so strange. She knew the name for it. Sick with love. No way. Her brain was trying very hard to shut out what her eyes were telling her. No way in the—

At that moment Harvey took half a step through the open door, blinking in the strong sun, his tufts of white hair as untidy as molting feathers, half of him still in shadows. He turned as if to talk with someone behind him, unseen in the dim passageway. Then he raised the bullhorn to his mouth.

"DADDY HAD HIS PECKER OUT!"

No one was certain they had heard it. Then they were certain they had.

Their voices rushed to fill the silence like water finding a hole dug in beach sand.

Josie Becomes Famous

There was a frying pan in her hand, and the hand was fisted around it. Now wasn't that totally stupid. Oh, what had she done? Gone and opened her big mouth. Out on the front porch there was the sound of feet shifting uncertainly. Nothing to do but follow through. Josie screamed again. She was getting good at it. "He says beat it, go away, or somebody's going to get hurt!"

They beat it. Got in their car and pulled out, fast. But they stopped at the end of the block. Josie watched them through the chink in the window shade, her small flare of courage sputtering out. She had a bad feeling that things were only just beginning.

Harvey was still hanging on to the gun by its barrel, puzzling over it. "Here, you better let me have that." It felt heavy in her hand, slick and cold and heavy. The man on the floor coughed and moaned. She wondered if there were any bullets left. She wondered if she could shoot him if she had to. Yes, she decided. She could shoot anybody if they were going to hurt Harvey.

"We should tie him up," Josie whispered. Why was she whispering? She shook her head and tried to get her numb self in gear. The frying pan had a clot of red-brown hair stuck to its bottom edge; she dropped it hastily. "I'll take care of him, why don't you go lie down? I bet you're exhausted."

"He sure is a noisy noise."

"Well, he's quiet now."

"I whupped him."

"You sure did. You did great."

"I can whup the whole army."

"Who put a nickel in you? Go lie down, try to sleep." She watched him shuffle off. They wanted to take him off to some kind of Happy Home.

They might as well be sending a dogcatcher out after a stray.

Like it was supposed to be so easy to tie somebody up. There wasn't any rope, but Josie found a belt on Harvey's bathrobe and an extension cord. She was squeamish about touching him. He smelled like an empty chicken package left too long in the garbage. And what if he was only pretending to be knocked out, then he jumped up and grabbed her, like in a horror movie where nobody was ever really dead? She nudged him with her toe. His chest felt hollow, his ribs like twigs. Once, when she was younger, they'd had a cat who killed birds in the yard. Sometimes Josie had to pick them up and put them in the trash. It was the same fluttery-sick feeling of touching something smashed and unclean. Plus she had no idea about the knots, how to do anything fancy. But she got his hands tied behind his back and trussed his hideous feet together.

He groaned again. He was coming around. Josie scrambled to put the couch between them. Raspy phlegm sounds, breath fighting its way through slag. She hadn't tied him up so he'd choke, had she? His eyes opened and he squinted at her upside-down.

"Who . . ." His tongue seemed swollen. "Who are you?"

"Me? That's a good one. Who the hell are you?"

He wriggled against the cords; she was pleased to see that they held. "Shit, why you tie me up?"

"Duh! Because you were trying to kill us!"

"I never did nothing to you, turn me loose, you crazy?"

Josie waved the gun at him and he squawked and flopped.

"See? You don't like it much when people do it to you." She heard something outside and crossed to the window. Two police cars converged and the officers, neither of whom was Mitchell Crook, got out and hitched up their pants and rubbed their chins, talking. She wished she could just roll this guy out onto the front porch. Here, take him, will he do?

He managed to raise his head so he could look at her right-side-up. "I swear, I never seen you before in my life."

"Oh, right, who was that running around here, your evil twin?"

"Run around where, where am I?"

"This is my uncle's house, he lives here. He's trying to sleep, so keep it down."

He was quiet for a moment. Then he said, in a smaller voice, "Yeah, but where? This place have a name?"

"Springfield, Illinois. United States of America. Planet Earth. Ring a bell?"

"You're shittin me."

"I don't think so."

"Is Illi . . . noy near Detroit, Chicago, one of those places?"

"Chicago's *in* Illinois, but Springfield's the capital." Like he would care. She watched him narrowly. He was a lot calmer. They were even having a conversation, sort of, something that had not happened before now. Was it some kind of trick? "Where did you think you were, huh?"

"Din't know where I am."

"Well why not?" Josie asked reasonably. "Where did you come from?"

He muttered something. "I can't hear you."

"L.A."

"L.A., California?"

"Ya."

"You weren't watching the road signs?"

"Don remember." Very small.

She was getting a creepy rush. The hairs on the back of her neck were rising as if she'd gotten a charge of static electricity. "Why don't you remember stuff?"

"I don feel so hot."

"Well you don't look so hot. You don't remember busting in here and screaming and shooting things and trying to rob us?"

Even wedged on his side as he was, he managed to shake his head.

"Bull, you don't."

"My head's killing me."

"Yeah, we hit you pretty hard."

"You hit me?" He was outraged. Then he began sniveling. "Tie me up . . . beat on me . . ."

Josie looked at him, disgusted. He was such a wimp all of a sudden. It was so weird. "Hey, really, tell me what you remember."

"I gotta scratch my nose."

"Later." There were more noises from outside. Josie went to the window. One more police car. And, as she watched, her father arrived, brakes tearing up the pavement and the car's tires all mashed against the curb. Her father got out and started waving his arms. The police didn't seem nearly as excited. They let him stomp around and carry on and give orders and they probably said Absolutely, Mr. Sloan, they'd get right on it, or some other polite way of ignoring him. Her poor old clueless Dad. Always trying to be the most important person in the room. Even when, as now, there was no room. Because he took himself so seriously, no one else did. Because he made so much noise, he never heard anything else. And he'd never figure it out, his whole life was like some trick mirror that didn't reflect anything straight on. She felt sorry for him, mostly since he was the last person in the world who would think anyone should feel sorry for him. And because that was sad and awful, and because she knew that, in his own dorky way, he was worried about her, Josie pulled the window shade aside and waved to him. Hi, Dad! Dad, hi! He saw her and his arm shot up right away. Then, more cautiously, his fingers uncurled in a wave.

The tied-up bundle at her feet was bumping and thrashing around. "Just let me out of here, OK?"

"Unh-unh."

"Maybe I was drunk or sick, something. I'm all right now, I don hurt you."

"And what if I let you loose and the next minute you're Mr. Screaming Maniac again? Besides, you can't leave, the police are watching the house."

"You called the police on me?" Something in Spanish, curse words, probably.

"Not exactly. It's complicated." Oh boy was it. Everything about to crash and burn. Her parents, Mitch, Harvey, school, the rest of her life. Not one thing that wasn't bad and going to get worse. "Look, what's your name?"

"Rolando Gottschalk."

Josie couldn't help it, she busted out laughing. "That's a name?"

"Shut up." He struggled against the ties. His clothes were so ragged, Josie was afraid they'd shred from the friction. Then he stopped, tilting his head from one side to the other. "Whad you do to my hair?"

"Your hair? Nothing, I wouldn't touch that nasty mess." Which reminded her, she needed a shower in the worst way.

He was quiet now, his face turned away. He was silent for so long that Josie said, "Hey, Rollo . . ."

"Rolando."

"Don't die on me over there."

"Think I'm already dead."

Josie waited, but he was curled up with his face turned away from her. "Well that's different. Why do you think you're dead?"

"Don remember my hair growing."

She thought about this. "It's not the kind of thing you really pay a lot of attention to."

But he was done talking. Fine. She decided to take a shower before somebody broke down the door or shot her or both. If she kept the bathroom door open a crack, she could make sure he wasn't gnawing himself loose. She peeked into Harvey's room. He was asleep on his back, mouth open as if sleep had seized him in the middle of a surprise. A trail of wet silver at one corner. She wouldn't be able to keep him safe forever, or even for very much longer. The police would come in, one way or another. No one would listen. They'd already made up their minds about Harvey, about her, and about her bad behavior, which had now crossed some unforgivable line.

Thank God for hot showers. They revived you, made you feel you weren't whupped yet. Josie pulled her wet hair back with a rubber band, scrambled into clean underwear and jeans and a black T-shirt that she thought made her look tough. She picked up the gun from the back of the toilet and held it up to the mirror, pointed it this way and that and tried on some expressions that went along with that sort of thing. Recklessness had brought her this far, recklessness was all that remained to her. She had fallen in love in a desperate, impulsive way because she believed it was the only way to do such things. She had been—she leveled the gun straight ahead—trigger-happy. And maybe that meant you ended up in a blind alley with one shot left, like in the movies and songs, but what else was there besides an ordinary fucked-up life?

Even with all the horseplay she'd been quick, she'd hardly been in the bathroom five minutes. The gunman who no longer had his gun (she found it difficult to think of him by an actual name, let alone such a peculiar one) was still curled up on his side, looking like he'd invented bad moods. The Weather Channel, which she hoped she lived long enough to never watch again, was showing pictures of the retreating hurricane. It was finally moving up into New England and pooping out, leaving the state of North Carolina to the insurance companies. Everything in the world a giant disaster.

This time when she lifted the window shade she saw her mother and father standing toe to toe on the sidewalk, acting out a perfect pantomime of one of their arguments. You never. You always. Well you. No you. She dropped the shade and backed away. It was probably safer inside.

Behind her on the floor the gunman said, "Driving."

"What?"

"I remember driving."

"Well, I could have told you that. Your car's right outside."

He groaned. "What kinda car?"

"Red Camero with Kansas plates."

"Kansas," he said, like he wasn't sure where that was either.

"You just couldn't be more messed up, could you?"

"Leamme alone."

"So you're saying you have, what, amnesia? I didn't think that was a real thing."

Just when Josie thought he'd stopped talking again, he said, "It's like when you know you seen a movie but you forget what it's about."

Josie looked at him, feeling curious in a repulsed sort of way. "You do a lot of drugs or something?"

"Maybe. I don know. Remember . . . somebody talking to me all the time, this stupid-ass mean stuff . . . except sometimes it was me talking . . . and things was happening . . ."

"What things?"

"Bad things."

For the second time Josie felt that static electricity prickle of hair on her neck. "You did some bad things, huh?"

"I guess so. Or maybe, it wasn't me. Like I was inside myself and outside too."

Josie wished someone else was there, so they could trade significant looks. He was psycho. And she wished she could give his creepy self another knock on the head, but she wasn't cold-blooded enough. Plus he actually seemed sorry about things, not that people always weren't, once they got caught. At the end even Darth Vader had turned all sad and regretful about going over to the dark side, which she'd thought was just ridiculous.

Another peek through the window showed her how large the crowd had grown. In the kitchen she looked out the backdoor. She was pretty sure there was a squad car idling in the alley, just a couple houses down. She felt light-headed, sweaty. She got a Coke from the refrigerator and carried it back in, the gun in her other hand. He hadn't moved. "You want something to drink? Coke, water?" She thought the situation required her to be a hostess, sort of.

"Just tell me what day it is."

"Friday. Oh, I bet . . . What do you need, month, day, year? It's the seventeenth of September, 1999. That make a big difference to you?"

"I missed my birthday."

"Yeah? When is it?"

"Ten August."

"Well, Happy Birthday." No response. "August, that makes you a Leo, right? I'm Aries. They're both fire signs. If you're into that stuff. I don't take it very seriously, but I think it's interesting."

"Yeah. Fascinatin."

"I bet your horoscope says, 'Conditions are excellent for making new friends.' Ha ha."

"Go ahead an shoot me so I don hafta listen to this."

"I wish horoscopes really worked. The ones in the newspaper are so lame, they never get it right." The Coke had a metallic taste, or maybe that was just her mouth gone dry, from fear, from not being able to stop talking. "The old-time astrologers, the ones who set everything up, they had to go by the stars they could see. But now we have these telescopes and we know there's a million million stars out there, and how do they figure in? Aren't they all exerting some kind of influence of gravitational pull? Even from light-years away. How would you calculate that, what kind of horo—"

More commotion outside. Josie ran to the window. Of all the sights she didn't expect to see on this day of freaky sights. She hollered for Harvey and had just enough time to reach the front door.

"Rosa! Rosa!" Josie couldn't keep herself from jumping up on her like a puppy. Harvey was rubbing sleep out of his eyes and smiling his wacky blissed-out Rosa smile, Rosa happy to see him too, and it would have been a real nice reunion except for half of the Springfield police force out on the lawn and the psycho tied up on the living room floor.

Rosa saw him and shrieked and said, *"Dios Mío,"* and something that clearly meant who in the world is that? *"Bandido,"* said Josie. Rosa was staring at the gun in her hand. "Oh, it's his, I took it from him. And what's this?" A bullhorn? Had Rosa been deputized?

Rosa took a cautious step into the living room and spoke to the gunman. He answered in Spanish. Then Rosa again. Then him. A regular conversation. Josie tried to follow the back and forth of it. Rosa, stern and skeptical. The gunman, sullen and injured-sounding. Harvey touched Josie's arm.

"Does she know him?"

"No, they just speak the same language."

"He should go away so we can eat breakfast."

The Spanish conversation stopped. The gunman addressed them. "The *señora* says you can untie me."

"Yeah, right."

"I promise her I don make no trouble."

"She doesn't know you like we do."

"It's so I can get myself cleaned up."

"Now that I might believe," said Josie. Rosa was already flicking bread crumbs from the couch, gathering ceramic fragments of coffee mug, and making indignant noises. Josie felt a little bad about the uses to which they'd put her good skillet. "Did you tell her about breaking in here and carrying on and shooting things?"

"I tell her the truth, I'm a poor lost man, I don remember nothing. Hey, my nose still itches."

"Tough."

"All the bad stuff happen to me, it's on account of this ghost. A ghost was after me. The *señora* says it goes away now."

Unsure what to make of this interesting information, Josie asked what kind of ghost, who was it, but he just muttered into his beard and complained about his nose again.

"Oh, for God's sake." Josie got a Kleenex from the bathroom and, with shuddering care, applied it to his nose. It was harder to touch him now that he was acting more like a human being. His eyes fixed on hers, furious and humiliated. "There, how's that?"

"Turn me loose, you're not doin it right."

"Don't be such a baby." She gave up on him, took another peek out front. There was a TV news truck there. Unbelievable. They were actually hoping somebody would get shot.

Harvey and Rosa were fooling around in the corner. Harvey kept trying to walk his fingers up Rosa's neck and she kept slapping his hands and scolding him in between giggles. Josie couldn't believe them. Was she the only one who cared that they were under seige here?

"You guys, we seriously need to decide what to do. Harvey!" She had to tug at his elbow. "You know what those men were here for? You know what this is all about? They want to cart you off to some crazy farm, because you won't have this simple, dumb operation so you won't go blind. Blind, do you get it?" She waved a hand in front of his face. If she started crying one more time, she was going to lose her last ounce of self-respect. She never should have let things get this messed up. She'd tried to help and only made everything worse. She never should have come here in the first place, why stop there, she could unfurl her life like a roll of carpet, follow every bad decision back to the one before it. Never should have picked a giant fight with her mother, never should have fallen so willfully in love, never should have thought she was anything special, looked down on anyone, mouthed off, made snotty judgments, hurt people. She should just take a step outside, salute, and shoot herself in the head. Send the news crew home happy.

Rosa was speaking in her soothing voice. She wished she was Rosa. Rosa always knew the right thing to do. If something was dirty, you cleaned it. That simple. Cleanliness next to godliness. Maybe she could follow Rosa around, scrub floor tiles on her knees with a toothbrush, ruin her hands with bleach. Atone for her sins. She was losing it. Brain cells starting to strobe and wink out.

"She says, tell him she'll marry him."

It was the gunman. He'd managed to wriggle himself around until he was sitting upright. "That's what she said. Don look at me."

"Marry Harvey? She said she'd marry Harvey?"

"She says, tell him if he gets his new eyes, she'll marry him. That supposed to make sense?"

Josie leaned against a wall. "Oh wow." Rosa was watching her with her bright, birdlike gaze. "What's 'married' in Spanish? Quick!"

"*Casado*. What is this, the damn Love Boat?"

"Rosa, you mean it? *Casado?*" Was she serious? Good Lord. Harvey married.

Rosa put her hand over her heart and delivered another earnest speech. The gunman said, "They should do it. They both a couple of old crumbly types."

"Shut up and tell me what she said."

"Says the two of them will be happy because it is fate they come together, and a lot more flaming crap."

Josie tried to think it through. Could people like Harvey get married? Was it legal? She didn't know anybody else like Harvey who was, but then, she didn't know anybody else like Harvey. He was canting his head from side to side as the others spoke, as if trying to make hearing do the work of seeing. Getting married was one thing. The operation was another.

"Harvey, Rosa says she'll marry you if you have your operation. You want to get married?"

"I do! Yup."

"Married. You know what that is?"

"Herecomesthebride."

"That's right. And it's a serious, serious . . ." Josie decided to leave a legal explanation of marriage to somebody else. "I'm talking about your eye operation. I want to make sure you understand. You'll have to go see a doctor, you have to go to the hospital and get shots and do whatever the doctor tells you. You'll have to be very brave."

"Braver than Frank?"

"Yes, Harvey. If you do this, you will be braver than anyone I know." She held her breath as the idea of bravery took hold, rooted itself, then spread across his face.

"And you'll have to take better care of yourself. You'll have to let Rosa and me and Mom and everybody else help you. Can you do that? Can you go out and promise everybody you'll do it? Can you start being brave right now?"

"Ain't scaredy."

"That's great, now you have to go out and tell them that. Is that why you brought this, Rosa? You are too much! Uh, congratulations, you guys." Harvey turned his head this way and that, his smeared eyes blinking, smiling his watery smile. "Here, you push this button and you talk through it. Can you hold it like this? Just go outside and tell them everybody's OK in here, and you'll get your eyes fixed."

Josie prodded him toward the door, unlocked it and pulled it open. "Show time."

Harvey lagged behind in the hallway. The bullhorn dangled at the end of his arm. "No, hold it up to your mouth, see? Tell them what I said."

"Ain't scaredy."

"Sure, you can say that too, just hurry up."

She watched him take one step, then two. After being shut up for so long in the stale house, the slice of fresh air made Josie's lungs expand. The crowd noise rose and fell in a wave. And then, as if his was the only face worth seeing in any crowd, she saw Mitch. Oh goddamn him. Could he see her? Her skin burned. Her heart clamored. She hated that someone could do this to her. She didn't want to be in love anymore. She wanted to pick it off like a scab. Harvey raised the bullhorn to his mouth.

"DADDY HAD HIS PECKER OUT!"

In the brief, silent space of her echoing disbelief, Josie thought, I'm glad Rosa can't understand this.

"NOBODY BETTER HOLLER AT ME ANYMORE!"

"Sss, Harvey!"

"I GOT MY OWN HURRICANE!"

"Give me that thing." Josie dragged him back by his shirttail and seized the bullhorn. Then she was out on the front porch, trying to focus on the mass of shape and motion before her. It was like one of those pictures made up of a million colored dots that if you looked at it one way, it was just a blur, but if you shifted your eyes, you saw the picture. So it was that one moment Josie saw nothing but confusion, then the next she was able to pick out Mitch, his expression one of stony dread, her mother looking like she was the one who'd spent a week wandering the Utah desert, her father scowling into his tie. And if she tried, she knew she could see all of them, every human face, just as clearly. She raised the bullhorn to her mouth.

"EXCUSE ME."

The amplified force of her voice made her rise up on her toes. It was an electric wind, carrying her along.

"MY UNCLE'S NOT REAL USED TO TALKING TO A LOT OF PEOPLE, SO I WANTED TO EXPLAIN . . ."

The TV cameraman edged closer. Every face in that sea of faces, listening and waiting. Her head seemed to expand and drift away like a balloon, and there was a moment of slippery panic before she grabbed it and hauled it back and took courage from the new, electric power of her voice.

"THERE ARE PEOPLE HERE WHO HAVE BETRAYED HIM! HIM AND ME BOTH! THEY KNOW WHO THEY ARE! SNEAKING AROUND DOING SNEAKY, DISHONEST THINGS! WELL, THEY SHOULD BE ASHAMED!"

So there. Her mother was crying. That just wasn't fair. Your mother crying was a secret weapon, it naturally made you feel like a lowlife. Mitch was trying to look like she didn't mean him. She wanted him to feel scummy, and then she wanted to learn not to love him, and in spite of all that she still wanted to fasten herself to every inch of him. Her father was talking to the police, who were beginning to mill around and size her up. Josie didn't like the way they were putting their heads together, so she hurried on.

"HE SAYS HE'S GOING TO COME OUT NOW, AND HE'S GOING TO HAVE HIS EYE OPERATION, BUT YOU HAVE TO PROMISE NOT TO TAKE HIM AWAY SOMEPLACE HE DOESN'T WANT TO GO. MOM?"

Her mother was crossing the street and Josie came down from the porch and met her halfway. Her mother hugged the stuffing out of her and called her Baby and her father was there too, slapping them on the back like they were in some football huddle. Josie kept saying she was fine, really. "I have to tell you about Harvey, it's the most amazing thing. Tell the stupid police to back off." Harvey and Rosa were peeking out the front door.

"See, everybody's fine."

Her father said, "What's she doing in there anyway, windows?"

"No, Dad, she's like his girlfriend. They're gonna get married and he can keep living here. We got it all worked out."

"Married? What kind of stunt is this?"

"Frank, I'm going to have you arrested for public idiocy. You just let me talk to Harvey. Sweetheart, I'm sorry, you believe me, don't you?"

Her mom was blubbering. Well, Josie was blubbering too and of course she said she was sorry, you had to say that, and sort out all the hard part later. She hated that everyone was watching them. And where was Mitch?

He was gone. No, going. She left her mother in mid-blubber and chased after him down the sidewalk. Her last official reckless act. She didn't care if he got fired or she got sent to the home for depraved girls. She wasn't going to let him just *leave*. "Mitch!"

He stopped and turned halfway. "I know you don't want to talk to me, but you have to."

He was trying to give her his cop face. The impassive one he used on criminal types. She said, "Boy, it kills you to have to admit you know me, doesn't it?"

The cop face wasn't holding up real well. "That's not true. I just figured you were still mad."

At least they weren't on TV at the moment. The news people were back at Harvey's, pointing microphones at the police lieutenant. Josie said, "Right. Like you're so happy to see me." She didn't want to keep sounding all sarcastic and mean, it was only part of what she felt, but she didn't know how to start over some other way.

"I am, I'm happy you're all right."

"Yeah." Josie shrugged. She felt self-conscious and grubby. "Still have all my fingers and toes."

"I really was worried about you."

"You didn't have to be." She wasn't going to let him say anything right for a while.

"I didn't know where you were, nobody did."

He was wearing a blue shirt with a frayed collar. She loved thinking about how many times that shirt must have been on him. Why did she always go barmy over his clothes, she was such a basket case. She couldn't look at him and not fall back into all that crazy wanting. But she was tired of it as well. "I wasn't at the police prom, that's for sure."

"Look, I made the date before I even met you, and you couldn't have gone anyway, and I figured it would only upset you more if you knew about it."

Josie didn't even bother with that one. Just stood there and let the bullshit rain down. She could admit to herself now that he'd always been a little dense.

"It was a date, that's all. A dumb date."

"And what am I, your dumb . . . Oh shit." She'd forgotten all about the psycho. "Never mind that now, you gotta come with me."

She turned and fled back to the house, dragging Mitch along, dodging the enterprising TV crew now headed in her direction. Her mother and father and Harvey and Rosa were in the front yard with a bunch of grumpy-looking cops. Josie galloped past them, tore up the front steps, and whacked the screen door open.

"What's the big deal?" Mitch bumped up behind her as she skidded to a stop in the hallway. The extension cord and bathrobe belt were tangled on the floor. No psycho.

There wasn't any point in looking for him but she did anyway. In the bathtub she found his nasty clothes, a great wad of oily, burnt-brown hair, and a wet towel smeared with grime. It was as if he had slipped down the drain and left nothing but dirt behind. She wondered if Rosa had turned him loose or if he'd managed that on his own. She guessed it didn't matter. He was gone, good riddance, one more thing she never wanted to think about again.

"Never mind," Josie said, backing out of the bathroom before Mitch could see. "I thought I forgot something"

"Where's the gun, I should get that secured."

It was gone, of course. "Oh, there wasn't any, I just made that up so they wouldn't snatch Harvey." Which was sort of true. Besides being the easiest answer.

Now he was the one passing out the dirty looks. "You brought the department out for no reason?"

"I didn't bring anyone," Josie reminded him.

"You provided false information."

"Oh, come on, Mitch. You're mad because I caught you doing something sneaky, and now you want to work it around so everything's my fault."

"I still don't think you should have said that about the gun."

Josie sighed. Her parents were going to come in any second and one or both of them was likely to get arrested. "Let's just call it a draw." Foolishly, she stuck her hand out.

Mitch stared down at it. Josie said, "I think things are getting awfully complicated."

"Well . . ."

"No hard feelings."

"Of course not." He seemed glad to be agreeing about something.

"And I'd use the backdoor if I were you."

They shook hands. Mitch said maybe they could talk sometime. Josie said, "Sure." He didn't get it. After he'd left, she squared her shoulders and took stock. She still had all her fingers and toes. She would go back to being her parents daughter. She would cry some more and mope around and call herself an idiot and other names. She could see it all coming. It went along with her messed-up heart, and the carelessness she kept confusing with love, and life going on, in spite of everything, in its good old ornery way.

Lonesome Road

Rolando Gottschalk, heir to all the Americas, was seated in the last row of an eastbound Greyhound, traveling light. The window of the bus produced a landscape of gray highway and long stretches of useless green punctuated by cows. He breathed in exhaust and other mechanical perfumes. He was scared to drive anymore. He would stay on the bus until his money ran out, and then he would walk, and maybe by the end he'd be crawling. He tried to pay attention to the road signs so as not to lose himself again. The signs said SPEED LIMIT, YIELD, CAUTION. The towns were Decatur, Paris, Terre Haute, Indianapolis, Richmond, Dayton, names that were only collections of streets and crosshatched wires and storefronts. Whenever the bus stopped he got out and shuffled around the terminals, with their sad restrooms and vending machines dispensing puddles of coffee into styrofoam cups. He spoke to no one and no one spoke to him. In one of these places he stuffed a paper bag containing the gun into the mouth of an anonymous trash can.

His new hair prickled. It made his head feel too small, lost in the oversize shirt collar that kept sliding over his shoulders. All the clothes were too big, especially the shoes. He had to creep around real slow so they wouldn't fall off. He felt like a cat or a dog that had been shaved down to its skin and didn't recognize itself anymore.

When he tried to think about all the places in between Los Angeles and this bus, it was like taking too big a step in those loose shoes. He lost his balance and had to stop right where he was. There was probably some very good reason he couldn't remember clearly. That meant the next face he saw on the street might have a score to settle, know him better than he did himself, know what he deserved and why. He fell asleep in his seat and his head rolled like the bus's wheels. Awake or asleep, dread followed him.

Dreaming his muddy dreams, he woke up with a shout in his throat, unsure of whether it had come all the way into his mouth. He must have made some kind of noise, because a voice from the next seat said, "You all right, son?"

It was solid dark inside and out except for the safety light on the bus's floor and the occasional car passing, dragging its own darkness behind it. The voice was a woman's voice and Rolando could see the shape of her but not her face. He thought the voice had color in it, although he couldn't say for sure. "Yeah, I'm all right."

"You was wrestling the devil. What it looked like."

"Huh." He swallowed the shout down and forced a laugh. "The devil, sure."

"All souls in trouble be wrestling him. Our Lord Baby Jesus will help you if you call on him."

Rolando tried to will himself back to sleep. He was too tired to answer back or argue with her foolishness. His spine jolted as the bus ground through its cycle of gears. He kept losing his balance in the seat, had to brace himself with his elbows so as not to slide into the woman. She was singing a Bible song, softly, but in such a way as was meant to be overheard: *Didn't my Lord deliver Daniel, Didn't my Lord deliver Daniel, Didn't my Lord deliver Daniel, so why not any man?*

Always it was some voice breaking into his silence. Always he had tried to ignore it or shout it down. His own voice convinced no one. He had no outside words for his inside self. The song wasn't so bad, he decided, or maybe it was the singing itself, breathy and damped down, but ready to tear loose if you gave it enough space. He might even have sung along if he knew the words, and who the hell Daniel was. He was a lion guy, he gathered that much. Like Siegfried and Roy.

Didn't my Lord deliver Daniel, didn't my Lord deliver Daniel. He was at a big Las Vegas–type stage show where the lion was made to float overhead on a cloud of pink smoke. Our Lord Baby Jesus wore a white tuxedo with glitter in his hair. The angel girls were there, belting out the song. They did a little shimmy dance. Everybody booed and hissed when the Devil came out in black tights, stomping up and down and scowling. He never even laid a glove on Our Lord Baby Jesus. Bolts of holy lightning knocked him flat. Wrestling was always such total bullshit. Even in the middle of his dream, Rolando had to laugh.

But he woke up sad. The woman was gone, maybe she had only changed seats, but she felt gone. Her song was gone. It was one more lonesome thing. The bus was still moving, like he'd already died and gone to hell and hell was a Greyhound going nowhere. The darkness was turning grainy. Morning out there somewhere.

Could any man be saved? Had he ever in his life known anything besides meanness and fear? They had been the fuel that propelled him, and now he had used them up. Simple fact. End of the damn line. He touched something on the empty seat, paper. He brought it up to his face but it was too dark to see.

Mile after mile, he waited while the light grew. First he could make out the pictures, the cross and the crown, with a number of energetic lines to indicate radiance. Two hands emerging from a rainbow cloud, palms up in heavenly welcome. Then the words.

He read that Jesus Christ had died for him and for all sinners, was buried, and rose again from the dead. And that if he turned away from sin and invited Jesus into his life to become his personal Savior, and placed trust in Him alone for his salvation, and read his Bible every day to get to know Christ better, and talked to God in prayer, was baptized, worshipped, fellowshipped, and served with Christians in a church where Christ was preached and the Bible was the final authority, and told others about Christ, then he would be born anew.

He started in praying right then and there. He prayed for the bus driver and the people in the seats ahead of him, who kept turning around to look at him. He prayed for everyone still asleep in the houses along the highway, and in the cities and towns and farms both ahead and behind, everyone who was grieved in mind or body, everyone lost, forgotten, heartsick, burdened, tangled up in hatred as he himself had been. Everyone and everything, prisoners in their cells, soldiers fighting in cruel wars, fishermen at sea and the fish beneath the waves, all that hungered or thirsted or labored. He had reached out in darkness and found light. He pointed himself at the sunrise like an arrow, and Jesus loosed the bow.

Hurricane Party

There was lemonade tinted pink with a bottle of maraschino cherries, and a white-frosted angel food cake with a bride and groom on top, and that was for Harvey and Rosa. The old kitchen table was covered with a pink tablecloth; garlands of paper flowers and paper butterflies hung overhead. Someone, probably Josie, had gone to the party store and brought back a dozen pink flamingos, palm frond hats of the sort favored by village idiots, some painted coconut heads and other tropical touches. That was for the hurricane, even though Harvey was really only a tropical storm.

They were all crowded around the television, watching the Weather Channel and rooting for the winds to strengthen. But they peaked at a measly 50 miles. The storm dodged Tampa and dumped its rain on the Everglades and Miami before it crossed the peninsula and trundled out to sea. Elaine explained to Harvey that this was actually just as well, since the Everglades needed the rain and nobody farther north did, on top of the misery of Hurricane Floyd. "You wouldn't want anybody to get hurt, would you? Of course not."

She couldn't tell if he was disappointed. He was wearing his postsurgical dark eyeshade, leaving his face half-masked. He and Rosa sat next to each other on the new couch, a wedding present from Elaine. They seemed a little shy about all the fuss. Someone had put two of the silly hats on their heads and heaped the brims with paper flowers for wedding crowns. If not for that, they might have resembled those dour nineteenth-century husbands and wives, staring down the camera for a formal portrait. Elaine hoped that once everyone left them alone, they could be a happy, loving couple. There were such things as loving couples, weren't there?

It had turned into a fairly large party, most of it Rosa's family: Lorena and her mother and father, *hermanos y hermanas, tíos y tías,* and probably some cousins thrown in for good measure. A dozen small brown children ran in and out, inventing games with the coconut shells and trying to feed bits of the turkey in mole sauce to Fat Cat. A group of husky men in open-collared shirts slapped Harvey on the back and offered marital advice.

Harvey's side was represented more meagerly by herself and Frank and Josie and, in an effort to pad things out, Ed Pauley. Elaine nibbled at one of the powdered-sugar wedding cookies that Lorena's mother, Nereida, had baked. Everything had happened so fast. Their own private hurricane. Elaine felt like one of those cartoon characters shown clinging to a lamppost in a high wind, feet blown out from underneath them.

"Mom?"

Josie waved a hand in front of her face. "You in there? You look totally spaced."

"I'm fine, Sunshine. Just trying to catch my breath. This is quite the fiesta."

"Yeah, I guess it's not every day Grandma gets married."

Rosa had been a widow for almost thirty years. Elaine learned this, and other interesting facts, during the ceremony at the courthouse. (Everyone had agreed a church wedding would be pushing their luck.) Harvey had worn a gray tweed sports coat and a red tie purchased for the occasion. He was awkward but respectable in his new clothes. He could have been a retired farmer.

Rosa had a much-frilled blue dress and a corsage. Elaine and Frank were there as witnesses, as were Nereida and her husband, Jorge, a short, serious man who looked as purely Indian as if he'd been on hand to greet Cortés.

Harvey had needed only a little prompting to get the words out of his mouth in the right order, while Rosa tackled English syllable by syllable. The justice of the peace presided equably, as if he had seen stranger things, and even managed to imbue the proceedings with some of the grandeur of the law. Nereida took pictures with a disposable camera and confided in Elaine that they had been concerned because Harvey was not Catholic. But Rosa had told them that he was very devout in his own way, even if he was unable to receive the sacraments, and that at her age, God made allowances. Elaine said that she was glad it would not be a problem. She had mostly been concerned with getting Harvey through the ceremony before he could make any embarrassing announcements. That, and his surgery the next day. Theology hadn't been one of her big worries.

Josie said, "All the women look like Rosa, but different sizes. I was talking to Lorena, she's awesome. Did you know she didn't speak English until she was ten years old?"

Elaine agreed that this was remarkable, although she was unsure if Josie meant that Lorena spoke very well considering her late start, or that there was some shocking deprivation involved here. As if she sensed them talking about her, Lorena turned and waved at them from across the room. Her hair was piled up and curled on top of her head in a glamorous fashion, and she was looking very pretty in a lace blouse and short black skirt. Elaine said, "I'm going to ask her if she'd like to come work at Trade Winds. I could use her."

There was a moment when Josie might have been thrown off balance by this, but she came back from it. "Really, sure, she'd be great."

Elaine couldn't tell if Josie felt some tinge of jealousy or dis-
placement. "You know, if you ever wanted . . ."

"Nah. Not the business type."

"Maybe once you see the dye works."

Because Josie was coming with her to India. It would mean she
might as well forget about school this semester, and she wouldn't
graduate with her class in June, but none of that seemed as important as it once had. Elaine was thrilled she was going. That
she'd agreed to the trip, that she even seemed excited about it,
was more than Elaine could have imagined only a few days ago.
They would have time together and conversations that would not
have to be arguments. They would have all of India, its dust and
flowers and river of faces. She would present it all to Josie, watch
her be amazed.

It would be just as well to get Josie away from here for a while,
even though her mysterious uniformed true love didn't seem to
be in the picture anymore. Not that Josie had said anything about
him, nor had Elaine asked. But the climate between them had
shifted in some subtle way. Instead of her usual sullen silences,
Josie had been determinedly cheerful, as if to demonstrate how
over it all she was. And even if Elaine wasn't quite ready to believe that, she had to consider the possibility that Josie might finally be growing up.

Perhaps Josie would decide to tell her everything. But even if
she never did, Elaine wouldn't feel obliged to say anything. She
felt a tenderness toward Josie's secrets, perhaps because she no
longer had any of her own.

Well, she was going to have lunch with Bob Kellerman. That
didn't count as a secret, and it was only a lunch. But it was something new, someone new. A small exploration of possibilities. It
made her feel she wasn't entirely old and used up yet.

And she was getting her new car next week. It had a sunroof
and a killer CD player. She could drive around with the windows

down, belting out old rock and roll. Silly how happy that made her, as if she'd bought into all those car commercials promising luxury or fun or cute families or the freedom of the open road. The all-American crass materialistic etcetera. She didn't care. Happy was good.

Frank and Ed Pauley were having a conversation in one corner of the kitchen. Elaine went over to them and stood until they were forced to break off their talk about municipal bonds or whatever it was they found to say to each other, and acknowledge her. "You boys aren't mingling."

"I don't speak Spanish," Frank informed her.

"I'll get you some language tapes."

Ed Pauley smiled and turned his glasses from one of them to the other in a way that made Elaine wonder if he'd heard them, if he might be going deaf. Frank hoisted his lemonade, stared at it as if he wished it were something else, then lowered it without drinking. Elaine said, "We have you to thank for all this, Ed."

"Me? How do you figure?"

"You told me we should be worried about Harvey. You were right."

Ed regarded "all this": the cake and shrieking kids and flamingos and dressed-up ladies gossiping in Spanish over the sink, and shook his head to disclaim responsibility. "Now you know I didn't do anything."

"You got the ball rolling." He'd been the starting point, the first sequence. But because that was nothing you could say, and because Ed was smiling his deaf smile again, she said, more loudly, "We're getting the roof fixed next week. Frank is, I should say."

"Hey, don't mind me. I just pay the bills."

"That roof's been bad for years."

"Next week. They can't get started any sooner."

"And something ought to be done about this kitchen. Don't you think they deserve better?"

She dared him to say no, right there in the presence of the funky linoleum and weeping paint and lopsided stove. But he surprised her by agreeing. Perhaps he didn't want to look cheap in front of Ed. A little while later, as Elaine was tidying up the discarded plates and napkins, Frank came up to her and said, "I really didn't want to see him locked up or anything like that. I'm glad things worked out."

"Did you mean that about the kitchen?"

"Sure, why not. We'll make it a damn showcase. Put it in magazines."

"That's very nice of you, Frank." Meaning it, or trying to. Frank being expansive always made her cautious.

"What the hell. You know how much the nursing home would have cost?" He swatted at one of the butterfly garlands, which was drooping low. "I don't suppose she married him to get her green card, anything like that?"

Elaine might have chided him if she hadn't had the same unworthy thought. Along with wondering if they'd only gone along with the marriage in order to provide Harvey with a caretaker. But she didn't want to always believe the worst about people, herself included. She said, "I don't think so. Rosa's been here such a long time already, and besides . . ."

She was distracted by Josie, who was standing in front of Harvey and Rosa, coaxing them to open a bundle wrapped in tissue paper. They'd already received a number of gifts, items both useful and decorative: a gold-scrolled picture frame, a set of linens, a microwave, an electric knife-sharpener, a clock that announced the hour with bird calls, a pair of wrought-iron candlesticks, and dish towels trimmed with rickrack. Josie was shifting her weight from one foot to the other in a swaying half-dance, and she was explaining something Elaine couldn't hear, using her hands to fill in the gaps between English and Spanish. She looked cheerful, unself-consciously beautiful. Rosa was shaking her head in protest, and the others were laughing, and Harvey had perked up, was trying to bite Rosa's ear, getting all tangled up in the hats and eyeshade. Cries of encouragement from the crowd. They were a nice family; Elaine supposed they all had some loose tribal connection now, which pleased her. Rosa opened the package and shook out a white satin nightgown, very fine and lacy, and a matching robe.

More laughter and cheering. Rosa hid her face. Frank and Elaine looked at each other, then glanced into the bedroom, the neatly made-up bed and its plain chenille spread, where Harvey and Rosa slept as man and wife.

Frank said, "Do you wonder . . ."

"I don't think we'll ever know."

The Wide Blue Yonder

Rosa wanted them to go to Mexico. She wanted him to see it with his new eyes. She showed him on the television when the map came on. She said: See? See? Mexico was brown, like Rosa. The map floated just above the screen. His eyes still didn't work quite right. Things weren't always where they should be. Sometimes smears of rainbow dazzle crept into the corner of his vision, and at night the darkness was fuzzy. But other times it was like a window opening up.

He was trying to learn Rosa-talk. 'Sky' was see yellow, 'blue' was a zoo. He wanted to talk to her about Mexico. How did you get there, and what did you do once you arrived? Was Mexico a place that had good or bad weather? You never heard that much about it, like it was too far down on the screen for anyone to see.

Rosa-talk was like a different channel on the television. You didn't always get good reception. A lot of the time it was Ya ya ya. Other times it almost came together. He had to let his ears slip down into a different place. Then watch Rosa's face and how she moved around the room. She said: She was old now, but Mexico was where she had been young. If he came with her, he could imagine her when she was a little girl, a young bride, pretty, she hadn't always been such a dried husk. What use was an old woman? All you could hope for was to keep yourself clean and pray for mercy. But her heart was still red and Mexico was her heart.

He said: Rosarosarose . . . I've never been anywhere. How do you start?

The girl said they should do it. "It would be like a honeymoon. You could ride on an airplane, would you like that? Oh don't worry, everything will be right here when you get back. What do you think, you could fly through a cloud. In the real sky, not the one on the dumb TV."

Off we go, into the wide blue yonder

"Now where did that come from? Did you hear it on a commercial? But it's *wild* blue, Harvey, it's the Air Force song."

Off we go, into the wide blue yonder
Flying high, into the sun

"All right, have it your way. Wide."

Da da da, dumpity dumdum dumdum

"You have kind of a nice singing voice, did anyone ever tell you? I bet my mom would help you buy the tickets if we asked her."

It would be his first and last trip. Would he see the ocean? Did the Air Force sell the tickets? Did the sky want you up there? Did Rosa know which direction? What did the map look like from that high up?

He was excited, thinking about it. You Are Here was going Someplace Else. He ran up and down the back porch stairs just to let off steam. Some of Rosa's friends would go with them. He liked her friends. They had names like hurricanes: Alberto, Carla, Eduardo, Juana. They took him and Rosa for rides in their car sometimes.

It would be his first trip because he had never taken one before, and it would be his last because you didn't live forever and forever was right around the corner. He could tell. The window opening in his eyes seemed to look inside as well. Some mornings he didn't feel like he'd woken all the way up. Some nights his sleep was thin and foggy. Different parts of his body announced themselves like clocks, like the new one in the kitchen that said robin oriole song sparrow meadowlark. Except his clock said knees neck heart breath. Then, sooner or later, the clock stopped. Off we go!

Oh don't be scairt. Nothing can stop the U.S. Air Force. It beat the army hands down. He flew loop the loops in the wide blue yonder. The air was as clear as water. At night when he couldn't sleep, he reached out his hand to Rosa. Rosa was like a map you could touch. She stirred and spoke to him from her dreams, in a kindly cross voice: Ya, go to sleep, baby, baby, let Mamma sleep. Love was a more, a more, a more. When he stretched his hand over the Weather screen, it covered everyone: Rosa and Fat Cat and the girl and Yoo Hoo and Frank Junior and Football Ed and Lorena and Ramon and Juana and all the names ever invented. Everyone he loved was underneath the same sky.